FOURTH OF JULY CREEK

FOURTH OF JULY CREEK

A NOVEL

SMITH HENDERSON

ecco

AN IMPRINT OF HARPERCOLLINS PUBLISHERS

This book is a work of fiction. The characters, incidents, and dialogue are drawn from the author's imagination and are not to be construed as real. Any resemblance to actual events or persons, living or dead, is entirely coincidental.

FOURTH OF JULY CREEK. Copyright © 2014 by Smith Henderson. All rights reserved. Printed in the United States of America. No part of this book may be used or reproduced in any manner whatsoever without written permission except in the case of brief quotations embodied in critical articles and reviews. For information address HarperCollins Publishers, 10 East 53rd Street, New York, NY 10022.

HarperCollins books may be purchased for educational, business, or sales promotional use. For information please e-mail the Special Markets Department at SPsales@harpercollins.com.

FIRST EDITION

Designed by Mary Austin Speaker

Library of Congress Cataloging-in-Publication Data has been applied for.

ISBN 978-0-06-228644-4 (hardcover)
ISBN 978-0-06-236111-0 (international edition)

14 15 16 17 18   OV/RRD   10 9 8 7 6 5 4 3 2 1

FOR MY FAMILY

If I knew for a certain'ty that a man was coming to my house with the conscious design of doing me good, I should run for my life.

—HENRY DAVID THOREAU

FOURTH OF JULY CREEK

ONE

The cop flicked his cigarette to the dirt-and-gravel road in front of the house, and touched back his hat over his hairline as the social worker drove up in a dusty Toyota Corolla. Through the dirty window, he spotted some blond hair falling, and he hiked in his gut, hoping that the woman in there would be something to have a look at. Which is to say he did not expect what got out: a guy in his late twenties, maybe thirty, pulling on a denim coat against the cold morning air blowing down the mountain, ducking back into the car for a moment, reemerging with paperwork. His brown corduroy pants faded out over his skinny ass, the knees too. He pulled that long hair behind his ears with his free hand and sauntered over.

"Name's Pete," the social worker said, tucking the clipboard and manila folder under his arm, shaking the cop's hand. "We're usually women," he added, smiling with an openness that put the cop at ill ease.

The cop just replied with his own name—"Eugene"—took back his hand, and coughed into his fist. The social worker pointed at the cop's badge with his chin, a seven-pointed nickel star with MONTANA chased inside it, mountains on the left, plains on the right, a sun, a river.

"Lookit mine," Pete said, pulling out a flimsy laminate from his wallet. "I keep telling them I need a badge that don't look like it came out of a damn cereal box."

The cop didn't have a ready opinion about that. He burnished a smudge off his own shield with a plump red thumb and turned toward the house. It abutted a steep hill and was poorly maintained, if at all. Peeling paint, a porch swing dangling from one rusting chain, a missing windowpane taped over with torn cardboard. Couch cushions, half a blow-dryer, some lengths of phone cable, a plastic colander, and broken crockery littered the yard. Pieces of clothing slung up in the cedar shrubs like crude scarecrows, and the grass erupted in tall disordered bunches, stalks shooting through the warped porch boards, at places window-high. The screen door hung open behind where the mother and her son sat.

"Shit," Pete said. "You had to cuff them."

"That or they's gonna kill each other."

The mother called out to him—"Pete! Pete!"—but he shook his head no, and she looked off, pissed and muttering. The son didn't even glance up, but must've suggested something to her because she turned away from him and spat out some words. From where they were, Pete and the cop couldn't hear what hateful thing she said, and they watched a minute to see if the bickering would flare up. It did not.

Pete affixed the open folder to the clipboard, clicked his pen, and started his incident report. The cop let out his pony-keg belly a little. They always relaxed when the social worker got involved, soothed by the scritching of his pen, relieved that Pete would be taking it from here.

"So what happened?" Pete asked, pen aloft.

The cop snorted contemptuously, lit up another cigarette, and told him. They were at it again, and the neighbor'd finally had it with the two of them broadcasting to the whole row of houses precisely how they'd kill each other, what appendages would be hacked off, and into what orifices they would stick those dismembered parts. There were children about, the neighbor said, so he went over. He pounds on the door. No response. Cups his eyes to see in the window. Sounds like the argument has spilled out the back door of the house. The neighbor jogs around to the side gate, where the boy is standing with his air rifle. The two of them halt at the sight of one another. Then the kid starts crossing and uncrossing his eyes at the neighbor. To unnerve him or because he'd at last gone bonkers, who could say.

"Did he actually threaten the neighbor with the gun?"

The cop blew smoke out his nose.

"This guy, he knows a pellet gun when he sees it."

"Right."

"But it ain't like he pointed the gun at the guy or said anything threatening at him exactly. The neighbor says he was more worried about the kid going after the mother."

Pete nodded and wrote some more.

"So then what?"

"So he says 'fuckit' and calls it in."

"And the situation when you got here?"

The situation was a perfect fucking mess. The situation was the kid climbing up onto the slanted, dented aluminum carport and stomping on the rusted thing like an ape. Just making the whole unsound shelter boom and groan under his weight. The mother saying so help her if that thing falls on her Charger she'll gut him, and the kid just swagging the carport back and forth so that it was popping and starting to bow under his weight. Now the cop was about ready to shoot the ornery shit off the goddamn thing.

Then the situation got interesting.

"The mother has the air rifle and—"

"No way," Pete said.

"Yeah, fuckin way," the cop said.

"She shoot him?"

"Before I get to her, yeah, she shoots. You can see the big old welt on his forearm."

Pete started to write.

"And then what?"

Then the kid leaps off the carport just as the cop has taken the air rifle and ordered the woman inside, but the kid and his mother are already tearing at each other like two wet cats in a sack. Right in front of a goddamn cop, mind you. Like he ain't even there. All the neighbors are out on their nice, normal lawns in their bathrobes clutched closed at the neck watching the cop trying to disentangle the two of them, taking it in like the fucking rodeo. And the bitch—"pardon my French" the cop at last says about all his cussing—won't desist, and the kid won't desist, so the cop wrangles the first one he can get a hand on—the woman it turns out—and wrestles her onto her belly and into the cuffs, but not before the kid makes a run to kick her in the face, which the cop just barely stops with his own body. And realizing he's just kicked one seriously pissed-off police officer in the chest, the dumbshit turns tail and flees.

"And you ran him down," Pete said.

Smoke leaked out the cop's pale yellow smile.

"See that pickup?" he asked.

"Yeah."

"So he's looking back to see if I'm coming and he runs smack into the open tailgate."

"I imagine that was satisfying."

"Your words, brother." The cop took a drag, and blew it at the ground. "Anyhow, by the time I get him up on the porch, she's blubbering about how she has a social worker who knows the whole history of everything and would straighten them out. 'Please, please, would I call the social worker,' she says."

Pete nodded and wrote. His arm was tired, so he bent to finish with the clipboard on his thigh. The cop said something.

"I'm sorry?" Pete said.

"So what's going on with these two?" the cop asked again.

Pete scoffed, not at the question, but at the enormity of the answer. How to sketch it. Shorthand it. A great many things were going on with them. Went on and would keep going on.

The mother collected unemployment but her full-time occupation was self-pity. She slippered around the house in sweatpants and smoked a lot of weed and took speed and tugged her hair over her face in a shape pleasing and temporary and dumped forth her old bosom and smiled prettily for herself and discovered nothing in the mirror to recommend her to anybody for anything. Or so you could imagine, the way she mooned her eyes at you until you told her to knock it off, you wanted to talk about the children. She ventured out only to get her SSI check and visit her dealer somewhere up on the edge of the Yaak Wilderness. Sometimes to get cereal. She could be seen around town powdered white and made up in slashes of red around her mouth and blue around her eyes like an abstract of the American flag, some kind of commentary on her country, which of a sort she was. Mostly she cloaked her grand paranoia in aviator glasses and lavender feather boas and, when she was ripping high, imagined herself some kind of fairy, and when she was low, imagined herself some kind of persecuted witch.

Pete closed the manila folder.

"The mother's a disaster. Most of her disability goes to speed."

"I recognize the kid," the cop said. "Got a good run of priors going."

The kid dangled his head between his knees. A recreational gas huffer, who smelled like gasoline, but with an undertone of minerals like a rotting pumpkin in hot dirt. Other times of Cheetos and semen. With that acne-potted skin, you initially felt sorry for him. He came and went but not to school or for long or for good. He owed restitution for an arson (equipment shed, track field), had a pending court date for burgling pickups.

"He's about one infraction away from a stint at Pine Hills," Pete said.

"Like assaulting a cop."

The thing was, Pete suspected the onset of something diagnosable, a condition or combination of disorders that a good therapist would home in on. But Pete could never get the fifteen-year-old to an appointment, either because of the boy or his insane mother. He told them there was a new drug called Ritalin in the literature. Regretted saying the word the moment it slipped out of his mouth and they looked at him like he'd broken out in French. *Literature.* What drugs and literature in the houses in and around Tenmile, Montana. Louis L'Amour and

James Michener, and comic books, furled and foxed *Penthouses*, some marijuana. *Popular Mechanics* and some truckers' speed. The Bible, if you were lucky. Good God, what this dotty bitch and the punkinhead son would make of Revelations. It'd look like something painted on the side of a van. The cranks and drunks up here took to Jesus (in jail, if it pleases the court) and worried creases into the spine of the good book, consulting it like the I Ching or a Ouija board. For a good five or six months, they'd follow the Ten Commandments and hand out Jack Chick tracts like they were lucky pennies or rabbits' feet. But soon they were chipping, they were sneaking a drink or a joint or some uppers on the sly, thumbing the thin pages for answers to the little questions as if following the better part of God's law was achieved by divining from Leviticus what to have for supper or what color socks to wear.

"He could maybe do all right in a stable environment," Pete said. "Maybe not."

On the porch, the mother and son sensed things approaching a head. Their social worker had his clipboard under his armpit and he and the cop were talking. The mother watched, read the men's body language, a language with which she had some fluency from previous arrests, other times she was made to wait. In court. At the SSI office, signing up for disability security. She chinned herself toward them trying to hear, but the kid was untroubled, mute and deviceless as a glass of lukewarm water.

"So do you feel like throwing a mom and her son in jail today?" Pete asked.

"I surely do not. But these two are full idiots." The cop dropped the butt and mashed it neatly with the point of his boot. "I thought the mama was plumb full of shit."

"About?"

"You. Dispatch didn't even know if we had a Department of Family Services in town."

"My office is in the basement of the courthouse," Pete said amiably. "Next to Records."

"So whaddya usually do with them?"

"There's no usual. What can I say? The kid's got priors. I'd like to keep him out of Pine Hills. There gonna be any charges?"

"I dunno. Resisting, I guess. Assault if you wanna go there."

"Do you?"

"What I don't want is to come back." The cop pressed closed a nostril with his finger and leaned over and blew furiously out of it.

"Let 'em off with a warning?"

The cop nodded, wiping his nose with the back of his index finger.

"Okay. But let me talk to the girl first," Pete said, bending to look in the squad car.

"The girl?"

There was no girl in the squad car. Pete had assumed there would be, but there wasn't.

"What girl?" the cop asked.

Pete ignored him and charged through the yard and up the steps. The mother leaned over whining at him, but he stepped around her and she fell over—"Hey!" she said—but he was past her and into the house. The light laddering through the blinds was morning light, cleaner and brighter. Not that what it shone on was much worth seeing. Styrofoam cups and paper bags and dirty clothes in the windrows of their comings and goings. Ashtrays on the gnawn armrests of the couch were filled to overflowing with butts. A dark jar of liquid sat on the coffee table atop a stack of unopened mail.

"Katie?" he called. The catch in his throat surprised him. Sweet Christ, he really gave a shit. The way he charged up in here. That he was here at all.

"Kate, it's me, Pete."

He set down his clipboard and stepped into a small cloud of fruit flies off the kitchen and waved them away from his face, his eyes. Into the narrow hall. Bed sheets with rust-colored stains and rectangles of particleboard rode along the wall. A pacifier. A Happy Meal box filled with twine. Sacks of sand and cans of open paint. A hammer and a stack of eight-track tapes.

"Katie?"

There were families you helped because this was your job, and you helped them get into work programs or you set up an action plan and checked in on them or you gave them a ride to the goddamn doctor's office to have that infection looked at. You just did. Because no one else was going to. And then there were the people who were reasons for you to do your job. Katie. Why.

Fuck why. She just was.

He stepped past the boy's room and called for her again. She wasn't in her room. Just a mattress on the floor and a thin sleeping bag and a cup of water. Pink nude dolls. He stepped over a crushed cardboard box and pulled on the cord to a bare bulb. Her small clothes lay on the floor. The cop's shadow passed by the window. Shit, she might have run away and into the woods out back.

The sliding closet door rattled on its track. There.

"Katie, it's Pete."

The door slid open. His heart was actually pounding. She stepped out into the room, slight and shy and stinted. Hair nearly white, and scared white too.

He knelt.

"Hey," he said.

She turned her head away.

"Hey," he said. "It's okay. I'm here."

She put her head down and charged at him and threw her arms around his neck. He gasped, and her hair sucked into his mouth with his breath, and her heart thrummed in her little birdcage chest, the little pumping bird that raced in there. His own racing too. He could feel the relief behind his eyeballs, his face, shuddering in his body like exhaustion.

"So she was in here," the cop said from the doorway.

Katie pressed her head tight against his, and he tried to unclutch her, but she closed her eyes against him, grabbed one of his ears, gripped his neck, and squeezed as hard as she could. Pete stood, the girl affixed to him. The cop scratched himself.

"It's okay," Pete said to the girl and then again, louder to the cop who departed, nodding sheepishly.

"Katie," he said. "The policeman is gone."

She looked to see if it was true, not at the door but at him. A skinny blond thing so small in his arms. She put her hands inside his coat.

"This was scary, wasn't it?"

She didn't move.

"The policeman came, didn't he? Because your mom and Cecil were fighting, right?"

She murmured yes.

"It was scary, wasn't it? I'd be scared. Not knowing what your mom is going to do to your brother or what your brother is going to do to your mom? Did you see the policeman?"

"Uh-huh."

"And is that when you hid in your room?"

She nodded against his chest.

"It's okay now. That was a good thing to have happened, because the policeman called me. And I'm here now and we're gonna get this all straightened out, okay?"

She wasn't ready to straighten out anything. She needed him to hold her. He rubbed her back, the laced bones of her spine. She shuddered out a terrific sigh. He wondered what she was thinking. He wondered did she wish he would take her away. Did she wonder what his house was like. What kinds of food he had. What he would play with her. What kind of father could he be.

He knew what kind of father he was.

But he knew too that it's nice right here to hold a small frightened girl and be strong and necessary. Times he took children from a bad home when it was almost worse on him than the child. Times they crushed up against him like this and he thought the work all came down to sheer rescue.

He carried her through the house and to the porch. The sun was full up, and the birds were out making their singsong rounds. The cop was talking to the mother and Cecil and he acknowledged Pete with a nod, looked under his fingernails, and kept talking to them.

"Now, I could put both of ya's in jail. I oughta should." He winked at Pete. "But, uh—"

"Pete."

"—Pete here says you're good folks having a spot of trouble is all, and I should be lenient."

He uncuffed them, the mother first. The boy rubbed his wrists. The shamed woman's chin quivered, but she didn't say anything.

"I don't wanna come back, you hear? If I do, somebody's going to jail. And I mean if I come back tomorrow, or next week or next month. I don't *ever* want to come back, you understand?"

The woman nodded. Cecil seemed transfixed by the indentures on his wrists.

"You all right here?" the cop asked Pete.

"Yeah. Thanks, Eugene."

The cop tipped his hat, and walked to his car, lighting another cigarette. When he left, a thick cloud of dust bore up from the road and washed over the porch and enveloped them. Pete covered the girl's face and went inside.

Pete had come up from Missoula to work in Tenmile a little over a year before, in the fall of 1979. Most of the people he actually knew in the town and in the region were his clients. In Tenmile everybody knew everybody else or at least one of their kin or where they liked to get good and peppered on a Friday night. Thus far, Pete had maintained a low profile. Anyone who met him outside of work knew only that he had an office at the courthouse, maybe something to do with easements or water rights. Some kind of comptrollery that went on in the basement.

But his anonymity would not last for long, he knew that. The past Saturday night he'd seen both the boy and the mother out and up to no good, Cecil in the bed of a pickup with a broken baseball bat, and Debbie on a stool at the Dirty Shame bar in an open-backed top that exposed her razorous shoulder blades and a dense constellation of moles. He'd managed to avoid speaking to either of them, but Tenmile shrank with every case.

Debbie followed him inside the house, dropped onto the couch, and commenced quietly sobbing. Pete sat on a wooden chair by the door. The room stale with the smell of flat soda and body odor. The mother glanced at him in intervals. Pity me. Poor me. Angling for his sympathy.

Let her dangle a minute. Let her see how well that works.

He got up and carried Katie into the kitchen, still nuzzled to his chest. He didn't even know if her eyes were open. He tried to catch their reflection in the window, but couldn't make her out. Five years old and light as a toddler. He might have been holding a long doll for all she moved or weighed.

"You hungry?"

She nodded against his chest. Plates crusted with dried mustard and mayo and ketchup crowded the countertops like discarded palettes. Fruit flies teemed over a bowl of old fruit, fruit he might've brought two weeks ago. Jesus, it was the fruit he'd brought. For fucksake. You try and help and she doesn't even give them the fruit. She doesn't even pretend. You put the fruit in the bowl for her and you say to her to make the kids eat it and she nods vigorously like she learned to in school, in detention, at what few jobs she's had, she's only ever learned to nod and say yes. Fucksake. You could picture her getting pregnant that way. Yeah, sure, it's not my time of the month, don't worry about it, I ain't getting pregnant. I do too much speed. My ovaries are broke.

There was cold pasta in the sink that looked halfway fresh. He touched it and it was still moist. It smelled okay. He set the girl on a plastic lawn chair by the table. She watched him fetch a bowl from the stack of dirty ones and wash it with hot water and a bar of soap from the windowsill. He washed a fork the same way, grinning at her. He sniffed the noodles again, and then forked the stiff spaghetti, but it came out of the colander like a halved basketball, and so he rinsed it and pulled it apart with his hands into a saucepan. He searched the cupboards and fridge and at last simply emptied a ketchup bottle over the pasta, and put the red mess on the electric stove. The girl tucked her knees up under her armpits, gazing at him as he turned the noodles in the heat. When the pasta sizzled, he carried her and the steaming bowl out to the living room. On his lap she blew on it, ate, and was otherwise silent.

The mother had ceased crying and stared at him grimly.

"I just can't get you all off my back," she said.

"I'm not on your back, Debbie. You told the cop to call me." He covered the girl's ears. "I'm nowhere near your damn back."

He could feel the girl chewing under his palms.

"You let things get so out of hand, the cops come? Jesus, Debbie."

Her chin crumpled like a can again. He uncovered Katie's ears and whispered he needed to talk privately to her mother, and she nodded and blew on her food. Lovely girl. He'd take her. He would. He covered her ears again.

"I know. I know. Just nothing works out for me." She picked through the junk on and around the coffee table for something—a cigarette probably—and knocked a metal pipe to the floor.

"We talked about that."

She nudged the pipe under the couch with her foot.

"About self-pity," he said. "Not the pipe you're trying to hide."

"You said you'd help me," she said, searching the cluttered table with roving hands.

"What do you think I just did with that cop? That's helping. That's exactly helping," he said.

She found an empty pack, and crushed it, sighing hugely.

"Not enough it ain't."

She looked at the cuff-welts on her wrists and started in crying again. Katie twisted spaghetti around her fork.

"Debbie. You're not the only one to ever fuck up. Everybody's got their troubles." Pete kissed Katie's hair. "Even me. I got problems just like you do. I mean, hell, I'm only up here in Tenmile because I needed to get away from some bullshit where I was at."

At this, Debbie looked at him.

"Just take him away." She tried to work up some tears. "He's an ungovernable."

"You can parent him, Debbie."

"I got a note from his school that he ain't been for weeks."

"We can deal with that. Why don't you just tell me what's going on here at home."

She rubbed her face. She was coming off of whatever she'd been on and her spindly hands worked her head like they were trying to dig into her skull. Her legs quietly pistoned.

"You know what all goes on. He's crazy."

"I've made numerous appointments to get him in to see the psychiatrist in Kalispell—"

"He won't go! What am I supposed to do? He's biggern me!"

"You can hold your own, Debbie—"

"He hates me."

"He doesn't hate you."

He hates her, Pete thought. I hate her.

She balled her fists and crushed them into her eyes. For several moments.

"Okay, Deb. Why don't you take it easy on your head there?"

"What?"

"Your head. You're digging into it."

She set her jaw and shook her head.

"Take him. Just take him."

"Where? Where am I supposed to take him, Debbie?"

His hands had slipped off Katie's ears.

"Wherever you take kids when you take them. Ain't that your job? I'm asking you to take him. Do your fuckin job. I'm a taxpayer."

Katie twisted around to see him, alarmed. A touch of want in them too. Would he take her away. Take her with him.

"Nobody is going anywhere." He put his hands back over her ears. "I don't know what you think I do, but let me tell you, the world is not filled with people waiting to raise your children."

"His uncle then."

Just then, Cecil entered. Air rifle in hand. Pete shunted the girl into the recliner and stood. The boy leaned the air rifle onto the couch. He wore a backpack and was expressionless and heavy-lidded and it occurred to Pete that Debbie was probably a raging drunk when she was pregnant with him. Had to name him *Cecil* of all things. And now this mess of a person.

"I'm leaving," he said. "You can forget about me."

"Hold on—" Pete started.

"Go already!" Debbie screamed, outsized for the situation. "Just leave me! Leave me here with no man in the house!"

"Debbie . . . ," Pete said.

"You ungrateful piece of shit!"

"Fuck you!" Cecil roared, and he slipped by Pete and had his mother by the hair. Both of them shouting, Debbie kicked him in the groin, and he let out a low moan, released her, and fell to his knees.

"All right, all right, enough!" Pete hollered, but the boy quickly stood and punched her in the face. She wheeled backward arms flailing, and tripped into the television, which fell onto the corner of the flagstone fireplace and cracked open like an egg. A snotty tendril of smoke rose out of the picture tube. The boy lunged, but Pete pushed him down and pressed his knee into the middle of his back.

"Get out!" he yelled at Debbie. "Go!"

She cupped her eye as though the pain had at last occurred and further enraged her. She stepped back to take a run at kicking her son in the head. Pete grabbed at her leg, but she skipped out of range. Pete pointed toward the rear of the house.

"Get out, goddamnit, or I'm calling the cops."

"You piece of shit!"

"Debbie! Go or the cops again! Your choice."

She wasn't listening. Cecil struggled and yelled, and Pete jammed his knee in harder—but then Katie gathered her mother's long fingers and tugged on her, and Debbie followed her out of the room calling Cecil a sonofabitch, sonofabitch, holding her crying eye.

It wasn't yet noon and no one was much about on the square in Tenmile or around the Rimrock County Courthouse or the shops. The only person they saw as they drove across the tracks and then the river was a man pumping gas at the station on the way out of town. They were soon in a narrow alley of serried pines that gave way to mowed pastures. Pete turned onto an unsurfaced road that was shortly a ruck of graded dirt and vibrated them silly in their seats until they pulled in front of a white ranch house. Their flesh and ears buzzed in the sudden stillness. Out of sight atop the flagpole before them snapped an American flag in the wind.

The ugly pumpknot on Cecil's head glowed like an ember. His nose whistled. He gripped the air rifle. Pete had agreed to let him take it, just to get him out of the house.

"You can't bring that here with you," Pete said.

Cecil stared straight ahead.

"Now look," Pete said. "This isn't permanent. You're going back home."

"Like hell."

"You mother is your mother."

"I'll cut her cunt out. How's that sound?" Cecil asked.

Pete rubbed his face.

"It sounds damn awful, Cecil. You can't talk like that. Not here."

"Like what?"

"Like a psycho."

"I ain't a psycho."

"All right, look. Look at me." Cecil turned. "I need to know that you'll be good to these people. They don't want no trouble and I don't want to bring them any. They wanna help."

"Just drop me off on the highway."

"You know I can't do that. Let's just get you and Mom apart for a little while, and see if we can't get things figured out when everybody's cooled off a little bit."

Cecil raised his palm. Whatever. Fuck you, Pete.

Pete got out. The house was set back from the fence and the flagpole, and in back were outbuildings and beyond them an empty pasture. Cecil stayed put. Pete went through the gate and then up the path through a trellis to the house. A regal old hound brayed responsibly at his approach but didn't get up from inside the doghouse. Pete was almost to the front door when an older man came out of the garage, wiping his hands with a red rag, which he stuffed in his back pocket before he pumped Pete's outstretched hand. The man's great white mustache twisted out like longhorns. He and Pete exchanged greetings and were now looking over at the boy.

"Thanks for this," Pete said.

"Not a problem."

The aproned missus stuck her head out the front door, ruddy and cheerful as a gnome, and said howdy and that she couldn't come out, they were just about to pour the jam into the jars, but would Pete want one. Pete said of course, and turned back to Cloninger.

"There he is there in the car," Pete said.

"We looking at a shy fella or a tough guy?"

"Around grown men, he's pretty docile. But him and his mom are in a bad way."

Cloninger laced his fingers together, hung them below his belt, and tilted his ashen head at Pete.

"He's got priors, but they're *sneaky* priors. Arson. Breaking and entering. He was with those kids that were busting into pickups outside the basketball game last spring," Pete said. "He's older and bigger than that Rossignol kid you took in last time, but I think he's more bark than bite. That said, you never know. He might could be a handful," Pete said.

"I see."

"Really, I just don't know how he'll act in a different environment. Probably quiet for a few days and then we'll just have to play it by ear?"

"They Christian?"

"Not even close."

Cloninger nodded.

"I hate to ask this, but what's the longest you can have him?" Pete asked.

Cloninger unlaced his hands and pulled out a small black calendar and a small pencil from his shirt pocket. He thumbed through the little book to the place he needed. He squinted without his glasses.

"We're going to Plains in two weeks. Marta's sister. If he gets along, he can certainly come with."

"Nah. I'll get something sorted out before then. There's an uncle. I just didn't have time."

"Okee-dokee," Cloninger said, putting back his calendar and pencil. "Let's get him set up."

"One thing," Pete said, touching Cloninger's elbow. "Obviously, he isn't going to be grateful for your hospitality. But please do accept my gratitude."

Cloninger clapped Pete on the shoulder.

"We'll feed and shelter him, body and spirit."

From the car, Cecil observed the man holding Pete's shoulder and bending his head at him, like they were praying with one another. Then Pete and the man were at the car and opening the door, Cecil going along with it, handing Pete his air rifle, shaking the man's hand, and then already in his house which was a cloud of sweet moisture and the dog was sniffing his groin, and the mother squeezed his hand, and their children lined up to greet him too, and this was really happening. Pete was already out the door with a jar of jam, and Cecil was shown a spare bed and where to put his things. Then they were sitting down to eat. He was just in time for lunch, they said like it was pure kismet, and the dog would not quit sniffing his pant legs under the table even though he moved his feet and tried to shoo him with his hand.

What was her name?

Rachel Snow. But she wanted to change it.

To what?

Rose. "Rose Snow" said something deeply true about her. About her soul. She was a frozen flower. It was so sad, her almost-fourteen-year-old heart throbbed with feeling. Gushed.

And there was this bitch at Rattlesnake Middle School named Rachel.

This other Rachel.

Why'd she reach over with her foot and stomp on the gas as she and her mother idled at a light?

Because her mother was taking too long.

Because she couldn't stand the way she drove.

Because she didn't know why, all right?

Because she just always felt now like she needed to go go go everything was taking too long she was missing it all. She was thirteen already and she was missing everything.

Everything.

Did they nearly have an accident?

No.

Did her mother slap her?

She tried, the bitch. Just caught a bit of her hair.

Did her mother say that this was it? That she could go live with her father she was gonna act like this?

Bitch always said that.

What did Rachel think of going to live with him?

It's Rose.

What did Rose think of going to live with her father?

She thought, whatever. That it was all talk.

A *break* they called it. Hilarious. He bought a house up in the woods.

No, she didn't even consider it a possibility.

Why not?

She just didn't.

Why?

This wasn't why, but you wanna know something? What she remembers about him? Like an oldest memory?

Yes, of course.

A party at Greenough Park. Her father and mother and uncle Shane and some of their other friends. Uncle Spoils makes his dogs take a bath in the creek, coaxing them into the cold water. Working the clots of hair. He slips, goes all the way under and when he pops up he's yards downstream and only just manages to get to his feet and clamber out. Coughs up sprays of water, eyes wild with fear. Walks sopping wet back up to his dogs barking and nipping at him in their excitement, and says you kids stay away from the water. It's too high to play around. Don't go near it. Go on. Go play over in them trees or somewheres.

He's from Butte. He's totally hilarious. Big ears and a big nose and big eyes. Mustache, hair like red straw.

So later. It's almost dark and time to go home and her daddy is calling for her and she goes. She's five or maybe six. And he's in a hurry about something, about getting Mommy home, they had a fight because she was being foolish. Daddy had begun saying that some-times about her, that she'd get foolish at parties, sometimes grown-ups acted silly he was saying, no, not like Spoils silly, but Mommy has her own kind of silly, it's—we gotta hurry. And he says come on, the bridge is too far, the car is right over there, the lot is across the creek, come on. And he picks her up and they go into the dark water. And she tells him Spoils said to stay out and he wasn't being hilarious—

They are already up to his waist.

He's breathing hard, straining against the water. Footing the rocks now, slow steps. The water is cold through her shoes. She says she's scared Daddy and it's cold Daddy and she pulls her feet out of the water and it changes his balance and he stumbles and she clutches and screams.

He stops in the middle of the stream. Says for her to be quiet.

Be still.

He's breathing heavy.

Water's not that deep, not over my head, but it's fast, okay, he says. You gotta just hold on. I got you. His breath burns her nostrils and the smell of his sweat is bitter.

She realizes much later—when she got that bottle of crème de menthe with Kim and Lori from Lori's dad's liquor cabinet—that he was drunk. But even at the time she thinks I don't trust him, I don't believe him.

He doesn't have me.

And the next step, he slips, they go over into the roar and churn and she's so shocked by the cold and the outrageous fact of this even happening that she isn't even upset, she's just this thing being acted upon, totally helpless as a dolly, that it isn't until he's got her at a cutbank and pushes her up through the brush, handfuls of wet dirt falling away, shoving her into the poking sticks that then, right on the heels of relief, she is so so so mad. She slaps him when he comes out after her.

That your daddy could drown you on accident. She's shaking with the cold and the last of her fear and then her warming anger, her daddy almost killed them both.

Come on, Applesauce, he says. You're okay, he says.

And when he touches her, she won't let him, she says you're foolish too you're foolish Daddy too.

TWO

Tenmile was set in a triangular valley at the confluence of the Kootenai River and Deerwater Creek. A ghost town shared the creek's name, a settlement abandoned in 1910 when the last of the fifty thousand ounces of copper had played out. Before that, gold and silver. Miners by the hundreds and then the thousands blasted it free with dynamite and high-pressure water hoses, melted the mountain into muddy and runneled hillocks that from the bird's eye would have looked like a red and brown cavity furiously attended by denim-blue ants. Deerwater was never easily gotten to, and the town of Tenmile sprung up, first as a canvas-tent trading station the name of which was lost to memory but eventually became known as Tenmile because of its distance on the perilous switchbacks from the mining camp.

By the time the last of the miners left Deerwater's muddy sluices, Tenmile boasted a town square with an area for a courthouse. The town swelled to 3,500 souls. The citizens incorporated and sent money to the legislature to be named the county seat and within the year broke ground on a courthouse and jail. Timber and the vermiculite mine in

the nearby town of Libby kept Tenmile populated through the world
wars and well into the 1960s before the grown children began to move
away, the elders started to die, and the town settled at a suspect equi-
librium of about 2,500 people in 1975.

It was home to many loggers and around a hundred men working at the mill. A few guys made more than fifteen dollars an hour at
plumbing, machine work, and sporting goods. A used-car dealer did
fair competition with his rivals in Troy and Libby. There were a pair of
service stations and two churches (both Protestant), four steamy cafes,
and ten bars. About three hundred citizens made the haul to Libby for
the third shift at the vermiculite mine and came back looking like they
were dipped in flour, bloodshot in the eyes. Fervid coughs kept their
wives and children up nights.

There was a single lawyer who handled all the defense work, a
rotund judge named Dyson, and a profoundly alcoholic district attorney on whom even the old sots looked down. Two pastors and two pastor's wives and a gaggle of ever-present old ladies threw bake sales for
various charities and gossiped about everyone in sight. Self-important
nepotists manned the fire department and police station, the kind of
men who sometimes turned handily heroic in the histories of other
small towns and were no different here, having thwarted a bank robbery in 1943 that could be pointed out in places where ricocheted bullets had lodged around the square. There was even a piano instructor
who lived in a small, well-kept cottage that looked like it just might
house a piano teacher and from which issued an incompetent plinking
that proved it. And there were twenty-plus teachers in the town and all
were women save the gym instructor and the principal who managed
the elementary and adjacent high school.

The children were like children from anywhere, maybe a little
less so. Which is to say they watched very little television and lived
in trailers and cabins. In the main, they behaved themselves, but that
didn't mean all of them were suited for much more than seventh or
eighth grade. Nurturing a child's intelligence was still considered a bit
indulgent—the sooner they got to work, the better. It was well known

that Principal Pemberton didn't brook troublemakers—he simply expelled them into the meager economy. So it was something of an intrigue when Pemberton called and asked if Pete could come down to the school right away.

SOME OF THE OLDER children said they'd seen the boy on the playground but no one talked to him as he edged his way along the fence to watch the kids on and around the jungle gym. He sat on one of the halved dump truck tires in the wood chips, bonging his enormous boots against the rubber. The kids who noticed the boy didn't speak to him.

Some thirty minutes later Principal Pemberton found him on the second floor, outside Ms. Kelley's art class. The nurse was with the child now. Pete and Pemberton regarded them from behind the glass of the door.

"He turned to run, I grabbed his arm, and he bit me."

Pete looked at Pemberton. He showed Pete his hand.

"Didn't break the skin."

Pete looked through the window at the kid. He wore brown camouflage pants that were rolled at the cuffs to fit him and a darker brown sweater that hung on him holey as netting. Leaves and pine needles stuck to the wool and his knit cap. His eyes scanned the room, lighting on Pete behind the glass only long enough to look away and study the nurse or the room.

"I got him wrapped up, but just barely," Pemberton said. "The kid's strong for his size."

He tapped on the glass and the nurse came out.

"He's got bloody gums," she said to Pemberton. "I think he has scurvy?"

"No one's seen him before," Pemberton told Pete.

"He reeks," the nurse said.

The boy stood with his hands on his hips. He ran a sleeve under his nose. His movements were swiftly mannish, as though he were another species and full-grown for it, a pygmy or some other reduced people.

"Get a name off of him?"

"No. He wouldn't tell me."

"How's he been?" Pete asked the nurse.

"Sweet as a little bell."

"And no one has any idea where he's from? None of the other kids know him . . . ?"

Pemberton shook his head.

The boy sat back on the exam table and unlaced his enormous boots, and after he pulled them from his feet, plucked out the rags balled into each to fill the space after his toes ended. He sniffed the second of these rags like it held some information, shook it out as he had the first one, and laid it to the side of him. He tugged off cheesecloth socks. His bare feet were sickening. A thin flap of soleskin hung from his foot and he pulled it off like a piece of wet sack paper. He smelled this too, held it up to the light, and tossed it onto the floor, where it set like a gray cold cut. The rest of his foot like an etiolated stem, a rotten tuber or root.

"My word," the nurse said.

The boy looked up at their blanched faces and resumed the crude debridement of his feet.

Pete opened a notepad and wrote down the name of a pediatrician, tore off the paper, and handed it to Pemberton.

"This guy's retired and a little deaf. Let it ring and he'll eventually answer. Ask if he can come down."

Pete opened the door and went in. The nurse was about to follow, but he asked her to let him see the boy alone. The boy glanced up, but kept picking at his feet. Pete took a chair across from him.

"Hi. I'm Pete."

Pete leaned down and saw the gray sags under the child's eyes on an otherwise clean pale face. There was a taupe grime of dirt and ash all over his clothes. He smelled like a burnt match and salted fatback. His chopped hair shot out in brown shocks.

"What's your name?"

"Benjamin."

"Mind if I ask how old you are?"

"Go on ahead."

Pete grinned.

"How old are you?"

"Eleven."

"Really? You don't look more than eight or nine."

The boy licked his fingers and seemed to be pressing loose skin in place.

"Where're you from?"

The kid tossed his head.

"In town somewhere?"

The kid shook his head no.

"Where's your mama and daddy?"

The kid began to roll down his long socks. Light could be seen through them.

"Your feet hurt?"

"Not bad."

"You must've walked a long way for them to get like that."

The boy pulled on the socks and then began to stuff the rags back into his boots. A vinegar odor wafted across to Pete.

"Listen, I'm from DFS. I can take you home."

The kid pulled one of the great black boots onto his foot and began to lace it.

"Sorry. Department of Family Services. That's what the letters mean. I'd like to see if you and your family need anything. Help with groceries or maybe some medicine or something."

The kid tugged on the other boot and laced it.

"What do you think?" Pete asked.

The boy stood on his newly booted feet and rocked in place on them.

"I gotta shit," he said.

The kid walked bowlegged and with his chest forward like he was breasting his way across a river, observing with badly concealed interest the panoply of animals and plants cut from construction paper and taped to the walls. He looked through an ajar door at a classroom taking a quiz and at the lockers and up into the staircase with the mute fascination of an ambassador. In the bathroom, the boy entered the doorless stall and regarded the sculpted porcelain a moment before locating the upright seat and pulling it down. He shat with Pete watching, shameless as a dog. When he washed his hands, he lathered promptly, and then rinsed with wary pleasure, turning his hands in the hot water and looking at Pete in the mirror as if he had to keep an eye on him, and not the other way around.

The child didn't have hot running water. And he'd never set foot in a public school.

The boy wouldn't let the doctor examine him, but the doctor said scurvy was certainly possible. Said to check his belly and legs for liver spots, if the boy'd ever let him. He told Pete to get him some vitamin C, asked after the boy's stool, and when Pete described the quality of it, wrote a prescription for the giardia he'd probably gotten from drinking the mountain water.

There was no trace of the boy's earlier violence against the principal. If anything, the child radiated studied calm. He spoke in the clipped cadence of a POW, announcing at one point that he'd renounced his citizenship. He stated plainly that he'd kill anyone who stuck him with a needle.

Pete took the boy with him into the pharmacy for the medicine and vitamin C. The kid suffered a few stares for his clothing, the lengths of tattered sweater hanging off of him like witch-hair moss. His ears turned red. Pete took him around the corner to Jessop's Sporting Goods and by eye sized a winter coat, jeans, and a pullover because the boy wouldn't try anything on. He bought him socks, a bag of undershirts, and a pair of boots. For good measure, he grabbed a first-aid kit with gauze, bandages, salves, and aspirin, and had the clerk fetch a bottle of iodine tablets.

He half-expected the child to run, but he followed Pete faithfully.

When they got to the Sunrise Cafe, Pete guided the boy into the bathroom and set the sacks of clothes on the counter. He pulled out the bag of T-shirts and opened it and tore the tags off the pants.

"Let's get you in these new duds, huh?"

The boy swallowed, regarded the clothes like a person might a growling dog. With stillness and fear.

"Nuh-uh," the kid said.

"Why? What's wrong?"

"I need to go home."

"And I'll take you. But you could use some new clothes and something to eat. Then we'll go right home."

Pete picked up the shirt and started toward the boy. An outsized fear gripped the child and he backed into the wall and slid down against it and closed his arms around his head.

"Hey, hey it's all right," Pete said. "I'm not gonna hurt you. Here—"

But when Pete set the shirt on the tile before the kid, he clutched himself, pressed his face in his folded legs. Pete stepped back.

"Come on," Pete said. "You're wearing rags."

The kid didn't move. Five minutes like this. Ten. Flatware clapping together in the kitchen. Someone tried the door and Pete shouted that the bathroom was out of order.

The kid muttered into his legs.

"I can't hear you when you talk into your lap like that."

The kid looked up at him. "I can't."

"Sure you can. Then we'll eat—"

"He won't . . ."

"Who won't? Your father? He won't want me helping you and your family?"

The boy traced the lines of the grout in the tiles between his legs.

"Does he hurt you?"

"No."

"Does he hurt you mother?"

No answer.

"Look, Benjamin. Let me tell you what I see. I see a kid who's sick and small because he hasn't been getting fed enough. And now you're telling me that you can't put on some new clothes. I'm starting to wonder if it's *safe* for you to go home—"

"You're not gonna take me home?!" the kid screamed. "You can't keep me! You have no right!"

"Whoa!" Pete shouted. "Just calm down. I'll take you home. But I want you to—"

Pete was going to tell the child to just take the clothes home with him, but the boy tore off his sweater and began unbuckling his belt.

They lived in the woods some ways north of Tenmile in the rolling and dense forests of the Purcell Range. The boy didn't know the way to town by any of the county roads or which logging road he crossed coming down from their camp. He emerged from the forest behind the IGA grocery. Beyond that was an uninterrupted series of ascending ridges bisected by an old railroad track that was no longer in use. The kid said he went along the backbone of the ridges until he descended to and crossed a creek and then finally up a logging road. Determining what logging road was the problem. Pete had an idea from his map in the glove box, but it was old, and the new roads were not on it.

Of course, the kid had no idea how you drove there, didn't know if it was a Forest Service road or a Champion Timber Company road or what. It was coming on evening and they had been all over looking for any markers the boy might recognize. Outcroppings of rock. But there were only trees, miles and miles of green larch.

"Maybe this one," the boy said, pointing to another turnoff marked with two yellow reflectors a mile or so from where Separation Creek joined the Yaak River. The child had eaten lunch, drunk a large glass of orange juice, and even smiled at some of Pete's jokes.

They went up a disintegrating road, grown over with timothy and cheatgrass. The potholes were disguised by banks of unmelted snow at the higher elevation.

"This road's gonna swallow my car."

There was a closed gate ahead.

"That's the gate there," the boy said. "It's got that dent in it."

Pete stopped the car and turned it off. The engine ticked under the hood. The larches and pines sighed.

"How far?" Pete asked.

"A ways."

"A couple miles, what?"

The boy didn't know. Pete told him to wait in the car and got out and began to inspect the area around the gate. There would be a key somewhere around here. There always was—biologists and surveyors for the Bureau of Land Management, the Forest Service, and Champion Timber were always coming and going. He looked in the crooks of trees at about eye level and under stones that were about the right size. He heard the kid get out of the car.

"Just wait," Pete said. "I'll have this gate open in a minute."

Pete spotted a flat rock that sat conspicuously atop another one the size of a dinner plate. Bingo. He turned the top rock over. Nothing. He looked under the plate stone. Nothing.

"The key's gone," the kid said.

Pete stood.

"Papa throwed it in them bushes over there, but good luck finding it."

Pete looked up the ragged road. He couldn't even see the first switchback. He looked up for the sun, which had already ducked into the trees.

"How far are you up this road?"

"I dunno. A ways."

"A ways," Pete said. He ducked under the gate and told the kid to come on.

The sky and the snow they walked over turned everything the sleepy blue of evening and the gelid air burned cold into their lungs. Pete's lungs at any rate. You're in terrible shape, he thought. The boy trudged just ahead of him and by the second switchback could have bolted and Pete wouldn't have pursued him. But instead, the kid stopped against a stump where the road was half washed out and a steady trickle of water ran down a gut carved into the dirt.

Pete gripped his knees gratefully. Walking he'd pondered what he would say to the boy's parents. He'd tell them that he brought Benjamin

back just as fast as he could, that nobody wanted to mess with them or
their boy. He was working on what he'd say about the clothes, the prescription, and the vitamin C. But as he played out the scene his positiv-
ity set with the sun, and his decision to take the kid up here seemed
more absurd. Then fully stupid. Pete had been motivated by a certainty
that keeping the kid overnight was not an option. He had no place to
put him. Cecil was at the Cloningers', and he couldn't ask them. There
was nowhere else.

But Pete still felt a surging anxiety as he sat there, then a dread realization of the possibilities, in particular the chance that the boy's father
would put a bullet in him. Violence became in his mind an ever-likelier
outcome. There was the shelter in Kalispell. Pete could've run the kid
down there. At least called around.

The boy watched him, and for a moment it seemed he'd been reading Pete's thoughts.

"What's your last name?" Pete asked.

"Pearl."

Pete had caught his breath but wasn't ready to start hiking again.
He didn't even want to know how much farther. His legs knocked. He
squatted.

"Benjamin Pearl. That's nice."

"Mama said our name reminds us of how rare we are."

"What's her name?"

"Sarah. Before that, it was Veronica."

"Before what?"

"I dunno. Just before."

"And your daddy?"

"Jeremiah Pearl."

"You got any brothers and sisters?"

"Yes."

"How many?"

"Five."

"Five? Wow. That's a lot. Are you the oldest?"

"Nah."

"What are their names?"

"Esther, Jacob, Ruth, Paula, and little Ethan. I come before Paula and after Ruth."

"I see. Are they up here with your parents?"

The boy stood and tugged a sapling from the side of the hill and beat the dirt out of its roots. Pete looked around. He'd scarcely noticed that they'd walked into an area that had been replanted in the summer. Waist-high green pines grew up and down the hillside. The Pearls had chosen a good place to be away from society. The traffic up here—from the timber company at least—would be minimal for some years.

"Why'd you go into the school today, Benjamin?"

"I dunno."

"Just sort of wandered onto the playground?"

"I don't know."

"Well, what were you doing in town?"

"Getting some things."

"What things?"

"Food and things."

"You have a house or some friends in town or something?"

"No."

"Dumpsters?"

The boy pulled another sapling out of the ground.

"They throw a lot of perfectly good stuff away behind the grocery stores, don't they?"

The kid shrugged and beat the dirt out of the sapling and tossed it over his shoulder. He pulled on another. It was almost as tall as he was.

"I don't think Champion Timber'd be crazy about you doing that." The boy had no idea what Pete was talking about. Pete said they should get going.

"He's coming."

"Your father? Where? Here?"

"He's been watching the whole way."

Pete turned in a full circle, looking in the short trees for some sign. Again, it was well thought out. There was cover in the saplings, but they were short enough to provide ample sight lines from any of the surrounding ridges and peaks. The revelation of his own exposure annoyed Pete.

"Let's go meet him then. It's getting dark."

The kid started up the draw from where the water washed out the road. They climbed up over stumps and rocks and the water ran under kernel-corn snow that was a year old and knee-deep in this hillside cavity. They achieved the rim and walked it, slipping on icy hidden roots. They rested and went on in the falling dark at last arriving on the ridge. There was starlight to the east. A dark vista of trees and still more trees.

Pete massaged his side. An ache there. He was cold and short of breath in the lashing wind, and his eyeballs floated in little pools.

"So," he panted. "Where the hell. Is he?"

A deafening crack drowned out the boy's answer. A flash, a light in his eyes. Pete crouched in a beam of light and the gunshot was echoing back off the mountains. The light remained in his eyes like bear spray, and finally the shot died out and still he hunched and covered his eyes against the light. He looked over and the boy stirred on the ground. He thought the child had been shot.

"Get up," a man said from behind the light.

Pete splayed his fingers in front of his face as if to filter out some of the glare, but it fired into his eyes all the same, and many-colored coronas burned in his vision when he looked away.

The boy started to walk toward the light, and Pete was trying to decide if he should reach for him, hold him back—*of course not, you'll be shot*—when the man spoke: "Stay right there."

"Papa, I—"

"Stay right there!"

The voice boomed of its own signal magnitude, a thunder.

"Mr. Pearl? I'm from the Department of Family Services." His voice sounded high and fearful in his own ears. He carried on and hoped that his timbre would improve: "I'm not law enforcement or anything like that. May I show you my badge?"

The light offered no response.

"I just come across Benjamin in town and he said you all were living up here and so I brought him back."

The light swept over to the boy.

"Take off those clothes," the man ordered. Benjamin immediately complied and the light swung back into Pete's eyes.

"Wait," Pete said. "It's gotta be thirty, forty degrees out. There's nothing wrong with the clothes. They're *new*. Look, you're not on the hook for them. They're gratis. Free."

"I know what *gratis* means."

"Of course. I just meant that it's my job. I have a budget for this sort of thing."

The boy had dropped the coat and the shirt into a pile in front of him and was undoing the pants. An insistent logorrhea poured out of Pete as the kid pulled off a brilliant white T-shirt.

"Look, if it's a matter of you wanting to not take a handout, that's fine. I can certainly arrange to, you know, accept payment for the clothes. I, I didn't mean to offend you or overstep my bounds. Benjamin didn't ask for the clothes. I *insisted* that he take them."

The boy unlaced and kicked off his new boots and tugged off the new socks and then pulled down his pants and stepped out of them onto his wounded bare feet.

"Mr. Pearl. Please. He's just a boy out here in the cold. I wouldn't have—"

The light swung over to the boy and then back into Pete's face and stopped him short. The boy stepped gingerly in place on the pine needles, wincing.

"Please, sir. *Mr. Pearl.* Your son's got giardia poisoning from drinking out of the streams up here. I figure you and your family might have it too. I have some medicine here in my jacket. Enough for all of you and I can bring some more. In fact, I was hoping that you might let me bring up some oranges. He's got bleeding gums and we think . . ."

He trailed off. Benjamin was naked. All knobs and knots, white and gaunt, and he put Pete in mind of creatures that lived in caves, albino spiders and eyeless fishes and newts. A white boy with purple and brown bruises and dirt and pink scar tissue and all those jaundiced whorls, all of the colors so faint in the whelming whiteness of him. He was nacreous, mother-of-pearl, this son of Pearl. And about his thighs and stomach a leopard dappling of liver spots, his penis scotched in his new pubes like a gray node. You thought not of flesh at the sight of his body, but minerals. It was a small astonishment that he was mobile, that this pearlescent boy clutched himself with bony arms.

"This isn't necessary," Pete said. "There's no reason he needs to suffer."

"You go," the light, the elder Pearl, said. "You come back, you can expect a fatal wrath. You tell the same thing to the feds."

"The feds? Nobody's coming. Nothing like that is going on here."

"You've come, haven't you?"

The fact that the man spoke settled Pete's nerves some. He could interact. Pete could do his job.

"I'm just returning your boy. I'm not bringing any trouble. All my job here is to help."

"You come clothed in weakness, but I know what stands behind you. You insinuate yourself among good people and you rot them from the inside with your diseases and mental illnesses."

Crazy talk. What to say? You don't push him. You don't test him.

"You need to put these clothes back on this boy," Pete said plainly, astonished at the brazenness of it. Despite the rifle, the light, his fear. "If I thought you were going to make him strip naked in weather like this, I wouldn't have brought him back at all. And if you think I'm just going to allow this boy to *freeze*—"

The beam shot into the trees and Pete followed it as it skittered to rest and lanced the black canyon, realizing too late that the man had simply dropped the light and was coming at him. Before Pete could recover his vision, Jeremiah Pearl was on him, had him by the jacket and was lifting him with one arm and pitching him backward to the ground. Pete lay there stunned. His vision a waterfall of sparks. His head rang. Those black angry eyes, even now striking fear into him. Pete threw up his arm helplessly and scuttled backward into a tree.

He now made out Pearl squatting right over him with his rifle in one hand. The man's breath, body, and beard stunk like a smudge pot.

"I'll put one in that boy's brain before I let you have him. That is a *solemn* fuckin promise."

He leaned forward. Pete flinched. The man spat on him. Then he whipped around and heaved his naked son up onto his hip and jogged into the brush.

Pete could still hear them moving across the mountainside and the boy sobbing, and Pearl saying something to him, not harshly, something firm and measured. Pete's impression of it was that they were very scared, as if they'd had the same nightmare and he was assuring the boy that they were awake now, that everything was okay.

He listened until they were gone. Then he gathered the clothes, folded them, put a business card in the pocket of the pants, and set them under a cleft in a rock where they would be dry and could still be seen. He walked carefully down through the dark woods to the road and to his car.

Another day at the office.

THREE

Pete drove west into Tenmile out of the absolute black behind him where there were no lights or residences in the Yaak Wilderness, where only a black horizon rose up unevenly to the constellations that pulsed from their cupola over the lightly spangled valley bowl below. Tenmile's scarce illumination—neon bar signage, a few porch lights, the four streetlights flashing yellow—could not dim the stars in this plain and blank night country.

And though Pete was from another small town, or rather, a ranch outside of one, he liked it in Tenmile.

That is, he liked particular places in Tenmile.

He liked the Sunrise Cafe for its coffee and smoky ambience and the way his arms stuck to the cool plastic tablecloths in the summer and how the windows steamed, beaded, and ran with tears when everyone got out of church and came in for breakfast on a cold morning. He liked how Tenmile smelled of burnt leaves for most of October. He liked the bench in front of the tobacco shop on the square and how you could still send a child to buy you a pouch of Drum from inside with no problem from the proprietor. He liked the bowling alley that was sometimes, according to a private schedule kept only by them, absolutely packed with kids from the high school and the surrounding hills who got smashed on bottles of vodka or rotgut stashed under their seats and within their coats. How much a girl was always a girl and would turn bonkers when the correct boy took her coat, how she would bend over at the waist like she could not move her feet, as if she were rooted to the spot, desperate for him to come back and take something else so she could squeal again. How much that was like a pheasant flopping on the ground as it tried to lure you away from her hatchlings. How much biology throbbed and churned here—the mist coming off the swales on the east side of town and a moose or an elk emerging as though through smoke or like the creature was itself smoking. How the water looked and how it tasted right out of the tap, hard and ideal, like ice-cold stones and melted snow. How trout looked in that water, brown and wavering and glinting all the colors there were and maybe some that didn't really exist on the color wheel, a color, say, that was moss and brown-spotted like peppercorns and a single terra-cotta-colored stone and a flash of sunlight all at once. That color existed in the water here.

There were also people here with secrets. A thief. A homosexual. People who mistreated their children, and whose houses stood out in Pete's mental map of the town like amber beacons because he knew. Their secrets he kept.

The judge—a fat man named Dyson who recalled President Taft with his gray mustache, vest, coat, and pocket watch—knew Pete's family back from Broadus (before Pete was born) and then Choteau where they now lived, and he introduced Pete to the town's luminaries, the business owners, and the local color when Pete took the open position in the western half of Service District One. Pete met them all, the president of the Cattlemen's Association, the union rep for Local 292, and a series of thin cowpoke noblemen who all shook his hand and said howdy when they saw him at the little Safeway or at the Sunrise. It might be years before they really felt they knew him, before they talked familiarly with him.

But the bars. In the bars was another class of people, fast friends

who came in for a dollar burger and a fifty-cent beer and free peanuts for lunch, and sometimes blew off the rest of the day and just
got wrecked. There was Ike who had a glass eye that would often as
not be in somebody's beer glass. Jerome and Betsy who fought, made
up, fought, and let Pete crash on their couch if he wound up there
for a nightcap. Demented Harold who always needed a ride home.
The other Harold, a Blackfoot Indian they sometimes called "Indian
Harold" who was always good for a round, no one knew where he got
his money.

You went to the Fizz if you wanted to see Ike and his glass eye,
and laze about at the low tables and plush chairs on rollers. You went
to Freddie's for burgers and beer, the long black griddle shimmering
behind the bartender, and the War Bonnet for fishbowls of an unholy
red concoction that was ice, liquor, and lurid grenadine. The Nickel was
only just wider than a restroom stall and the bar ran the length of the
place, and you peed out back into a cement trough that the gutter ran
into. You drank elbow to elbow, and when a fight broke out, you couldn't
see it because of the narrowness of the chute you were in, and people
climbed on the bar to get a look and the ceiling fan knocked off your hat.
And at the Ten High time stopped and at some point you toppled over,
and when you stood your back glinted with pull tabs and peanut shells
and people sometimes cut their hands wiping you off. And, like tonight,
it was dark when you were done with your work, and to get there you
drove by the dimmed hardware store—the bags of lawn seed under the
awning next to the lawn mowers padlocked to one another—the Dairy
Queen, the firehouse, and onto the square proper, past the Ten High,
then right on Main and into the dark alley behind it.

Tin gutters rattled in the wind and voices rebounded from the alley-
mouth, their figures already past when Pete looked up. He pulled on the
back door of the bar and entered. In the hall, wainscoted with laminate
tile, starkly lit by a bare bulb he flashed on a memory of himself from
when he first moved to Tenmile, passing in and out of awareness, holding a Blackfoot woman fast by the waist, his head buried in her pure
black hair. Where they ended up, what became of her, he couldn't recall.

He pushed through the swinging doors to the bar proper. Old men chatted at a back table, a few more shot pool. A pair of the decrepit in their fine suits of polyester, brown and powder blue with matching vests and white piping, sat by watching from sunken eyes, sipping red beers on a row of stools along the wall. They leaned in to listen to what was said, pulling the toothpicks from their mouths as if that might help them hear.

Behind the bar Neil unloaded a box of beer into the cooler.

"Drink?" he asked, seeing Pete.

"Dyson been in?" he asked.

"Nawp."

Pete went out the front door and looked across the street at the courthouse. The light in the judge's office was out, but Judge Dyson and another man stood under a maple on the courthouse lawn talking politics in the light of the moon. The judge gestured animatedly. Dyson the old Democrat, fighting the good fight for the sinned-in-his-heart President Carter. Pete had read the race was close, but it wasn't close here in Rimrock County. The people who lived up in the Yaak in their tar paper cabins and half-finished log homesteads weren't political— they were perfect anarchists. Most of them lived here because the government was a negligible presence. They cut down their own trees for firewood. They hunted and fished whenever they wanted. Most trucks had a snowplow. Some even objected to the delivery of mail.

Dyson could generate a plurality of straight-ticket Democratic votes with state and federal employees and union guys, but he only prevailed on Election Day because the better part of the county actively avoided voting or mocked it, submitting *Mickey Mouse* as a write-in candidate.

But this year something was off. Hand-painted REAGAN COUNTRY signs had bloomed up in the pastures along the highway. Places that weren't even hamlets, just little outposts of fierce individualism. The people the judge tried to cajole now didn't care how long he'd been in the legislature, what committees he'd been on, or what pull he may or may not still have. They may have liked him personally, but not his pedigree.

Now the judge talked with his hands, threw wide his arms, touched the man's chest, and pointed at his open palm. Pete willed him to ease off. But the judge now buttonholed the guy—literally hooking his fat finger through the man's open buttonhole—as though turning this man alone would deliver Rimrock County to President Carter.

Give it up, Judge, Pete thought. We need to keep our heads down. We need us a stiff drink. The man spoke and the judge crossed his arms and tilted his head back in a mime of listening. Pete had seen this move in court and it always preceded a redoubled harangue.

Could be hours.

Pete went back inside. Neil had his foot all the way up on the cooler and leaned over it shelling peanuts, watching the television over the end of the bar. The president and Reagan behind their lecterns. Reagan's wrinkled cheeks ruddied with makeup. Carter and those outrageous lips.

Pete put his hands on the bar and leaned in.

"Do me a favor and turn it off? I don't want to hear from him all night about what a Republican dupe you are."

Neil smiled and got up on the cooler and flipped the channel. The debate was on all of them. He killed the sound and climbed down.

"You want a drink?" he asked.

"Better get me a boilermaker. It's been a long-ass day."

Neil selected a bottle, held it up. Pete nodded that it was fine as he took out a twenty.

"When the judge comes in, bring the bottle over before he can give you any money."

Neil clucked his tongue and took Pete's cash.

A couple of the judge's friends along the wall held up their beer cans in greeting, and Pete settled into a booth at the back of the bar. A quiet night. The poker table was covered with a black blanket. Pete sloshed his whiskey around, watched it cling like oil to the side of the short glass, and then took a drink. Hot and lovely. He quickly finished the whiskey, drank his beer, then got another from Neil, and when he'd finished that one, the judge came in fuming. Pete called, and the judge stormed over and slid into the booth, his gut taut against the table. Pete nudged the table away so the man could fit in. The judge frowned at him for it.

"Apparently we got us a real problem with welfare queens," the judge said.

"Is that right."

"You can't throw a stone without hitting one. Even out here in Rimrock County if that sumbitch Johan is to be believed."

Neil came up with the bottle and a glass. The judge grabbed them away from Neil and poured and then reached into his suit coat for his billfold.

"This goddamn Reagan— Where you going, Neil?"

The judge held up a bill. Neil pointed at Pete, and the judge scowled at him and put the money on the table.

"I drink your good stuff all the time," Pete said. The judge took a sip, held up the drink to say thanks, but left the bill on the table. Then he narrowed his eyes at Pete, studying him up and down as one might a horse or an engine block. He reached across the table and pinched some of Pete's hair between his fingers.

"Get a haircut," he said, tossing it away. "Why do these people let you into their homes, I have to wonder."

Pete smiled and poured more into his and the judge's little glasses.

"Because they know I'm not a cop."

The judge smirked into his whiskey, then swallowed. Asked how was business. Pete told Judge Dyson about the boy he'd taken to Cloninger's.

"Got 'em a Reagan sign up in their yard?"

"Not that I saw."

The judge took a fresh can of snoose from his vest pocket and snapped it in his hand while Pete told him about the Pearl boy and the gunfire and his father.

"These people," the judge muttered, more about the general electorate than Pete's clients.

"The guy made his kid take off the clothes I bought him. I'm not sure what to do now."

"Let them rot, the ungrateful sons a bitches." Dyson ran a fingernail around the diameter of the can, and twisted it open.

"Noble sentiment there, Judge."

"You go back up there, you'll get yourself hurt."

The judge took a pinch and tucked it in front of his bottom incisors. He licked his fat lower lip, picked black motes off his tongue.

"If I go alone," Pete said.

"You'll get some deputies hurt then. Just help the ones you can. It's not like you got nothing else to do."

Pete went and retrieved a coffee cup from Neil for the judge to spit in. The judge turned the cup handle away and aligned the can of chew next to it and his glass. He was not as neat a man since his wife had died, but habits remained.

"I seen your father's new old lady . . ."

"Bunnie."

"That's right, Bunnie. When I was in Great Falls a few weeks back," the judge said.

"How was that?"

"Evangelical. No match for your mother, rest her soul. The judge raised his glass and they sipped. "Bunnie had a couple bags on her arm. I assume that means the ranch is still doing okay."

Pete scoffed. "That ranch is a hobby."

"Your old man makes more of his hobbies than most people do with a whole career."

"He's just mean, is all."

The judge was going to say something about this, but Neil came over to check on them, and the judge shoved a fat finger in his face.

"Don't let this guy buy my drinks, Neil."

Pete slid out of the booth and the judge grunted his way out too. They watched the debate on television for a minute. Carter's sallow aura was evident, more so with the sound down. Reagan's turn to talk. He shook his head, said something to his lectern, looked up and smiled at Carter like he'd turned over a royal flush in a movie. It occurred to Pete that no one wins a close hand with a royal flush in real life. Ever. But in the movies, royal flushes were always coming to the rescue. These remarkable turnabouts, reversals on the turn of a card.

The front door boomed open. The judge scurried through it on his fat furious legs.

FOUR

Pete's cabin sat on five acres in the Purcell Mountains fifteen miles north of Tenmile, a two-mile walk from some decent fishing in the Yaak River. He'd put down two thousand dollars and made payments to the doddering codger who'd built it and now lived with a sister in Bozeman. A kind old guy who showed him all the little kinks of the place, what doors wouldn't latch, which window wasn't true. White sandpaper stubble and watering eyes when he left.

Think of getting old.

Think of being only thirty-one yourself and having gotten so much already dead fucking wrong.

Pete had running water and was to have electricity in the spring if the county could be believed. He had a new water heater from Sears on the porch, still wrapped in plastic, which he couldn't install yet; unlike the electricity, it was unclear when or if the county would bring gas, but he got a deal on the water heater. He'd hoped some surveyors he'd seen farther up Separation Creek were in the employ of developers, but a Forest Service truck met them and he couldn't be sure the men weren't from Champion Timber Company. He foresaw another year showering at the courthouse.

Next to the water heater was a nearly spent stack of firewood, but he had a pile of rounds out back of the house that he could split to get through the spring. The layout inside was simple, ample. A bedroom where for now he chucked his empty cardboard boxes, a front room with his bed, a leather chair, a kerosene lamp and an electric lantern, two shelves of books, and a bureau. An olive canvas bag half-full of clean or dirty clothes for the Laundromat in Tenmile. In the kitchen a separate woodstove cooked his meals just fine, and a hatch in the floor led into a root cellar where he kept his milk, beer, and vegetables. Problem bears broke into places up around here, but he hadn't had any trouble. The very idea of problem bears. A problem for who. Did the bears talk about problem people.

Pete was already up in the freshly broken dawn boiling water and watching out the window for whatever was there. There were times he saw down through the tamarack to the meadow a whole gang of elk, steam and reedy cries issuing from their throats as they moved through the sheets of mist. He scanned the woods, the morning light not yet lancing through, the tree boles black in the dark morning. No elk. No bears, problem or otherwise.

A time in his childhood when he went to Yellowstone Park. His father paid for them to sit on a bench in front of a dump with about fifty other people. The garbage trucks rumbled up and emptied themselves, and the grizzlies lumbered out of the woods one by one or paired with cubs to nuzzle through the trash. Their tongues scoured the insides of tin cans. They devoured cardboard boxes whole for what had once been inside. Sometimes they scuffled explosively, their fur coats shuddering as though they could throw off their carpets of fat, and thus disrobed show what bears looked like underneath all the garbage they'd been eating. No one said these bears had problems.

The kettle whistled. He turned to get it and when the whistle died, he heard a truck clattering up the road. He went to the kitchen window to see it was his brother coming. He set the kettle on the counter and massaged his face. The things his brother kept in the bed rattled and the diesel engine knocked as it quit.

They met one another out front, Pete on the porch in a T-shirt and robe, his brother down from it, in a plaid jacket and his hair combed flat across his skull like he was just from an interview or court date. The porch boards were cold on Pete's naked feet.

"What do you want, Luke?"

Luke smiled. It was Pete's smile—Pete's body just about too, the same wiry frame and rib cage and the same derelict heart underneath.

"I need a little money."

Different kinds of dereliction.

"Fuck you."

"I'm kidding. You gonna let me in?"

"No."

"C'mon. I ain't high or nothin."

Luke pulled at the skin under his eyes to show Pete the whites.

"You don't need to be high to steal."

Luke shook his head and smiled with one side of his mouth and frowned with the other, wry and bittersweet.

"Why don't you just get yourself back in that truck," Pete said, but Luke slunk up onto the porch, made for the front door. Pete intercepted him. Luke grabbed Pete's hand where it pressed on his chest. They were identical in height, but Luke was bigger in the arms from mending fences, bailing hay, and other handywork. Jobs he could land on parole.

"I about kicked your ass last time, big brother," Luke said.

"But you didn't."

"I'm feeling spry this morning."

Luke poked Pete in the gut smiling. Pete knocked away his hand, and Luke tried a short roundhouse that glanced the back of Pete's ducking head. Pete slugged him in the ribs, and Luke gasped and jabbed Pete square in the face, setting him back, and then Pete charged at him, robe billowing out behind him like a cape. Neither landed a good blow in the following short volley. They breathed heavily a moment, and then Pete closed on his brother, shoved him into a porch post, palmed his brother's entire face, knocking his head against the support. Luke had gotten his hands onto Pete's head and endeavored to peel away his cheek like one might a rind. A coffee can of nails went over into the dirt. Pete yanked himself free of Luke's grip and they got one another by the nape, their heads joined at the ears like a pair of hung-up deer. They panted there. Pete's face was numb on the one side.

"Will you just get back in your truck and go?"

Luke twisted away, and they stood apart, each of them trying not to show how winded he was, rolling his head on his shoulders, shaking out his arms, sideways to his brother like a pair of prizefighters. Then they slowly lowered their arms. Luke pressed his mussed hair flat against his skull. Pete pulled his robe back around his shoulders. He searched for the belt like a dog after its tail, and angrily knotted it after he found it. They panted still. Regarded one another across the six feet that separated them.

"May I sit on that milk crate at least?" Luke asked.

Pete kicked the crate over. Luke sat, yolky sunlight leaking through the trees now.

"There's two reasons you ever come to visit," Pete said, breathing heavily. "To get something out of me . . . or to tell me about Jesus and get something out of me." He paused to catch his breath. "Even though I ain't interested in neither one."

"I know it," he said. "Mine's been a crooked path."

"Don't romanticize it. You're just another asshole—"

"Pot, meet kettle."

"—and a thief. I told you we were done. I meant it."

Luke rubbed his face, pulled his hands across his eyes.

"I know. You're right. You're *right*. I can be frustrating."

"At this point, even Jesus and Satan just wish you'd choose a fucking side."

Luke uncrossed his arms and nodded. Ran his hand through his hair and then remembered that he wanted it flat, and pressed it back down.

"I know."

Pete abruptly went inside. He returned rolling a cigarette.

"How's your old lady?" Luke asked.

Pete pointed a wooden match at him.

"Leave it alone, Luke."

Luke sat up straight and looked off into the woods. There was nothing out here except trees and stones and animals, and though the forest was alive with the sound of those trees swaying in the wind and the small critters moving in them, you could tell he was bored already of it. The woods made him antsy. Land and nature gave him no peace. Never did.

"It's nice out here," Luke lied. "I wish I'd have gotten my shit together to get a place like this."

Pete turned a large piece of firewood on end and sat unsteadily on it.

"Bullshit. You hate it in the sticks."

"So do you."

"What do you want?"

Luke grinned a private grin that Pete knew hid a secret he was about to hear. Something Luke connived.

"Should I bother asking?"

"Bunnie wants you to come out to the house. Dad's been sick. That cough."

"Gosh, he has a *cough*? Why didn't you say something?"

"You should go see him. Bunnie and him."

"Let me just get my coat," Pete said, dragging on the cigarette.

"You need to check up on them," Luke said.

"You check up on them."

"I ain't going back that way."

"Here it comes. I fuckin knew it. What'd you do?"

Luke ran his hands over his thighs, his fingers arched into tines. It was something bad.

"I knocked out my parole officer."

Pete began to cough, he was laughing so hard. So hard he dropped the cigarette and stepped off the porch and gripped his knees.

"I had a knife on me that I'm not supposed to and Wes saw it and started talking all this shit. 'Serious violation of my parole.' Fuckin asshole. Way up in my face. Way up, Pete."

"So you clocked him."

"I beat the lovin hell out of him. I couldn't stop my fists," Luke said, holding up his hands with some wonderment.

"You dipshit."

"Stop laughing. I had to spend two nights in the damn woods. It ain't funny."

"Yes it is. Yes, it truly is." Pete got back up on the porch and just beamed at his brother. "This beats everything."

"I ain't going back. I can't do no time again, Pete."

"Shit, it can't be that bad. Eighteen months? What are you gonna do instead?"

Luke stood and rocked back on his heels.

"Right. You have a *plan*," he said.

"I need someone to know where I am. In case anything happens. With Dad."

"Nothing's gonna happen with Dad."

"You really need to go see them, Pete."

"I said I would."

"No, you didn't."

"Well, now I have."

"This week?"

"Where you gonna run to?" Pete asked.

Luke reached around to his back pocket and handed Pete a slip of paper. Penciled onto it was an Oregon post office box and a map with directions to a spot not far from the coast.

"What's this?"

"He's a decent guy. Met him at church. He was coming through giving a pretty interesting lecture."

"Sounds like you got everything under control."

Luke smiled the beneficent little smile he'd acquired with religion.

"You should go sometime. It's done me a world of good."

"That's evident. Nobody would debate you."

"Sarcasm is just anger."

"You're an idiot."

"Pete."

"I got your information here." Pete held up the paper. "Anything else?"

"I don't think there's a phone, but if there is, I'll call your office."

Pete mashed out the cigarette smoking on the porch with his bare heel. He didn't feel anything but a small spot of warmth.

"Give yourself up, Luke."

"I have, my man." He pointed upward.

"To the Teton County sheriff."

Luke put a hand in the air, his eyes floating off, a helpless expression on his face, and paid out a long sigh, that taken together meant that Pete was right, and running was foolish and would just escalate things, but also that Luke had made up his mind and there was no talking him out of it.

"I got to get away from this trouble," he said. "It'll blow over."

Luke stretched out his hand for Pete to shake and to the surprise of both of them, Pete took it.

"It ain't gonna blow over, Luke. Not this time."

Luke pumped his brother's hand and pulled him in, clapped his palm onto his neck, and hugged him. Then he bounded into his truck, waved, and backed out. He turned around on the dirt road and then trundled down the mountain. For a long time Pete could hear him going.

He drove his Corolla with the windows down, but pumped them back up when mammatus clouds popcorned over the Flathead Valley and gumdrops of rain began to splash his windows. He turned onto Highway 28 and the clouds quit raining altogether and shortly thereafter broke up like a crowd after a fistfight. He drove into mature afternoon sunshine. The yellow valley slicked and glistening where the haymows stood in the fields like wet yurts. Coveys of birds rose in folding fans and closed to the ground, pecking where the rainwater had flushed up worms and bugs. The highway bore south, and at Paradise, Montana, he crossed just down from where the Flathead joined the Clark Fork River candescing in the sun like a sheet of copper tapering off up the valley toward Idaho. He eased along the water and rolled down the windows again. The cool fresh air poured in. The papers in his car fluttered like a rookery.

The wheels slipped on the wet dirt road heading into Billie Gulch and slipped again up the steep drive to the Short house. The drive was as pitted as a shell range. A pollarded goat drank from a halved oil drum and watched through its rectangle pupils the car slowly pass by and was trotting after when Pete glanced in the rearview. He leaned forward to get a better look at the house and when his car dipped into a severe pothole, Pete stamped his chin on the steering wheel. The car stalled out fifty yards from the place. His tongue throbbed and smarted sharply at once. It hurt so badly, he shuddered. He looked in the mirror, and the gaps between his teeth turned bright red.

Pete climbed out of his car and weaved up the drive working his jaw, which was sore too, and the ram trailed after, its yellow demon eyes unnerving him. He shooed it away. He said something like "Muthathuck," and spat blood. The goat nickered at him and stopped to sniff where Pete spat and it ate the dirt, saliva, and blood, the godawful animal.

The Shorts kept a brace of black and tan Rottweilers, which were the nicest things they owned and that now lifted slobbering heads and growled in a low rheumy register in near harmony. They had met Pete, but always with Tony Short. Now Tony Short was nowhere about. They watched Pete sway heedless through the thin, gray mud, spitting blood. To the dogs he was merely some bent and slipping man, muttering and scraping off his shoes on the edges of the flagstone approach to the fence, now walking upright to the open gate. He was thirty, forty feet away from the porch when they barked. Pete halted, regarded them, and clapped his hands, beckoning them to heel. They might have recognized him. They might have not. His voice was suspiciously garbled. He might have sounded wounded. Definitely hinky.

He peered around and over them at the windows, what trodden hardpan littered with broken toddler bikes and rubber toys that passed for a lawn. Now the Rotties barked in unison and stood. They took quarter steps in his direction, quivering, teeth bared forth in the slow peeling back of their faces.

They had Pete's full attention, and he tingled up and down his back. The air between his skin and his shirt was charged, as was his entire torso. He wondered did the dogs sense his electric fear.

"Eathy boys, ith me," he said, and they charged, brimmed hearts pounding, hot throats open. Pete yelped and swung closed the gate, and they slammed into it. The latch rattled but the gate held. They fell over one another and clambered up snarling, spittling and furious. Pete backed away, palms up, and they reared hindlegged at the gate like dwarf landlords, upright dogmen now whimpering in fury. Pete halted his retreat. It was okay. He was okay. He grabbed his own chest in relief. Heart still rattling in its shallowed brisket.

Their barking continued unbroken, and they seemed to need no breath to do it. Pete flipped them off. He turned and walked back to his car, dodging puddles, happily hopping over them, quite giddy at this point, coulda shit myself, sweet Jesus that was close—

Of hot white sudden he realized that the barking was halved, that the rhythmic tread of dogfeet was at least one of those fine animals loose and headlong at him.

He didn't even look.

He leapt potholes to where his car had died, yanked open the door, and flung himself inside in terror just as the dog hit the open door, skidded past and immediately recovered, lunging, snapping at his hand before he could close it. For a moment the dog just barked at him as he dared not reach for the door handle. Then he did reach. The dog clamped its watering maw onto his outstretched hand. He yanked it free of the animal's mouth, but the dog was able to budge into the car with him.

From the yard, the less clever of the two animals stood and barked in high agony, completely forgetting the gap in the fence. The vehicle rocked at the combat within it, and the dog watched the man spill screaming out the passenger door, and leap atop the car. The Rottie followed him out, ran back into the vehicle, and out the driver's side door, bewildered that it didn't somehow arrive on the roof.

Pete quaked and nearly retched with fear as he checked himself. Dark blood pooled in his palm and dripped out the back of his hand. Abrasions seethed under his coat. A long tear in his pant leg where the dog's jaws had snapped closed like a sprung trap. Which the animals were. Hatred for Tony Short swelled in his breast. Fucking hill people and their fucking dogs lying around like loaded guns.

The vehicle shook under him as the dog began tearing the upholstery. The second Rottweiler had found the hole in the fence now, and sprinted over and joined the other in the car, and from the sound of it, the two of them fought one another for a moment. Then they circled Pete's car and Pete on top of it, heaving themselves up, whining and smiling at him, circling, until at last one attempted to scramble up to him, claws slipping on the bumper and hood as it slid off with a grunt. It would not be long, though, before one of them simply leapt onto the hood and drove him off the roof and into the jaws of the other.

The moment to move was now.

Now.

Okay now.

They're going to get up here, you don't do something—

Pete slid over and shut the passenger door from above, and the dogs closed in on him, jaws clacking at his hand, and then he flung himself over to the driver's side, dropped off the car, sprung into it, and slammed closed the door.

The Rottweilers scratched at the door and window, and then snapped at one another again, hindlegged in an outraged dance. The gnashing inches from him on the other side of the window like some-

thing you wouldn't even see at a zoo. Buffeting the car with their muscle, Pete's keys jangled in the ignition.

He opened the glove box and soaked up blood from his hand with a
paper napkin. He grabbed a flask and opened it against his chest with
his good hand and dribbled liquor onto the holes in his bad hand. It
burned, and he winced hugely. He pressed the saturated and ripping
napkin against his hot wounds until it finally stanched the bleeding
and clung poulticed to his palm. The dogs crazed and slicking his window with slobber the whole time. He yelled at them, but naturally they
could not leave him be.

He dropped his head back and tried to cease shivering. Pictured
the Short house in flames. How he'd do it. He didn't even care about
the Shorts' children anymore, children who'd turn out just like Tony
or get pregnant by guys like Tony who bought and bred dogs for sheer
destructive power. Raze the thing. Scatter the Shorts to the winds.

He grabbed their case file from the seat, and bloodied the case log:

*The Shorts breached their agreement with Agency and were again (fifth
time) absent for a previously scheduled from this agent. Agent believes
that the Shorts are evading inspection as ordered by the Rimrock County
Family Court and Rimrock County Office of the Montana Department
of Family Services and may again be involved in criminal activity (see log
7/30). Agent was unable to survey house due to attack by the Shorts' wild
dogs who were left unsupervised at home location and may pose considerable danger to Short children. Agent was bitten on the hand and—*

Pete set the paperwork aside. He reached into the open glove
box, fetched the canister from within it, and cracked the window. He
paused a moment in sympathy for the guileless animals, genuinely
touched by the raw beauty and ideal breeding snarling wildly at the
inch-wide gap in his window. Then he maced one dog square in its
snapping face with exquisite joy. It bucked back and twirled coughing,
fell, scrambled up in the mud, and then careened blind until it col-
lided into a metal shed at full speed with an explosive bang. For a time

it did not move. The second bore into the field after Pete sprayed it, simply trying to outrun the hot torment. Peace settled over the scene. The hornless billy chuckled like an amused codger. Pete stashed the spray and wrote some more:

> Agent recommends to the Court that the children be remanded to their aunt's (Ginny Short) until such time as Crystal and Antonio Short can demonstrate their willingness to work in good faith with the State of Montana and as per their plea agreement with the District Attorney's Office and the Office of Child Protective Services.
>
> —Agent P.W.S.

◆　◆　◆

Did her father call?

Yes. She'd answered the phone assuming it was Kim or Lori and hoped maybe but probably not Kevin calling her back.

God, if it was Kevin. A soph-oh-more. Yes, more please.

Hey Applesauce, her father said.

Oh.

Yeah, hi.

Hi.

Look, I can't make it down today. I'm really sorry. I got bit by a dog. I need to have it looked at—

She asked him did he even have any idea what was happening.

He said what, what was happening.

She said she couldn't believe he didn't know. She wanted to get back at him. Intuited that she had some power in knowing what he didn't: her mother was in her bedroom, shoving clothes into garbage bags.

What is it, honey? What's going on?

What is wrong with this family?

He said Rachel. He said come on Applesauce. He said to put her mother on the phone.

She placed the phone on its silver cradle. She ran her hand

through her hair over and over and hated her tiny head in the reflection of the toaster. The phone rang again. She stood from the table and walked on the balls of her feet to her bedroom. Her mother said for her to get it, but Rachel closed her door.

Jesus, Rachel!

YOU GET IT! she shrieked. *I'M PACKING LIKE YOU TOLD ME TO! GOD!*

An empty suitcase. She heard her mother's voice veer into a fighting pitch on the phone. She opened a drawer and pulled out an armful of shirts and threw them onto the bed. In the back of the half-empty drawer was a saddening fifth of vodka.

Was it for a party? Was it for showing how grown she was and practically sophisticated?

Yes. It was for sitting with Kevin. She'd seen his stomach once. His bare stomach.

God.

Soft. But hard.

Oh.

More.

It ached to think about.

Was that so over now?

Duh.

FIVE

H e drove four hours to the city of Missoula to see his wife. He didn't eat or stop for gas. No radio. Like when you were a kid. The old man treated every road trip like a moon shot. You brought your grub for the trip or you went hungry. You held it or you pissed in the milk carton. Wasn't anything on the radio anyway.

He took Orange Street under the railroad and went up Front. It was strange visiting the city again, their city. The specific feeling of this small western city geography. He'd done his undergraduate at the university. A liberal arts degree in seven semesters. He'd done three semesters of grad school before he couldn't afford it anymore. All of it right out of high school with a wife and newborn daughter. No small pride in that.

There were cars around and people on the sidewalks. Buildings higher than two stories. He'd grown acquainted with smaller rhythms.

He turned onto his wife's street and parked near their cottage apartment by the river. Her apartment now. Late morning now and the sun had warmed off the frost except in the shaded lee of things. The aluminum screen was propped open with a broken brick, the door ajar. An open U-Haul trailer sat hitched to her little pickup, and his wife's clothes, his daughter's box spring, and even some of his old things were visible in it. A fierce hammering commenced in his chest and temple at the sight of his leather chair. He started up his car and then turned it off.

When she saw him come in, she set down a cardboard box, took the bandana off her head, wiped her brow, and put it in her back pocket. She already had a beer on the floor near her that she picked up and drank. Put her palm on her hip. The loose beauty about her—the way her smile cracked across her face, her wide lopsided curls rigged into a bun that seemed liable to topple down—reminded him of a tooth about to come out, a button about to fall off. Everything about her always on the verge of falling down or out. Made a body want to screw her heart out. Even now. Even after she'd cheated on him and even though it still hurt like a purple bruise, he could see falling into bed with her. Just look at her. The beer, eyebrow cocked, her condescending grin.

She said his name plain. Even that ached.

What it must be like to go about in that body, to think with that mind. It occurred to him that even if he didn't forgive her, it was possible to not blame her. Some narrow country existing between recriminations.

"Fucking Texas?" he asked.

He looked about. Bright squares of fresher paint where the pictures had been removed. Indentures of the couch feet in the rug.

"Yeah, Pete. Texas."

"And you don't ask me."

"I don't gotta ask you where I can live."

"The hell you don't, Beth. She's my daughter."

"You're welcome to take her up into the woods with you. If she'd go."

Backlit from the sunlight in the kitchen, his daughter appeared or might have been in the doorway the whole time. Nearly featureless in the shadows, a cutout. Knobbed at the knees, holding her kindling arms across her. Knowing if he went toward her she'd bolt to her room and slam the door, but he did anyway and she did, of course, run to her room.

"Applesauce, come on."

She was thirteen. She hated him.

He stood in the kitchen. Beth's keys were on the table. She saw him looking at them and she picked them up and chucked them at his chest.

"Keep us in the pumpkin shell. Right?"

She crossed her arms. Dare-faced.

He shot out the door with the keys.

"Ah hell, Pete!" Beth yelled.

She pursued him around the house, and catching him just as he reached the lilac bush, landed small blows to his head with her little pool-ball fists, and then all atangle they trundled through the brush and down the sharp incline to the rocks by the river. She clung to his arm so that he couldn't get a good throw, and the keys plunked into the water not far from the shore. He shucked her off. She pelted his back with river rocks, and he climbed the bank wincing, and sprinted to the house, flung open the back door, and strode down the hall and into his daughter's doorway.

Rachel folded clothes kneeling on the floor, stacking them in little piles. Sparkling denim skirts. Striped shirts the colors of candy. She shoved things into a neon grip. She wore lip gloss and blue eye shadow, and her thin wrists were bangled with colored bands.

"Tell her you don't want to go," he said.

Homosexuals postered to her walls in blouses and fishnet gloves pouted at him. She stood up and walked calmly to him on flounced pink socks. Almost balletic in the precise placement of her feet.

"Come here," he said, throwing his arms wide. The contempt shimmered off of her like actual heat, as though he'd opened a furnace.

She closed the door on him. The small clatter of the hook-and-eye lock.

He was muttering promises against the door when Beth's tennis shoes slapped on the kitchen tile. She could see him in the hall from where she sat at the kitchen table, little puddles at her feet.

"You're a son of a bitch, Pete."

She pulled off her wet shoe with effort and chucked it at him.

"You buy her all that makeup?"

"And beer and rubbers."

"You're not kidding."

"Christ, Pete."

"Not much. You're not kidding very much."

"You don't get to social work me!" she yelled. "You just don't. You split. It got rough here and you went to live in Tenmile. That was your decision."

"You made decisions too."

She threw her other shoe at him. He leaned away and it spanked the wall.

"I'm not apologizing again. I'm not. I'm done trying to get your forgiveness. And I tried, Pete. Oh, I tried and tried and tried. I called you and called you and we went up there to see you. And what happened when we went up there to see you, Pete?"

"Just don't go," he said to the floor.

"Did you come out of that shitty cabin? Did you come out and see your own daughter, Pete?"

He looked up at her.

"You're like an accident," he said. "You're like I was hit by a truck."

"Oh my God."

"I'm not looking at a person right here in front of me. You're more like a bad thing that happened to me."

Her laugh was sharp, a bark.

"That's really deep, Pete."

She grabbed some mail from the table and went through it, tossing what was addressed to him at his feet. Then she tore a bill open and wrote on the inside of the envelope and handed him the scrap. She said it was the address in Waco. That he could write to Rachel if he wanted. That he could start to send money if he was worth a shit at all.

The bartender at the Stockman's knew him, and Pete turned around and exited onto the street to avoid him. He was so inconsolably angry. He crossed the street behind a truck stamped FISH and was nearly hit by a Chrysler Imperial that screeched to a stop kissing his hip. Pete leered through the windshield with his hands on the hood of the car, the occupants dimly cognizant of his rage. He went up the block on Higgins scarcely aware of the foot traffic, the few ladies window-shopping the jewelry at Stoverud's, a pair of businessmen slapping shoulders. He ducked up the alley and tried the back door of the Missoula Club, but it wouldn't open for him. He scowled at the backside of the Howard Apartments. Some windows thrown open to the warmish noon, revealing the top of a television and a pair of naked feet a floor up. An argument broadcast from another of the upper rooms. Pigeons cooed and shook and bickered in the brick eaves and let fall a sleet of white shit and feathers. He pounded until a grim aproned barkeep unbolted the door. They looked at one another with mutual irritation.

"You open or not?" Pete asked.

The man stood aside and let him in. Pete sat at the bar and fingered the coin-scored divots in the pine, waiting for the bartender to pull his beer. He had most of it pumped down his throat by the time the man had extracted his change from the old-fashioned black niello register. Pete left the money where the man put it, and slid the glass at him. The bartender chewed his cheek.

"Chop chop," Pete said.

The man poured another, and Pete burped silently and drank under the man's gaze. The bartender went to the small cutting board near the griddle and cut onions and came back wiping his hands on his apron and filled Pete's beer and held up a bottle from in front of the mirror. Pete nodded. He poured them each a shot. Glasses clinked, the liquor hot and smoky. The bartender sucked the bourbon from his mustaches and then cooked Pete a burger and put the paper plate in front of him. Said for him to eat something.

"That's all right," Pete said.

"It's eleven o'clock in the morning, pal. Eat something, you're gonna drink like that in here."

Pete swallowed the last of his beer and slowly fingered out his change to the man, and told him he'd take a pint of Redeye. The bartender just stood there. Pete took a bite from the burger and chewed enormously.

The man fetched down a pint bottle from the shelf, sleeved it in a paper sack. He snatched it back when Pete reached for it.

"I don't want to see you in here again. Not today."

On the sidewalk he looked around for a place to open the bottle. He turned and went to where Ryman Street quit in a parking lot by the river. He hopped down the riverbank clutching the alders for balance and pushed through a brake of Russian olive. He perched on a stripped cottonwood worn smooth by the water, the wood warmed by the sun. The Clark Fork River churned heedlessly past. Paper litter garlanded the thin trees nearby. A rufous barrel shipwrecked on the rocks. He uncapped the bottle and drank from the sack, visible in his seething to the pedestrians and the cars crossing the Higgins Street Bridge. Kingfishers chittered. Water skippers skated on a puddle by his feet.

There was a time with his wife on this river or a river just like it, it can't be this river, but in his memory it is this one. A time on a wash just like this where he lay shirtless with her shivering in the August night, jeans pasted dark and wet to his knocking legs, his torso white to glowing in the moonlight. Her hair tendriled and framed about her face like an outlandish black tattoo. Her wet dress like a sleeve of molting skin, which of a sort it had been that whole night in their dancing. Her heart in its red and white cage knocking just inches from his own, like two young prisoners tapping out simpleton Morse I am here I am here I am here. Here I am for your pleasure for you forever. On a river like this where he impregnated her. A river promise too, he said I love you I love you. Seventeen years old. A pleasure so total that even then he knew he had mortgaged years to her and he did not care.

A derelict who was either Indian or sunburned so often that he looked like one emerged from the foliage downstream, togaed in an unrolled sleeping bag. This man nodded at Pete like he recognized in him a shared trouble, and came over and sat on the fallen tree next to him. Pete willed him away, but the man didn't move or speak. Pete drank. The man leaned over to say something, but stopped, leaned away. He leaned over again, and back again, as if there was some confidence he could not evict from his brain.

"Get away," Pete grumbled.

The man stood. Outrages having little to do with the present situation beginning to roil his features.

"Wait. Sit down." He patted the log. "Sit down."

The man dropped and Pete handed over the bottle. The man drank and then began to stutter out whatever it was he'd been trying to say.

"Just let's be quiet a minute," Pete said.

In Flipper's Casino, Shane, Spoils, and Yance hunched around the machine where Spoils was on a tear at nickel keno. Laughing among pale patrons on the stools in front of the machines arranged along the walls. Not a soul played pool or sat at the tables or ordered or ate any food. All perched like ghouls in front of their machines.

Pete now deep in his cups stumbled in and sidled up to them, and Shane doubletook him and said, "Holy shit, Petey!" and grabbed him with his big hands. He shook him and hollered joyfully in his face. An ugly, gap-toothed, red-haired giant.

"Where you been, professor?" Shane asked.

Pete grinned. He smelled of the river water and whiskey he'd been in.

"Over . . . ," he mumbled, throwing a thumb above his shoulder. "You know. Down by the river."

"Drunk by the river," Shane said proudly to Spoils and Yance. "Old Pete. Lookit you."

Shane's paws on his shoulders held him forth to Spoils and Yance, who took turns looking him close in the face to see his eyes swimming and dishing like half-full shot glasses.

"You got a puddle down around your feet there, Pete," Yance said.

"So I do."

"Oh, you are good and peppered."

"Been in the river, have ya?"

"Old Pete. Gosh."

"Get him to a table."

"Whishkey."

"Get him a *beer*. You need to sober up a skosh."

Spoils printed out his ticket, and together they led Pete over to the cage, where Spoils collected his winnings and then to the bar where he ordered a pitcher. They sat at a crooked table that spilled the heads off their beers. A thing you couldn't rest your arms on. The beer in eight-ounce plastic mugs.

"Easy Pete, the table's crooked."

"My arm's . . . my arm's all wet."

"Look at this guy. Grab another table, Spoils."

"Isss all right. I'm a keep my beer in my lap."

"You still up in Tenmile?"

He gestured in some way that suggested he was indeed still in Tenmile.

"You okay, Pete?" Spoils asked. "He don't look good."

"No he don't."

"M'aright."

"Your eyes are a couple of setting suns, professor. Here, drink your beer. Gotta get some fluids in you. There you go."

A cadaverous good-timer of the sort usually clutched to the back of a motorbike appeared in the door. She sized up the room and beelined for Pete. She put her arm on his neck and began to deposit herself in his lap. Her elbow was like a shiv in his breast. He dropped his beer.

"Fuck, lady. You spilled his beer," Shane said.

Shane pulled on her, but she wrapped her arm around Pete's neck. Yelling commenced. For her to get out of here. Pete still wondering who this guy was.

The crone snarled at him as the bartender lifted the hinged section of the bar. Her fingers dug in when the bartender and Shane tried to unhook her from Pete, and he cackled until she cut off his air. He yelped when she had a fist of his hair.

"She ain't lettin go. Come on, bitch, let go."

Yance handed him a fresh beer and he took it as though he might simply observe these happenings. She yanked and Pete dropped his cup. He swore then and took the woman's fist full of his hair and mashed her knuckles into his own skull until she cried out and let go, a technique he'd been trained to deploy with raging children. Muscle memory. Shane and the bartender dragged her out, kicking the whole way like a dancing skeleton. Violent promises exchanged in the entry-way by the gumball and cigarette machines. Shane returned, utterly unfazed, so happy to see him. Saying his name over and over. Pete, ol Pete.

The keno music dinged idiotically. Spoils counted his money.

"It's a good thing I did so well at keno today. I was about busted."

"Get a fuckin job, dummy."

"I have one. A couple three days a week for that fencing outfit in Lolo. I don't get paid shit."

"Why in the hell are you working *three* days, Spoils?" Shane asked. "Goddamn."

Spoils did numbers with his thumb and forefinger, some math that involved his knuckles. Shook his head.

"Shit. I don't think I can get by on just two."

They laughed at Spoils who didn't let on whether he was sincere, and there was shoving at the doorway where the bartender still argued with the woman, and in spilled Gator and Kev with three gals laughing through squinched faces and tottering on high heels. Tight jeans sideseamed to their legs. Gator and Kev going "Ho! Pete!" and slapping his back and making fond introductions. Ursula, Kimmie, and some girl else. Ursula's T-shirt lashed across her tremendous boobs, reading I WISH THESE WERE BRAINS. Kimmie spanked her eyelashes at Pete, and he lit up from within and resolved to fuck the first thing that would let him. Kev pulled Kimmie to the pool table. Ursula and the other one weaved through the crooked tables to the bar. Little rosy bottles fetched up out of the cooler and spiffed open. Pinkies aloft, the ladies sipped fancily.

Shane took the back of Pete's neck in his palm.

"We need to go to a bar bar. Liquor."

Pete nodded loosely.

Time began to pass unheeded.

They assembled themselves giggling in the backseat of a Plymouth

Gran Fury. Ursula settled onto his lap. He spread his legs some to accommodate her.

"I'm not too heavy, hon?"

He patted her leg to say no, she wasn't.

"I'm crushing this poor thing, Nancy. With my big fat ass."

Nancy ceased cleaning Gator's ear with her tongue.

"He looks all right," she said.

"Something better than all right," Ursula said to him.

Shane fired up the engine. A leonine roar and they reversed and screamed out, tires and women both.

Ursula pushed his hair behind his ears. His chin pillowed on her perfumed tits. A bitter smell from her armpits. We're all animals. Just dancing bears in tutus and monkeys with cigarettes. Painted up and stuffed into clown cars.

"You're a handsome thing," she whispered. "Is your dick skinny? I bet you have a fat one."

Even in the depths of his stupor, Pete blushed. She tilted his head back and kissed his face and then deposited a sluggard tongue in his mouth. She moved the lukewarm thing about and detached herself and checked for the effect on him. This close she was rather unlovely, but he took a handful of her tit and groped for an elusive nipple under all that fabric of shirt and bra. "My" she breathed, and slavered about his mouth almost like she was looking for something. Gator watched, his woman constantly turning him by the chin to kiss her. The one named Kimmie over with Kev or maybe Spoils too, who could tell, the whole backseat a rolling cart of near to fuck.

The pop and ping of gravel. Skid. Shane killed the engine, and they tumbled out of the car and into the sun rebounding off the white gravel.

"Have a pull of this here, Pete."

Palming the flask, and taking a swallow, he retched it all burning back into his mouth. He spat into the weeds in back of the Eastgate Bar expecting them to ignite. Pivoted gracefully and went through the open door. The inside was as cool and dark as they were loud. He hopped onto a plush green stool and drank all that was proffered him. The candy cinnamon Hot Damns! that coated his lips and little glasses of Redeye that stripped his throat. The jukebox glowed green, red, and lurid blue. When a bass line curled out, Ursula pulled him up. He lay into her bosom as they slow danced among the squat tables. Knocking the candles in their red beaded teardrop holders to the carpet. She straddled his leg and ground herself on him. The girl behind the bar told them to get a room, that that wasn't dancing. They groped against the wall yet. He ran his hand between her legs. It came away hot and moist as something from an oven. The girl behind the bar said she was calling the cops, they didn't knock it off.

"You're pale."

"M'aright."

"Where you going, baby?"

"Minute."

This moronic sunlight. Pete wheeled around the side of the building away from the dinnertime traffic on Broadway and leaned his head against the building, his arms quivering, and opened a faucet of rainbow vomit. The earth misted through his tears. Great sweeps of his head, steps taken, keeling into the backseat of the Gran Fury. Nodding out on warm Naugahyde, he had dreams of little narrative or figure or action. Colors. A whorl of sickened faces. The sense everybody needed his help.

He is lifted by his armpits out of this car. Steps less articulate than a puppet's. Coming to. His feet furrowing the dirt, bouncing over tree roots, dragging pinecones. Darkness. Smoke.

"Here you go, buddy." A can set in his lap. Somehow he's been shaped cross-legged by the campfire. Shane opens the can, squeezes his hand around it. Man is clay, he thinks.

"A couple sips of that'll bring you around."

"Man is clay."

"He sure as shit is, buddy."

Every pained divot in his crushed and wasted features he can feel. He sets the can by and crabs behind him and draws himself against a stump.

A body between him and the fire now.

It is Great Ursula, hands on her hips.

"You dance with me, baby?"

"Just let him alone, Ursula."

"You just stay right there, honey," she says to him. "I'm a dance for you."

Great Ursula standing in front of him, a black amphora against the fireshards, the upflung sparks. She tells no lie. She is dancing.

SIX

He woke in the dark, sat up, and wondered where he was. He recognized the orientation of the windows in the walls but was for a moment lost in a rough draft of a place dear to him until he remembered all that had happened. Missoula. This, the cottage they shared. Where they tried to stay married. The place was empty. Beth had cleared out already, taken Rachel.

He got up and rinsed his face at the kitchen sink.

Spoils snored on the living room floor. In a sense, his last friend, the last one who thought of him dearly. Shane, Yance, and the others—they missed him, but they didn't know him.

Nobody knows me but me. Where had he heard that. Was it true.

Spoils awake of a sudden and peering up at him.

"How you doin, professor?"

Pete coughed. Bolts of phlegm rattled loose and he spat them onto the wall and sat on the carpet with Spoils.

"Where is everybody?"

"I said I'd stay out here with you. Almost left you on account of you were punching at anybody'd touch you."

"I got hammers in my head."

"It's good to see you, Pete," Spoils said.

Pete nodded.

"Where's Beth?"

"She's going to Texas."

"Texas?"

"Yeah."

"Jeez. But Rachel . . . ?"

"Yup."

Spoils sat up against the wall.

"We seen him at the Stock's one night. Playing poker."

"I ain't even mad at that fucker."

"Shane kicked his teeth in anyhow."

"I didn't ask him to do that."

"You'd a done it for him."

"No, I wouldn't."

"Well, Shane, he does like to pound a motherfucker."

They sat in the squares of streetlight and looked at one another like a pair of prisoners in a cell.

"What are you gonna do, Pete?" He nodded toward the door.

"About Beth and Rachel?"

"Yeah."

"I dunno. I should go get 'em. I just don't know how."

Pete's eyeballs throbbed in this screaming gale of a hangover, of a life. He said to himself to quit feeling sorry for himself. Bed, lie in it.

"It is real good to see you, Pete."

"You too, Spoils."

It was five in the morning. He told Spoils to go back to sleep and he sat in back of the cottage listening to the river behind the bushes, slowly deciding things. Deciding to quit his job and chase down his wife.

At least get Rachel back.

Something. He wasn't sure what.

Just quit the job first.

He entered an annex of one of the county buildings, and through a door into Western Service District Headquarters of the Department of Family Services regional offices. Three rows of cubicles under low-hung ceilings the color and texture of saltines. The only person around on this Saturday was a woman nursing a baby from a bottle in a chair in the middle row of cubicles. She lit a cigarette, then hefted the child over her shoulder to burp it, turning her head to exhale smoke away from its face. Under a nearby desk, a boy turned over. Asleep too. From somewhere in a rear office another woman emerged with papers and went into the cubicle where Pete couldn't see her. A moment later the mother toted the baby down the divide between the cubicles toward the front door. The social worker woke the child under the desk. The boy sat up dazed, then fearful and unrecognizing. She coaxed him out, took his hand, and walked him toward the front door after his mother. The boy, now alert, inspected Pete as he passed, whose own attentions had drifted to the social worker guiding and coaxing the child along.

She was someone new to the office, or new to Pete at least. Long dark hair done in a loose ponytail. A warm grin spread over her open and pleasing face as she led the child, and noticing Pete, she asked him would he wait, said she'd be right back. He said he would. Thinking I'd set a car on fire if you asked me nice. I'd eat a shotgun shell.

He sat on the plastic chair near the door. His hand throbbed and itched under the filthy bandage gone brown with dirt, blood, and discharge and he scratched the wound absently. The dog bite had begun to heal, but after a few days the pink folds of skin around the scabs had turned bright red and hurt to touch.

He watched through the blinds as the social worker put the woman and her kids into a cab, and then met her at the door when she came back in. Smiling, her hands shaped into a little basket. She asked what she could do for him.

"I'm looking for Jim," he said.

"He's the supervisor." She glanced at his bandage. "Are you working with anyone? Or is this a referral?"

He chuckled. He had not showered. The awful bandage. He said that no, he wasn't working with anyone.

"Maybe I can help you."

He noticed then that a pine needle was suspended in a tangle of his long hair. He hadn't shaved, hadn't so much as glanced in a mirror. He surely looked as sorry as anyone who'd been here for services.

"Are you all right?"

He laughed outright now. Looked at her and cackled again.

"Is something funny?"

"I'm actually DFS. Out of Tenmile."

"Oh God." She covered her mouth. She blushed and was altogether fetching that way. "I'm sorry, I didn't . . ."

"It's okay. I know I look like hell. I'm Pete."

"I'm so embarrassed."

He stuck out his good hand. She took it. He held up his other hand.

"I've had a rough couple days. Dog bit me. Visiting a client."

She took his bandaged hand and inspected the filthy thing.

"Did you see a doctor?"

"No."

She pulled him into a harshly lit break room that smelled of the melted plastic someone had burnt in the ashtray. He sat in the chair she pulled out for him. She got a first-aid kit out of a drawer and sat in front of him.

"Take it off," she said.

He tore away the bandage with his teeth. The black arc of punctures against the white of his hand. His yellow bruises smelled like wood smoke. She sucked her teeth and looked hard at him.

"You didn't even wash it out?"

"Sure I did."

"Well, now it's infected."

He cowered mildly at the reprimand in her voice. Rather liked it.

She ripped open a bag of cotton balls, soaked one with iodine, and sopped the back of his hand. He gazed at the ceiling, breathing through his mouth. She opened a sterile gauze pad, cut it to fit, and taped it in place. Told him to get to a doctor for antibiotics.

"Thank you."

She gave him a curt nod.

He could smell himself, a tinge of dirt, sap, sweat, and beer. How repellent he must be. He started in chuckling again. She quit putting the first-aid kit back together and crossed her arms.

"Stop laughing at me."

"I'm not. I swear."

She searched his face, like she wondered was he telling the truth. He thought perhaps she liked him, might at least be intrigued despite his foul fettle.

Then she stood to leave.

"Hey. Wait. I'm sorry. This was real nice of you. I just came in to tell Jim I gotta take some time off. I didn't expect all this." He held up his fresh bandage. "So thanks."

"You're welcome."

"What's your name?"

"Mary."

"I'm Pete."

"You said."

"I wasn't laughing at you."

"I'm not bothered."

"Sure you are."

Mary touched her throat, then noticed she'd done it, and abruptly shook Pete's good hand.

"You want to have lunch? The Palace."

Her turn to laugh.

"Ouch."

"You're all bandaged up. You'll be all right."

"Still."

She stood and looked at him a minute and then shook her head. He thought maybe she was deciding to join him, but then she said it was nice to meet him and that she'd tell Jim he'd been by.

Two cops standing outside squinted at him for a moment like he might be their man. He loped across the courthouse lawn, then crossed Broadway straight for the Palace. Cafe, bar, and poker joint. Many small hours in here playing cards. Old boys on fixed income who sat lively as stones. Guys who sheriffed every hand because they couldn't stand to be bluffed and the pushovers who quit at the sight of a raise. The guys who didn't say a thing and felt acutely some mistake they'd committed in antecedent games or hands, and who now played with premonitions of coming disaster. A percentage at every table arrived simply to do some sort of penance. They shot hot racing glances around the table that would only mellow with muted relief when you took their money. Some drunk freshmen. Some lawyers. Saps who paid for Pete's books, his rent. Diapers and burp cloths. Because, above all, poker is a congress of punishment.

ONE WINTER PETE is playing every night. He has a job as a janitor on campus and is making up the difference here. Rachel is about two or three.

His father appears in the doorway of the Palace, and the cold air blows in around him such that everyone in the place turns and says to get in or get out. He steps just inside. The snow clots to his cowboy hat red and obscene in the neon. He takes the hat in his hands, brushes it off. He peers into the gloom. Can't see that Pete's at the rear table, by the wall, waiting to fold.

But Pete sees him, sees everything in the poker room.

His old man slaps the hat against his thigh, comes in palming it to his chest. Pete's not exactly avoiding him. Just wants to see how he acts. And he acts like he's been in a place like this, but never for long. He frowns at the scoundrels and when he's about ready to give up, Pete chucks his cards and stands. His father sees him then, and Pete points to an empty booth up front. They sit together. His father observes Pete, these surroundings.

His silver hair glistens with pomade. His father looks older, and Pete realizes that it's been a couple of years. Since Rachel's first birthday. His father deigns to undo the top button of his coat. He's sweating. A couple drunks neck in the booth behind Pete and the old man frowns.

I see you've found your level, he says.

Got rent to pay.

As though it were some surprise.

I thought you wanted me to go to college.

And here I did not realize this was a class.

This is how I'm doing it.

My understanding is that people finish school.

I'm in graduate school.

Graduate school.

Yes. Jesus, what do you want?

Tell me the degree I paid for.

Liberal arts.

Tell me what does a person do with a degree in liberal arts?

He gets a graduate degree.

The old man shakes his head demonstratively. Pete wonders what Ma ever saw in him, if ever he was so much as pleasant.

And I don't suppose you have any concern whatsoever about that child of yours.

We can't all be paragons of fatherhood like you.

The old man's eyes flame up like they'd been blown by a pair of bellows.

Let me just write that down. He takes out his little Moleskine, the black pencil. *How do you spell it?*

Pete tells him.

And it means . . . ?

Model of excellence.

The old man jots this down and condescends to grin at Pete. Garlands and tinsel and blinking Christmas lights play on the wall behind him. Crude cartoon Santas on the windows. Reindeer play poker.

What do you want?

His father reaches into his coat and slides forward a check. A great sum.

Your little brother worked summers. In high school he worked the whole school year.

He's been arrested three times—

Just for fighting. And he never asked for a dime of bail.

No, you're right. He's a perfect angel.

Are you bitter that you're the oldest? Is that it? Do you tell yourself I was too hard on you?

Pete doesn't answer. He won't say shit. Let the old man figure out what went wrong. Pete takes a cigarette from inside his coat and lights it with a match.

Your mother heard you were playing cards for money. He taps the check. *About put the old gal into a tailspin.*

Just then Spoils comes over, almost on cue. The guy can smell money, it's why they call him Spoils, even though it goes through him like beer. Oftener as beer. He greets the old man who doesn't remember him from the wedding, and says he hates to ask, but does Pete have a dollar. Pete and the old man enter a silent exchange about this. Then Pete says to go over there on the table, go on over. Pete waves to the dealer that it's okay, and Spoils takes up a chip and shuffles over to the cage. The old man's burning up in myriad objections.

Pete slides the check back toward him.

I don't want it.

The old man smiles.

Oh, I ain't giving it to you. I come to see you tear it up.

You came all the way from Choteau to—

So I can bring the pieces of this check back to your mother. Yep.

I won't disappoint you.

That would be a refreshing outcome.

Pete rips the check in half, rips the halves in half, and snows the table with them. Then he heads back to the poker table, back to work.

The bell over the door tolled her unexpected arrival. He kicked out the chair in front of him.

"Have a seat, Mary."

She looked at the chair a moment.

"Have lunch with me."

"There was a call."

"Look, I think you're very pretty and I can tell already you're interesting as hell. Just sit down."

She grinned and shook her head at some thought and glanced at the door. As if debating something. Maybe she was thinking of her boyfriend.

"Soup," he said, opening his hand over his bowl like he was teaching her the word.

"There was a call. From Tenmile. Somebody named Cloninger. He says the kid you left with him isn't welcome anymore."

* ✦ ✦ ✦

What was it like on the way to Texas?

It was Wyoming, which means to drive forever through ugly scrubscape the color of dirty pennies.

It was just wyoming along. They were wyoming forever. You could wyom all day and not make any progress. To wyom was to go from nowhere to nowhere. Through nowhere. To see nothing. To do nothing but sit. You turn on the radio and wyom through the dial slowly, carefully in search of a sliver of civilization only to find a man talking about the price of stock animals and feed. You listen to a dour preacher wyoming about your bored and dying and wyoming soul.

Did her mom wyom too?

Mom wyomed all through Colorado. She smoked, she drank coffee and Tab and then beer, wyoming her fingers on the wheel sometimes and stopping to wyom to someone on the pay phone, maybe Daddy but probably that friend in Texas. The truck driver.

Is he your boyfriend?

It's an old friend, Rachel Leslie.

She said Rachel's name to annoy her.

Old friend from when?

From when I worked at the trucking company. He's a trucker.

Is that why we're going all the way to Texas?

He said we could stay with him, yes.

What's his name?

Jimmy.

How do you know him?

I told you. From when I was a receptionist.

Did you do it with him too?

What is that supposed to mean? Him too *what?*

Come on. I know why Daddy left.

Did her mother hit her or pull over or give her some kind of talking to?

Worse.

What did she do?

She cried. Drops big and quiet racing down her face.

Did it unnerve Rachel?

Rose.

Did it unnerve Rose?

Yes.

Why?

Because her mother's heart was wyoming, it was wyoming hard, and she was days and years and maybe forever from a good man.

exual deviancy came as little surprise anymore. Nymphomania, satyriasis, pedophilia, coprophilia, telephone scatologia—there wasn't a particular paraphiliac that hadn't crossed Pete's path at one time or another. He'd worked with a six-year-old girl who'd been so sexualized that she would grab at passing groins, grope and cop feels like a brazen pervert, and could never be left alone with other children.

At first, he was shocked to discover whole rings of kids who practically orgied in group homes and psych wards, doubly shocked to find out how uncommon it wasn't. There were kids he worked with who'd routinely been molested by parents, teachers, and staff at various institutions, as if some dark chaperone escorted them from consort to consort. He'd worked with panty thieves, serial peepers, and Lolitas who found and fucked Humbert upon Humbert on the way to school. Not a few of them touching him on the leg, trying to tongue his ear.

So Pete had no trouble imagining Cecil squatting over the Cloningers' dog, reaching under it, and asking the dog how was that, and the dog yelping and then licking his hand, and Cecil doing it again, getting the casing between his fingers and expertly coaxing the lean member out.

The dog barking in earnest now.

And Pete had no trouble imagining old, kind Cloninger peering around the upraised hood of his truck to see what all was the rumpus, seeing the dog drop its front paws and bark a question mark—a sound Cloninger had never heard his dog, any dog, make—and the boy crab-crawling on the grass around the animal. And this time the dog being into it. Whatever it was. Cloninger's eyes, they could not yet see this thing entirely new to his experience, there being no word for what was occurring.

And then all at once he understood. The coolness of his reddening face, a bracing ice water outrage, and he charges into the yard where the dog is now on its back, and there on the step are Cloninger's dumbstruck daughters and his squinting dim son, and Cloninger kicks the dog, who snarls in alarm and then slinks off in shame or even guilt, because dogs, they do feel guilt, yes they do, they may not have souls but they have one point on the moral compass, the due north of masters like Cloninger, so the dog now goes to the ground low and backward-glancing. And Cloninger takes great heaving breaths just to keep from laying Cecil out, saying you're gone, go get your things.

Pete and Cecil had lunch at the Seven Feathers Truck Stop outside of Columbia Falls. The kid said he had to take a piss, slid out of the booth, and slouched off to the bathroom. Pete could tell immediately that he was going to run. When the boy slunk out of the bathroom, he broke for the front, hitting the postcard rack next to the register. It pinwheeled over, spraying cards.

The customers at the counter ceased sawing into steaks and chicken-fried specials, set their silverware, wiped their chins, and regarded the boy's flight with interest. He careered into the parking lot, was nearly struck down by a skidding compact, and alighted running on the pavement, skittish and bantam as all get-out. He juked as if someone were in hot pursuit and sprinted around the gas pumps. The folks at the counter leaned to watch him disappear from view.

"The meat loaf wasn't that bad," the plump waitress said to laughter. The cook taking a smoke break at the counter said to go on and just keep it up, and they all laughed again. The other waitress came out from the kitchen and asked what was so funny.

"That kid he was with"—the first waitress nodded toward Pete— "just took off like a maniac," she said to the other. Then to Pete, "Your son, or . . . ?"

"I'm from DFS," he said.

"DF whatnow?"

Everybody in the place was watching Pete.

"I'm his caseworker," Pete said. "Department of Family Services."

Some silence. A coffee cup set back in its saucer.

"Well," the waitress said, stuffing her pad into her apron and taking up plates. There was a low mutter somewhere along the counter, and a muffled, snorting laugh.

"You just gonna let him run wild?" someone asked. They looked at Pete, this Long-Haired Organ Where Their Tax Dollars Go as he crammed a cold handful of the boy's fries into his mouth. They waited for him to do something.

"You want I should call the highway patrol, hon?" the waitress asked.

"Let's not throw our skirts over our heads just yet," Pete said. There was no good in letting her or the truckers, loggers, and farmers think this was an emergency, because it wasn't.

The folks mumbled, resumed eating, lit cigarettes. The hostess at the register gathered up the postcards that had fallen into a harlequin floor mat of glaciers, geysers, jackalopes, and cottonwooded sunsets on the Missouri Breaks. She set them on the counter and righted the display. Pete pinched a toothpick from the dispenser when he paid. He silently burped and picked through the cards.

She gave him his change. One of his nickels had a hole bored into it. She began sorting the cards. He showed her the nickel.

"You want a different one?" She opened the register. She was annoyed about the postcards.

He knelt and gathered up the remaining cards and set them on the glass countertop.

"No, it's all right." He pocketed the coin. "I'm sorry about the mess."

A cold gale ripped at him when he stepped out and the high thin clouds marbled the sky where the sun was placed in the middle of it like a heatless, gaudy stone. Pete leaned into the wind and started in the kid's direction. He passed the convenience store adjoined to the diner, peering through the tinted windows for any sign of the boy's passing, for fallen and spilt things, someone on the floor being told to just lie still.

Pete moved on and nodded howdy to an old rancher pumping diesel into his dually. He wasn't near enough to ask about the kid. He surveyed the rest of the empty plaza, passing by the air pump, the pay phone, and restrooms. Cecil couldn't have gotten far.

He cornered the building and came on a small herd of diesel trucks idling in the cold norther. Chromed long-haulers glinted like showgirls among logging trucks caked in oatmealy mud, white exhaust thrashing flamelike in the wind from their silvery stacks. Pete unfolded his shirt collar up around his neck and stuffed his jean pockets with his fingers. Cecil would be chilled by now in only the T-shirt. Pete wondered would he sneak into a cab to hide. Was he that brave. Was he otherwise inventive.

Wending through trucks, Pete crouched at intervals to look underneath for the boy's shoeprint, a handprint on a cab door or in the road dust on the perforated stack sleeves. Nothing. He stopped near a livestock trailer and was startled to see himself in the black orb of a beef cow's eye. The animal nudged its stanchions.

He went where the timothy swayed around a sagging, nominal fence and behind there the furrowed land, a cutbank striated by crimson bands of clay. It was Saturday and out there on the prairie somewhere were hunters. It would be a trick figuring how much to compensate in all this shifting wind. But with the noise and the scent-clearing gusts, you might could get right up on a deer, an antelope.

A long squeal of tires. He ran to the front of the truck stop. A green pickup westbound on the frontage road kicked up a huge pennant of dust.

Shelby was east.

Cecil was on his way.

"Well done, Pete," he muttered. "Well fuckin done."

Pete went to his car and got his flask from the glove box. Then he opened the trunk. Cecil's air rifle was in there next to some blankets, stuffed animals. He reached under a shovel into a bag of clothing. Felt around for the bottle, looked this way and that, and then dunked his torso into the trunk and took a long pull. His throat burned and hot fumes ran out his nose and burned his eyes. He took another drink, and then filled the flask and put it in the interior pocket of his coat. The world clicked up into place when he closed the trunk. He felt all right. It'd be all right. The boy ran. He'd call it in, someone would pick him up sooner or later. No big deal.

From within the restaurant the hostess tapped the window and pointed back at the register. The big old rancher who'd been pumping diesel had Cecil in a standing full nelson just inside the door.

"Huh," Pete said.

He walked through the gale to the restaurant. His arrival occasioned deeper interest among the customers, arms crossed and so on.

The hostess said, "There he is."

The rancher turned around with the boy. Cecil's arms splayed out, and his head was forced down under the man's laced fingers. The man's liverspotted skull was red with effort. The two of them breathed heavily, twitched as they strained against one another.

"This yer boy?" the old man asked.

"I'm his caseworker," Pete said, reaching out for a handshake. The rancher forced a grin onto his granite face, as if to ask if Pete thought he was an idiot. Pete dropped his hand.

"Are you responsible for him or not?" the rancher asked.

"Yes," Pete said. "I'm taking him up to Shelby."

"The hell you are. I got a mother up in Shelby."

Pete nodded. Conveyed that he was listening, that the man had his complete attention and respect.

"I seen him run outta here, you know. And you go after him. Seen him sneaking up there to my truck when I was paying for gas. Little shit had the gall to fight me too. This young girl here talked me into waiting a minute to see if you come back before we call the cops. She said you's his parole officer."

"I said you worked for the state, that you were *like* a parole officer or something," the hostess clarified.

"Well, I thank you both," Pete quickly offered. "You did a good thing, waiting for me. I appreciate it."

The man grunted as Cecil squirmed.

"He about got himself tore up from earhole to asshole."

"I'm sure. I'd have not been able to restrain myself like you did. What say you remand him to me now?"

"Remand?"

"I can take him."

The rancher took long measure of Pete, his hands laced over the boy's nape like knurled stocks. Wondering should he trust Pete, whether Pete looked capable. Cecil tried to twist and slip free but the rancher simply clenched the boy all the more tightly, lifted him up onto his tiptoes.

"Just hold still, Cecil," Pete said.

"It don't look to me like you finished the job correcting this boy. Course the government ain't been any good at fixing anything, has it? Probably had him sitting on his ass all day, didn't ya? Hold still, godamnit."

Pete and the man at the crux now. How long until the boy raises his arms, drops, and wheels free. Or kicks the old man in the nuts with his heel.

The rancher looked at the top of the boy's black thatch of hair as though he could derive an intent from it. A bead of sweat traced the ridge of his nose and fell from the tip.

"Take him before I change my mind," he said as he unthreaded his fingers, sprung loose his arms, and Cecil stumbled forward. He remained arms out, head down, like a mold of the old man's action on him. He smirked up at Pete.

"He's bleeding," someone said, and the hostess ran outside after the old man with a dishtowel. Behind the big man's left ear was a long fresh scratch, the rust-colored blood from it in the forking wrinkles at the back of his neck. They all watched her call to the old rancher and point at his head. The old boy touched his neck and grimaced at the blood on his fingers. He snatched the towel from her and stormed off to his pickup with it pressed to his wound.

Pete thanked the hostess when she returned, waved vaguely at the patrons. Everyone looked on Pete and his cretinous ward with annoyance approaching disgust. Muttering anew. Pete yanked Cecil out of the restaurant backward.

He left the keys in the ignition unturned while the wind buffeted the car. He turned to say something. Cecil held a single middle finger in his palm, lifted it before him like he'd found it on the floor and showed it to Pete.

"Back at ya, buddy," Pete said.

Cecil took back his finger, set it in his hand, and regarded it crazily. Pete started the car.

They went along the southern border of Glacier Park, followed the Middle Fork of the Flathead River. Turquoise pools and red and rusty railcars curling out of tunnels. Just over Logan Pass Pete spotted a pair of mountain goats at a mineral lick and pointed them out to Cecil, but the boy was having none of it. Fuck him then. No idea how good he had it. The pines shifted in the wind up to the tree line where great escarpments loomed gray and black. Past the Silver Stairs chuckling out of the mountains like mercury. Through East Glacier and out of the mountains and onto the endless plains of the Montana Hi-Line. Winter wheat chaff and dirt conjured up into curling sheets across the stubbled fields in five kinds of brown.

Up a rise, the Sweet Grass Grain silo peeked over at them. Tucked in hills the color of toast, Shelby spilled up in intervals. They descended into the town proper and passed a church where parishioners milled and children ran orbits. Another and another church. Mighty silos, a water tower, and they climbed another hill to see the rail yard.

Pete checked a piece of paper on the dash, turned at the next light, and headed north, scanning the right side of the road for the relevant mailbox. It was a trailer, once red, sunscalded pink. He stopped at the gate and got out, opened it, drove through, got out, and closed it.

In the large outbuilding Cecil's uncle knelt next to a snowmobile. A dog on a chain strained and leapt at the edge of the stamped earth circle around the stake to which it was leashed. Silently gnashing the air ten feet from where they parked. Pete caught himself rubbing his bandage. The animal's vocal cords were cut. Docked like its tail.

"Howdy," Pete called to the outbuilding, fetching his jacket from the backseat. The man looked up, stood, and wiped his hands on his jeans as he strode out to meet him. His hair was shaved into a flattop and he had the look of large, hale men who shoot straight and mean well, but probably nurse a good many resentments. They shook.

"I'm Pete. From DFS. Spoke to your wife."

"Elliot," he said, peering over Pete's shoulder at Cecil still in the car. "What's wrong with him?"

"Nervous, I suppose."

"Is he gonna get out?"

"Let's give him a minute."

"Because he don't have to be here. Favor to his mother is all this is. He don't like it, he can shove off."

"He'll stay."

They started for the house. There was an add-on covered in tar paper at the back. The fence terminated in a stack of posts some ways off and added to the air of incompletion about the place. A thin woman emerged from behind the screen door. She leaned on the porch railing, shielding her eyes from the sun, and peered toward the car trying to get a look at Cecil.

"There's the wife," Elliot said gruffly.

They went over together. She was a hard thing, taut in her arms and in her face. She was cross, at Elliot or the situation, maybe perpetually. She looked older than her husband. Wind-chapped lips. She nodded toward the car.

"What's with him?"

"A little cold feet. He'll come around."

"This is a favor to his mother. He don't like it here, he can shove off," she said, just like her husband.

"He'll warm up to it," Pete said. "He's at that age. Wants to get out on his own. But most of all, he needs stability."

She looked meaningfully at Elliot. She was about to say something—probably about the boy's mother—but the car door opened and Cecil climbed out. The dog lunged against its chain, whining airily, as the boy walked just at the edge of the animal's limit up the drive. Pete called to him, but Cecil ignored him and went into the outbuilding.

"Let me talk to him," Pete said.

"Hold on, mister," the woman said. "You got our check?"

Pete was already on the steps, and he turned to face her.

"You know, I didn't get your name," Pete said pleasantly.

"We was promised two-fifty a month for him."

"The stipend. Yes, they will send a check just as soon as the paperwork is processed and everything. No more than a week or two."

"What are we supposed to do now?"

"How's that?"

"How is what?"

"I mean, what are you asking."

She shot Elliot a look, and he bowed his head. "We're flat broke is what I'm asking. That kid don't live on grass is what I'm asking. Elliot ain't had no shifts since he got out of the National Guard is what I'm asking."

"And I got until Christmas to decide to re-up or not."

"He might have to re-up," she said with a practiced outrage.

"I'll contact the folks in Helena just as soon as I get back to Tenmile," Pete said.

She crossed her arms like she didn't believe any of it.

"Maybe they can put a rush on that check."

"Maybe they can put a rush on it," she said to Elliot, and then to Pete, "You ain't hearing me. We ain't made of money. Of any money."

Pete looked over at the garage for some sign of Cecil.

"I oughta go get him," he said.

"And when you get him, you can put him back in that car," the woman said.

Pete looked from Elliot to his wife. She turned to go back into the house. Pete raced through the things to say, resisted the urge to ask why the hell they had him come all the way out with Cecil if they were going to commence with this horse-trading bullshit.

He felt his pockets.

"Tell you what," he said. "I got about fifty bucks in petty cash left from taking him out here. What say I give you that, put a rush on the check—pay my own way back to Tenmile, mind you—and you all write me a check for the fifty, which I'll cash once you get your check."

"We don't use a checkbook," she said.

"Not for bills or anything?"

"No."

"Maybe," Elliot said, "this ain't such a good—"

"Look," Pete said. "Fifty is all I got. You can have it."

The woman shook her head. She and Pete both wiped their hair out of their eyes. Even this seemed to annoy her—that it was windy, that Pete had long hair.

"That kid's as weird as a three-dollar bill. A couple Christmases ago he's riding his cousin's tricycle like he was five. Carrying on like a retard. Wouldn't give it back when he was told to, neither."

The door slammed behind her, and the breeze through the cheat-grass filled the silence, and there wasn't anything else to blow over that would make a sound, not a tree or clothes on the line or anything.

"Maybe this deal ain't such a good idea," Elliot said, looking off across the yard. The dog turned in concentrated circles before he set in the dirt. Pete reached into his wallet and pulled out the cash.

"I got forty-eight here," he said, pressing the money into the man's hand and folding closed his palm. Elliot took a pack from his front shirt pocket and shook out a smoke and offered it to Pete. Pete took it and Elliot took one for himself and they each lit them and smoked together without talking.

"I'm a see what he's up to," Pete said.

He jogged across the yard, past the lunging silent dog. He felt light-headed from the cigarette, and when he got to the doorway of the huge outbuilding he was panting. A rusted combine filled the main area. A snowmobile was off to the side. Cecil sat on a big round of pine. His hand fell gently from his face. He held a filthy red rag in his hand, and a bright red plastic gas can sat hard by. The boy's huge dumb grin. Eyelids half closed like broken window shades.

Pete stepped into the outbuilding and the aluminum walls all around ticked in the wind like a cooling engine. He spat at a copper pipe, and it toned back at him for a long moment. The boy's eyes lolled.

"You would love it at the treatment facility," Pete said.

Cecil licked his lips as he turned toward this voice from the ether.

"They knock you out for days in that place. Just have to kick or hit or bite somebody. Whip out your dick. I know it. I seen it. And when you come to all groggy and fucked-up, they just wait and see if you do it again. And you will. They all do."

Pete peeked out the doorway to see that Elliot still smoked on the porch of the house. From inside his pocket, Pete removed his tiny flask. Finished and replaced it and approached the boy.

"You know the worst part about treatment facilities, Cecil? The freedom. It's what they call a paradox, Cecil. No longer being afraid of ending up there is what makes you free to do anything. And all the anythings you can learn. How to fight with a toothbrush or a spoon. All the drugs there are to take. How to molest other kids. You won't believe the appetites you got inside."

The kid snorted or choked a little or coughed. From the stump Pete lifted Cecil, who swayed and giggled. His actual breath stank of gasoline.

"You laugh? Go on. But let me tell you a secret. Kids like you, they become the worst ones. Maybe because it's too late to send in someone your age. I dunno. But something just quits in kids like you and you become bad men. You go in wild ungovernables and you come out bad men."

Pete balled a fist and slugged Cecil in the gut and as he doubled over Pete grabbed his face with his right hand and hit the boy again just under the opposite rib, dropping him to his knees. On the ground, the boy quietly kecked. Pete knelt.

"You can't believe it, can you?" he asked. "How could this be, you ask yourself."

Cecil looked up at him, flushed and gagging. Pete had never laid a finger on a client before. Not once done a thing in anger. And he wasn't angry now. He was as astonished as the boy.

"All right," Pete said. "Quit moaning. You're all right."

He lifted him up and brushed the pebbles and twigs from both their knees. He straightened Cecil's T-shirt and met his tearing, enraged eye.

"Your mama doesn't want you anymore. The Cloningers are good people and you ruined that. Maybe for other kids too. But you have this uncle. So I want to know: will you stay here?"

Cecil balled and unballed his fists. Bewildered and scared and angry.

"Look, I ain't the one that hit you," Pete said.

The kid blinked at the naked lie.

"I ain't," Pete repeated. "Those punches sure as shit come through me but they were not mine. As meant for you as they were, they were not mine."

"Fuck you, man," Cecil whispered.

"I am not just an agent of the state. I'm an agent of your future. I'm a goddamn time traveler. And, I promise you, that little tune-up was just a preview."

Elliot was lighting another butt off his second or maybe third cigarette when Pete got to the porch. He let the man take the reins of the situation, handing off the boy to him like a half-broke horse. He fetched the boy's things from the car and followed them through the house as Elliot's wife crossed her arms and asked why he smelled like gas. Cecil glowered at her, hunched and miserable. Elliot patiently showed Cecil where he would sleep and keep his things, as patient as a man taking his sister's son, at least as patient as a man who needs money to do such a thing.

The kid might run. Pete might have to find him again and bring him back. You couldn't know.

Pete crossed the brown and blasted grass. The dog heaved up at him, wheezing through the cut cords of its voice box. The chain went taut. The animal's pads rose and patted the hard dirt. Its teeth snapped in the air.

Pete sat in the utter quiet of his car but for the fond wind and the ringing of the animal's chain.

　　　　✦　　　✦　　　✦

Was Jimmy nice enough with a big harmless face and so excited to see them that he'd ordered pizza and beer and Cokes?

He called them Cokes, but they were 7UPs, said would you like a 7UP Coke, I also have some Dr Pepper Cokes. Rachel was confused and said she'd have whatever kind of pop he had and he looked funny for a minute and checked the freezer and said they could run out for pops or ice cream after dinner.

What were pops?

Popsicles.

And pops were called Cokes?

Or sodas, yes.

Did Rachel and her mother and her mother's "friend" go out for Popsicles?

They were gonna. They didn't. They got to talking and talking and Mom laughing at every last thing he said and drinking Lone Stars and him showing them the tub where he kept his turtles and saying he just showered with them or in the truck stops mostly but he was fixin to have to get them an aquarium on account of them staying with him, *staying with him* he called it, not moving in and it was obvious from the get-go.

What was obvious from the get-go?

They weren't staying.

Why?

Because. You could tell.

How?

He was terrified of them. Him asking did they want to see the inside of his semi-truck, and they all climbed in, and Rachel crawled into the sleeper cab and he turned on the lights and said he'd sleep in the truck, there was a room for Rachel and Beth could sleep in his room, and her mother said he didn't need to do that, but he went ahead and did it anyway.

Was there a room for them?

There was a room for her and a fold-out couch and a dresser a closet half-full of boxes of Jimmy's things about a hundred sweat-stained baseball caps and some old calendars of women splayed over machines, and in the middle of the night as she tried to sleep her mother went out to the truck. Rachel pretended to be asleep when her mother came in to check on her and kissed her good night with beery tobacco lips before she went to Jimmy's bedroom.

What was it like in Waco?

Who knows? They never went anywhere. McDonald's sometimes. She just watched TV.

What shows?

Love Boat. Fantasy Island.

The Facts of Life.

Venturing sometimes out into the trailer park. Signs of children, a Wiffle ball bat flattened as though hammered into the dirt drive, toddlers toddling, the women watching her grow uneasy under their gaze. She runs away when they ask her is she living at Jimmy's.

And then Jimmy is gone. A week.

And then when he's back, they are always *just talking* in the kitchen and she needs to play outside. Then when dinner's ready they put her in front of the TV and talk in the back room. Then they talk outside in the dark. In his truck. Then Jimmy's yelling at her mother to go inside, just go inside the damn trailer, it's enough already.

Mom coming in to wyom in the trailer. Days and days wyoming.

Jimmy on the road all the time, treating her like she's lucky to be here. Goddamn turtles in the tub. This ain't no Taj Mahal. Jimmy saying what does Beth have to complain about, living high on the hog, rent free and everything.

What about school?

Don't ask. It's horrible. Texas girls with big hair and cliques. She'd skip, but she doesn't know where to go, the girls are awful. Jealous, her mother says.

Of what.

Of your breasts. Of the boys wanting you.

Tells Rachel to come here and let her have a good look. Turns her about and then crushes out her cigarette and hops out of bed in her underwear and opens the closet and Rachel thinks she's going to get her a shirt or something to wear but she pulls down a shoe box from the back corner of the top shelf and inside is a pistol.

What's it for?

To sell. It's an antique. They're gonna pawn it and have some fun, her mother says.

So they shop together?

Yes, and get their hair and nails done, and they talk about the boys loping through the mall, her mother saying watch now how they are looking at us, the two of us all done up.

But they aren't looking at her, she's too old.

Flirting with the shoe salesman now. God.

And does she keep Rachel home now, say for her to cut class and stay home?

Yes.

And do they watch TV all day and go for long drives and was it like they were always just waiting for Rachel to get old enough so they could be friends and tell each other everything?

That's what her mother says.

And what is the everything Rachel tells, on the porch in the cooling of the evening?

Nothing. Her mother does all the telling. Starting off abstract.

The thing about men. The things about men. How Jimmy always wanted her when they worked at the trucking company in Montana, you can tell the way a man will drink half his coffee sitting on the edge of your desk. And leaning over your desk to look at something, but really he's just trying to get the smell of you.

Does she talk about Pete?

She does. On the two-by-four porch of Jimmy's trailer, drinking a sweating beer. She says your father was once so affectionate, but when we had you it killed it or started to kill it, something about having children—you're old enough to hear this now, you're a young woman and you need to know this now—a child changes the love between two people. A baby makes it harder to keep the fire going. Don't have a baby, Rachel.

Does she ask her mother if she regrets her?

No.

What does she ask?

Can she have a beer.

And can she?

Sure. Just promise me you won't have a baby.

EIGHT

A few weeks of Indian summer gave way to a sudden chill, snow-fall that melted in the last warm days of the year. A moose wandered into Tenmile. The town's dogs surrounded it and not a few of them got kicked and nearly gored. The sheriff shot it dead in the middle of town.

There was a fistfight in the War Bonnet that spilled into the street and ended when Ike's glass eye popped out and disappeared into the alley. He came back an hour later with a .22 and shot the miner he'd been fighting in the back of the head. The man was two days dying.

A few other deaths. An old woman collapsed in the IGA bath-room. Indian Harold had a heart attack in his apartment, his hot plate glowing a malevolent red for two days. When they found him, the plastic tile on the wall nearby had melted and the underside of the cupboard was black as burnt toast. Lucky the whole building hadn't gone up, they said.

The weather turned fully cold, highs in the thirties, and Pete got his firewood finished and put plastic over the windows, and weather-stripped the door nice and tight with shims and half a roll of duct tape.

A bear had tried to break into his place, tore up the window over the kitchen sink pretty good. He could see a little rust-colored blood and tufts of black fur in the sash, on the porch posts. A problem bear. When Pete opened the front door, chipmunks dashed about and vacated through the new kitchen egress. A box of granola on the counter sat blasted open like a firework pagoda. He found his other stores in the cellar under the house unmolested.

The only other curiosity was his loose change: cooking dinner one night, he accidentally tipped his tin cup of coins into the sink and noticed an inordinate number of coins with holes in them. Just like the nickel he'd gotten at the Seven Feathers Truck Stop. He sorted out ten of them, recalled that he'd half-noticed the phenomenon in his comings and goings, but only just now, turning them all over to the obverse side, did he see the Lincolns, Jeffersons, Washingtons, and FDRs all shot through the temple. Dead presidents. He wondered how he'd come by so many.

A pickup pulled in behind his car and disturbed these speculations. His brother Luke. Pete went out wiping his hands squinting into the headlights. The engine died.

"Just get back in the truck and go," Pete said.

A chickadee fee-beed lonely in the rising dark, and a breeze kicked up.

"I don't got a single thing for you."

It wasn't his brother's shape limping from the darkness.

"Who is it?" Pete asked. He tugged a hatchet out of a round of pine on the porch.

"It's just me, Pete." His brother's parole officer faltered into the light. "Give me a minute."

His name was Wes Reynolds. His bitter, hardscrabble people had come from Minnesota, before that, Sweden, settling in Choteau where he grew up, a year behind Luke in high school. Wes and Pete and Luke Snow had been friends, or friendly, mainly by necessity, as Wes lived near the Snow spread west of town. He was always on the porch when they finished dinner, waiting for them. Saturday mornings too. He told outsized lies about his father's whereabouts, vehicles the man allegedly drove, and missions he'd been assigned. It got to where he annoyed even their mother. Pete and Luke dared him to eat and climb all manner of things. The summer he broke his leg, they were relieved to be rid of him, and after Luke started high school, he quit coming around. He had a child with a woman who left him inside of two years, taking the boy with her. He still wore the wedding ring.

Pete fried burgers in a skillet as they completed their pleasantries. Wes wore a cylinder cast from his shoulder to his wrist, a neck brace, and turned his whole torso to look around. He ate with his good arm, and they listened to one another chew, Wes all but wincing with the effort. He caught Pete lingering on the bloody bloom on his eyeball and the yellow contusion around the socket.

"Where'd you and my brother fight?" Pete asked.

"Wasn't no fight," Luke said, swallowing. "More like an ambush."

"What happened?"

"He was shitfaced at the Buttreys, holding up the line. Harassing this high school sophomore to let him buy beer with a check. Even though they don't take his checks and everyone in town knows he ain't supposed to have beer as part of his parole."

"Christ," Pete muttered.

"And everybody knows I'm his PO. I'm supposed to stand there? I'm supposed to worry about embarrassing him? Or getting crosswise of the almighty Snows?"

"I hear you."

"He's been by."

"No."

"It wasn't a question."

Wes extracted and extended a pointer from his shirt pocket.

"He came by after."

"After what?" Wes asked, probing under his cast for the spot that itched.

Pete tried to figure out how to put it.

"After your run-in."

"Say where he was headed?"

"I wouldn't let him tell me."

"Why?"

"In case someone come looking."

Wes smiled revealing a chipped front tooth. Pete took up their plates and pulled the coffeepot off the stove and brought over two cups.

"Milk?"

"Nah."

He poured them some coffee and nodded for them to go outside. He rolled cigarettes and by the time they were smoking the coffee had cooled off enough to drink.

"Look, Wes, I'm really sorry. But Luke . . . he'll turn up sooner or later. He always does."

"It's not the same back in Choteau," he said. "People ain't as impressed with the Snows as they used to be."

"Meaning?"

"Meaning it ain't like high school. Meaning the cops aren't gonna just tell Luke to go home and sleep it off. Fucking meaning"—Wes stepped off the porch and twisted awkwardly to see Pete around the beam—"when I catch him up here, you're going down for abetting."

Wes articulated himself into his pickup and rattled down the road. Pete went inside. He stood in front of his bulletin board empty save the map and post office box his brother had written down for him. He took it down, folded the paper, and put it in his wallet.

He investigated a family in a trailer park outside of Columbia Falls. A cadre of thieves who edged about the walls of the trailer like suspicious feral cats. Audibly sighing at his departure.

He stopped in town for gasoline, parked the car, and walked to stretch his legs. He could eat. The streets were empty, scarcely a person at business or play. He wondered was it Sunday. He passed a squat building made of stones and mortar from the city's founding or nearly so and then a butcher's shop with brown tile walls that were warm to the touch from the sun. The butcher notched up an eyebrow at Pete going by, switched the toothpick to the right side of his mouth. The Columbia was just up ahead, across from a chapel. He hastened up the street. The red vinyl upholstery on the inside of the door. The cleavage entryway of smoked glass bricks. He doubted there existed a bar between Tenmile and Choteau he hadn't been in. Brisk business took place inside.

Here's the church, here's the steeple, he mused. *Open it up, where are the people? Across the street in the bar. Open it up, there they are.*

Elbow to elbow with some old boys at lunch. The man next to him finished up and left, and a sot dropped in at Pete's side, alcohol fumes pouring off him. The bartender set both palms on the bar and asked the drunk did he want him to come out from behind the bar or did the drunk want to leave of his own volition. The man drew a circle on the bar with his finger, pounded it with a fist by way of a hex, and spun off his stool and out the door.

Pete held up his beer glass.

The bartender returned with a fresh lager mildly bubbling. Pete dug crushed bills and coin money from his jeans. Counted out the amount with his index finger, stopped and picked up a quarter. There was a hole bored through Washington's temple.

"You seen these?" Pete asked. "I got a bunch of these with holes in 'em at home."

"May I?"

Pete slid it over, and the bartender held it up, handed the coin back to Pete, and went and said something to a fellow a couple barstools down. An old boy leaned forward to get a look at Pete, then rose from his stool and waddled over, removing a tucked-in napkin from his plaid shirt.

"This is Gene," the bartender said.

"Can I see?" the man asked.

Pete handed the coin over. The man held it up to the neon light on the window and squinted at it. He showed some feature of the coin to the bartender. They murmured like a pair of diamond merchants.

"Give you three dollars for it," the man said.

Pete laughed.

"It's a quarter."

The man set the shot-through quarter on the counter and reached into his back pocket for his wallet. Three old dollar bills that fell over his fingers like pieces of faded denim.

Pete covered the coin with his palm.

"Well, let's just hold on," he said. "You start out at three, maybe I can get you up to five."

The man sighed out his nose and had a little trouble negotiating the old dollars back into his wallet.

"I'm just joshing." Pete slid the coin toward Gene. "You can have it."

When Pete wouldn't take the man's three dollars, he handed them to the bartender for Pete's tab. He removed a small cloth pouch from his jeans, and dropped the coin inside.

"How many of those you have?" Pete asked.

The bartender and Gene shared a quick knowing glance, and then Gene emptied the little sack onto the bar. Dimes, nickels, pennies, quarters, all of them shot through.

"That's about eight bucks in broken money," Pete said.

"I'm of the opinion that these are a warning."

"A warning of what?"

The man scooped the coins back into the pouch.

"Trouble."

"From?"

The man looked up from the pouch at Pete.

"The man who made them."

"Who's that?"

"Goes by the name of Pearl."

"Not a Jeremiah Pearl," Pete said.

"You met him too?"

"Yeah. For my work."

"Me too."

"No shit."

The man nodded, exchanged another silent communication with the bartender.

"Can I buy you a drink?" Pete asked.

Gene pulled closed the pouch, said maybe they should go to his shop instead.

The early afternoon light swept in the open door and then the fluorescents lit the place in full. A rack of leather jackets, stacks of speakers and stereo components and turntables, a display case of bone-handled knives. One wall was given to taxidermy, deer and whole foxes in posed dioramas with dusty eyes and spiderwebbing among the antlers. There were scimitars. Columns of paperbacks. A Nazi flag among other flags.

Gene explained that he'd been in the pawn business thirty years, inherited the building from an uncle. He ducked into a back room, returned grunting with several large plastic tomes, which thudded on the glass.

"What are these?" Pete asked.

The pawnbroker loped out from behind the register with his key and locked the front door, and pulled the roller blind all the way down. He took a stool behind the counter. He looked mildly insane. He had the same strange gray eyes of certain huskies or goats. He explained to Pete that he'd already told all of what he was about to say to the local cops, but that nothing had come of it.

PEARL HAD FIRST COME in the summer last. Not looking too hot, neither. The beard on him blown out and thatched with bits of leaves and sticks like he'd just crawled out of the brush. It'd be no surprise to hear chirping issue from it. Pearl was got up in a black outfit that on inspection was a dark medley of filthy flannel shirts, denim pants, and a leather or canvas coat, you could not tell. Boots black and black laces too. The pawnbroker could smell him when he opened the door, a pungency of smoke, and up close stinking like an outhouse.

"Was his boy with him?"

"Outside. He come in once to say he saw a police car, and what did he want the kid to do should the cop come back. His old man told him to wait inside by the door."

"How'd the kid look?"

"Compared to the old man, about near a regular human being."

"His clothes? You mind if I write this down?"

Gene nodded it was fine, and Pete pulled his small notepad from his jacket. Helped himself to a pen from a cup on the glass display case.

"The clothes was probably cut down for him. Big baggy man-pants cinched up with a belt, you know. He had on a down vest, I remember. One of them thermal underwear shirts. He looked okay, I guess."

THE PAWNBROKER TELLS. Pete writes. That Pearl looks at the coins in the cases and not seeing what he wants, asks does the pawnbroker have any buffalo nickels. Gene fetches out a box of them he has in a drawer, more valuable coins than those under the glass. Gene sets the box on the counter and Pearl paws through the coins, nodding. Pleased. Asks does he have any more. Gene says nah, but they aren't too rare. That Pearl can go into any pawnshop, there's probably a box under the counter just like this one.

Pearl says he'll take them, but only if Gene gets some more. Says he can't be going around to pawnshops all over the place.

"What did you say?"

"I say, *Sure, fine, whatever.* He's stinking up the place. I just want him out."

"I see."

"But here's the queer part: he pays in gold. From a little satchel of Krugerrands and Canadian Maple Leafs."

"He doesn't have any cash."

"He don't *want* any cash. Won't let me make change on the Krugerrands."

"What's he say?"

"That he'll take his change in buffalo nickels. When I get more."

"And it's weird to trade rare gold coins for less rare buffalo nickels?"

"Yes."

"He give a reason?"

"Well, hold on and let me get to it."

"Sorry."

PEARL'S BACK A FEW weeks later. Gene has another box of buffalo nickels he's managed to pick up. No kid this time, Gene doesn't ask. Pearl doesn't reek as bad or maybe Gene's just expecting it. But this round it's like Pearl's had a couple pots of coffee. Pacing around the place, idly fingering the pawnbroker's wares, expounding. About money. The history of money. Starts all the way back at the Byzant, the original gold coin. Does the pawnbroker realize how much gold in circulation is as old as that Byzantine coinage, Spanish doubloons, Aztec sovereigns. *Imagine this.* Seems to wait to see if the pawnbroker does, in fact, imagine it.

Does the pawnbroker realize that no metal has such little real application as gold? Unless you count the generation of greed an application.

The pawnbroker says to him, *I thought you were here for buffalo nickels.*

Gold is woven into our history, even these nickels, Pearl says. He says that humanity is an alloy of itself and gold. Or something like that. He goes on at length, so much history you can barely keep up. The de facto adoption of the gold standard by the founding fathers. Lincoln's Scrip Act to get greenbacks to fund the war. The Brand-Ellison Act. The Sherman Silver Act. The Crime of '73. The suspension of the gold standard to pay for World War I. How the commercial banks convert their dollars for gold, causing the Great Depression. All of it a long conspiracy to abandon the gold standard in 1933, to remove any real value from currency at all.

"Sorry, but I'm lost. What is all this he's talking about?"

"Hysterical numismatics."

"Pardon?"

"Horseshit. Nothing you don't hear at trade shows. Every time there's a recession someone goes on about it. How the whole game is fixed. How bullets and seeds are the only really real currency. Only, with Pearl, more intense. You can tell he's brewing trouble the way he talks."

"The way he talks?"

HE SAYS WE'RE AT WAR, that fiat currency is a permanent state of war. He makes the pawnbroker pull a dollar from the till. Pearl holds up the bill, says, *This company scrip is a boot on your neck like all company scrip. Good for a shit sandwich. It's written on the damn thing, look here now.*

Pearl explains the meaning of the descending capstone, how the thirty-two feathers of the dexter wing of the eagle correspond to the number of ordinary degrees in Scottish Rite Freemasonry. How the stars above the eagle's head form a hexagram, a Star of David. Witchcraft and Hebrew magic.

And what could be more magical, more alchemical, than a soft yellow metal that derives from itself currencies and wars and then more complicated magics like markets and exchanges, loans, interest, compound interest, mortgages, credit cards, lotteries, futures, bonds, derivatives, short stocks, all manner of financial spells burgeoning out in ever increasing complexity and intricacy like a heathen mandala, all of it originating in a substance that has no physical application save as a symbol of itself in coin or bar.

Then he starts in about tulips.

"Tulips?"

"Something about tulips and markets in Europe. In the past. I dunno."

"What did you say to all this?"

"I get a lot of cranks in here. People who can't even see Fucked from where they are. Desperate to get some cash. People liable to do anything. But this guy . . . I couldn't wait for him to leave. I just sold him the coins."

"And then?"

"Then nothing. I never seen him again."

"Never?"

"Nope."

The pawnbroker opened the books on the display case. Pages of coins in plastic slots.

"What are these?"

The pawnbroker pointed at the first nickel in the sleeve and flipped the book around for Pete.

"A couple months later, this fella I know comes in, says have I seen one of these before."

"I says, 'Sure, it's a hobo nickel.' These old-timers in the Depression, they'd use a buffalo nickel because they were struck with more relief to them—the images aren't as flush with the surface of the coin as your dimes and quarters and pennies. With small tools you can make the Indian look like some hobo or your riding partner. Put a knit cap on him and a train in back of him. Turn the buffalo into a horse or a camel."

Pete examined a nickel that had been crudely altered into a Jewish banker. Hook nose, yarmulke.

"Pearl?"

The pawnbroker nodded.

"What's ZOG?"

"Zionist Occupational Government. A lot of the older hobo nickels have your standard anti-Semitic signs in them. The Depression, and all. Though I did think it was a little bold that he'd put his name to it."

The pawnbroker turned the page for Pete to see where Pearl had etched his name in the buffalo.

"Where'd your friend find it?"

"In a phone booth."

"No shit."

"Then they start appearing everywhere. Cigarette machines, newspaper boxes outside of the Osco Drug. You can see his work get better and better. Like this one. See how he turned the buffalo's hump into a mushroom cloud? I'm partial to that one. Here's one he turned into a crosshairs. Got pretty damn good in a short while."

The pawnbroker opened the second book, and the two of them scrutinized the coins. He showed Pete pages of Hasidim with wavy beards and long payos.

"What's the inscription on this one?"

"Oh yeah. This is when he started working small. Here, take the magnifying glass."

"*The plague . . .*"

"*. . . has come.*"

"*The war is here. It will last until . . .*"

"I think that last part is ' *. . . the seventh year.*' Amazing. I don't know how he got the letters so small."

"What the hell does it mean?"

"Well, that he's gone apeshit, for starters. These books hold three hundred coins."

"Christ, how many did he do?"

The pawnbroker turned up his palms.

"These are just the good ones." He touched the books. "This is months of work right here."

"But now he's just putting holes in any coins."

"It would appear."

"It's easier."

"No, it ain't. These holes look *punched* in. I got no idea how he's doing it. I tried, it's not easy. Not with just a hammer and a bit, even if you can get everything lined up. And it's not just circles. That quarter you gave me, it's got a pentagon-shaped hole. There's triangles, squares, ovals, and now, pentagons. But, yes, he's churning out a lot of coins."

"And you're collecting them?"

"People are actually coming in asking for them. You turn on the CB and you'll hear truckers saying they just got one of Pearl's square nickels out in Great Falls, who's got a roundy dime?"

"So they're really worth something?"

"Yeah, but it's more than that." The pawnbroker's stubble on his chin sounded against his fingers like sandpaper. "This is a strange kind of genius. This lunatic has taken money and turned it into another kind of money. His own money."

"Kinda brilliant for an act of rebellion," Pete said. "But what for?"

"I take him at his word. He's at war. Sooner or later he's gonna give somebody a reason to go after him."

"You think people will die."

"Yeah." The pawnbroker swung closed the book of nickels. "For starters."

◆ ◆ ◆

Why were they fighting?

Jimmy said for Rachel to put on some clothes she said you're not my dad and her mother said to listen to Jimmy and she ran to her room and then Jimmy and Mom were fighting and everyone was pissed at everyone such bullshit jesus.

What was she wearing that ignited the incident?

Shit her mother bought for her in the first place. A halter top. Cutoffs.

Why did her mother tell her to change then?

. . .

Is this when he started looking at her like that?

. . .

Like he was supposed to look at her mother? From across the room, taking whole rude draughts of her with his eyes? His tongue moving like he was working something in his teeth loose?

Gross.

So was the fight about that? About Jimmy looking at her that way?

More or less. But also her mother going to the bars in Waco. Afterparties in Jimmy's trailer. All the strangers up from Austin.

Did the neighbors complain?

Some did. The cops came one time. Checked IDs, went room to room. Ran a flashlight over her in bed. She screamed.

Jesus.

It was fucked.

So was this when she first ran away?

No. There wasn't anywhere to go yet. Besides, this was nothing new. Her mother was always "having a few people over tonight" or "going out for a little bit" even back in Missoula. Even before her father left. The both of them sometimes. Her father carrying her from the couch where she'd fallen asleep. His tobacco whiskey whiskers, good night Applesauce.

Did she miss him?

Of course. But not exactly. Everybody wants freedom.

Meaning?

Meaning she sneaks a bottle of vodka to school.

For what?

To make friends. She wants to be grown. She wants to have a few people over too. She wants to go out for a little bit.

Did she make friends?

In the grove of live oaks between her school and her house. There was a place where kids went to smoke, listen to music, and make out.

And what did these kids make of this tiny thing only on the cusp of fourteen and walking up with a handle half-full of vodka?

They asked her what did she have there. She said, does anyone have a cigarette, I'd kill for a cigarette right now.

All maturelike. Had she even ever smoked before?

A couple times. Lori and Kim smoked back in Montana. She used to sneak them some of her mother's cigarettes. It's how she made friends with them too. She pulled on the vodka and passed it to a boy who lit a cigarette and gave it to her.

Did Rachel like that?

Rose.

Did Rose like that?

Like what?

The boy giving her the cigarette?

She loved it.

NINE

A scant shadow dressing in the dark, thin arms, narrow chest, tugging his shirt over his head against a brown moon hung low outside his window. He ceases his dressing to listen, his silhouette turning to, halting, turning fro. Nothing. Cecil bends. Pulls shoelaces through the eyeholes, doubleknots them.

He pads over to the light switch but doesn't turn it on. Produces a small tool from his pocket. Flat head in the flat head screw on the switch panel. The screws fall into his hand, into his pocket. He removes the plate, removes a twenty-dollar bill folded and pressed into the box with the wires. He slips the bill neatly in his shirt pocket and replaces the light-switch plate.

He slides open the window, removes the screen from the frame with practiced ease.

The dog in the yard stands, wags what should be a tail. She made Uncle Elliot have the animal's cords cut. His balls too. *Would like to do a little work on her with a knife. Stack her own damn firewood.*

He moves Indian-quiet through the yard to the outbuilding, the dog padding along, her chain dragging to its limit, whereupon she leaps making that awful airy bark, that rude longing aspiration. The out-building. The tarp. The under it. The old single-speed Huffy. Tires he patched himself on the sly.

He pedals down the drive crunching over the gravel to the gate. Bike over gate, Cecil over gate, Cecil back onto bike. Stark cyclist glid-ing on the blacktop, the countryside of tilted fence posts and barbed wire and small bitter wind. He is cold and nearly miserable.

Pedal. You'll warm up.

Shelby itself is still, yellow lights ablink at the intersections. You couldn't be farther from anywhere. He wheels in behind the Hi-Line Bar to ditch the bike. Blows his hands, pacing. A cur wanders by startled to see him, growls, cuts a wide path. He shakes stones in hands like dice, pitches them at the railroad tracks. He walks the ties, he walks the fishplates.

Two hours, the pink surge of dawn.

He hazards out to the street. *Dude'd said meet him in back, but maybe . . .* No.

His ride is not coming.

He sets awhile in the South of the Border, idly mincing his eggs with his fork.

They've told you to rise and shine by now, idiot. You could go back. Say you'd taken a bike ride. No. Rather they'd drag you out of here than ride back there under your own power.

A Blackfoot Indian comes in, orders a coffee and a donut to go. Rancher by the look of him. Brown denim jacket. Cowboy hat, beaded hatband.

Go.

Cecil follows him out.

He asks the man is he going west. The sun in his eyes from the dusty shop window opposite. He shields them to see the Indian's face the texture of pitted wax, looking at him out the open door of his Ford. He shields them from showing his fear. The Indian scarcely nods. But nod he does. Cecil hops to.

A whole day to just get from Cut Bank to Kalispell. A buffet lunch he can neither really afford nor resist. A box of saltines.

Where did all your money go, you should have more.
Someone shortchanged you, stupid.

He skulks, a black bogeyman at night in the Kalispell alleyways behind the old railroaders' cottages, walking to stay warm, running from barking dogs. He sits in a coin-op laundry for as long as feels safe. Catches a southbound Kenworth.

"You got the fidgets," logger says.

"I'm all right." He stiffens, deepens his voice. "M'aright."

He walks to the rail yard in Missoula. See him dashing out after the departing train at sunset, slipping off the low rung, tumbling. He lies there, everything inside him rattling around, settling. Agony all over. He pushes himself up by the palms on the sharp white stones. A swollen pulsating lip. He checks to see that he has all his loosened teeth. His goddamn hair hurts.

"The fuck are you doing."

He sits on the ties, sobs.

"Do you even know."

"Quit being sorry for yourself. Get up."

He finds the bums on Jacob's Island the way an eight ball finds its pocket. Jackpot or scratched the game, he can't tell. He gets fed, a tarp to lay on or under, up to him. Wonders what this foretells, is shit lookin up for once.

He sits cross-legged with the tarp gathered and crinkling around him every time he moves, and tells lies to the men here. There's a cackling and breaking of bottles in the near distance and the sound of water as he falls asleep.

He wakes though it seems like he never slept at all. A dust of hoar on the tarp over him, the stalks of grass like blown milky glass. Steam issues from the dirty granite visages of the men around, their bloodshot eyes like molten rock.

He volunteers that he needs to pee. He never goes back.

He paces the grocery store unable to get warm, buys eight ounces of Colby cheese from a skeptical clerk, and realizes outside that he has no way to cut it. He peels away the plastic walking into the downtown gnawing it like a banana.

In the Army Navy store he looks at the garments with an admiration bordering on lust. The puffed ski jackets and the heavy canvas army coats with fur hoods. Wool gloves with leather mittens that fold over. Everything out of his range. He counts his money to be sure.

"How much for these blankets?" he asks.

The clerk folds closed his paper and comes out from behind the counter and takes the blanket from him, and then moves a blanket in the bin aside to show him the sign.

"Ten dollars?"

"How about that? He can read."

Businesspeople and day shoppers on the sidewalks. He searches their faces like a stray cat mewling at the window. Nothing comes of it, the pleading in his face. He could cry.

He passes a blond girl on the sidewalk, busking with a bamboo pan flute. Something to consider, this.

An hour later, he is across the street next to the Army Navy store tapping out rhythms with sticks on the side of a bucket. A discarded shoe box in front him. She's watching him from the first moment he sets to pounding. An hour of mounting discouragement. She rises, looks both ways, and crosses the middle of the street straight for him, a hand to her belly.

"I'm Ell," she says. She squats. Wool socks, unshaven calves of blond down, her dress is bunched so that he can see.

"Hi," he says.

"How old are you?"

"Nineteen."

"Sure you are."

He sets down the sticks.

"You make anything at this bullshit?" he asks.

"Depends. Should get a little more foot traffic as the holidays come on. Thanksgiving's a good time to be out, if it ain't too cold."

"Thanksgiving? Hell. It's fuckin freezing now."

She looks up the street.

"You got a spot?"

"What kind of spot?"

"A place to bed down for the night."

"I'm just trying to make enough to get a blanket."

"My man is in jail today."

"He is?"

"Yeah. Are you a raper?"

"A what?"

"I'm pregnant with my man's baby. So you can't mess with me. He'll fuck you up. You a raper?"

"You're the one come over here. I ain't done shit to you."

"My man's in jail."

"I know. You said already."

"I got a spot. But I don't want to be there alone. But I don't put out too. But if you need a spot, it would be good there were two of us and one of us was a guy."

He puts his sticks in his shoe box and his shoe box in his bucket and his bucket under his arm.

"Let's go already."

TEN

Pete hiked beneath scudding thunderheads up past Separation Creek where Jeremiah Pearl had threatened him, threatened to kill the boy. The clothes were still lodged in the cleft of the rock where Pete had put them. He stashed a few cans of beans there and the giardia medication. He thought the vitamin C might attract animals, so he'd wrapped the bottle in plastic, put it into a paper sack, and stuffed it in under the clothes with his card.

He surmised that it was all certainly pointless.

One weekend he drove down to Missoula as there was no longer any chance he'd run into Beth. Traipsing out of Eddie's Tavern with Spoils and Shane when he spotted Mary across the street heading into Warden's Market alone. He told the fellas he'd be along and hoped that he was lying. Inside she was looking at the beer and the wine like she couldn't decide what on earth to have. She sensed his approach and his attention but didn't recognize him right away. He wavered there, a little drunk.

"Pete," he said, touching his chest. "You bandaged up my hand."

Before she could reply, he palmed a bottle of red and asked her did she have a place they could drink it. She smiled at the ceiling as if to say not again, not again was this happening, was she going to take a man home. She put the bottle back on the shelf. He swayed in the air in front of her like a song was playing. She fetched a better bottle, and let out her arm for him.

She lived some blocks away in the Wilma Building. They went in through the door next to the theater lobby and to the elevator. A gray-skinned elevator operator in a vestigial red suit with epaulets requested her floor, though he must have known. Pete asked him what he was looking at, and the man took in Pete for a moment longer. He told Mary no overnight guests allowed.

"Who do you think is staying overnight?" she asked.

When they made her floor, Pete dug in his pocket and gave the operator a ten-dollar bill. The man folded it several times, put it inside his coat, and wished them a good night. The accordion gate rattled to. Pete watched the elevator operator's silhouette descend with low-grade delight.

She leant on the wall, the bottle of wine dangling in her hand like a short club.

"So you're the one who thinks he's staying over."

"There could be more gatekeepers. A jealous cat. I make no assumptions."

"Shut up," she said, striding toward him like she might brain him with the bottle.

They were at it when the elevator opened again and discharged one of her neighbors, who rushed past them, Mary's dress opened to the navel. She clutched it closed, took up the wine bottle from the floor, and led him inside.

When Pete woke he had no notion of the layout of her place. The window was covered by an opaque blanket or quilt, and when he pulled it away from the window the light from the street wasn't much to see by and the blanket fell back anyway. She breathed thick with contentment next to him. He touched her through the sheet and she arched toward him, the warmth of him, in the tropism of desire, and when he stilled, she ground against him in her sleep, moaned, and paid out a sweet winey sigh.

He got up and made his way blind as a mole. Glass things on the dresser tinkling as he bumped it. He stepped on what seemed like a paper sack, and found the door by chancing upon some hinges. A closet. Jesus. He moved along the wall, found the light switch, the door molding, the glass doorknob. The hinges screeched and he stopped and listened. She breathed on as before. He slipped out of the bedroom.

The neon light of the Wilma marquee illumined her tiny living room and kitchen, said too that it wasn't even late, that movies showed yet. They had simply fallen asleep like old lovers. What a nice idea.

He padded into the kitchen for a glass of water. A dull ache, the onset of a hangover. He thought he'd handle it with the wine.

He popped the cork and there was a knock at the door. The elevator operator. Maybe the manager. There was another soft knock like the person was using a single knuckle, like the knocker was getting discouraged.

"What are you doing?" she asked. Crimson hued and nude.

He held up the bottle. Whoever was at the door tried the knob. He glanced in that direction, did she want him to check it out. She gestured vaguely, as though people were always knocking, and shucked on a silk robe and yawned.

"You hungry?"

"I could eat."

"Pour me some of that."

She kissed him and he put on his underwear and T-shirt and they drank wine out of little juice glasses as she cooked, and she batted her eyes at him in mock affection and he stood behind her and kissed her neck as she worked. Hot fumes drove him to an open window with the view of the marquee.

"Jesus, what are you making?"

She smiled, strained noodles. Her robe fell open more than once and he caught sight of the lattice of white scars on her belly and over her heart that he'd felt in the dark. She caught him looking and came over and sat him on the chair and filled his mouth with her heated tongue and moved over him until he was splendidly awash in an opiate stupor and didn't move at all when she went back to finish cooking. The marquee winked out and in a bit she turned on a lamp, scented the bulb with something from a dropper, and came back with two steaming bowls.

"Come on," she said, patting the floor.

They ate facing one another cross-legged. He was starving.

"It smells like hell, but I could eat this the rest of my life."

She grinned and told him it was lo mein.

"Where did you learn to cook like this?"

"Not sure."

"Really?"

"Yeah."

"Why are you looking at me like that?"

She started to laugh, covered her face with her fingers, and peeked through them at him.

"I can't remember your name," she whispered.

"It's Pete."

She mouthed the words *I'm sorry.*

"It's fine. I like that you forgot. Mary."

She blushed. He held up a glass and she clinked it with her own.

"You're adorable, Pete."

"Thank you."

She pushed some of his hair behind his ear.

"You're welcome. Another helping?"

He nodded and she took his bowl and filled it again and his small glass of wine too. She watched him eat approvingly, lustily. Like the witch fattening him up. And he would have let her eat him, feed him to whatever animals she kept, whatever. When he finished, she asked did he need another.

"I'm full."

"You sure?"

"God yes."

"You're going to need your strength," she said, taking his bowl and setting it on the coffee table. She got astraddle him. Hiked up his shirt and began to run her nails along his torso. He gasped and it embarrassed him, but she didn't care or notice. She bent down, her robe was open already, and he swooned like a drunken woodland god. He started to pull her up, she fell back.

"It's cold on the floor."

"You'll be warm in a minute."

He was due some vacation days and he took them. A week of noons he woke and went downstairs to watch matinees in the Wilma or up the street to the Oxford for a late lunch and a little poker with tight-assed old cowboys. He had her key but he still paid the elevator man to let him up. Groceries and a bottle of something waiting for her when she got back from work. He liked having the place to himself. Waiting for her. Cracking the paper seal, ice in the glass, glug splash, ah.

He woke to her sitting on the bed, watching him sleep.

"Hey you."

"Hey yourself."

He sat up, the springs in the bed groaning and then tocking to stillness. How the contraption had clattered, bounding like a stagecoach. Fucking her you felt like you were really getting something accomplished, like you were a team, you two were good at it, that it was a thing that could be won.

"I feel like this bed is just gonna disintegrate," he said, patting the mattress.

She smiled. He noticed just then that her eyetooth was gray and too that her smile was no less lovely.

"What time is it?"

"Almost five."

He took a breath so deep it made his throat sore.

"I guess it's supper what I'm buying you."

They ate in a bleary cafe with weeping windows. Shared a tapioca dessert, spoons clinking in the pudding.

"So you've been at this awhile," she said.

"What this?"

"The pudding."

"What?"

"The *job*, dummy. I looked up some older cases in the records and saw you in there, in Missoula County. After you visited the office that day."

"What did you do that for?"

"I wanted to see about you before I fucked you."

He grabbed the check when the waitress set it down.

"You're up in Tenmile now."

"Yep."

She sat back in the vinyl booth and regarded him. It had become something of a pastime, this just looking at him.

"What?"

"What made you run up there?"

"I didn't run."

"Those rural gigs are tough. Hours on the road. Not a lot of support. I'm sure you were on track for supervisor down here. So why go up there?"

He was in his wallet and set a twenty on the table. The waitress came and got it and made for the register. He asked would she bring him another cup of coffee, and she waved over her shoulder that she would. He folded his hands together and leaned forward.

"Can we talk shop just this once, and not anymore?" he asked.

"I don't want to talk shop."

"Then what are we talking?"

She waited until the waitress dropped off his coffee and change. He noticed there were no holes in the coins.

"There's a party tonight, and I want you to come."

"All right," he said.

"It's a work party."

"Ah."

"Over at Tricia's."

She waited to see if he would say anything else, and when he didn't, crossed her arms. He reached across the table and got her wrist. A pair of hairline scars there too. He rubbed the groove they made. He did not wonder at all about why she'd done that. It was past.

"What is it?"

"I feel stupid."

"About what?"

"I like you," she said.

"I like you too."

"I want to go to the party with you."

"I'd like to be gone with to the party."

She looked off.

"Mary, what the hell is it?"

"I'm new."

"And?"

"And I'm gonna feel stupid when all the girls you've been with from the office are talking about me."

He grinned and took her cold hand and rubbed it and told her that he'd never been with anyone from the office.

"I haven't so much as kissed one of them under the mistletoe."

He took a hand away to sip his coffee and held hers with his other one.

"I'm not a jealous person," she said. "But people talking, I hate it. I need things to be separated. Work. Life. Separated."

"Okay."

"I don't even care if you have somebody else in your life—"

He'd let go of her hand.

"Do you have somebody up in Tenmile?"

"I left my wife a while ago."

He sipped his coffee. Before he could set it down, she took it from him and had a drink too.

"A wife."

"She went to Texas."

"Texas."

"You're repeating me."

"Sorry."

"Now you're apologizing."

"Fuck you."

"Now you're swearing."

She set his cup back down in front of him.

"Do we need to talk about her?" he asked.

She scratched behind her ear. Smiled when she looked at him.

"No."

He sipped his coffee and she took it from him again.

"Let's go to this party."

"It's not for a while."

He slid out of the booth and stood.

"Let's go to this party slowly."

They are drunk when they arrive, an almost empty fifth of Montana Redeye. She climbs a wrought black spiral staircase ahead of him, he keeps trying to put his mouth onto her lovely ass as she ascends before him. The lively throng upstairs. So much cigarette smoke the house may be afire. A guitar boils out a crude blues through overworked speakers. She leads him to a card table sagging under bottles, faceted half-empty goblets of red wine, and a fondue pot with a burping neon orange skin. Someone has placed olive eyes in the thing. Pete pumps a spittle of froth from a keg floating in a garbage can of ice water and gives up. Faces spin out of the mass to recognize him and shake his hand and say things to him he cannot hear.

Now Mary is gone.

He wheels into the kitchen to find her. People he knows from work, guys from the Attention Home slap his back.

"Pete, my man. What's that you're drinking?"

Pete hands the bottle over. Accidentally knocks a playcastle of cans off the counter.

"Christ, Pete. Nobody actually *drinks* this."

Pete shrugs dreamishly, coughs creamishly, hawks into the sink.

"Got a cold there?"

"I'm runnin' a temperature, all right."

"How's the wife?"

"Texas."

"What?"

"We're splits."

"I'm sorry."

"No one quits a good thing," Pete said.

A loud record now, something new from the plinky tinny keyboard sound of it. Mary dances in the living room. Alone. Swaying about in that dress, a satiny red and white thing that fits her all over.

"That Mary is just . . ."

"Yes. Yes she is."

Someone hands Pete a can with a screwdriver stabbed into it.

"Did you hear about her?"

"Hear what?"

"Shotgun that thing already."

Pete removes the screwdriver and puts the can to his face. A cold bubbling snake liable to choke him. A long foaming burp. He sets the empty by. Burps again.

"Hear what?"

"She has a file. Jake come across it. She was in and out of foster homes and state hospitals her whole life. And it wasn't no good run neither. Fuckin bonkers. One placement, they kept her in a goddamn closet most of the time. This was two years. Two years of getting beat and raped. All before she was twelve years old. And the shit at the state hospital? With the guards fucking the girls? She was up there too. It's still like a goddamn brothel up there. I *never* send a kid there, I can help it."

She dances, and Pete is not the only one watching.

"Looks great on the outside, but under the hood. Another story."

She touches her stomach with a palm and closes her eyes and sets her hips in a pendular swing as though her pelvis depended from a point somewhere near her heart.

The system knows this girl.

Which is to say that you know this girl.

All her homes are group homes and all her sisters and brothers are fosters in placements, her fathers and mothers are social workers, and when she ages out of care, she ages into the job. Your job. Only she gets inappropriate and benched, or no one trusts her with any real cases and she sits in the break room rearranging packets of Sweet 'n Low.

She is proof that there is nothing that cannot happen to someone. That the world doesn't need permission, that there is no novel evil it won't embrace.

And so you're in a mood now, watching Mary dance and taking shotguns of beer and then riding in a car with her and people from the party and you're both too drunk to notice the other is too drunk and you're kissing in the flicker of a dying neon sign, hiccupping, kissing hard and sloppily, teeth clacking together, inexpert, tyro.

Innocent, be untroubled a while longer.

He hurt all over, the sunlight frying him through Mary's window.

He thought he should just quit. The job or drinking or both.

Her note said she had drawn a Saturday shift and so he quaked alone in his hangover among her spider plants and wicker, staring for some time at the phone or the number Beth had scribbled on a scrap of envelope. He'd memorized it by the time he folded the scrap into his shirt pocket and went to Al's and Vic's. He took the beer the bartender pulled for him and watched him clean glasses and left when his head quit pounding.

He went to the Army Navy store for a new pair of bootlaces, to the bookstore, and for lunch. Didn't speak to a soul. It was two o'clock when he finally returned to the Wilma. He lay down on Mary's couch, couldn't fall asleep.

It was five when he woke.

He pulled the phone onto the coffee table and regarded it, muttering. Then he dialed and it rang twice and he was about to hang up when she answered.

"Hey, Applesauce, it's Daddy."

"Why don't you have a phone at your house?"

There was music in the background and people talking and Beth too, he thought. Her laughter.

"It's Dad," she said to her mother.

"How are you doing?" he asked.

"Mom says to tell you to send some money."

"Okay. I will. How are you?"

"Sucky. I hate it here."

"You'll meet some kids your age. It'll get better."

"I don't like kids my age."

"What does that mean?"

Beth was talking to her.

"Mom wants to know if you're going to send at least two hundred dollars."

"Tell her I'll talk to her in a minute."

His daughter covered the mouthpiece, and then it flooded with sound again.

"Pete?"

"Damnit, Beth. Put her back on."

"I need that money right away. At least a couple hundred."

"Yes. Put Rachel back on."

"Your *daughter* needs things. Shoes. School clothes. Notebooks and shit."

"Beth. Put Rachel back on."

"You don't have any right to talk to her if you aren't gonna support her."

"You're fucking kidding me."

A hand cupped the receiver and it sounded full of ocean, full of Texas. Thirty seconds he watched the clock. A minute. He wanted to pitch the phone at the window, but it was Mary's window, Mary's phone.

"Mom says I only have a minute because of the long distance."

"I'm the one who called, Rach. It's my bill."

"Daddy?"

"What?"

"Can I come live with you?" she whispered. "I won't need a lot of room and I'll be good, I promise. I hate it here. It's hot. It's fall and it's still hot. Hot hot. Like a thousand degrees."

"It'll cool off."

"I *miss* you."

"Honey, I miss you too—"

"I hate it here! There's all these people over and I don't like any of them—"

"What people?"

"I want to come home!"

"Rachel, listen to me. I'll make you a deal. Just try it out for a couple months."

"A couple whole months?!"

"I want you to try. We all need to try. And then if you still don't like it, we can talk about you coming back up here."

"You hate me! Why don't you just say it? You hate me and Mom."

"I don't hate you."

"You hate Mom."

"I don't hate your mother."

"This is so fucked."

"Come on, Applesauce—"

The line clicked.

"Rachel."

The line clicked again. Then the doleful dial tone.

+   +   +

What the hell happened? Wasn't she starting to make friends?

She made a lot of friends. The older kids in the woods. But she made enemies too.

Who?

Goody girls. Cheerleaders and bitches like that. Teachers asking was everything all right at home.

Was everything all right at home?

What home? Jimmy's trailer? That wasn't their home.

Is that why she wanted to go back to Montana?

She didn't want to go back to Montana.

Then why did she ask to live with her father?

Because her mother was letting her have friends over and of course the kids wanted to drink beer and her mother would be having people over too and there was this one perfect night when her mother didn't stop any of them from getting beers from the cooler and nobody got in trouble or called the cops or anything, but the next day she was being such a bitch and said they couldn't do that again.

Because it was inappropriate. Because she was her mother, not her friend.

Because she was hungover. Because she was jealous, to be honest.

Of the attention Rachel was getting?

Rose.

What kind of attention?

Just looking at her. Not looking at her mother. Talking to her. Jimmy always finding an excuse to lean over her just to get something from the shelf, rub against her in the narrow hall. One time fetching her a beer even though she didn't really drink that much, she didn't like being drunk and sick, she could nurse a beer for hours or pour it half out when no one was looking she was drunk enough on the attention the attention the attention like a drug.

So she liked Jimmy?

Ick.

The attention then.

Yes. The older guys in the woods, car stereos blasting. She knew the girls didn't like her that much, but she didn't care, she just talked to the guys, her mother's friends, a suntanned blond saying they should go to his boat. Guys her dad's age. Her whole life became more interesting. Every minute charged with her new participation in it.

But her mother, she hated this.

Jealous.

Surely it was more complicated than that.

They'd shared cigarettes and talked about men. They'd cried when they talked about Pete and Jimmy and what were they gonna do now, they couldn't live here. Waco was terrible. They were broke. They were friends. Her mother didn't know how to navigate backward to motherhood.

Or Rachel wouldn't return to being a daughter.

She ran away. Two days.

Where did she go?

None of your business.

The Waco cops spotted her after curfew smoking at a Dairy Queen picnic table? She didn't run?

No.

Why not?

She thought maybe her mother would be so glad to see her that she would let her get away with anything.

Was she?

She slapped her. Right in front of the police. Then kissed her and held her and cried and asked why and answered her own question that she was a bad mother and they needed to leave this place, they needed a fresh start and in a week they were headed to Austin where she had a job waiting for her.

What job?

A guy knew a woman who had to go back to Charlotte and needed someone to sublet her place and even better would Beth take her shifts at the bar down there, it paid good enough, hell yes.

What did they tell Jimmy?

They just left.

ELEVEN

He went back to work. He visited the Shorts armed with mace for the Rottweilers (gone), called Cecil's uncle Elliot to check in on them (no answer), and paid a visit to Cecil's mother, Debbie (skittish, defensive), and Katie (hale), but Pete was distracted. His mind kept turning to the Pearls, the boy, the coins. He watched for coins.

The cache of clothes and medicine was as he left it in the cleft of the rock. He sat listening to the forest, the chipmunks scurrying over the duff, the sky yellow with thin clouds and high smoke from a forest fire in Canada.

On his way down, Pete encountered a man dragging a travois of marijuana plants out of the cedar. When he spotted Pete, he dropped the plants and marched straight up the road toward him. Pete's only options were up or down the mountain, or back up the grade behind him. He took his hands out of his pockets and waited. Told himself the guy just wanted to check him out. Tried to appear harmless and fearless at once.

The man was a panting six foot five, two-fifty. Not exactly fit, but formidable and aptly paranoid. He'd stripped his torso to a sweat-stained thermal undershirt. He wore leather gloves and a three-day beard and he looked like he meant business a little more than Pete expected.

"Who . . . the hell are you?" he asked.

"My name's Pete Snow. I'm a social worker."

"A social . . . worker . . . ," the man panted.

"Yes. There's a family up here. . . ."

Clearly the man had no idea what that could mean. He scanned Pete up and down and then stepped closer to him. Pete balled his fists at his side and backed up. The guy halted his advance and squinted sweat out of his eyes and dabbed them with his sleeves.

"I'm a need you to let me pat you down," he said.

"What for?"

"Weapons. Whatever I find."

"Would I be making fists if I had a weapon?"

The man sighed like he'd done this dozens of times, like a bouncer.

"I ain't up here growing vegetables," he said. "I gotta know who we're dealing with."

"My badge is in my car down at the gate."

"Fuck," he said. "Really?"

"What?"

"You're parked at the gate? At the end of this road?"

"Yes. At the end of this road."

He turned around and gestured for Pete to follow him. "Come on."

"Like hell."

The man stopped, turned around.

"One way or another," he said wearily, "you're coming with me."

The grow was at the north end of a meadow where the uninterrupted sun nourished a dense half-acre of unremarkable cannabis all the day long. Two men halted chopping down the rows and stood straight up with their machetes at the sight of Pete and the man escorting him to their tiny plantation in the forest.

"Who the hell is this?" the nearest man asked. He'd gone bald, and an outsized Adam's apple moved in his lank neck. The one behind him was from the looks of him a relation, bigger and with a full head of hair. A son or much younger brother or a cousin from one of those families

where the kin bear too much resemblance and together seem like itera-
tions of an old idea.

"Was coming out of the woods. Some kind of government worker."

"The hell you bring him here for, George?" the bald man asked,
chucking his machete into the earth and walking to them.

"He's parked down at the gate."

The other two men groaned. The bald man quickly looked at his
watch and swore.

"Well Tom ain't coming back."

"I'm sure he's spooked."

"He's *cautious*," the bald man said pointedly. He addressed Pete:
"What are you, Fish and Game?"

Pete wondered if he appeared scared. How not to.

"I'm a social worker. I told your friend I left my badge in my car."

The bald man looked at the other two. Pete couldn't see the George
who stood behind him, but the one with a head of hair shrugged in
what Pete hoped was a benign indifference.

"Look, I really don't have any sort of legal requirement to do anything," Pete said. "I'm not a police—"

"Does your car have any kind of decals on it?" the bald man asked.
"Like from your office?"

"Nope."

"Give George your keys," he said.

Pete hesitated. Thought he should break for it.

"I gotta see that badge," the bald man said. He stepped close enough
for Pete to see that maybe he could trust him. Close enough to hit him too.

Pete dug into his jeans and handed the keys over. The bald man
told George to hurry, and George sighed and jogged off flatfooted in
the direction of the road. At a gesture from the bald man, the other
resumed chopping down the plants. The bald man pulled his own
machete out of the ground and pointed with it at a place for Pete to sit.
After a few minutes, he came and squatted in front of Pete, his arms
across his thighs, the machete dangling between his legs.

"So what's a social worker doing up here?"

Pete breathed through his nose, and studied a place just below the man's eyes as he spoke clearly and without a trace of fear or impatience. As if all that mattered were facts, and with facts they would avoid all unfortunate outcomes. He explained about the Pearl boy coming to the school. How the boy said he lived up here, up this road, in these woods. How he returned the boy to his family.

"There aren't any families up here, man."

"This was some weeks ago," Pete said flatly.

"There are not any families up here," the man repeated.

"I can show you where I left them some clothes and food."

The bald man searched Pete's face for some sign of a lie.

"Stand up."

"Why?"

"Stand up."

"I'm afraid of what you're going to do," Pete said. "I won't cooperate if you're going to hurt me."

The bald man looked at his partner, who had come over to see whatever was going to happen. The bald man half-laughed and half-sighed and said, "I'm just gonna pat you down. C'mon. Up."

"Your friend already did that. Look, I'll take you up to where I met Pearl," Pete said. "At least let me show you the things I left."

The man stood in alarm, as if a rattlesnake had emerged from between Pete's legs.

"Did you say 'Pearl'? *Jeremiah* Pearl?"

Pete nodded.

The man looked at his cousin or brother and put his palms to his kidneys and arched his back and looked at the sky. Then he grabbed a handful of plant stalks and started toward the trail.

"Come on," he said. "We gotta move ass."

They folded and stuffed as many of the grown plants into Pete's trunk as would fit, and then laid several out on the backseat and floor and left many of the plants by the side of the road. Pete didn't hazard an objection. They covered everything with their coats and climbed in. Pete backed down the road to the blacktop, turned the car around at the roadside, and asked them where to. The car was already pungent with sweat, dirt, and the aroma of their cargo.

"Left. Go left."

The bald man kept checking the mirror as they drove. After a time, he settled down and picked through the things on Pete's floor—clipboard, an accordion folder of case files, a plastic sack of baby bottles and rubber nipples. His lips flattened into a warmer expression. He said his name was Charlie.

"So you really are a social worker."

"Yes."

"Sorry it had to get a little heavy back there."

"It's okay. I'm accustomed to it."

The dope farmers' camping trailer was an hour and forty minutes away, up a remote logging road that hugged the shore of a nameless tiny lake impinged on and all around littered by a haphazard selection of boulders the size of small cars. Pete parked and they hauled the plants into the trailer and tossed them into the narrow hall, and when it was done, Charlie went down to the lake and came back with four bottles of cold beer. Pete made to go, but Charlie said for him to stay a while. That they'd all feel more at ease. They sat around a fire pit that was itself nearly encircled by boulders and drank the beers. Across the water a moose walked in muck and drooled into the lake heedless of them making a fire. Pete was put to shucking corn. Charlie took a few trout from the lake that they gutted, wrapped in corn husks, and cooked on the coals. They ate them with the corn and when dark fell, passed around a bottle of bourbon and a small ivory pipe carved into the shape of a naked woman whose mouth was the carb and whose blackened crotch Charlie stuffed with a plug of pungent purple weed.

"This your stuff?" Pete asked.

Charlie laughed. "The shit I grow is shit."

They leaned against the boulders sated as Cheshire cats. Pete became altogether absorbed by the gill-like pulsing of the coals and the stoned epiphany that fish and fire shared a profound correspondence. He chuckled morosely at how high he was, that these guys could still decide they didn't trust him. Now too stoned to make a break for it. The moose could still be heard across the water, the occasional suction of a hoof in the shallow mire. He thought he was just being paranoid. Except he wasn't. Not exactly. He couldn't tell.

Charlie leaned back to reach into the front pocket of his jeans and flipped a coin that flashed in the firelight and plopped in the dark somewhere between Pete's legs. Said for Pete to look at the quarter.

"I already know," Pete said.

"Where'd you get yours?"

"All over."

Charlie sucked his teeth. "I've heard of them as far south as Polson and west in Bonner's Ferry," Charlie said. "A couple in pay phones on the Hi-Line."

"There's a pawnbroker collects them in Whitefish," Pete said.

Charlie nodded and gazed into the fire.

"So," Pete said. "How do you know Jeremiah Pearl?"

THEY MEET PEARL one spring at another grow location, a place not to be disclosed. It has rained for several days and they have been waiting for good weather to plant the seedlings. They're playing cards in their tent when they hear a man call out. Pearl, in a hooded poncho, a rifle covered with clear plastic slung over his shoulder. He wears a large beard and the rain is coming down so hard you cannot make out his eyes or his expression.

He asks what is their business up here.

Charlie says they are camping, jokes how it's just their luck to be out in such weather.

Their saplings are in apple crates and covered by a makeshift tarpaulin of plastic bags. Pearl inspects them, ignoring Charlie's protests. He studies their seedlings and nods, as though he now understands everything. They think for a moment they are caught, that he is law enforcement or some grizzled official with the Bureau of Land Management. But the rifle. Maybe he's a crazy misfit, a poacher.

Pearl shouts through the rain that they have a crop in another location.

Charlie says it's none of Pearl's business.

Pearl describes the location exactly.

The tent is small for three men playing cards and now more so with Pearl, who has simply entered it uninvited. He tracks in a great deal of mud and badly reeks. Dark water runs off his filthy pants, and getting a close look at him, they can see now a face of staggering intensity. Eyes a mineral shade of blue, an unnerving cold potential in them.

Pearl introduces himself. Asks if they would like to parley. There's some discussion about what that in fact means. Pearl has a strange way of talking. Grand, with out-of-date words and diction. He explains that he does not believe the land he walks is his own, but also that no one knows all its features as well as he. He allows there are old-timers who might know more. He's met such men in their cabins and cruder mountain redoubts but knows several of them to have died or moved on.

He insists that he has not one issue with cannabis and discusses with them the history of the plant and its role in the early Republic, the rope, cloth, and paper that were made of it and the wide variety of its applications on land and sea. He outlines what interests had lobbied for its criminalization. He says that growing the plant is a demonstration of man's inherent freedom.

Charlie offers to smoke with him. Pearl declines. Charlie asks Pearl does he mind if he and his partners partake, and Pearl says go ahead.

Pearl talks as they smoke, almost as if he has held forth with them many times previous and has come back to at last finish the story. He speaks unbidden about his wife's visions, dreams of the mountains, explosions and bloodshed, and how they prayed and realized that God was telling them to make ready for the End Times. How they sold off everything. The house, the cars, the boat, the motorcycles. Pearl travels out here, finds a piece of land. It has the exact features that his wife has dreamed, a south-facing hillside, a bench of rock on which they will build a house. He buys the property, goes home to fetch his family.

They know the dollar will be worthless and so they convert almost everything they own into bullet, gun, or seed. And gold, Pearl adds. Krugerrands and Maple Leafs and smaller denominations.

There are signs of betrayal and of what will be completed. They are followed by a black sedan. The president of Italy is murdered by the Red Brigade. Their car is sabotaged in South Dakota. The heat wave, the hot blacktop as they wait for the tow truck, the hot blacktop as they wait for the mechanic.

A hundred and thirty dollars for an alternator. The mechanic says the tires look pretty wore out. Jeremiah checks for his wallet in his back pocket as if the mechanic were reaching for it, which in a way he is. They are about out of American scrip. They camp a stone's throw from the car in a dry swale next to a cornfield. No fire. They sleep on the ground in their sleeping bags and wake up dewy and stiff. A bag of green apples for breakfast.

They drive on. It's too hot to even muse. The children doze through a short cataract of rain, a rough draft of a storm. When they wake, they bicker. The mother has migraines along with her visions, and the children's voices are like trumpet blasts, the wind a plague of static in her ears. Her mind becomes a slide of falling boulders, and all at once she's gripping his arm, telling him to pull over. She runs barefoot over the sharp macadam and up a berm to retch and roll onto her back in a brief respite. She casts up her eyes and sees a baleful gray skein of movement that at first she takes for geese or ducks in flight but which turn in her painful gaze into a field of hammers. A sky full of hammers. The pounding behind her eyes begins anew.

Jeremiah helps her back to the car.

Gassing up in Sioux Falls, she pumps down the window and calls for him, and thrusts out her hand, fingers bloody to the palm. He is alarmed, of course, wondering what fresh evil is this.

She hasn't menstruated in over a year. A little spotting some months between miscarriages, not enough to even keep any pads in the house. She was a different woman the last time she had an honest-to-God flow. They were a different family then. They didn't observe the Law. Back then they didn't know any better. But now they know that she cannot be among the children and her husband as she is unclean.

She says for Jeremiah to get her to a hotel. She sits alone in her room and bleeds. She ponders the sky full of hammers. She listens to her children splash in the pool and calls Jeremiah on the phone next door. He worries. They are almost out of cash. They will need to sell some of the gold. She says the money doesn't matter, how they are all going to have to go through these tribulations, how she can take it, all of it, anything Satan wants to throw at her. Cover her in boils. Take her sight. Pester her with lice and fleas. But the children are our true treasure. Promise me, she says, they stay with us until the end.

They pass by Mount Vernon and White Lake, which are neither mountain nor lake but a gas station and the interminable field of quietly steaming corn, worms turning in the hot loam and humus. None of these places have pawnshops to trade Pearl's gold sovereigns.

Now the tank is nearly empty. In the town of Kimball, Jeremiah unloads the trailer to get at the safe and opens the safe to get the gold coins. Takes a few inside to show the old crone behind the counter. He explains that taken together they are a bit more than a troy ounce of gold. He opens the McEwan's Index of the London Fix on her counter. He explains that he will let her have these for last year's price, that she can see for herself right here that they are worth at least ten dollars more right now.

The woman's face goes cross as she pats herself for her reading glasses and she screws up her face looking at the figures, her bottom lip out over her furry old chin. She asks him does he really expect her to give him a hundred thirty dollars for those gold coins. She says this here's a gas station.

Pearl asks is she reading the papers. Does she know that the dollar will be worthless with what is coming to pass? Precious metal will be all that's left for Christians to trade.

She looks askance. She whispers to him does he have no cash whatsoever.

He digs a dollar and eighty-five cents out of his jeans. Says, *Look here at these dimes. What are they worth? What are they made of? Copper sandwiched between zinc and tin alloy. Money of tin, can you believe it? In and of itself virtually, literally worthless. It's just scrip,* he tells her. *Company scrip.*

She looks at him a minute and then at his children outside in the lot and in the store. She tears a piece of paper from a pad nearby and writes her name and address on it and slides it to him.

No charity, Jeremiah tells her, but she says she's turning on the pump, he likes it or not. She ain't interested in buying no coins.

Jeremiah beside himself at the woman's insanity. After all that he's just explained. Can she not see. Can she not hear.

She asks him does he want the gas or not. Well, does he.

Pearl asks Charlie can he believe this. Charlie is at this juncture quite confused as to Pearl's point. If there is a point. The rain abates somewhat, and inside the damp and stinking tent there is no answer to Pearl's question from Charlie or the others. Pearl says that the irony is not lost on him, coming all this way and having all this gold and no one with whom to trade. Incurring a gas tank of debt. He says he'd come to understand that it was already under way.

What is? Charlie asks.

The war, Pearl says.

Pearl is quiet now, grinning faintly it would seem like a man partway into a good drunk. In any case, Charlie offers him a belt from his flask. Pearl's eyes flash at some memory of whiskey, and he nods yes he would like a drink.

He doesn't say how they made it. Perhaps he thinks it and thinks he says it. There is more than paranoia at work here. His mind isn't right. He bobs to the surface of human connection but resides mostly just under like waterlogged driftwood. Steadily saturating and sinking. He drinks again, wipes his beard with his dirty palm.

Every place is an East Berlin, he says. *A Russia, and there is no West to be gotten to. Only these mountains, this Masada.* He says he is dreaming of the Jews in their mountain caves, the Romans implacable as Romans building their siege embankment. *I'm the kakangelist,* Pearl says. *Bringer of the bad word. The plague has come and the war is here.*

Charlie knows a lot of religion, was himself taught by nuns, but these rantings amount to nonsense. He asks Pearl what he wants.

He says he wants to be understood.

Understood about what?

Pearl says he wants his efforts to be perfectly clear.

What efforts? Charlie asks.

Pearl says that Charlie and his partners undertake their enterprise in a war zone and he will require payment in gold to protect it.

They smile. At last a joke. He must be joking.

He is not.

Pearl is told he can go fuck himself. Get the hell out of here.

What thought makes the queer expression on his face is not clear. Is it sheepishness that the gambit has failed? Is it malevolent calm? Is it keeping his anger in custody?

He leaves in a slighter rain than the one that gave him up.

Pete sat up. Charlie went quiet. The fire had burned down to white flaky ulnas. George rose and disappeared into the encroached dark and fetched some lightwood and stirred the coals with a stick and put the sticks in. The flames danced up. He left the noose of new light again and Pete quietly worried what he might return with, he was such a long time gone.

"I should go."

"I'm not done," Charlie said.

"I need to go."

George returned with firewood proper. He fed the fire, warmed his hands at it, and sat back down.

"You're scared of us," Charlie said.

"I feel like you're keeping me here."

"It's Pearl you should be afraid of. I'm trying to help you."

Pete gazed grimly into the flames. The moose was gone.

"Did you ever see him again?" Pete asked.

Charlie looked at the others, back at Pete.

"Not exactly," he said.

THE RAIN ABATES. The soil drains, dries out, Charlie and his partners till and plant. They prepare another small field in another small meadow and yet another. Then they go home, back to their regular lives. Charlie washes trucks in Libby. Theirs is not a sophisticated operation that reaps a high-grade product. They plant, and Charlie or one of the others checks the crop when it suits him.

A few weeks later, he goes to see one of the small fields, takes a fishing pole by way of a disguise for game wardens, Forest Service, whoever. He arrives at a field of yellow knee-high stalks, dead and dying. He turns the soil. It's been salted, literally salted with rock salt. He knows it is Pearl, and is certain when he gets back to his car: three quarters, evenly spaced on the front bumper of his van. A coin for Charlie and each of his partners. A hole in each temple.

Charlie is angry. This motherfucker. He doesn't own the wilderness. Who does this cocksucker think he is.

A hole in his windshield. He's still inspecting it when the report of the rifle washes through the air. There's another and another and another, each only as loud as an egg cracked on a skillet, and he's just hit the dirt when the shooting is over, the reports echoing off the mountains. He cowers a good ten minutes before crawling in the back doors of the van. Pale yellow mushrooms of stuffing out the back of the seats. He leaps behind the wheel. Keys, ignition, backing out, gas pedal to the floor. The windshield is so spiderwebbed he has to drive with his head out of the window to see his way home.

"Pearl could've dropped me at any time," Charlie said. "He wanted me to know that."

Pete looked at the quarter in his palm. The hole was neat, perfectly round, with a barely flared lip on the reverse. The exit wound.

If you asked around in Tenmile and Libby and in the offices of the statehouse in Helena and the professors of wildlife biology and the forestry departments of the universities, you would find men and women who had received these coins in the mail, Charlie said. It was in the paper. That they were in circulation meant that Pearl had declared war on everyone.

It had grown quite cold, and even near the fire the chill wrapped around the better part of him and Pete had to turn his back to the fire and then his front to stay warm. Charlie sat hatless loading the pipe again.

"How did you meet him?" Charlie asked.

Pete told him about finding his son in a school, taking him to his father. The pipe went around again. Charlie said he was damn lucky to be alive.

"What about you? You're still out here."

Charlie toked thoughtfully on the bowl, the smoke leaking out his open mouth like a gun barrel. He explained that they'd moved off some thirty miles or so and hadn't known Pearl was about until Pete came along.

"Fuck it," Charlie said. "We'll go back and get the rest of the crop tomorrow." The prominent cartilage in his throat was like an arrowhead that hadn't made it all the way through his neck.

"Pearl might not believe in the dollar," he added, gently tapping the ashes out of the pipe into his palm and then blowing them away. "But I sure as shit do."

TWELVE

It was an empty rail yard building. She'd pried away a plywood board and then hacksawed all but one of the nails away, leaving the zinc heads on the other side so that the board still looked like it was nailed fast though it clung from a single nail in the middle. You slid it up to the side and climbed in. There was batshit and birdshit, and mice crawled in the walls, but it got them out of the schizoid weather here in the Missoula Valley, good grief it couldn't make up its mind, cold, warm, colder, freeze your nuts off, warm. They covered the gaps in the boards with rugs, old carpets, packing material, and a foam rust-stained mattress, and the room just about warmed up from their body heat in the pitch-black alone.

Their busking, pathetic as it was, brought in about a buck and a half a day, sometimes more. Sometimes they begged outright and sometimes that worked better.

So, sleeping together: one night she coaxed Cecil under her blankets.

"No funny stuff," she said.

He slid out and took his blankets back to the discarded rug he slept on. She said don't be weird, who wants to mess with a pregnant lady anyhow. He said it wasn't about that. Or her. Or whatever she was thinking. He was an inarticulate person. An angry person. She said what's eating you. Chrissakes. He said there was this other time. He was quiet. She waited.

The building was right where the trains joined up and they crashed outside tremendously, unexpectedly.

He said to never mind.

They were quiet.

She said she could feel the baby inside her now. Moving a little bit. She said Bear was the first and only one she'd ever been with and it could've been the first time they'd done it she'd gotten pregnant.

Cecil had sat up in the pure dark.

"It's okay," she said. "I wanna have a baby. I don't care I'm young. The clinic lady said they could take care of it for me and it took me a minute to get she meant to kill it. I said that don't sound like taking care of it at all."

Two train cars coupled outside with a boom that rattled the walls, sent down little bits of plaster or bird droppings. Times it was like being trapped in a collapsing mine.

"Why don't you get over here in these blankets and help make us warm enough we can sleep?"

He didn't move. Not yet.

"It's all right," she said. "My old man Bear—you'll meet him when he gets out—he knows I love him and nobody else. He won't care about you and me. It's not like you're some sketchy dude'd pull something." She snorted a weird laugh. "He'd open up on a guy like that something wicked."

"I can be pretty sketchy."

"You're as sketchy as a daffodil."

"Fuck you."

"You're probably a virgin anyway."

He lay down.

"I'm joking. It's okay you're a virgin. If you are. It don't matter."

She asked him was he gonna be like that. She said she was cold.

They listened to one another ball up in their blankets alone. She said he was being an idiot. He felt tough and that to go to her would be weak and he wouldn't know what to do with himself in any case.

It was a whole week. But it got so cold. He didn't want anyone touching him, but it was freezing and now she was angry at him wasting his heat like that, enough to throw him out maybe. They didn't have enough covers to be fucking around like this. He finally took his blankets over and they snapped them out one at a time over them. He made her promise to keep her hands on his shoulders, not any lower. There were things happened to him just by getting in bed, things that spread out and changed ugly colors in his brain. To be honest, he was afraid he would hit her. He said so. He faced away from her and couldn't sleep and started talking, he didn't know if she was listening, he just went on about it.

"Might as fucking well tell you."

HIS MOTHER WHINING for hours in her bed, calling for him as he passes the door. She's all fucked up. He finally goes in. *Cmere baby. Cmere in here with Mama I'm so sad.*

"I understand what happened," Ell says.

She says, *Mama needs someone to hold her no one ever holds her.* And so he does. He has his arms around her. She sleeps. He falls asleep. He comes to and she's facing him crying, the whole pillow is wet and she's stroking his face, *My sweet sweet boy,* she says, and he pretends to sleep, and she kisses him on the forehead, then on his lips. She's tongue kissing him. Then she's touching him all over, his stomach and his legs. He's not wanting to, but he's responding. His body is. He isn't. He isn't not. He's just there. Then it's going. It's happening. He doesn't want to but she's pulling him into her, she smells like those peppermint cigarettes.

"How old were you?"

"Twelve."

"It's okay."

"Like hell it is."

"No, it's okay right now."

"I know it is."

"I mean it's okay to tell me."

"It ain't the worst thing I did."

"You did? Who said it was you that did it? You think it's only rape if a guy does it?" she asked.

She put her hand on top of his, he took a breath through clenched teeth, tensed his muscles. Then she said soft nonwords, and he released, went slack. After a while he said this is okay. She murmured that yeah it was, already half asleep.

"Maybe you're right," he said.

"Mm-hmm."

He told her about Cloninger's dog. He'd been wondering what the dog would do, wondering if all animals were helpless when it came to their peckers. That's why he did it. He had no idea it was illegal. It seemed strange to be illegal when you thought about it. No one was getting hurt, least of all the dog. It was an experiment. But he supposed that he knew it was wrong in his conscience. Or was there something broken about his conscience if he still didn't think it was wrong.

"What do you think, Ell?"

She'd fallen asleep.

He was all right with that, too.

THIRTEEN

He'd driven down to Missoula to see Mary, but she wasn't in, so he called Spoils. He wandered up to the Oxford to wait for him, drank beer with a rotating company of sidling inebriates, and hale, well-met drunks. A table of businessmen slumming it. Eventually Spoils.

Someone gripped Pete at the elbow, chilled the nerve in his arm all the way up his neck. A short old man with his hat in his other hand. Familiar. Pete searched for the man's name. An old cowboy from Choteau. Name of Ferguson. Part-timer on the ranch. Had a good arm, played minor league baseball in the 1950s. Could hit you with a coal of horseshit from twenty yards.

"Mr. Ferguson," Pete said, slipping out of the man's grip, standing, and shaking his hand.

The man's eyes were wet and he was moving his jaw around like he had taffy stuck in his molars.

"You tell your family how sorry I am," he said. "He was a helluva man."

Pete felt behind himself for a barstool and dropped onto it.

"Thank you," Pete said.

Ferguson panted out a few sentiments that Pete couldn't really hear for the rush of blood in his head and then Ferguson was shaking his hand again, replacing his hat, and heading out the front door.

"What is it, Pete?" Spoils asked.

He walked out without answering. He couldn't form the words to say that his father was dead.

Charles (never "Chuck" or "Charlie") Snow had been a respected if not especially liked hard-ass in and around Choteau, Montana. He hated Communists and liked to talk about Communists. He felt like there should be more ICBMs in the idle land to the east of Malmstrom Air Force Base and would arrange his business so he could drive out that way to be among the ones that were there. He had worked hard and married when he was good and goddamn ready at the age of forty. She had only just turned sixteen, but this was no scandal in 1947. He kept her in sea-foam and turquoise polyester dresses and made sure she didn't have to smell of horseshit or hay like the other ladies in town. By the time his sons were out from under her skirts, he had settled into a con-siderable cowboy barony, an outfit that used to have about two hundred head called the Purple T. He preferred work over every endeavor, and never really acquired a taste for the company of others. He had a stake in more than his share of things (timber, car dealership, and lately, natural gas leases) and never let a person forget it. He made rivals to vanquish. He'd seemed only able to stand people when they came hat in hand. For the most part, people mildly hated him but never said so to him and only rarely among themselves, which only fueled his misanthropy.

Pete pulled onto the property, his father's spread filling an entire canyon bisected by the Teton River, a stony and brachiate course that raced out of the mountains but ran slow and low across the property in the fall, and in the winter iced solid to the bottom in places. Medallions from the quaking aspen lay about in a golden hoard, blowing up in parade confetti as he drove through them. A few Indian paintbrushes still glowed red like small tissue-paper fires at a grade-school play. Pete felt a homesick sorrow at the little differences, at time itself. The barn's new coat of paint. A whole stand of pines behind the house had vanished. Where a humble orchard of apple trees had once been just a short walk from the back door, a white gazebo had been erected. The place looked shorn, fussed over like a toy dog.

Bunnie. These were Bunnie's improvements. Just like Sunday services at the Christ the Light nondenominational church on the east end of town. Charles Snow had been as spiritually curious as a fence post, and Pete doubted that his father had ever changed in any meaningful way, even after Pete's mother died. But there was an aptness to his late conversion, as though he always knew that at the end of his life he'd have to do something to avoid going to hell.

It was a new truck in the field, not the old man's. Seeing Pete, Turner pulled alongside the fence, but the fence beam blocked Pete's view of Turner up in his pickup, so he stopped and got out. Turner leaned over and rolled the passenger window down.

"Howdy, Pete."

He looked older. He was older. Whiskers gone completely to white. The saggings under his eyes like two tea bags.

"Mr. Turner. Nice truck."

"Had it a couple years now. But thanks."

Pete stood back from it. Whistled.

"Not a mark on it."

"Well, yeah. I don't do much these days."

"Lucky you."

"Well now." He didn't like much being told he was idle.

Pete cleared his throat.

"Ken come up, and me and him got the cows hayed," Turner said. "You're gonna want to check their water in the morning. Might could have a freeze."

"Thanks for coming out and looking after the place."

"Bunnie's staying up at her people's. We'll be by tomorrow. Hay 'em again for you."

"It's all right, I can do it."

They looked up at the empty house.

"So'd you hear it from Bunnie, then?"

"Yeah," Pete lied. If she'd called, it was probably to the old number in Missoula. Even Ferguson assumed he knew.

"It happened right out there?" Pete gestured toward the middle of the pasture.

Turner sniffed, nodded.

"With his own pickup . . . ?"

Turner shook his head.

"Me and Ken think he was haying the cows all by himself. There was a rock on the gas pedal. He prolly fell out the back and broke his hip."

"If he fell out the back, how'd it run him over?"

"The alignment's all out of kilter. The pickup was still doing big, slow loops in the pasture when Bunnie come back from her trip to Billings. I figure it swung back around on him."

Pete set his chin on the fence post, looked out over Turner's hood into the pasture. Turner took off his cap and ran his hand over what was left of his hair and tugged the cap back on. He coughed uncomfortably, and Pete raised up and thanked him.

"My number should still be penciled on the wall by the phone."

"All right."

"Call you need anything. If you get busy with the arrangements. We'll come out."

"Will do."

An odor of leather, sawdust, and lilac and some ineffable scent of the house or his parents themselves that was the smell to him now of longing and dread at once. What had come to seem like the smell of passed time. Pete took in the kitchen, the old man's last day. A half-cup of coffee where he'd left it, Bunnie didn't touch the stuff. Usually there was a hint of manure wafting off the old man's boots from the mudroom, but not today. His jacket and boots were at the morgue.

Pete sat at the table in front of an unpromising game of solitaire. His father had gotten up when he saw he wouldn't win. Went out to the barn. Pitched hay out of the loft into the back of the pickup. That alone made him ache. Or was he coughing, hacking up bloody bullets of snot. Did he try calling Turner. No, too proud to call anyone. But didn't want to be heaving himself in and out of the cab, coughing, sore. Figured he could clever himself out of this little predicament, just idle his way across the pasture.

Then, stars. Found himself lying in the frozen mud, the old clover. The pain in his hip, astonishing.

And in all that pasture, the truck orbits back to him. Did he find that ironic.

What it would feel like, a pickup on your chest.

Pete went down the little hall to the den, descended the short landing into his father's lair. Fish and fowl on the cedar walls, and pictures of the same. A framed collection of caddis flies and stone flies surrounded by a dozen plaques and plates from fraternal orders and associations.

Next to his father's easy chair was a half-full ashtray and a box of .22 rifle shells, the rifle near the window for shooting gophers. Paperbacks on the floor. Louis L'Amour and James Michener. A Bible and a few religious tracts of Bunnie's.

His mother's things were in a basement closet. He sat for a long time on the concrete floor turning through albums. There was a picture of five children arranged like nesting dolls on a dray horse. There was a picture of a young woman sidesaddle on a bicycle, her father or uncle or perhaps her new husband holding it upright by the seat. There was a morbid picture of a child on a bier, his or her hands composed around a black, shiny Bible. So many albums peopled with old Scots and Germans who stiffly stood in their canvas and gingham, in wind-blasted straw hair and dun hats like people hewn from wood. Like life-sized dolls or approximations. Pete could scarcely believe these stern apparitions were his people, that any part of them had been handed down to him, that they had ever existed at all, and yet they had, and many had come to novel ends, death by dynamite by rope by fevers by horse by broken hearts by suicide now by pickup.

. . .

THERE ARE PICTURES of the wedding. Of Beth, young. A lean, mean girl who can make your head boil with jealousy when she wants. Girdling pregnancy, smoking, and making a bad impression. You say you love her, but how can your father understand? He won't even look you in the eye anymore. The old man can scarcely be bothered to interact with her or her mother in the weeks before the wedding.

Right before the ceremony, with all the guests gathered and the reverend waiting, he takes you out to the barn and lights a thin cigar, leaning against the palings of the horse stable and regarding you for what feels like a punitive duration. Just smoking at you.

At least she's pretty.

You've taken a pill for your wedding day nerves, and you're not sure you can close on him and land a fist.

I'm not marrying her because she's pretty.

You're gonna tell me this is the right thing to do, are you now?

I'm not gonna tell you anything.

The old man smokes, picks bits of ash off his suit sleeve.

Look, I am the way I am, you offer. *Let be the bygones,* you're saying.

Ah, but how did you become this person? he asks academically, blowing smoke at the rafters. *And your brother? Did he follow your example?*

I wasn't even out with him last night.

I see. You're not his keeper.

I'm getting married today! Why is he my responsibility? Where were you last night?

I fed the both of you. Clothed you. He taps ashes off the cigar, makes sure to stamp them out in the straw. *But I cannot listen to your conscience for you, Pete.*

My conscience—?! You slip off the stall gate, stumble like a rodeo clown. A half-smile curdles onto the old man's face. The look he has when he screws you over on a deal, when you owe him money, when he has you by the balls.

I'm not perfect. Not like you. I'm just a regular person.

Well, just don't be too hard on yourself, he says. He claps his hand on your shoulder going by, and to the people waiting in the yard by the orchard it looks like a gentle gesture, a pater's pep talk. You'd think he'd just given the newlyweds a car or a starter trailer, and the satisfaction radiates off him like it would a lord.

There was a noise upstairs and he heard Bunnie call his name. He called back that he was downstairs, and it was clear from the way she descended—gripping the railing, sideways, one stair at a time—that she resented his being down here. That she suffered him.

"You're going through old things," she said.

She looked around the basement like someone making an inventory. She sighed, set her face.

"We're going to need to sit down and have a talk," she said. "Me, you, and your brother."

"Luke's gone."

"When the time is right."

"You know where he went."

"I know he's in good hands."

"This man from your church."

"Our church, yes."

"Luke needs to come back. He needs to go to jail."

"The Lord will tell him where he needs to be," she said.

"Is that right."

Her posture stiffened. It was as if she realized of a sudden that she didn't need to talk to him, that she no longer needed to pretend to like him or want him in her life. He was just the son of a dead man.

She started back up the stairs. When she was out of sight up on the landing, she said that he was welcome to stay in his old room or the den, that there was plenty to eat in the fridge, and that the funeral was at ten, they should be at the church by eight-thirty. And would he bring a camera.

A couple hundred people from all around the state came to the little clapboard church near the railroad tracks. All his father's vanquished rivals. A bank of legislators in back pews pumped out handshakes and smiled and carried on inimitably. Squat Judge Dyson from Tenmile eased into the row behind Pete, talking bulls and politics until the preacher took to the pulpit. His brother's parole officer Wes Reynolds arrived with his own mother and father and throughout the service swiveled around, as though Luke were hidden in his periphery.

The preacher spoke at length about how blessed Charles Snow was in business. How well everyone knew this—how not a soul in the place was untouched by his financial activity. Some for good, some for bad. The preacher was young, and Pete and most of the assembled could only imagine what Charles Snow would make of this fresh reverend talking about the absence of Jesus in much of his life, of Charles's thirst for the blood of Christ. How he was at last saved in this very church. How happy it would make him if one other person got saved today. If his death could be an occasion for eternal salvation.

He was run over by his own damn truck, Pete kept saying to himself.

The old man's funeral procession rolled through Choteau and back to Charles Snow's considerable property. The pasture was full of cars. Everyone trudged out to the bluff where the old man had told his wives to bury him. A wind to take your head off as they commended him to the earth. Under the clear and polished sky the reverend's voice carried off like scraps of paper.

When Bunnie and a cadre of the congregants began to sing and sway, Pete stood and walked across the pasture and up the hill behind the house. The assembled watched him go.

The judge was a long time coming up, pausing, at times asking, then practically begging Pete to come down to him. When he arrived next to Pete he panted, furiously unbuttoned his coat and vest, loosened his tie.

"You're a goddamn ass," he said.

"You're fat."

"I can lose weight. What are you gonna do?"

The judge breathed heavily for some time longer and then procured a dip of tobacco.

"Where the hell's your brother?"

"On the lam."

"Because of the fight with the parole officer. I heard. But where is he really?"

"I don't know," Pete lied, in the vague wish that it were true that he didn't know, that he didn't have an address.

"He should be here," the judge said.

"I said I don't know where he is," Pete said. "It's not my job to know where he goes to ground when he fucks up."

"I didn't say it was, Pete."

"Sorry."

They could see various people eat from paper plates on the front porch of the house.

"Not a drop of alcohol down there," the judge said. "Reminds me of the time I was at a fund-raiser with these blue hairs out in Dillon. A little luncheon. I ask is there anything with a little kick to drink. And this old lady says to me, *We don't approve of alcohol.* And I says, *Well, ma'am, we need to remember Jesus did turn water to wine.* And she says, *And we're none too crazy about that stunt, neither.*"

The judge punched Pete's arm.

"That's funny."

"I can tell. You're in stitches."

"I'm at a wake."

"You're uphill of one."

Dyson arced a brown bullet of spit that plashed a plate of stone.

"Mom would hate this."

"Yeah, I don't think she'd be much pleased to bury your father."

"Bunnie. This Jesus stuff, I mean. When we put Grandpa in the ground, the preacher just said a few words and that was it. What was that gibberish they were singing when I was walking away?"

"I think they were talking in tongues."

"What the hell is that?"

"Like you've never been around religious people."

"Not in my own *family.* Even Luke."

"Well, that one could use a good dose of religion."

"No, he needs a dose of jail."

The judge put his hand on Pete's arm.

"Your pa just died. You're upset. It's all right."

"No, it's not. Let me tell you something about Charles Snow," Pete said. "When his truck ran him over, he wasn't thinking it was a great goddamned opportunity to get some other son of a bitch into heaven too."

A laugh escaped the judge and he tried to cover it with a cough.

"I never heard anything so stupid in all my life," Pete said.

Wes Reynolds exited the house. They watched him cross the yard, look up the hill, and then hike to them.

"Who's the fella in the cast?" the judge asked.

"The PO."

They watched him make his way up, and then try to stay balanced just down from them, teetering on the incline, his cast throwing off his balance somewhat. Pete introduced him to the judge.

"I know Judge Dyson. One of your father's friends," he said, hiking the last few feet up to shake the judge's hand. A red yolk of blood on the white of his eye.

Pete thanked him for coming.

"It was a good service."

"I didn't care for it," Pete said.

"I can imagine. It's a sad time," Wes said. "But it's good to get everybody together. To see people you haven't seen in a long time. Friends and relations. Most of 'em anyhow."

"He ain't here," Pete said.

"Who's that?"

"You know who."

Wes sniffed, looked off.

"We just come to pay our respects, Pete. It's like a whole era ended today."

"What in the hell is that supposed to mean?" the judge asked.

"It means what it means. It means Charles Snow can't protect his sons no more."

Pete stood, grabbed Wes, and pushed him backward so that the only thing keeping him from tumbling down the steepness behind him was Pete's grip on his belt. Wes paddled the air trying to regain his balance.

"My father never called in a single favor for us. Any slack we were cut was because he was a mean fucking son of a bitch, and I'm glad he's in the goddamn ground."

"Pete," the judge said, perhaps more at the disparagement of Pete's father than at what he was doing to Wes, who now grabbed Pete's wrist with his good hand.

"And Luke," Pete went on, "was in jail on my wedding day and has just missed his own father's funeral because he couldn't stop himself from kicking your ass." Pete swung Wes into the hillside, where he winced, landing on his shoulder instead of his cast. "I'm not protecting anybody."

Pete hid in the outbuilding until the last of the mourners and condolers left, sitting in the quitting light with the discarded horse tack, bits and bridles, coils of rope, wooden pallets, old glassware, carboys, and reams of tar paper. Then he went up to the house. Bunnie's cats dashed under the porch at his approach. She was at the dishes.

"I'm gonna head home."

"All right," she said, drying her hands.

He didn't know what to say to her. She set the towel by.

"I don't want anything from here," he said. "If Luke ever comes back, you can work it out with him. But you won't get any trouble from me."

She turned to the sink and seemed to be crying or about to, but when she looked up, all he saw was ferocity and fear, like he'd come to take something from her rather than just the opposite.

How is Austin?

It is a cute little bungalow in a funny neighborhood of hippies and college kids. A room for each of them and their things and otherwise furnished throughout, colorful towels and antique furniture, cacti and pots and pans and spices. A cat that comes and goes. Bright Mexican tile. Tins and colored glass in the trees. A bird feeder and hummingbirds.

It's shining water at Barton Springs, the two of them lazing on the grass, marveling at this Texas October.

It's brunch. Huevos and tortillas.

It's her mother leaving at four in the afternoon to work her shift at the bar and not coming back until three in the morning.

Is Rachel alone?

There's a deal. Her mother calls at ten to see that she's going to bed. Says, *You better be getting in bed.*

I will if you let me off the phone.

You have school in the morning. You can't skip tomorrow.

You're the one who always wants me to stay home with you.

What?

Nothing. Good night.

Go to bed.

That's what I said.

What?

Good night.

Are there already people at the house?

Not yet. But in the coming weeks there will be. She is getting good at this.

At what?

At making introductions, fast friends. At playing host. At pretending the place is all hers. At kicking everyone out at two in the morning and cleaning up.

Covering her tracks.

Yes. She won't drink. She will hold the same can of Lone Star all night. She likes being part of something, even just a party, a clique. But of her choosing. Not just mother, father.

Does she think of her father?

Yes. Certain guys will remind her of him. A laugh. A build.

Does she miss him?

She will remember with a certain curiosity that she used to.

In Waco?

Before that.

When he went to Tenmile.

Before that.

When she was a little girl. She used to favor him, the way girls sometimes favor their fathers over their mothers. She would pine for him when he was gone all day and into the night. And later, when she was older and started to understand what he did for a living, she would wonder why does he help these other families when I miss him so much when I need him here why does he have to be the one?

Does she feel that now?

No. She quit a while ago.

When?

When she realized that he chose the job, that he wanted to be there for the other families. That he didn't want to be there for the one he had.

That's not true. Does she really think that?

What else could she possibly think?

FOURTEEN

They often slept deep into the day so complete was the dark, but come this morning bars of light cut the room and woke him. Ell was sitting cross-legged in front of a guy, a skinny blond guy with a wispy dandelion mustache and beard, tattoos on his long fingers, fingers that were feeling her arms, her hair, her face. Cecil stifled a cough. Ell looked over. Then the guy, slowly turning his head to Cecil but not looking away from her until the last second.

"Bear, this is Cecil," she said.

"Cool," he said.

Bear had a little money. They went to the Safeway for donuts. Bear and Ell ate on a spot of grass by the road and held hands, and from time to time Bear put his head on her belly and listened. He cupped his hands over her bump and spoke into them and tapped out soft beats on his baby's entire world. He tickled her. The leaves were quitting the trees.

Cecil was scared. He knew they were going even before Ell asked did he want to come with them to a place out in Hamilton. A little house they could stay in. They were set for a few months there if he needed a place. Bear was rubbing her neck as she explained these things and his fingers made her eyes roll back in her head like she was a puppet. This was distracting. He wanted Bear to quit touching her and knew he had no right to want that. Still, it didn't seem okay that you could touch a person and they'd be helpless to it.

The taste of his mother's mouth, wet burned peppermint, was always on his tongue.

"I think I might just stay in that spot of yours, try my luck here in Missoula. I'm gettin' the hang of downtown," he said, spitting onto the curb.

"You sure?"

He nodded. She smiled dimly at something Bear did behind her ears.

"Bear and I think you should come," she said. "You don't got anybody here."

"Neither do I got anybody in Hamilton."

That this hurt her feelings was plain, which made him feel better, briefly. Then mean.

"I met you," he offered. "I bet somebody else turns up."

She went into the grocery. He and Bear stood together, not much looking at one another, let alone saying a word. She returned with a pen and came back with an address written on a piece of sack paper.

"It's not far," she said. "You can catch a ride out there and find us, you want to."

Bear shook his hand and thanked him.

"I owe you," he said.

Cecil asked for what, but Ell hugged him, said something in his ear, but he was too far gone to hear it.

Cecil watched the department store ladies undress the mannequins in the windows of the Bon Marché. They took off the arms and set them on the floor. An old hunched cowboy walking spraddle-legged with his wife winked at him and jerked a thumb at the nude armless bodies in the window.

Cecil walked along the river, down through a tangle of brush for want of anything at all to do. He came upon a pair of men at something by the water, but it wasn't fishing. One spotted him upstream on the broken concrete and rebar that made the upper shore of the river. The men spoke and then they both stood watching him. Cecil was afraid they would follow him if he left, so he hazarded a mild nod and squatted and looked innocently out over the water.

One of the men called out something Cecil couldn't hear. The man said it again or something else entirely. Cecil shook his head no, and started to climb back up through the Russian olive and bullrush. He heard the man shout and he scampered up the rocks and flailed through the small trees and didn't stop running until he made West Broadway and all the traffic there.

Two nights later the board to his building had fallen. He held the bag of produce he'd selected from a Dumpster and stood in the alley facing the building for some time, unsure what to do. His blankets and few utensils. He set the sack under a small tree and crept to the hole. The board had been put aside and shadows wavered in the laughter of the men who made them.

He walked up and down the tracks working up his courage. The men went quiet before he reached the hole, were already regarding him with candlelit bearded faces, hazardous eyes.

"Hi. I left some things . . ."

The men drank from their beers. None spoke.

"I think I left some things in here."

"Come in and have a look around," one of them said.

Cecil hadn't thought that far ahead. How he'd negotiate his things out of the room. If objections arose. You go in, you might not ever come out.

He trotted away. They didn't even laugh, he was so insignificant.

He went up Orange and over to Higgins heading toward the river again. It was cool, might not be too cold to find a spot under the bridge.

He eyed fire escapes, the unlit windows of the offices above the street. Then he spotted Pete and a pretty woman inside the Oxford at a poker table. He couldn't believe his luck, was in fact afraid to mess with it, and so he just looked through the window at him, but Pete was hunched over his cards, the woman talking in his ear. A cup of coffee appeared at his elbow, and he drank it and never once looked out the window. At last Cecil opened the door, but the bartender happened to look up from his wiping and shook his head no at him.

He waited outside in the blue neon of the beer signage, watching an old drunk wrapped in a sleeping bag shout absurdities at passersby. *I am that guy,* he thought. *Far as anyone else is concerned, just another guy on the street, nowhere to go, no one to go to.*

When Pete didn't come out after a time, Cecil returned to the window. Pete and the woman were gone. He remained in front of that window like a dog. Then he searched around the side of the building. There was an exit there that Pete may have used. He scoped around the place some more. Looked in the window. By now no one was on the street.

He slept a few hours in the window well of a church on Myrtle before the frost came, and then he rose and walked across town to Buttreys. Pissed at this point, just furious. He loaded a cart full of things he had no intention of buying and made sly egress through the loading bay in back of the place with a loaf of bread and a summer sausage.

Not a soul truly saw him, maybe not that whole day.

Come dark he's full of meat and bread. He walked by the Oxford again and waited, but Pete was not there and did not pass on the street. He walked to the university campus and admired the people dining with utensils in the cafeteria. In the commons among the smoking and reading students, he warmed up, wondering what on earth they could be reading for so long. He found a room with long low couches and slept on one until the building was closing.

He asked a college kid on the footbridge how far it was to Hamilton. The kid said it was maybe forty miles. Forty fuckin miles down Highway 93. The wind out of Hellgate Canyon was a rapid, cold astonishment to him. He hurried across the bridge to at least get in the lee of the houses and buildings. He thought about trying doors, explaining his pitiful state.

He found himself back downtown watching the high school kids cruise Higgins Avenue. It was a Friday night, and they drove up and down the street, up and down, their engine racket rebounding off the bricks. Small crowds spilled in and out of the bars and a carnival mood prevailed despite the cold. He'd been in Missoula for some weeks but never downtown at this hour on a Friday. The giddying spectacle of cars sometimes speeding by, the girls inside shrieking, girls calling out to him as he walked alone. Something that radiated off him from his few weeks of vagabondage, a new way he bore himself up. A vague optimism overtook him.

Near the old train depot the cars turned around and headed back down the street. Some parked on a gravel lot, idling or barely rolling in the cold, and teenagers clung to and ran between them. He watched from across the street, wondered what kinds of lies he could tell that would get him to Hamilton. He settled on a few of the less outrageous, took a deep breath, and started to cross. He shoved his hands in his pockets and sauntered over like they'd called him by name.

FIFTEEN

Pete kept an ear to the ground for the Pearls, but heard only rumors. He called the pawnbroker from time to time, but Pearl had not been by, and the pawnbroker said he didn't expect him. Nevertheless, Pete asked around in truck stops and cafes, and nearly always someone knew who Pearl was or something about his coins, but of the man's whereabouts, nothing. There were rumors and apocrypha. He was dead. He lived with a band of Métis Indians in Canada. The government had disappeared him. But never an eyeball on the man personally, save the dope farmers and the pawnbroker.

A bitterly cold day with two new calls, one in Trego and the other up someplace called Thirsty Creek. There was no one at the former and he couldn't locate the latter. When he returned to his office, there was a message from a logger by the name of Vandine. The man had had an encounter with a boy and his father up at a place called Freckle Creek or Tinkle Creek or some such. Pearl. Pete rang up the man at home, and learning that he lived in Libby, asked if he could come down.

Vandine was slick to the elbows in engine grease and he apologized, said he was just about done lubing his self-loader, would Pete mind waiting inside, his old lady'd put some coffee on. Pete went through the crooked picket gate to the house and no one answered the door, so he smoked on the two-by-four stoop in front of the trailer until Vandine was finished. When Vandine saw him still there and coffee-less, he grinned succinctly, stepped inside, and shouted at his wife for not fixing Pete anything, for not answering the goddamned door god-damnit. Pete waited among the motor parts the man had set on news-papers for later tinkering. Vandine beckoned him into the kitchen and scrubbed his hands at the sink, a five-minute job with gritty pink soap that dripped from his elbows as he looked about in increasing irritation for a towel. He yelled for his old lady, and Pete stood against the wall as they argued again.

The man wiped down his thick and poorly inked arms and went out, and Pete followed him down a trail to a shed where a box of cold Rainiers sat in the dark. Vandine turned over two buckets in the door-way and handed Pete a beer unbidden. He cracked his own, threw the tab in a jar of them, and sucked down half of it before Pete had even situated himself on the bucket.

He said cheers and tapped Pete's freshly opened beer with his own, and began to explain that the pawnbroker over in Columbia Falls was an in-law, and that they'd had supper the other week. When Vandine and the in-law got to talking about what happened, the pawnbroker said there was a social worker who would be plenty interested in what he, Vandine, had to say.

"About what exactly?" Pete asked.

Vandine placed his hands on his knees and looked between them a moment. He eventually made a small preamble about how he wasn't exactly thrilled to be sharing this story with Pete, because it didn't reflect well on him. He looked up and said that there were legal ramifications.

"You ain't a police officer or anything right?"

"No."

"Do we have confidentiality?"

"Yes."

"Gene says you folks'll take information anonymous."

"Absolutely."

Vandine ran his hand through his black and white hair deciding.

"Truly," Pete said, "if the police need to get involved I will say I got an anonymous call."

Vandine scowled like someone fresh out of choices. He dangled the beer can between his legs.

"We was going through a rough patch last spring. Financially. I have to tell you this because it's why I didn't go to the cops about it."

He took a long draft on his beer, observing that Pete did not sip his own. Pete drank then.

"Tell me what happened, Mr. Vandine."

"I's up on Tickle Crick, where Champion was cutting a new logging road," he said. "Maybe I was up there making off with the right-of-way logs."

"Right-of-way?"

"The ones they cut down to make the road. They leave them alongside of the road there. You seen my self-loader."

"Right."

Just then Vandine's wife called out to him, and he hunched his shoulders at the incoming artillery of her voice. She shouted his name some more, and when they heard the wooden screen door clap shut, he sat upright again.

"So it's May eighteenth I'm up there. You remember what happened last May eighteenth?"

"Mount Saint Helens."

"Exactly. Ash falling on Tickle Crick and I had no idea what it was. This weird gray snow coming down. You remember.

"Well, my partner—the son of a bitch shall remain nameless—jumps on the CB and all the truckers are saying get indoors and don't breathe it, it's toxic. And don't run your vehicles in the stuff, the air filters can't take it. They're saying to wait until it's all done falling. Well we don't want to get waylaid, not up there, so we decide to park, hump it down to his pickup, and leave my logging truck for when it all blows itself over."

Vandine swirled the dregs of his beer in the can.

"Next day everything's covered in ash, and I got a truck up Tickle Crick where it ain't supposed to be. Day after that they're still saying don't drive if you don't need to. It's the next next day and I'm still up there with my dick hangin out. So by now I figure I better haul ass and get my truck down before Champion sends someone up there to check on the Cat and skidder they got up there. If they ain't already. If they ain't got my license plate and calling the cops already. You couldn't be more red-handed than we was. But my alleged partner won't go because they're saying we ain't supposed to be driving except for emergencies. I says it is a emergency. Not to me it ain't he says. I says I get in trouble so do he, I says. That got him moving. So next day we get up early and head out."

Vandine polished off his beer and fetched another one. He was slow to getting back into the story. As though he were sorting through the events.

"What happened?"

"My brother-in-law says you're looking for this guy, name of Pearl?"

"Him and his son, yes."

"The boy," Vandine said, shaking his head.

"Yes. You saw them?"

"Matched my brother-in-law's description in every detail."

"Where?"

VANDINE SAT UP and explained what happened. The timber country all around coated gray and otherworldly and looking like a tintype or a still from an old western. Feels like you're smack dab in a John Ford movie. And Vandine's on a long dirt road straightaway and nearly misses in his rearview the waving hand in the truck's wake of ash. He just sees an arm swallowed in a cloud the color of cigarette smoke. He says, *Didja see that?* Partner says, *See what?* Vandine stops the truck. *Somebody come out of the woods,* Vandine says.

Vandine pulls over, gets out. The kicked-up ash a red fog in his brake lights and out of it emerges somebody, this boy, bandana over his face, coughing. Vandine reaches in the cab and kills the engine and as the truck dies, he hears the click of a cocked gun right behind his left ear. A voice tells him, *Don't fuckin move.* He glances over at the passenger seat and his partner's eyes wide as dollar coins at whoever's there behind him. The voice says for Vandine to move over and put his hands on the hood of the pickup and for the partner to get out and come around front of the truck or Vandine gets it in the back of the head.

The partner slides out real slow. Vandine can tell he's thinking of running. *Don't do it,* Vandine says.

The partner ducks behind the open door and runs low and into the dust cloud, and then over the lip of the road, you can hear the sumbitch crashing through the ashy brush. You can hear the sumbitch coughing.

Don't kill me because of that idiot, Vandine says. *He's miles from anything. He can't hurt you.*

The boy comes up, he's coated in ash, except for his eyes, which gleam red like open sores. He's about as jumpy as a fart on a skillet, and the voice behind him tells him not to worry about the other one. The kid hops in the truck and gets to ransacking. Efficient at it. As the man pats him down, Vandine says there's a thermos of soup and a can of Coke. That they're welcome to them.

The man says for him to put his hands behind his back and take three steps backward slow and then sit down.

Something tells Vandine he does this, he's a dead man. Something else in him has the courage to say, *Fuck that I ain't moving from my truck.*

Now the kid's eyes are the ones wide as dollar coins—whether it's that the man is about to shoot him or the kid is just scared of what Vandine might try—and it wilts Vandine's courage, the boy does, and Vandine says, *All right all right, I'm a do what you say.*

The man comes around front of Vandine, pistol trained on him. Vandine gets a good look at him. Hair that's been hacked away to see by, but otherwise long like gray stalks of straw. A blue bandana gone to black from moisture and ash mixing into a thin wet layer of concrete over his nose and mouth, a bushy beard under it. Same red eyes as the kid, same ashy, tattered clothes. The man stifles a cough. Chokes it back.

The boy sacks the soup and the Coke.

Vandine volunteers he's got some paper filter masks there under the bench seat, the kid's probably seen 'em, they can have 'em. The man says to shut up. The kid's watching the father, the pistol in his hand.

The man asks, *How many are left?*

Vandine says the box hasn't been opened yet.

I asked you how many are left goddamnit.

Vandine shook his head, ran his finger around the lip of his beer can.

"How many what?" Pete asked.

Vandine wiped his nose with his sleeve and said, "People. He's asking how many people. He thinks there's been a nuclear war."

"You're shitting me."

"I wish I was, because he didn't believe me. He asks why I'm up there. I tell him to get a logging truck, he says, *Bullshit,* he says, *you got a bug-out place up here.* Says things about martial law and where are the tanks and troop transports."

"Jesus," Pete said.

"I remember there's a newspaper on the seat. I tell him to have a look for himself."

Vandine polished off his second can of beer, stood, and crushed it with his logging boot.

"What'd he say when he saw?"

"He didn't see. My partner shoved the paper under the seat and they didn't see it and wouldn't look for it." Vandine was at the hard part. He toed the can on the ground in front of him. "So then he gave his pistol to the kid." He looked Pete in the eye. "He told him to shoot me." Pete looked Vandine up and down, as though a gunshot wound would still be in evidence.

Vandine gazed off into the woods at a rusted trailer and broken sawhorses overgrown with lichen. A metal garbage can lid nailed to a tree and rusted and shot to hell.

"The kid come out of the truck and he's shaking and pointing the gun at me. And I'm saying to his old man, *Come on now, you don't need to do this, he's just a boy. . . .* Things of that nature.

"The boy, he was shivering—he's scared shitless like me—and I'm thinking maybe I got a chance to, you know, close on him and, I dunno, take the gun . . . but the old man has him nearby and I see he's got his hand on his other holster too."

Vandine squatted down on his haunches and began to draw idly in the dirt with the side of the can.

"A person can imagine begging for his life. And beg, I fucking did. And I'll allow that I was pretty cowardly in some of the things I said to this man and his son."

"You weren't a coward," Pete said. "You were trying to stay alive."

"It wasn't any pleasure to discover that I would behave this way." Vandine pitched the can spinning like a saucer into the woods. "In any case," he said, "that's not why I called you. I called you because of the boy. I'm a fuckup. But . . . I can't imagine a man making his boy kill someone for nothing."

Vandine reached for another beer, closed his hand around it. Again Pete waited for him to continue. But he did not. It occurred to Pete that Vandine and the boy had both been thrust into this horrible situation of Pearl's making. How there was nothing either one of them could do about it.

"So the kid, did he—"

"He shot at me."

"He missed."

"From ten feet. I don't know if it was on purpose or it was too much gun for him or the good Lord or what. But I didn't get killed."

"What about Pearl, didn't he—?"

Vandine held up his hand for Pete to quiet down.

"Next thing I know I'm half-deaf and throwing up, and when I finally get my head together, I see the old man and the kid running off into the woods."

Vandine stood, pitched his freshly empty can aside, and sat on the bucket.

"It was like some goddamned test. I wonder if the point wasn't even to kill me. Like that Old Testament story, the father who has to kill his son—"

"Abraham."

"Yup, Abraham."

Vandine opened the beer and squeezed the pull tab in his fist. He regarded the cut the pull tab had put into his skin, and smiled dimly.

"Do you know where they are?" Pete asked.

"I was going to ask you that."

"This was up Tickle Crick." Vandine drank and nodded and snorted at some amusing thought.

"What?"

"You sure you want to go mess with this guy?" he asked.

Pete leaned back against the jamb of the shed and ran his hands over his face.

"No, I'm not sure of that. I'm not sure of that at all."

SIXTEEN

The farmer rose before dawn and went out to chores. A broken chevron of geese honked in the high white air of morning, and he thought he might go down to the bottoms with the shotgun. The dog dancing at the sight of him in his rubber waders. He put the shotgun on the table, dropping shells into the pocket of his wool jacket.

"Thought I might head down the bottoms with the shotgun," he said.

His wife was making breakfast. She scraped his eggs between two pieces of toast and handed the plate to him. Told him she had that appointment at eleven. He nodded, already working a bite of the dry toast and egg in his mouth, taking a swig of coffee to wash it back. He put the open shotgun in the crook of his arm, let out the dog ahead of him, and softly closed the door like he was already down in the low land by the water.

He crossed the field as the sun struck the tips of the Bitterroots and down through the chokecherry and water birch to the path that led to the long pond where he kept a permanent blind. The dog bounded through the brake of wild raspberry and, snuffling at the soil, tore off into the trees.

He whistled for the animal when it didn't come back. Listened, whistled again. The dog barked. He set off into the trees.

He smelled smoke. Goddamned kids. Beer cans would be all over up there. He climbed the hill through the stand to the little clearing just off the dirt road. The dog bounded back to him and dropped a laceless hightop tennis shoe marked up in neon colors on the grass.

"Go on," he said, and the dog tore up the hill ahead of him. The farmer was panting and hot when he reached the summit. Charred grass around a circle of ashes and a few glowing embers where the kids had a fire but didn't even bother to dig a hole or make a ring of rocks. No beer cans to speak of, but, curiously, three plastic honey bears around in the dirt. And, so quiet it startled him to see, a young person sat on a log with his pants around his ankles, his head between his knees, hands palms up on the dirt in front of him. As if in a mortal bowel movement. The dog sniffed around his trousers.

The farmer set the shotgun against the tree and picked up a honey bear and held it up against a spot of sky. About half full of clear liquid. He sniffed at the nipple on the top. Alcohol. But something else.

Sulphur.

Shit.

He immediately pitched the thing aside and shook his hand in the air and wiped it on his jeans just below the knee. He asked the boy what the hell he'd been up to. Not expecting an answer. The kid's white legs like alabaster sticking out of the denim pooled around his ankles.

"Don't you be dead, now," the farmer said.

He went over and poked him on the shoulder. The kid moaned.

"Hey now," the farmer said.

Cecil suddenly looked up, bloodshot and bewildered. The dog barked at him and the kid let out a little shriek, stood, and managed to turn one leg of his jeans inside out with his first step before the tangle dropped him. The farmer was trying to get his barking dog by the collar, so he didn't see the honey bear lodged in the kid's bunghole.

Whenever Cecil mentioned his headache to anyone, they asked how his asshole was doing, or said they could only imagine how his ass felt, and so he stopped saying anything about his head. But it didn't matter. The cops continued to speculate. Would they need to administer the aspirin rectally. Did they have a suppository for him. Did he shit out the mouth. Thank goodness he wasn't a smoker, whatever that was supposed to mean.

He spent the day in the lobby of the Missoula police station with the desk officer, who was reading a paperback. Sometime in the late morning, the desk officer glanced up at Cecil and a funny look came over his face, and he left his station and returned with a paper lunch sack and set it on the chair next to the boy. He told the cop who came out of the restroom not to leave his lunch where the boy might could sit on it and eat it.

By evening, no one had come for him. He was issued a gray jumpsuit that chafed him and taken to a great white door and into the cells, which were painted cinder block and echoed with their footsteps. A sot with wasted eyes and a walleyed brute leered at him passing. The drunk closed his lids and curled up on the floor like a cat, but the brute walked to the bars and watched the deputies put Cecil into the cell.

The brute scratched his stubble and the wiry black hairs of his dark arms and regarded the new arrival thoughtfully.

Cecil looked around the cell. There were two bunks. A rudimentary chair and small table formed up out of concrete. A black stool banked in the lidless metal toilet had been there so long it had no odor. It was cold, and the clothes on him seemed unable to keep the heat of his intermittent shivering.

The brute watched him take in his surroundings with a pair of small black eyes, close-set in his pocked face.

"Boy." He stretched up on his tiptoes, tilting his head back and looking down a knobby protuberance of a nose at Cecil sitting on the bunk. "That's my bed, boy," he said. "Get off it."

Cecil climbed down.

He was nearly in the bottom bunk when the brute tsked his tongue. Cecil looked at him, and the man shook his head no.

Cecil sat on the concrete chair.

"Get out of it," the man said calmly.

Cecil put his head down.

"I said get up out of it, boy."

Cecil slid out onto the floor. Then the man began to talk to him. Steadily. How much trouble Cecil was in. What errors the young man had made. What all they would have to do about that. In time. In due time.

The next afternoon the cops had him change back into his street clothes, and put him up in a back room of the station to wait. The door was ajar and he heard when Pete came in, heard Pete talking to the officer who was in charge. He crept up to the door and peeked out.

"I'm the one he told you to call. The boy you picked up yesterday. He all right?"

The officer looked at Pete's badge with his reading glasses and then gestured for him to sit. He opened a drawer and set a honey bear in a plastic bag on the desk. Then he leaned back in his groaning chair and drummed his fingers on his fat stomach.

"That was sticking out his ass."

Pete rubbed his face. Couldn't help grinning.

"I don't know why everybody thinks this is such high goddamn hilarity," the cop said to the room generally.

"I've known kids to do it," Pete said.

"The hell for? Is the mouth gone out of style?"

Pete put his elbow on the desk, leaned in.

"The tissues down there"—the cop frowned disgustedly at the word *tissues*—"are very absorbent. A shot of booze straight into the bloodstream. You're drunk instantly and you don't smell like it."

"What kid knows this?"

"Information gets around."

The cop sat up and put the honey bear back in the drawer.

"You get drunk, your dad whups you, and you spend the day baling hay or mending fence puking your guts out. That's the way it's done. And you drink whiskey not fuckin vodka and you sure as shit don't do it with your puckered asshole!"

There was a small commotion of cops and a real criminal at the front door, chairs getting kicked around the tile near the desk. Grunts and the like. Then the door to the cells opened and swallowed up the noise.

Pete asked where the kid was.

Cecil knocked over a chair getting back to his spot at the table. Pete gestured wearily from the doorway for Cecil to follow him before he even made it back to his seat. They both signed some paperwork and walked out to Pete's car. Once again, they sat a minute together, Pete drumming the steering wheel.

"I got some people I can live with," Cecil said. "Here in Hamilton. We're in Hamilton, right?"

Pete looked at him.

"You're in Missoula. You were picked up in the Bitterroots."

"Her name is Ell and his name is Bear."

"Bear."

"Yes."

"That short for Honey Bear?"

"What? No."

Pete reached across Cecil to the far side of the dash for a lighter that had slid over there. It wasn't lost on Cecil that Pete wanted to keep him from winding up with it.

"What happened at your uncle's?"

"I never asked to go there."

"You didn't give me many options, Cecil. In fact, why'd you even have the cops call me? You clearly want nothing to do with the options I can provide you."

"I have one now. These people, Bear and Ell. They're *of age.* You can make it so I can live with them."

"I wasn't stopping you. Why didn't you just go be with them?"

"I was *trying* to get a ride."

"And wound up with a honey bear in your ass. Of course."

"You were the only person I could call. So now, just make it so's I can live with them."

"Just make it? I don't know them from Adam, Cecil. What is it you think I—?"

"Fine. Why don't you just punch me again? Made you feel better at least."

Pete sighed, laid his head back against the headrest.

"That wasn't right. It wasn't okay at all. But I was trying to get you to listen, to tell you that if you blow it with your uncle, I'd have to put you in a very rough place—"

"I have a fuckin place! Just check it out."

Pete turned to face him.

"Please. Please?"

"What about your mom?"

Cecil crossed his arms and wedged himself against the car door.

"The whole idea was only to get you two apart to cool off," Pete said. "Why don't we see about going back?"

Cecil shook his head and would not meet Pete's eye.

"Is there something you're not telling me? Is there something I can help—"

"If you want to help me, let me live with Ell and Bear. Otherwise just throw me in a hole or wherever you're gonna put me."

Cecil had to stay in the temporary shelter in Missoula for a week. Maybe two, Pete said. It was fucking bullshit, a brick dormitory with ten bunk beds on red tile that had been scuffed the color of Pepto. White cinder block walls with boogers on them and a chest of nappy stuffed animals, wooden toys from the 1960s.

When Cecil had arrived there were three boys and seven girls aged four to sixteen, and the majority looked to him to be related by their dishwater blondness and their odor, a piney scent that he shortly came to realize was the smell of the medicine shampoo they were all made to use.

The small children generally kept themselves apart from him because of his size and his ratty face, and the sixteen-year-old was a muttering Indian boy who only left his bunk to look out the window or watch television.

There was a little girl named Tracy who had bald patches on her head. Around her bed were long strings of hair that she pulled out in the night. You could hear her doing it, a barely audible tugging sound like someone yanking a sleeve or the drawstrings on a pullover. The other children seemed to have gotten used to it. Cecil told her to knock it off, but she never did, and he realized that no one was used to it, there was just no remedy for it.

There was another troublesome kid, an obese hysteric named Scotty. He stole a coffee cup from an attendant and after a two- or three-minute standoff, threw it at the attendant's face. Blood from the man's nose soaked his shirt, and the kid cried like a toddler when they restrained him. Screamed like they'd stuck him with knife.

Tracy and Scotty were taken away in the same hour, and for a day there, Cecil was high on the hog because he claimed both bunks and no one questioned it. Then several of the girls left and eight new kids arrived and he retreated to a bunk near the window and the rackety radiator. There were kids with scars that fairly glowed like pink wax melted across their naked backs in the showers. Kids who had no respect for personal property or space and who would take your toothbrush or touch you without warning. Kids who bit. Kids who arrived in the middle of the night. Kids who slept on blankets on the dirty runners and left at first light. These children cried at night, they spoke at night, they would not shut up and in the dark you imagined waiting until they were deep in sleep and then slinking over and punching them in the face. That you were ashamed of these feelings did not drive them away. Cecil even imagined what kind of places these kids came from—and these places seemed to him to be in a significantly worse category than his own sad, weird home—and felt the stirrings of pity, but good God they would not cease jabbering. It was like they could not help making themselves hated objects, magnets for cruelty. He wondered did all abuse simply come down to children so irritating that they engendered violence or neglect, the reverse of the way adorable children got toys, got spoiled, and got fat. Seven days and still no Pete.

They had outside time in a pavement play area where the staff tried to engage him in small talk, things about his family, did he have any brothers or sisters, and large talk, was he angry about anything, did he feel like hurting himself. He provided terse answers.

He felt guilty about his sister alone up there with his mother. When he was at his uncle's, he was actually angry at Katie that she could stay home, that she had all her things, that her life was less broken than his own. But now, he worried. Maybe Ell and Bear would take her too? Or he would go up to Tenmile and murder his mother himself—suffocate her with a pillow or push her down the basement stairs so it looked like an accident—and then Pete would have to let Katie come stay with him and Bear and Ell. They could both help take care of the baby.

One day the matron of the place had him pack his things and wait in the lobby for Pete or someone else, it wasn't clear. After a while, they were talking about him, he could hear his name, his fate partially announced in snatches as her door opened and closed. They brought him supper in the lobby and the heater made him painfully drowsy. He knocked his head against the wall steadily to stay awake, and the matron came out to see what was the matter. He tried to grin pleasantly. She told him to go watch television. He watched cartoons with the other kids asking him was he leaving or not. He ate in silence.

A new resident had taken his bed. He was to sleep in a cot.

A few days later, Pete arrived. He asked if Cecil had any idea where his mother might be. He'd been by the house a couple times, no one there. Katie hadn't been in school.

"There you go."

"There you go?"

"I'm abandoned," Cecil said. "Just send me to Ell and Bear's."

Pete rubbed his mouth in a gesture of feigned contemplation. There was something made up about his mind, you could see it. And Pete wasn't happy about it.

"What is it?"

"Okay, look," Pete said. "I went and checked them out. They're nice enough people, but Bear doesn't have any work and Ell's about to have a baby—"

"They said I could live with them!"

"Calm down. I have to think about what's best for everybody. Even them. If I put you in a bad situation, that's on me—"

"My uncle's was a bad situation."

"No, that was a *good* situation. Which you messed up. And now they won't take you back."

"So, what, I'm gonna live here for the rest of my life?"

Pete looked Cecil in the eye.

"We're gonna go see your father."

"Why? I can't live with him."

"Obviously. I talked to the judge up in Tenmile, he's a friend of mine, and he says if I'm gonna put you with somebody like Bear and Ell, I gotta get at least one parent to sign off. So."

"You go."

"It'd be good for you to see him."

"You talked to Bear and Ell?"

"Yes."

Cecil stood.

"Fine. Let's go to the prison. Let's get his signature."

"There's something else. Sit down a minute."

Pete pointed at the seat and Cecil fell into it.

"Ell told me about your mother."

"What about my mother."

"She molested you."

"Fuck that. She did not."

"She did. Or Ell's a liar."

"Ell's a liar."

"And you want to go live with someone who lies about you?"

Cecil narrowed his eyes and clutched the edge of the table.

"I ain't dumb. I see what you're doing," he said.

"What am I doing, Cecil?"

"You know." He looked down at his hands, let go of the table, crossed his legs, and thus composed, said, "I don't know what you're talking about."

Pete slid back his chair and put his hands together and wedged them between his straightened legs in a kind of countermove. They sat like this for a long moment.

"If Ell's telling me bullshit, how can I trust anything she says when I let you go live with her?"

Cecil closed his eyes just so he could avoid having to look at Pete anymore. When he opened them Pete was still there. Waiting.

"Come on."

"Oh my God, if you don't quit asking me this, I'm gonna lose it. For serious."

Pete and Cecil stood in the lot outside the prison. In the burnt dusk the black mountain horizon glowed like a hunk of charcoal. Two men exited the front of the building and walked purposefully toward the car. Pete got out, went around and opened Cecil's door, and clapped him on the shoulder. The men walked straight at the open car door. White, short-sleeve shirts, plastic ID badges. Cecil realized this could not be good.

"Where are we?"

"Pine Hills. It's a juvenile facility. I gotta put you in here for a little bit."

Cecil looked at the grim brick building, the flags snapping in the wind, the men advancing, with sickening incredulity.

"No fucking way. Just take me somewhere. Let me out on the side of the road."

"You know I can't do that."

"You can sign the papers. You can do it."

"There's no papers to sign, Cecil."

"You said I could go live with Bear and Ell!"

"You gotta go in juvie until you have your day in court. I can't keep you in the attention home. I got nowhere else I can put you."

"You fucking asshole! You fucking dick! You lied to me!"

Pete reached for him, and he knocked his hands away, slid over.

"This isn't my fault!" he shouted. Pete stood back, hands up.

Cecil was crying now. It was shameful to him, but the shame only made the sobs come thicker. Something burned in his stomach.

"You know that if you put me in there, you'll never get me out!"

He looked around, out the back windows, for somewhere to run.

"You'd make it as far as the gate."

"You're a lying asshole bitch! You just tricked me into coming up here so you could throw me away! I never should have trusted you!"

Pete squatted down in the open door in front of him. Cecil could launch himself at him. He could get him by his pretty blond hair and do some real damage. He searched Pete's face, imagined tearing it to shreds. But that was all he did, imagine it.

"I need you to calm down. Right now."

There were pins of light in the blackness around Cecil's vision.

"You're hyperventilating. Just calm down, and listen to me. You're not staying here. This is just where I gotta put you. I'll see if I can find someplace permanent. Some program. I'll find you something."

"Ellll . . ." It came out ragged, like the words were serrated.

"You gotta forget that. It ain't happening."

"My uncle's then!"

"It's too late, Cecil."

He fell against the dash, sobbed there.

"I'm sorry. I won't . . . I won't be bad . . . Oh God."

He flopped back in the seat. Either Pete beckoned them or the men knew just when to grab him. He screamed, but was too stunned to really fight. They were firm, the way they had him by his arms and torso and were extracting him from the vehicle. An excruciating pressure on the back of his hand and he couldn't hold on to the steering wheel and he immediately knew their competence, their experience, his own weakness. He sobbed anew as they walked him to the door. He tried to break for it, but so halfheartedly they simply steered him into the building.

They entered a small foyer that was filled with desks, and people in different uniforms watched him come in and even them looking on him made him cry that much harder and it was difficult to see in the wash of tears. The smallness of him. The smallness of his heart. No courage whatsoever.

"Can I stay with you? Pete?"

"It won't be so bad."

"That's not what you said. You said it would be very bad!"

"It's gonna be all right, Cecil."

Someone said for Pete to go ahead and leave.

"Pete!"

"I gotta. You'll be all right."

"No. No. No no no no no no . . ."

Pete was gone and Cecil panicked, he strained against several arms for a door, the door he must have gone through, and he was adrift in terror then, bleached with fear, a brine in his throat at the terrific realness of this. Someone had him down on his back. Blue black stubble against his forehead as they held him. They carried him deeper into the facility. He made out the metal beds. The boys in them. Pointing, crowding round like pigeons at feed, he'd seen pigeons in Missoula, sleet of white feathers falling from the underneath of the Higgins Street Bridge. The brake lights strung out like bulbs along an awning, and the cold and the feathers snowfalling down.

No.

I'm not staying.

I ain't gonna spend Christmas in here, I'll die first I fuckin promise.

SEVENTEEN

Your caseload is brutal and will get worse as the holidays steadily advance on the poor, deranged, and demented. Kids waiting with cops in the living room or the front seat of the squad car to stay out of the cold until you arrive. You run the children down to the crisis shelter in Kalispell. There aren't many beds. You have twenty-four hours to find a placement. Fortunately, the emergency placements that were so scarce in summer sprout by the gross come Thanksgiving. People ashamed of their good fortune come the holidays, meaning well.

But as always the calls are mostly bullshit. Ninety-five percent. Landlords ratting out noisy, alcoholic tenants. Divorcees fighting over Christmas-morning custody. Visit the little studio apartments or a trailer or a yurt up the sticks, confirm that there are Cheerios in the cupboard, frozen juice in the freezer, blankets, winter coats, and mittens in the hall closet. Ignore the bong hastily covered by a bandana and write out an action plan and get the hag with stained teeth and her balding homunculus to sign it and fare-thee-well out the door. Don't even bother with the paperwork for the state office because by noon there are three more new cases to replace that one. Just shove your pink copy of the action plan in a folder marked with the month and leave it at that because paperwork's the single least important thing you can be doing. You have a backlog of real cases to work into your real rotation, cases that are as slow to close as infected wounds. Like the real sweet twitchy and dysarthric kid with a miserable and uncomplaining nub of a mother, a woman so ashamed of any aid that you come by at night and park around the block where the neighbors won't see your car. You do her paperwork for heating assistance, Medicaid. Apply her for every program there is, because the doctor bills and insurance eat through her last motel-clerked penny like acid. Yes, you have bigger fish to fry than potheads and mileage reimbursement. Newly suicided fathers and their wreckage. The mother who calls your office wondering if you could take her child, God is telling her to kill him, you better hurry. Cecil in the fresh hell of Pine Hills. His sister, Katie, out there somewhere God knows, you can't think about her, but you do think of all the magnificent horrors that can befall a child in the shabby motel rooms and concrete rest area bathrooms frequented by her mother, her mother's shifting partners and adversaries, and the errant unattached freaks in those orbits.

You have what feels like an ulcer.

And the Pearls. Living on pinecones and squirrel gizzards waiting for Armageddon with their coin-scoring, apocalyptic old man.

And again circle back to your own life, like a pair of headlights in the rearview late at night, some trouble tailing you on the black highway. A brother on the lam in Oregon. Luke, you fool, just come take your medicine.

A daughter in Texas at an address where you send the checks. Should something happen to her, you know you underwrote it. You call but she doesn't much want to talk or there's no answer. After the holidays, this stretch, and it will slow down. You resolve to call. You don't as much as you should. Wonder how you're supposed to have a relationship at such distance. You worry.

You think, *No news is good news.* You think, *That's always true.*

At a court appearance in Missoula, Pete gave curt and frank testimony stating to the judge that the woman in question had not kept a single appointment with him in the three months she'd been in his district. The woman yowled like he'd stuck her, but all it meant was she couldn't have her kids back yet. The judge told her to quit it, and she fell to a stammered jag of weeping that had no effect on the proceedings' outcome. When Pete left the courthouse, she leered at him from her car but didn't say or do anything as he crossed the lawn. The groundskeepers bagged the leaves.

Mary wasn't in the office, so he walked to her place. The elevator operator at the Wilma wouldn't let him upstairs because she wasn't in.

"Come on, you know me."

"You have to be on the lease."

"This a new policy?"

The elevator operator sat on his stool, caring for his nails.

Pete waited outside the theater smoking. The wind poured out of the mouth of Hellgate Canyon and eddied where Pete idly paced on the tiles in front of the box office. The breezes sketched up little twisters of brown leaves and a puppetry of paper. The elevator man was watching him through the glass door and Pete opened his palms, as if to ask what his problem was. The operator drew back.

He went for coffee up the block and had just sat down when Mary strolled by wearing a long coat and a look of wry expectation. She was headed downtown—instead of coming from—and her expression seemed like that of someone who knew she was going to her own surprise party. He grew jealous of whatever was on her mind. He rapped the glass, startling her. She covered her chest and smiled when she saw him, kissed him when she came in.

"I was wondering if I'd see you again."

He put his hand under his T-shirt and made like his heart was visibly pounding. He could feel her smile like a heat lamp on his person.

Anyone would suffer corny sentiments in her presence, she was that dear, that comely.

"You went by my place," she said.

"I had a court date. I just stopped off for coffee."

She set her hands on her hips and looked at him skeptically.

"Here. On the block where I live. You stop for coffee."

He scratched behind his ear and admitted the elevator man wouldn't let him in.

"He's a fickle little son of a bitch," he added.

"You all right?" she asked.

"I'm fine."

She looked at her watch.

"Go," he said plainly. "Whatever you got to do. I'll come by some other time."

"It's just that I was supposed to meet some people."

"It's all right."

She searched his face. He asked her what for.

"I'm getting a weird energy off you."

"Look, there's nothing I'm wanting or not saying, okay? I just came by is all."

She tugged off her gloves, removed her coat, and sat.

The waitress came, and Mary ordered a piece of apple pie. Pete shook his head no when the waitress looked at him to see if he wanted anything to eat too. It had begun to snow. Just a thin powder as though from a nearly empty shaker.

"I thought you had to meet some people."

"You're sad," she said, and she touched his hair back over his ear and put the back of her cold hand on his forehead and cheek.

"I don't need you to take my temperature," he said, warming her hand in his. He remembered that she had terrifyingly cold feet. She loved to put them between his legs to shock him. She'd said she had poor circulation or thin blood, a real condition. Some quack told her to imagine pulling clothes from a dryer, to hold in her imagination a clean dishtowel, a warm pair of jeans with hot rivets.

The tiny brass bell over the door rang and the people who came in brushed the new snow off their hair and shoulders before it could melt.

"So, what's up?" she asked.

He thought for a moment, and then told her about his father.

"I'm so sorry, Pete."

"It's okay. We weren't . . . close."

"Still."

She held his hand, and he said that if he was upset about anything, it was leaving Cecil, that there wasn't much to be done about it, but how it had left a bad taste in his mouth. More than a bad taste. Putting Cecil in Pine Hills made him feel awful that he'd run out of things he could do for the kid. Then there was the courthouse today. The holidays coming on.

Texas.

"I guess I got a lot on my mind," he said. He smiled at the understatement.

She sat there, listening. That was all. In fact, as he was talking, he began to realize she wasn't as forthcoming as he would have liked; she offered no palliatives or even a mildly philosophical take on this being the nature of the job or the people they worked with or the nature of life entirely. These were things that he would have said to her, and he resented that she didn't offer them up.

"You're distracted," he said.

"I don't like the way you worked that case," she said.

"What case?"

"The boy you put in Pine Hills."

"He was going to juvie whether I was involved or not."

"You shouldn't have tricked him. He trusted you enough to call you and you lied to him. You don't know what that does to people. People who already don't have enough people they trust. Just because you were ultimately right doesn't make the way you went about it okay."

"All right."

"That's all you have to say?"

"I hear you. I could make excuses, but you're right."

She looked sidelong at him.

"What are your intentions with me?" she asked.

"My 'intentions'? What are you, your own father?"

"Pretty much, yeah. Yes, effectively, I am my own father. I was—"

"Look, I know. About you. What your background is. It's out. People know."

She laughed. A hard bark of laughter that doubled her over when she looked at him.

"Everybody knows, Pete. I told Jim in my interview. All my professors knew, all my papers were about it, my thesis. It's not a dark secret."

"Okay."

"I am *not* ashamed of myself. It's not my fault."

"Of course not."

"So then don't treat me like I'm a crazy bitch for asking you what's up with us."

He told her he was smitten with her. He said: "Let's call it smitten, what I am."

"Okay then. That sounds pretty good."

"Can you bail on your people tonight?"

"I don't want to go to the bar."

"Okay."

She told him he drank too much. He said for her to tell him something he didn't know.

The waitress brought coffee, and Mary turned some cream in her cup with a spoon. The waitress brought the pie. Two forks, just in case Pete changed his mind, she said. She put a fork in front of him, and when he didn't pick it up, Mary cut a bite with her fork and put it into his mouth. And it was good pie, and she was there, and he felt better. Simple.

She said he could take her somewhere, but it had to be somewhere special.

By the time they made it onto Highway 12 it was full dark, the motes of snow firing out of the black as though they were vaulting through stars. He pulled into an empty turnaround and took her across the still and empty blacktop and into the lodgepole forest and helped her up the trail slick in places with ice. The snow falling on the trees was a sound itself, so faint that it could be heard if they held their breath, and then lost in the thrum of their hearts and their panting as they hiked the grade. They found their way by his flashlight, and shapes of steam from the hot pools sifted lazily through the wet pines like robed ghosts of a sudatorium. Lurid mosses and mustard lichens grew here as in the rain forests of Washington, the near rain forest of the Yaak. They undressed on the wet rocks and put their clothes in a garbage bag. Flakes of snow alit on their bare shoulders, and he took her hand, and they stepped gingerly over the slick stones and down a few crude steps into the hot pool.

"Jesus," she said, wincing at the heat.

"Come on. All the way. There's a bench over here."

She took a breath, slid down to him with a slow gasp that whistled over her teeth, and joined him on the stone that sat them in water up to their necks.

"Nice, huh?"

"If my skin doesn't boil off."

"Come on."

She tilted her head back onto the rim of the pool and sighed, her breath convening with the cloud steaming over them.

"Yeah." She sighed. "Okay. I get it."

Pete reached for the flashlight and shined it around the boulders and trees.

"This would be a good place to spend the winter."

She laughed.

"Seriously. You got hot water. You set up your camp down near the creek. You could make it out here okay."

"If you don't mind all the naked people coming and crashing your camp."

"Well, not here. Something like this up around Glacier."

"Tenmile getting a little crowded, is it?"

"Not me. I was just thinking of this case. This kid. Sorry. I didn't mean to talk about work again."

"Get it off your chest."

She beckoned him to speak with her fingers. Pete took them, kissed them.

"This boy and his family are living somewhere in the sticks, and I was trying to figure out where they might be holed up for the winter. How in the hell they'll make it. Something like this would be prime. But I don't think there's any hot springs up there."

Her eyes were closed, and beaded water was already running down her neck to her clavicle.

"You have no idea where they are?"

"Not really."

"Do they have any previous cases on file?"

"Pearl's more the kind of guy you read about in the paper."

"You should check."

"I should've already. I'm losing my knack for this."

"At least you have a beautiful cock."

She didn't look at him or move, but a sleepy grin cracked across her face.

"I'm gonna have to wash your mouth out," he said.

"I can't help it. I'm just a product of the system," she said, tilting her head slightly in his direction. "I had a lot of foster daddies," she whispered gravely.

Her eyes were half closed and in the deep darkness he could not see what kind of craving rode in them, so he swallowed and took her outstretched hand.

She slid up to his ear, whispered, "A lot of staff who would check on us at night," and bit his ear. He wondered was this flirting. She grinned. Flirting. Should he play along. Could he play along. Did she think this would arouse him. She stirred vaguely under the water, and a grenade of lust boomed in Pete's chest.

"They took advantage," she whispered.

He got in front of her, and pinned her to the edge of the pool.

"They—"

He put a finger over her mouth to shush her, and she nodded and put her body to him as if to say she understood, yes, but would he still please, would he still.

For a period of weeks things were as good as ever between them. They took a drive to Livingston for interesting gourds from Hutterites, and on Halloween they handed candy to the few children living in the Wilma who raced the floors for treats in plastic costumes.

In mute astonishment they watched Reagan get elected on the television at the Union Club, where the Teamsters Local 400 had gathered to observe, crush their hats, and get mournfully plowed. When someone put on the jukebox, Pete and Mary turned slow circles on the dance floor and went home in a sleety snowfall that soaked and chilled them on the three-block walk to her apartment. An errant shout that might have been joy at the election's outcome redounded off the empty streets, and then it was quiet, as though all was well in the Republic.

"The judge is gonna be a mess," Pete said. "I should go home and check in on him."

"Take me," she said.

It was nearly 4:00 A.M. when they arrived in Tenmile, and the judge was heaving in his booth with Neil and the sheriff keeping watch. He had wept openly in the preceding hour. He'd been telling stories about the old days, outraged yarns of cattlemen riding up on shepherds and slaughtering the offending stock, hanging rustlers and innocents alike, and terrorizing the state generally. He inveighed against the Copper Barons. He sang the Montana state song and then a few bars of "The Battle Hymn of the Republic," drumming his tobacco-stained gut in a tuneless rage, cracked verses spewing from his voice box. Pete took a shot of bourbon with him and the judge agreed to let the sheriff drive him home.

Pete drove Mary up to his place and lit the fire as she looked the cabin over. Maybe wondering what it might be like to live there. What kind of husband he would be. He knew what kind of husband he had been, but felt—watching her touch his fishing pole, run her finger down the spines of his books, and idly inventory his cupboards—that he might be a different kind of husband now. She asked what happened to the window and when he said a bear is what happened to the window, she didn't believe him, and when she saw he was serious, she stayed close to him. He dragged the mattress out by the fire. The sun rose on the Yaak and they went to sleep.

He would take off to do his cases and come back to Missoula to be with Mary whenever he could. Long weekends. The days were shorter now. Colder. Days he cut work like he'd cut high school geometry, realizing with a soft embarrassment that he did so with no fear of consequences. That old Snow sense of entitlement. But this too: DFS could not fire him any more than they could hire someone to help him. He was as good as it got, and for the most part that was pretty damn good.

He watched it snow from her window, falling pink embers in the evening neon of the marquee. Nothing accumulated and the cars swished by in the street below as if it had rained. He napped on the couch like a hot cat and woke and moved away from the radiator and into the cool of the bedroom. He smoked in her groaning brass bed reading her books and it was usually dark when he finished. For hours he merely listened to the traffic down below, people about their business, utterly reft of his enjoinment, his sage advice.

It's almost as if they don't require your assistance at all. Imagine that, Pete.

It would be dusk. The lock would click open, she would come into the bedroom with a cup of wine, disrobe, slide into bed, and they would begin to harvest orgasms.

She would tell him stories sometimes of the group home. How the kids were, how the staff was. Times she snuck out. A time she ran away with another girl, hitched a ride from Spokane. They stayed with a Boeing executive for a few weeks. He gave them presents and money for letting him masturbate onto them. They stole his wallet, got picked up on Capitol Hill, sent back to Spokane.

On Thanksgiving Day, Mary needed an assist and a second car to do a removal, so Pete went with her. They rescued the kids simply enough. The jittery mother appeared almost relieved, saying to take 'em just take 'em, and the children were in various states of comprehension as Mary and Pete helped stuff what clean clothes and toys they had into duffels, and then through the yard muddy with snowmelt to the cars. But as they left, the guilt did a sudden number on their mother and she raced down the mountain after them, laying on her horn, flashing her lights. The kids bawling at the sight of her reaching for them at the stoplights in town. Pete pulled into the parking lot of the Kmart while Mary ran in and called the cops, and the kids howled against the windows of the cars, hysterical and hyperventilating, until the cops took their mother away. But then a slobbery, sniffling quiet and anesthetic relief washed over them, and they sagged like they'd been drugged. Some even dozed.

Pete and Mary shuttled them like their own harried brood into JB's Big Boy, and they ate burgers and shakes, and colored on the place mats. With nourishment came new anxiety, where were they staying, what will happen to us, and Pete and Mary could only give immediate answers.

The attention home.

Yes it's nice there.

Yes you'll all be together.

No we don't know about after that.

Someplace better.

You haven't touched your fries.

The eldest girl, at Pete's elbow, began to sob quietly and he was unable to soothe her dismay. Mary nodded at him to get out, and she slid in next to her, took the girl's wrist into her own long fingers and began to turn magic circles on the bones of her hand and then on her other hand. Her crying ceased, and in time the girl's eyes rolled, her head fell against Mary's shoulder, and Pete saw or imagined a ghost swim like a flagellate out of the little girl's forehead, a departing devil. Mary coaxed deep mind-wiping breaths out of this girl and she nuzzled against her in this warmth and peace.

Pete asked quietly how she did this.

"Acupressure," she said. "There are points on the body where the tension is physically stored."

"You know, I could use a little of that."

"Stop it."

"Serious. I got a lot of tension stored up in this one spot—"

She threw a straw at him. The children laughed. He made a face at them and invited a fusillade of french fries.

At Christmas he sent Rachel a box full of things he feared were all wrong. A gross of jelly bracelets and three pairs of earrings. Sunglasses. A belt. A book of e. e. cummings and *Jonathan Livingston Seagull* and *Lord of the Flies*. A short letter explaining that her grandfather died and saying how much he loved her. He wrote Mary's number and said if she couldn't reach him at work to try him there.

He finally wrote Luke too. One draft explaining that the old man had died that he pitched into the fire because he could not calibrate the voice or sentiments. His own corrosive thoughts. He wrote another short note just telling him to come in, get it over with and then on with his life. That there was bad news and that he loved him. To just come back.

Mary worked Christmas but came to his cabin the days after. Fingers of ice from the eaves. Opening gifts, many of them bottles, batches, vintages. A kind of hibernation. New Year's in Missoula. They skied Lost Trail. Hot cocoa and Rumple Minze on the lift, the sun shattering off the sheets of snow.

Then the succinct gray days of late January, February. The Yaak socked in with banks and clouds and cold. Shots of terrible arctic air, the useless sun. Everything under a nap of snow, and yet curiously alive.

A fox hopping after bunnies or mice in the meadow beyond the trees. A stillness at the heart of things, between the beats.

A night he came home from work to fresh tire tracks leading up the road to his place, but stopping short of his drive. Footprints going to and coming from the cabin. As he made a fire, he discovered the cup with a puck of frozen coffee on the table. His brother or his brother's parole officer. He wasn't sure which. Didn't care much, one way or the other.

Spring. Come March 1981 a spell of warm weather set the snow melting, everything dripping. Water running under the ice, the ice white and slick as enamel.

The temperatures squatted in the low fifties when he went to Butte for St. Patrick's Day. Pete and his friends woke midday with heroic hangovers and dragged themselves into the pitched revelry already spilling into the streets. A carnival of motorcycle noise and nakedness to rival anything in Sturgis, anything in New Orleans. The whole town a red-light district, funny, hinging toward ugly. They watched fights that Shane ushered to completion with his meaty fists. They arrived at a house party where a crowd of leathery enthusiasts watched an old slattern tug on a pair of thin cocks attached to two men as pink and shiny as basted hams. Pete had only just wheeled outside to retch when Shane walked out as calmly as a sheriff, punching the head he had cradled in his armpit. A skinny witch rode his back and tore at his ears as he stepped off the porch and dropped the man he was beating into the grass. He seemed surprised to find he couldn't work the gate latch with his broken hand, and once again they made for the ER, stopping for a six-pack, as if on the way to an afterparty.

✦   ✦   ✦

Did she receive Pete's gifts and letter?

She did. She didn't read the books or wear the bracelets or the earrings or the belt, just the sunglasses and read the letter about her dead grandfather to her mother.

You should see if he left you anything. Son of a bitch was rich.

There's another number here he wants me to call him at.

You can call him if you want.

Her name is Mary.

Whose name is Mary?

The number.

Let me see that.

Did her mother read the letter?

Just the last part with the number. The other woman's name in Pete's handwriting.

Mary, she said.

That was it?

She had people over that night and got rip-roaring after her shift. Then divorce papers. She would sit and regard her daughter in the sunshine on the porch that cut through the leafless live oaks, it was still warm enough to sit outside, and announce that she wasn't going to say mean things about her father to her. That she would find out on her own that he was cold. That there was something broken in him. That she would see for herself what a wreckage he was, how incapable he was, just like how he would forget her birthday, just watch, he will forget. You'll see.

And did he forget her birthday?

She didn't care. She was all about Cheatham by then.

Cheatham?

A college dropout who'd come over with some friends some Friday her mother was working and the first one she said to herself she wanted. Yes, she had been boy crazy before, but this was different she wanted to hit him and bite him and crawl up him and chew his ear off. She couldn't understand these violent feelings, but there they were she was nervous the whole night she actually drank and went up to him and said this was her house did he want to come inside and have a look around and he said he was okay on the porch having a cigarette and someone handed him a guitar and his long brown hair fell over his face as he played and she waited on him all night and two weeks later when he came over she made him walk with her around back of the house and then she climbed up him and kissed him and it was love he was nineteen she scared him but her birthday had happened and she said it was only five years' difference now but he wouldn't touch her anymore. He came by another time with some other people but didn't talk to her at all really and then a time after that around Thanksgiving or Christmas and her mother threw a party on New Year's and they did it in her room at last he had to leap under the bed when someone stumbled in and she screamed bloody murder and whoever it was slammed shut the door and she laughed at Cheatham for being so scared.

Was he sweet?

He really was. He wrote her a song and sang it in a whisper. A song about soft birds. He was worried it was so so so wrong for him to have slept with her.

Did she intend him to take her away?

Yes.

Did her mother suspect she was planning to leave?

Almost every night now it was a carnival of drunks and weed dealers and some speed dealers and these long-hair stoner guys and guys on motorbikes and artists and all sorts. Cheatham didn't stand out. Her mother was distracted by bar people, by new prospects herself. She'd lost weight doing the hours on her feet, doing some coke, staying up all night, her voice was reedy and hoarse as she was herself in the throes of something fresh and almost teenaged. Having her own crushes from those in the aforementioned carnival. She and Rachel passing one another in the hall like roommates, not mother daughter, not that they were fighting yet either but in a kind of mutually agreed improximity like two north-poled magnets, never to touch, to close, even side-hugging when they were out together and someone said they looked so much alike, side-hugging like rival sisters made to stand for a picture.

EIGHTEEN

A case had in fact been opened on the Pearls by his predecessor. Pete found it in the files in his office, but there were no notes and the forms were empty save an address: 22,000 Fourth of July Creek Road. Pete had gone up to see the place but couldn't find the turnoff and gave up. But when the snow melted, he hazarded up Fourth of July Creek one last time. He passed by Cloninger's house on the way and waved at him standing in his yard with a hammer. Cloninger only seemed about to recognize Pete and didn't have time to wave back, and might not have in any case.

This time he found the turnout, but the road was impassably muddy. He parked and hiked up through the old snow and cedar and larch, through the calling finches and kinglets to a meadow that gave onto a view of a large rock bench and atop it, a kind of house. The aluminum roof gleamed violently in the sun as he approached. All about the crude structure was the sound of melting snow weeping from it. The windows fogged gray with dust. He guessed it was a good thirty miles from the place in the woods where he'd first taken the boy. As the crow flies. They weren't crows. They walked all that thick, ragged country. He wondered where they wintered. How. Where were the others, the mother, sisters, brothers.

He decided to go back to the place where he'd first met the Pearls, up the unmarked Forest Service road. The hike past the gate was no less difficult, the kernel corn snow over his ankles, and on the last stretch he slipped on almost every step. When he made the ridge, he sat on the wet rocks, sweating under his coat until he was cold again. From where he was, the fabric of the clothing he'd stuffed under the ledge was visible, but he went over anyway and pulled everything out. It had been jammed back in a disordered mess. Not the way he'd left it. The bottle of giardia medication was still there, but not the plastic bag in which he'd wrapped the vitamin C. He searched through the clothing and felt around under the ledge for it. He searched the ground nearby.

"You fuckers," he said, smiling.

He stuffed everything back and hiked down to his car.

The next day, he returned with more vitamin C and a bottle of regular vitamins and several chocolate bars and cans of beans and chicken soup. He folded everything up together and replaced it in the crevice. He stepped back from the cache and then snapped his fingers and put the jeans in front so they'd know he'd been by.

Three days later he spotted the coat under the ledge instead of the jeans. He whooped and hoped they were somewhere about, to hear him. The vitamin C and all the cans were gone. He replenished the soup and beans and added some canned vegetables. He ate a bar of the chocolate himself.

"Hot damn," he said.

The boy came along about when Pete expected. Middle of the day. Some distance from wherever they were camped. He loped up out of the golden currant brush, glanced around, nearly missed Pete sitting twenty feet away. He ran. Pete waited.

In forty minutes, he could just hear the boy coming up the hillside behind him.

"You come alone," the boy asked or said, it was hard to tell.

The kid's face was gaunt. No child's fat. Mildly ghoulish cast to his skin.

"You take that vitamin C?" Pete asked.

The kid walked past him to the ledge and began to fill his canvas bag with cans. He put the chocolate in his coat.

"I'd like to come with you."

The boy looked down the hill.

"My dad," the kid said by way of explanation.

"I'd like to talk to him. There's got to be an easier way for me to help than leaving the stuff under a damn rock way up here."

"He doesn't know."

"Where does he think it comes from?"

"I go to town sometimes."

"The IGA?"

"Sometimes."

"And shoplift."

The boy sighed impatiently, worried a hole in the sleeve of his sweater with his thumb.

"You don't have to do that."

The boy hiked his bag up his shoulders and started down the hill. Pete followed through a thickness of broken cedar, new lime green ferns, and livid mosses. The child's wet warren. They trod into some new country, a stand of towering ponderosas. The long brown needles sounded softly under their feet. Cold breezes trundled invisibly over the moist and vacant understory of the trees.

The kid stopped walking. They leaned against pines, facing one another. The boy regarded him.

"You can't come."

"I know you're worried something will happen," Pete said.

"Something will happen. To you."

"Do you really think he will harm me?"

The kid pulled puzzle pieces of bark from the tree and flicked them through the air, sailing like blades. The distances he achieved. So much time in these woods.

"I talked to a guy who ran into you two after all the ash came down."

The boy's eyes flashed up at Pete.

"It sounds like you guys were pretty scared. Your old man thought the world had about ended."

The boy broke a stick with his foot.

"But it didn't, did it?"

The kid's lips constricted over his teeth. He scratched his cheek, but then resumed debarking the tree, sending the pieces whistling through the air.

"I don't want you guys to feel like that anymore. Like you're all alone out here. I can help you and your mama and your brothers and sisters."

Pete crouched against the tree trunk so he was at eye level with the boy. He leaned in the direction of the child's gaze to achieve some eye contact.

The kid turned and ran.

Pete's posture against the tree—his back wedged against it, no leverage—put him at an immediate disadvantage. He took a moment just standing upright, and when he started after the boy, he slipped on the slick carpet of pine needles. By the time he was at a jog, the kid was gone. The big pines weren't especially thick—not compared to the cedar—but after the quick fifty feet the boy put between Pete and himself, he'd disappeared. Or he was hiding. Pete slowed, searching this way and that, expecting to come across the child hiding behind one of the huge boles. No luck. If the kid kept at a dead run, looking for him this way only made his escape certain. Pete ran as fast as he could in the direction he guessed the boy had gone.

"Benjamin!" he shouted. "Come on! Let me just talk to you a minute!"

There was a blur ahead of him and to the right, some sixty yards away. Or it was his own movement shifting something up there in parallax. He broke after the figment anyway. Through his heavy breathing he could hear water. He stopped and listened, holding his breath. His heart throbbed. A creek somewhere ahead babbled. A snap, shuffling. Pete ran toward the water. He budged through the brush. The bank dropped suddenly, soil and rocks giving way until he had dropped into the drink, a knee-high pool that bloomed darkly with dirt.

The boy was upstream of him in the middle of the creek, a couple yards from the other side, stepping gingerly across a riprap.

"Ben!"

The kid glanced back at Pete, unhalting, and then leapt up onto the opposite bank and disappeared.

Pete slogged out of the pool and headed straight upstream, the creek shallows flowing around his ankles, walking the cold stones, arms out like a tightrope walker. He slipped on the tails of virid moss, vivid to glowing in the overcast. A thin sleet fell on him from the unobstructed sky. He made for the shore opposite to get under the trees, but it was all cutbank and deep eddies and he'd have to go where the boy had crossed or just about to exit the water.

He tottered upstream, ankles rolling like a child on ice skates. He slipped again, but close enough to the shore to reach for an overhanging branch of larch to halt his fall. It gave and gave under his weight as he pulled on it hand over hand, stripping away new needles, tipping and twisting backward until it gently, almost kindly baptized him into the water. He let go when his back was soaked and dropped into a four-foot pool. The cold evicted his breath and when he tried to rise, he slipped and fell again up to his neck and flipped over onto his knees and pulled himself up by the roots on the bank and stood. Stunned and dripping for a long moment. He moved upstream along the bank by handfuls of earth and flora like a man traversing a cliff face, until he arrived a few yards down from where the kid had crossed. There was a single wet footprint on the rock and then nothing, just thick green alder. He listened for anything at all, but there was only the water moving behind him and dripping off of him, and the whispering down of the sleet. He began to shiver. He pulled off his jacket and wrung it and wrung the shirt on his body and walked back across the creek. The going much easier this time because he was already soaking wet and angry.

When he got out of the water and back among the ponderosas the sleet had turned to rain. He trotted to warm up. His hands were bright red, his ears too. The long hair at the back of his neck was soaked through and like an icepack on his nape. He began to jog faster and his side ached but it was too cold to give a shit. He crashed the cedar, all numbness and genuinely worried he would get turned around and freeze himself to death. He wondered did the boy hear him fall. Was the boy following him now. Was his old man.

By the time he made it to his car, his jeans were stiff down at his ankles, but he was basically warm, if winded. He turned on the engine and cranked the heat and held his palms to the cold air blowing out of the vents. He blew on his hands and looked in the glove box. He turned off the engine, got out of the car, and went and unlocked the trunk. He squinted at the sliver of rusty Canadian whiskey, swallowed it, and tossed the empty bottle into the weeds.

The snow fell and fell and with it every fool's hopes for an early spring. Pete worked a few cases in the eastern part of his region. Hard-gotten-to cabins in the Flathead where the grim occupants paced and fumed like bulls at the sight of him. He had lunch with Cecil's sister in her school. He gently culled from Katie her and her mother's recent whereabouts. They'd taken a road trip down to Denver for reasons unknown to the girl. When he visited Debbie, he didn't even bother to try and get the whole story, just informed her that Cecil was in Pine Hills. She pantomimed indignation about Cecil's incarceration, but Katie was genuinely worried when Pete told her, asking was he okay and how long would he be in jail. He promised he'd get Cecil out as soon as he could.

When he got back to the courthouse, Benjamin Pearl was in his hallway, standing outside his door.

"My papa's gone blind," the boy said in a papery voice. He paced, and his words sluiced out faster than Pete could gather them up, all out of order.

The old man's screaming, hot pokers grinding in his sockets. They try water and he shrieks and writhes on the cold ground. He runs away. Ben has to go look for him. He's in the woods struck blind. Come morning his eyes are sealed shut swollen. It's snowing again. The snow's all over. Ben wants to know if this is his fault. He says God doesn't need to answer, Ben knows the answer already. He has to fix this. He finds Pete's card and leaves, his father calling after him, where are you going. Where do you think you are going. Can Pete help, he has to help.

This camp, yet another, was four miles in from the National Forest Development Road #645, most of it uphill and by Pete's reckoning not all that far from Separation Creek and his own house. Maybe a day's hike to the old logging road that wound out of the empty wilderness down to his place.

Jeremiah Pearl wasn't in the camp—a canvas tarp that disappeared into a hillock of young, dense alder, a few packs, some bedrolls, and a fire pit—but sprawled on his back near the runnel of a small headwater. Stones placed on his eyes for the cool in them. Pete searched for signs of the other Pearls, the sisters and brothers and mother, but there were none.

"Papa?"

The man sat upright and the rocks fell away. His eyes surely throbbed under their swollen lids, even at a distance a raging shade of red.

"Where the hell have you been?"

"I—"

"Get over here, damnit."

The boy came forward and his father had him by the arm and gripped his head and appeared about to do some punishment to him, but just grabbed him all over to feel that he was whole. A thing he could accomplish in a glance that assumed a new depth of expression by hand. The boy threw his arms around him and held him, as his father patted him.

Suddenly, the man shot up, pulling the child behind him, and still gripping his boy by the shoulder.

"Who's that?"

Pete hadn't stepped or moved at all, but the man perceived him just the same.

"Mr. Pearl, it's me, Pete—"

"You get the fuck out of here," he said. His face glistened with water, with tears. Suppurating pus hung like a maggot at the corner of one eye.

"I brought you some medicine."

"There's no remedy for God striking you blind, you fool."

"I'll bet you're just snow-blind," Pete said. "A real bad case from the looks of it."

"I'm not snow-blind! You ass!" He took a step, stumbled, and gripped the boy to regain his balance.

"There's snow all up here in the high country, Mr. Pearl. Not a lot, but everything's covered. You were out in an exposed area for a few hours the other day, I'm guessing."

Pearl's eyes moved about, unseeing.

"It doesn't have to be very bright out. Really," Pete said. He sat down and began to pull items from his backpack. "My daughter and I went cross-country skiing a couple winters ago. Completely overcast. You could make out the shape of the sun behind the clouds, but just barely. It was hours afterward when things went blurry. By supper we were basically blind. You don't need any direct sunlight, is my point. Fact is, it was probably worse on us because we weren't even squinting all day."

While Pete spoke Pearl rubbed his sockets with fingers of one dirty hand. The effort of it wrenched his face, and a guttural *gah* issued from his throat as he twisted his head in pain and tried to shake off the torment like an animal.

"Don't touch them. Please, Mr. Pearl. I have the eyedrops the doctor gave my daughter and me for the pain and some ointments too. There's no reason to think anything's amiss."

Pearl swagged from side to side.

"Papa," Benjamin said.

"You shut up," Pearl muttered.

"He's been leaving us the food, Papa. He's been helping us already!" His father turned and the boy slipped free of him.

"Don't be mad at your son, Mr. Pearl. It was my fault. He was just trying to make sure you and your family"—Pete glanced back toward the camp, wondering where he thought he might see the rest of the children—"were all right."

"Let him help you," Benjamin begged. "He's okay, Papa."

The man touched his temples with his fingertips and began muttering. Then he smiled, some teeth shone out from the thatch of his beard and he began to speak, and Benjamin knelt with him. To pray, Pete realized. They clasped their hands and hung their heads. Pearl spoke to God directly, asked was it His will for him to go blind or was it not. Would the restoration of his vision allow Pearl to enact His will, or was this thought vanity. Was this another in the series of tests, he asked, in a rueful half-grin like a man who'd won a bet with a good friend. Pearl stiffened and said he could take what God would dish out. That God must know this. That Pearl would reach into his mouth right now and wrench out his teeth was it His holy will. That He need only speak. One word.

They remained on their knees. Then Pearl raised his head and seemed to be at some long thought or perhaps trying to see Pete.

At last Pearl stood. He said it was all right for Pete to give him some medicine. What did it matter, what could any remedy accomplish if God didn't will it.

Pete had listened closely because he couldn't see, couldn't tell if Beth was paying attention as the doctor explained how to apply the drops and ointments. Hospitals made her nervous, and when they got home, he was right to have memorized what the doctor told them to do. But that was two winters ago.

He removed a canteen of distilled water from his bag and the packet of gauze and the scissors. He set these on his coat, which he'd spread open on the ground. He rolled up his sleeves and washed his hands with a fresh bar of soap and rinsed with the distilled water and dried them on a little towel from the bag. There were two ointments and a bottle of drops. One of the three was for pain. The drops. The doctor had said white pus meant the infection was bacterial. He said to use one of the ointments in that case. The antibiotic ointment. Or the other.

Pearl sucked air through clenched teeth at a fresh wave of pain.

Pete asked Pearl to lie down and rest his head in Benjamin's lap. He told him he was going to pour water into his eyes and wanted to flush them as clean as possible. Pearl did as Pete told him. He told Pearl to try and blink. The man's eyelids were swollen shut, and when he opened them they split like sausage casings, fat pus dribbling out. Pete poured water into his eyes and the man arched in agony, but he did not cry out. Pete told him he had drops for him that would ease the pain a great deal. He said to stay still, and firmly wiped away the pus so that he wouldn't have to do it again. The man whimpered. Pete told him he was going to pull his eyelids open and put in the drops. Pearl barked for him to do it already. Pete pried one eye open with one hand, the gummy lashes like a flytrap, and saw only the black sightless centroid of his pupil. He squeezed a drop onto the eyeball. Or not. He wasn't sure, the eyelid clapped shut and the man strained away despite himself. Pete said let's try the other eye, and the pupil was rolled up when he opened the lids and this time he saw the cool drop hit the ball. The man's breath heaved into and out of him. Benjamin ran his hand over his father's head as the drops did their work. Pete explained what the ointment was for, but as the pain diminished Pearl went pliant and let him run the ointment along the bottom of his opened eyelid like a line of white frosting.

They watched the agony go out of him. Melted excretions ran down his temples like white tears, but the man was still and Pete thought maybe he'd passed out—he'd been awake for two days in great pain—but he took Pete's hand and patted it. The boy sniffed and grinned gratefully at Pete. Pete went to the fire and let the two of them alone.

He was two days with the Pearls. The first night he cooked hot dogs but they refused them. The boy said they didn't eat swine. The pork and beans were out too. Pete ate the hot dogs himself and gave them buns and cheese and small tins of fruit cocktail. The man was sound asleep and snoring minutes after they wordlessly ate. They sat by the fire some, and Pete suggested the boy go to bed and then rolled a cigarette and sipped from his flask. He caught the child looking at him from inside his bag. They grinned mutually. Then the boy turned over toward his father.

On the first morning, the man's eyes were crusted shut and they performed the same ablutions, applied the drops and ointment. He sighed at the fresh relief and let the boy stroke his head.

Pete got up and stretched his legs and observed the campsite. They'd dug out and flattened the earth on a hillside that wasn't far from a good view of the canyon and which was only a short hike from the ridge that looked out on the northern approach to their position. They were close to fresh water, close enough that a blind man in agony could find it.

Pete inventoried their things, the collapsible cups and lightweight aluminum plates, forks, spoons, knives, a few small pots. They'd slept in the open air, but the area they'd dug out went some ways into the hillside. The shed they'd constructed of small logs was about four feet high on each side with a good yardage of canvas stretched taut over it. Pete spotted fishing poles, rifles, and a mishmash of garments, hats, unmatched gloves through the flap.

The only thing missing was the rest of the Pearls.

At supper the man sat up, beckoned his son, and softly said something to him. The child went into the shelter and returned with a bag he handed to his father. The man groped for it, set the bag in his lap, felt among the coins inside, and fetched one out.

"Where are you?" he asked.

"Over here," Pete said.

Pearl tossed the coin to him. It landed between his legs where he squatted. It was about the size of a nickel, pure gold, with an antelope on the back. An aristocrat on the obverse.

"That's a quarter-ounce Krugerrand," Pearl said. "For the medicine and the food and your trouble. I don't know what gold's at right now, but that's more than fair."

"I can't take this."

"Yes you can. You can change it into a hundred dollars. At least."

"I'd heard you didn't believe in the dollar."

Pete couldn't see his eyes to tell what the man might have thought about that remark. Pearl hawked up a plug of snot and spat.

"From who?"

"A pawnbroker. A dope farmer."

Pearl lifted his chin and turned his head to better hear Pete.

"Ever since I came across your son," Pete said, "I've kept my ear to the ground for you."

Pearl daubed the corner of his eye with the back of his hand.

"Really, I can't take this," Pete said of the coin. "Helena pays for everything. Reimburses me, anyway. And my salary."

"Render unto Caesar then," Pearl said.

"And what if you're right? What if the world comes crashing down and money's worthless? Won't you want this gold?"

Pearl smiled. Pete asked what for.

"Well, what is gold?"

"I don't understand the question."

Pearl leaned forward, resting his elbows on his knees.

"The metal isn't *for* anything, is it? It's soft and worthless. All we do with gold is stamp it with animals and dead men and Masonic symbols. Melt it into trinkets," he said, donning an imaginary ring. "We stack bars of it in vaults."

He laid gold bar atop invisible bar. One eye had come unstuck and was partially open, giving him the aspect of a demented vagrant or seer. A little of both.

"A can of Spam is a better hedge against the apocalypse," he said, smiling. "It lasts a thousand years, and you can eat it."

Pearl felt around his person and located some fingerless wool gloves in one of the many pockets on his olive army coat and pulled them on. He tipped his head at a noise he alone heard, some auditory figment of his own paranoia.

Pete turned the coin over in his palm.

"Why not put a hole in this one?"

Pearl smiled, presumably at his own infamy.

"That's a South African coin. I have no opinion of the images on it."

"But Lincoln and Washington?"

"Washington was a slaver and a Mason. And Lincoln issued fiat scrip to pay for his war on the states."

"And FDR?"

"Don't make me laugh," Pearl said.

The boy watched them talk and looked to Pete like he had a stake in the outcome. Like he wanted Pete to pass his father's test. Worried about it, in fact.

"I'm not a man," Pearl said, unprompted and like he was holding another conversation with a ghost or within himself.

"You're not a man," Pete repeated. "What are you, then?"

The child looked away from Pete. It slowly occurred to him that Pearl wasn't helpless at all, that the boy would do anything he told him to, that he had shot at Vandine—

"I'm dynamite," Pearl said, smiling. Tilting his head as if to better hear Pete's expression.

The boy would not look at Pete.

"What do the shapes mean?" he asked, as though they were talking about some harmless craft. "The square and the star and the keyhole?"

"Symbols," Pearl said, fluttering his fingers in the air.

"Of . . . ?"

"Of nothing. Like all symbols. Of themselves. Of a virus. As in the Tulpenwode."

"The what?"

The boy abruptly stood. Pete resisted the urge to stand himself as the child went into the tent.

"In centuries past, there was a market in Holland," Pearl said. "The country at the time was making advances toward modern capitalism. Trading currencies and commodities. Futures markets."

Pete wondered if whatever Pearl had said—*tool pen road?*—was some kind of signal. If the boy was even now fetching a gun.

"A new investor class," Pearl continued. "New ways of buying low and selling high. Paper fortunes. Betting essentially—and then bubbles and crashes."

The boy remained in the tent.

"Are you following me?"

He had failed to kill before. Maybe Pearl had insisted his son try again.

"Mr. Snow?"

"Yes, I'm following you."

"The Tulpenwode was such a bubble and crash," Pearl said. "*Tulpen* is Dutch for tulip. And *wode* . . . *wode* is mania."

"Mania. Yes," Pete said, absently.

"Now the tulip at this time was a new flower in Europe. Very popular. It should've been a harmless fad, but because of the Tulpenwode, it remains to this day a symbol of Holland.

"Now this flower had a virus, which expressed itself by streaking the petals with ribbons of color. Tiger stripes and flames. The Dutch classified them with a passion, gave them names like 'Viceroy' and 'Semper Augustus.' And these infected tulips needed careful cultivation. This only intensified the sense of their preciousness.

"Almost overnight, the growers who tended these flowers were charged exorbitantly for the bulbs. And this gave way to the second cause of the Tulpenwode: the speculative Dutch market."

The boy exited the tent in an oversize peacoat that he'd buttoned incorrectly. His hands tucked in the pockets.

"Contracts were drawn up to protect the growers with a set price," Pearl lectured, "defending them against rapid changes in the market. A 'futures' contract. And as the prices of the bulbs continued to rise, a surprising thing happened: the contracts *themselves* became commodities. As the prices for the contracts ballooned, the price of the flowers ballooned, and vice versa. Just imagine that. For the first time, the price of an object—a vanity at that—was sheer enthusiasm."

"Enthusiasm," Pete repeated, watching the boy.

"Perfectly sane people traded their horses and sheep for bulbs of the rarer varieties. Goods in excess of several tons—cheese, a bull, beer— were traded for a single Viceroy bulb. For a time, the tulip replaced the florin as the national currency. This was a fuckin *wode*."

"A *wode*," Pete said.

The boy sneezed, startling him.

"Bless you," Pearl said.

The boy wiped his nose with his sleeve, and then set both empty hands on his lap.

He picked his nose.

"Then one day," Pearl carried on, "it was as if everyone found their sense in a dresser or hanging from a nail in the barn. The tulip became just a flower again. The prices plummeted. Whole families were ruined, generations of wealth squandered on nearly worthless contracts for sick flowers."

The boy didn't have a pistol.

"So your coins," Pete said, "they're like this . . . tulip mania?"

Pearl didn't reply or move. The boy now unbuttoned the coat to fix it.

"The pawnbroker says people pay good cash for some of your coins," Pete said. "He told me that there are collectors everywhere. That they have almost become another money. He says you're a genius. That you're up to something major."

Pearl grinned and nodded sagely.

"I am the kakangelist."

"I don't know what that is."

"The bringer of bad tidings. The bad word."

"So your coins are a warning."

"The coins are a whimper when what is needed is a full-throated cry. We are in a different situation altogether now. The Lord has set me over nations that I might root out and pull down and destroy. I believe the pawnbroker is right. I will be associated with something incredible. My only fear is that one day I might be thought of as holy."

It alarmed Pete to realize that the boy was standing. He'd been drawn in by Pearl's inchoate charisma, his madman charm. Now the child was afoot and off into the woods.

Pete tried to silently rise to his feet.

"Are you going somewhere?" Pearl asked.

"I'm just stretching my legs," Pete said. "Where did Ben go?"

"He's only a boy. A boy you've come to aid," Pearl said. "You aren't afraid of us, are you? Us poor, backward people who need your assistance?"

"I didn't say that. I don't think it."

"Your presence here presumes it."

"No. I came to help. That's all. I know you're not people to mess with."

"Ah," Pearl said. "The man in the ash. Yes?"

The boy was behind Pete in the dark. He turned and peered into the trees, but could not see through the cedar and larch.

"Yes?" Pearl asked again.

"Yes," Pete whispered.

"The Lord needs us to be sharp," Pearl said.

The boy blithely stepped through the ferns and into the firelight, dropped an armful of firewood, and went back into the woods. Pearl's clouded eyes were half-opened, regarding Pete or his shape. He sat back down.

"You thought it was the end of the world," Pete said.

"Of this world."

"But it wasn't. Your wife. What did she think?"

"Of what?"

"Of everything . . . Where is she?"

The blind man gestured vaguely, his arm up and behind his ear, as if to say they were deeper in the mountains and many miles away.

"With the other children?"

"Yes. She is with the other children."

"She's alive."

"Yes."

The boy returned with more wood.

"It *will* be like that," Pearl said.

"What will?"

"The end. Fire, smoke, blood."

Pearl rubbed his temples. Pete asked if he was in pain again. The man did not say.

"I see your instrumentality now," Pearl said. "God is inscrutable and I don't know the end game, but He has made it clear that you are involved now."

"Okay. Does your wife need anything? The other children, are they—?"

Pearl said he needed news. On the way west, he said, they'd read about the assassination of Aldo Moro by the Red Brigade. He said that Revelations 13:3 predicted the Antichrist would survive a deadly wound. That he would yet rise to lead armies against God. He said he had a list of possible Antichrists. He said these were some of the things he needed to know.

The boy fed the fire, grinning pleasantly at Pete, oblivious to what all had been said. Or, more likely, absolutely accustomed to it.

NINETEEN

Again the elevator operator told Pete that Mary wasn't in and wouldn't let him up. Pete smoked in the theater lobby, watching through the glass doors for someone to come down the stairs—residents on the first few floors didn't bother with the elevator and the cranky Charon who operated it—but no one came down. He bought a ticket to a matinee and went up into the balcony. The movie let out and he made like he was waiting in the second-floor lobby for someone in the bathroom. A few teenage truants left the theater and an attendant came to clean. Near the top of the stairs was an open janitor's closet and next to it a locked door. Pete could see the apartment building's hallway through the little window in the door.

"You lock yourself out?"

The janitor was already sorting through his keys.

"Yeah, I was just . . . Yes."

The janitor gave him a peculiar look.

"You here to see Iris."

"Uh, yes."

The janitor found the key but he didn't open the door. He looked about and then rubbed the fingers of his free hand against his thumb. Pete gave him a ten.

"You tip the box office?"

"I didn't—"

"Tell Iris. She'll take care of it. Come back out this way. Don't use the elevator."

So there was a whore and the elevator attendant didn't like it or had been told by the building owner to do something about it. Pete climbed a flight of stairs. Curious as to which door was hers. Wondered would there be trouble when the guy in the box office didn't get his tip. He had half a mind to go down there and tip the man himself just to not queer any of their business.

Mary's room was at the corner of the L-shaped hall, and he came to it from the back stairs. A fresh angle on the place. A man stepped out, closing her door behind him. Pete's stomach dropped. The man walked straight toward him, looking down. Pete gazed at him—gray temples and a hundred-dollar suit—and then turned toward the nearest door and pulled out his keys. The man walked past and exited where Pete had just entered.

Pete found himself in front of Mary's apartment, just short of knocking. His fist in the air. He wondered what she'd say. If anything. His mind and heart fairly raced, but all his reasoned thoughts biased toward ignoring it. Not her type at all. Maybe she had some kind of business with him. Maybe it had to do with a case. Maybe he was her father.

She didn't have a father.

Maybe she was Iris.

He ran back to the stairs that exited off the theater lobby. On the landing above the elevator, he squatted to see the operator sitting in the open car on his stool. Pete jogged up to the second floor, summoned the elevator, and was back on the landing just as the elevator door closed. He ran down the last flight of steps and outside.

Pete waited in front of the theater for the suit to exit. The man didn't see him or recognize him if he did. Pete hung back, watching him. The guy was pushing fifty. A fit fifty. Trim, not unattractive. But still.

When the suit crossed the street and walked north, Pete remained on his side of Higgins and tailed him two blocks until he entered the Montana Building. Pete dashed through a gap in traffic and followed him into the lobby. The suit had just boarded the elevator. He stopped the door from closing.

"Thanks," Pete said.

The man nodded. Pete entered and stood to the right and just behind the suit. He scanned the man for the flush of sex. Faint scratches and blemishes. An aura of contentment. Every hair was in place. A pleasant cologne tinged the air between them.

"Floor?" the man asked as the elevator closed.

"Eight," Pete said.

The suit looked over at him, one eyebrow aloft. He gestured at the panel of buttons. There were only six floors.

"Top floor," Pete said. The man pushed the button and the elevator rose.

Pete wondered what it was he intended to do following this guy.

The man exited on his floor, Pete rode the elevator to the top, back down, and got off on three. A hall of offices with frosted glass windows. Law offices.

He went outside, stood on the sidewalk for some time. A woman in a car gestured at him to cross, as he was standing in the gutter. He got himself back on the sidewalk. He loitered in the entry of Butterfly Herbs wondering what to do. There was a deep ache of jealousy within him that surprised him. He watched but did not really see a policeman question and then arrest a vagrant.

He marched back to the Wilma. The elevator operator said she was in.

"No shit," Pete said.

She was fresh out of the shower. In her robe, steam coming off her wet black hair like a smoldering tire. He wondered did she look through the peephole to see was it him. Was it a surprise to find him there. They spoke, but beyond the usual pleasantries he could not say what of. He slipped into the bedroom as she bent over and towel-dried her hair in the bathroom. The bed was made. He smelled the linens. She spoke to him from the bathroom and he searched the wicker baskets. Her underthings. Shirts missing buttons. He searched the floor for used condoms. For a cuff link or billfold. A gray hair.

There was nothing. He thought of loose buttons.

Of Beth.

This was about his wife, about her fucking someone else.

Mary came in swabbing her ear with a Q-tip and wearing the towel on her head. He set a wicker lid back on one of her wicker baskets.

"What?" she asked, her head tilted sideways as she worked at her ear.

"I didn't say anything."

She righted her head and asked him what the matter was.

"Nothing."

"Why are you digging through my shit?"

He made an innocent gesture that asked what on earth could he be looking for.

"I've been in more group homes than I have fingers and toes, Pete. I can tell when my space is being . . . *inspected*."

"Who was that guy?"

"What guy," she fairly growled. Her face said he better have a pretty good answer. A whole detailed explanation.

Is one woman all women, he asked himself. Do they know what they do to us. Do they try on cocks like shoes, and keep some of them and put back others. Is she Beth again.

She is.

"The fucking suit who came out of your door just before I got here."

Her mouth fell open, only just.

She blinked.

"Pete, I'm gonna say this once because I can tell you're angry and it's freaking me out: I have no idea what you're talking about."

"Bullfuckingshit. Elevator Man said you were out. Wouldn't let me up."

"I *was* out. Asshole. I just got home, showered, and I just got out when you knocked," she said. She shook her head, as if to clear it.

"I saw him come out of your room, Mary."

"*Who?!*"

"The suit! Not thirty minutes ago."

"Wait a minute. How did you get in?"

"Fuck you is how."

"Stop it."

"Just tell me who he is. Don't lie to me."

"Okay, look—"

"Are you a prostitute?"

For a halted moment she looked like she was going to cry. Then she stepped aside and pointed at the door.

"Get out."

"Are you Iris?"

Her fists were like billiard balls. She was naked and the towel on her head unwound and fell over her eyes and he had her by the wrists, but only for a moment as she bit his hand. He had her hair, briefly. Something hard struck his temple, and he let her go, and again his head rang and he found himself marveling that she'd acquired a hammer. She reared away from him, and he could only see through one eye and double at that. The heavy ashtray hit him square in the sternum and he doubled over.

She sobbed behind the bathroom door. He looked in horror at the strands of hair laced through his fingers and shook his hands in the air like the hairs were spiderwebs. Knots bloomed all over his skull.

She stood in the bathroom doorway. In her robe. Maybe an hour had gone by, sitting in the ashes and cigarette butts on her floor.

"I'm not Iris."

"I know what I saw."

"No, you don't."

"Excuse me?"

"You went through the door off the balcony."

"So what?"

"Pete. You were on the wrong floor."

"You have to be fucking kidding me," he said.

"Asshole! Listen! You started on the second floor, you went up the stairs, but you counted from street level. You went up two flights to the *fourth* floor. Ass. Hole."

She closed the bathroom door. His head tingled as a fresh draw of foolishness rolled over him.

"Mary."

He heard water running and knew she couldn't hear him. Would that he'd never come. If he could take back the past couple hours. He sat on the bed and, when she returned, stood up and told her he was sorry. That he was an utter shit.

"That was fucked up, Pete."

"I know. I don't think that way of you—"

"I don't like being accused of things."

"Nobody does."

"Especially not me. Half my life I've been blamed for shit I didn't do. It got to where I was used to it. I carry that with me all the time. This guilt, Pete. Even now. Fuck. Fuck you." She pointed to the window, the world outside of it. "For you to come in here . . ."

A long tear ran down her face and to her chin and fell to the floor. The soft pat of it on the hardwood over the traffic, the creaks of this old building. An untroubled expression of resignation on her now. She wiped her nose.

"I'm a fuck," Pete said. "I'm hammered dogshit over here."

A slight grin at his choice description.

"I'm so sorry. It was a misunderstanding."

She wiped her eyes and swallowed and waited for him to go on. He didn't want to go on. He had to go on.

"My wife fucked this . . . guy."

"She did?"

He gestured away all the particulars.

"So I think that I'm half-expecting you to screw me over. Nothing to do with you. Nothing to do with your shitty background. Mary, I . . . I *marvel* at you. I know what your life was like, and I sit *in awe* of you."

She told him to shut up. He said he meant it.

There'd been too little praise in her life and she didn't know what to do with the degree of his compliments. His sincerity, he could see, was difficult for her. Her chin vibrated, her whole body then as well. And he could see how she coped when she came over to him, put her hands inside his jacket and her tongue inside his mouth and touched him down onto the bed with a fingertip to his bruised sternum. She undid his pants and pulled them and his underwear down and kissed his cock and she slipped out of her own panties and ground her confusing feelings into a slick pair of orgasms that she summoned for them with hot words into his ear like a filthy spell. And his joy ebbed into a ruminating silence, realizing that half of what she'd been saying to him these past months was expressed with her body, a restless logorrhea that betrayed depths of her that she could not put into words, whole anguished diaries she'd yet to write if ever to write if ever if ever . . . and Pete felt party to a conspiracy to keep her mouth shut against her own ears, and it wasn't that he suspected her of cheating on him that made him sorry and silent, but that what they'd been doing together all this time was not grow closer to each other so much as keep her at a safe remove from herself.

Her hair was still damp, and when she lifted her moist cheek from his chest to have a look at him it sounded like a good-bye kiss. She got up and went into the kitchen and then he heard music, and the sounds of her cooking put him in mind of his childhood, times he could hear his mother at the dishes. His father would be braiding leather at the table and occasionally they'd have a few words between them and their being there was a lullaby and how reliable was this lullaby.

A grim dream that he'd actually harmed a child. Furious digging into the hillside. He half-buried the marbled white body.

Mary shook him awake.

"Sorry," he said. "Nightmare. Was I talking?"

"It's for you," she said.

"What?"

"The phone," she said, slipping back into bed.

"What time is it?"

"Three something."

"Who the hell is calling me here?"

"Your wife," she said, tugging the covers back over her body.

He touched her shoulder in abstract apology, padded out to the living room, and picked up the phone.

"What is it, Beth?"

"Oh Pete."

"Look, I know it's late, but I did put a check in the mail yesterday. I tried to call the other day. You guys don't pick up."

"We moved to Austin, and—"

"What? Austin? When?"

"Pete, it's been four days—"

"Why? What happened in Waco?"

"—and I'm calling you now because I'm real scared, Pete. It's never been four days in a row . . ."

"Are you drunk?"

He heard a lighter flick and another voice in the room with her.

"It's been four days, Pete."

"What's been four days?"

"Rachel."

"Rachel and four days what, Beth?"

"She's *gone*, Pete. I think she's been . . . I can't say it, but I can't stop thinking it. Jesus, Pete. I need you to come. Please come. Just come."

TWENTY

When his flight touched down in Austin, the pilot announced that the president had been killed. Gasps hissed throughout the cabin, then angry murmurs. The passengers debarked, and in the terminal men with coats folded over their arms consoled weeping women, lit their cigarettes. A somber crowd assembled around the television in the bar, watching the news. The president hadn't been killed after all, someone said. They watched Reagan get shot on the screen over and over. A little old lady with wads of folded skin around her eyes, a little hat on her head just so, a print dress, took Pete's hand and smiled gratefully. Across from him stood more people holding hands. Before Pete realized what it was, the prayer circle closed as a man took Pete's left hand, barely glancing at him before he bowed his head. Pete was obliged to pray for Reagan.

The heat outside smothered him. The cabbie asked if he'd heard the news. Pete said he had. The cabbie said to watch out, we'd probably be at war with Russia by nightfall.

The neighborhoods teemed with black people and then with Mexicans and bright red and yellow businesses, and people went out in the heat in short sleeves and pants, and young girls in hardly any clothes at all, and boys in nothing but black shorts. The cabbie took him downtown along Sixth Street. At a major intersection hippies in flip-flops milled among the muttering homeless at the bus stops, and Texans in whole suits and ties strode along the pavement in waves of heat.

Beth's place was across a large river or lake. Even in the shade of great oaks Pete sweltered. The brightly painted clapboard houses silently quaked. Welded statuary and mobiles of glass shards, amalgamated junk pressed into the service of whimsy. The toilet flower box just made him mad. He wondered where was Rachel in this astonishing heat. It was only March. He wondered what was this place Beth had brought his daughter to. What kind of people these Texans were.

Through the screen door he saw box fans blowing. He pulled his hair back and knocked again.

Beth emerged from a back room, threw open the door, and cascaded onto him, hand, arm, whole body, her head notched in his sweaty neck as in the old days. A single sob juddered out of her like an engine turning over. When she pulled away, snot and tears ran from his shoulder to her face, and she grinned in embarrassment and wiped his shoulder and her nose, and wiped his shoulder some more. Touched his shoulder. She smelled like herself. He held her here, and he missed her.

It was hotter within her house and he set down his army duffel. She went into the kitchen and returned with two bottles of beer, both pressed to her neck, and handed one to him. She was in scarcely any clothes at all. Cutoffs and a tank and no bra. She'd lost weight and her breasts sagged down her chest some, but the thinness made her beauty stark.

"I don't want a beer," he said. "I want to find Rachel."

"Just sit. Pete."

There was a fan trained on the couch and he sat in its stream and put the unopened beer on the coffee table next to some empties. Bottles were serried atop the mantel and ashtrays everywhere and clothes and Styrofoam containers.

"Stop it," she said. "A week ago the place was spic-n-fuckin-span."

She drank from the bottle. He left his sweating on the coffee table. She'd been to the police, she said. She'd called all the hospitals and shelters and everyone she knew. Everyone Rachel knew. The school, her teachers, everyone.

"I'm going to visit them myself. When did you last see her?"

"Five days ago."

"What time?"

"Bedtime."

"Bedtime when?"

"Late."

"How was she?"

Beth sat in a plastic folding chair and leaned forward and swung the bottle between her legs from her fingertips.

"She was fine."

"Was anything going on?"

"Like what?"

"I don't know, Beth. Anything that . . . I mean she left under her own power, right?" He looked around the place. For broken glass or something, a sign of something. "No one busted in and carried her off, right?"

She drank. There was something she didn't want to say.

"Beth."

"There'd been a party. The night before. Supposed to be just a few people from work."

"What work?"

"The bar."

"What happened?"

"It just got to be a lot of people. Like some of the afterparties we'd have back home. Nothing out of hand. Just some people from the neighborhood."

"And . . . ?"

"Girls her age . . ."

"She's thirteen."

"She's *fourteen* now."

"Shit. That's right."

She set the bottle on the floor and rubbed her face all over.

"Tell me what happened."

She enfolded herself within her arms, and girded up to tell him.

"This fucking guy went into her room and he . . ."

"He *what?*"

"He just kinda scared her."

"Jesus, Beth."

"Nothing happened! I heard her yelling and I went back there—"

"Why was she yelling? What was he doing?"

"Look, I couldn't get a straight story out of her—she said he was on her bed."

"Jesus! Did he hurt her or touch her or . . . ?"

He couldn't finish the question. His mind couldn't complete the idea.

"I think she was just surprised. She didn't say he *did* anything."

"I can't believe you."

"He didn't hurt her, Pete. She was fine—"

"I'm supposed to be all right with this? It's just no big deal because you say so?"

"You weren't here! You do not know what happened."

"I sure as shit know enough. I know you put our daughter in a situation—in her own house, in her *own bed*—where she was afraid for her safety. Fuck, Beth! I can only imagine what this guy was like. The kinds of people you like to party with—"

"People *I* party with? How about people *we* party with? Like that thug, Shane? Or *Spoils?*"

"Fuck you. Shane and Spoils wouldn't lay a finger—"

"I'm telling you, she was fine. Nothing happened!"

"I've heard this before."

"Heard what?"

"That nothing happened."

"You're hilarious." She shook out a cigarette from one of the several packs nearby. "I never said nothing happened. I *could not wait* to tell you I fucked him."

He threw the beer bottle at the wall behind her, as astonished at the act as she was. He'd never touched her roughly in all their time together, and now a bottle flew centimeters from her ear and exploded against the molding. Did he aim for her or not, he didn't know. Did he miss on purpose.

She opened her squinched eyes, turned and looked at the suds running down the wall. The glass.

"Who's this shithead that was in my daughter's room? Give me a fucking name."

Pete went to the police station and was a long time trying to get with a detective because every idle officer was watching the news. Cops in cowboy hats gathered around the small black-and-white television set out on a folding table, forearms crossed, smoking, mashing out cigarettes on the floor.

He was finally escorted to a desk. A fat plainclothes officer came over with a file folder and a missing person's report. The detective read and then told Pete everything was in order. He explained that the Texas Department of Public Safety had his daughter's description and last known whereabouts. He asked did Pete have any new information.

"She was assaulted in her bed the night before."

The cop looked at the paper to confirm what Pete had said. Pete told him it wasn't in the report because his wife didn't file charges. For what, the cop asked.

"I don't know. I don't trust my wife to tell me what happened. A man broke into my daughter's room and scared her."

"You weren't at the domicile?"

"No. I was in Montana. We're separated. Divorcing."

"I see."

The cop sat there, his neck like a roll of dough over his shirt collar.

"So I want this guy checked out."

"The guy who is supposed to have scared your daughter."

"Yes. Are you gonna write any of this down?"

"Write what down?"

"The man's name is Booth."

He gave Pete a curt scowl and clicked open a pen from his shirt pocket.

"That a last name?"

"All my wife knows is he goes by Booth."

"Like phone booth?"

"Yes. B-O-O-T—"

"I can spell. That a last name?"

"Like I said, I don't know."

"So it's just a nickname?"

"No, I don't . . . I don't know that. It could be a last name. I *don't know*."

The cop wrote down the name and underlined it.

"Booth. Got it. Anything else?" he asked.

"I thought maybe he'd be known around here."

"Known around where?"

"That you'd have him in one of those books with the mug shots."

The cop fidgeted in his seat and underlined the name again.

"I can see if we got any Booths with priors."

"Okay."

"You leave me your number and I'll—"

"I can wait."

The cop constrained his irritation. Took Pete in entirely, his clothes, his hair, as though deciding whether to help him at all. At last he stood, and headed off into a back room.

Cops coming and going stopped by the television asking was there any news. Asked how the president was doing and where they were keeping this Hinckley piece of shit. Could they somehow finagle him into the basement of the Dallas Police Department and put a Jack Ruby on him.

The plainclothes detective came back. There were no Booths in the book.

Pete checked into his motel. He'd been wasting time with the cops. If Rachel was still in Austin, she didn't run to the guy who'd busted into her room. More than likely the guy was just a drunk. Pete had let his anger at Beth muddy his thinking. He wondered what else he was fucking up. What crucial thing he wasn't doing this very minute.

He contacted Child Protective Services and Austin Children's Shelter, explained who he was, who he was looking for, and asked where the runaways congregated. With the overnight lows in the sixties, he was told, she could be anywhere. Hanging around downtown or in any number of uninhabited lots overrun with bamboo. She could be sleeping in Pease Park down along Shoal Creek or staying in one of the run-down Victorian houses in West Campus. They said to bring a picture. They said to ask around. The kids on the picnic tables in the park. The bums in the bamboo.

He didn't have a car so he took a cab back to Beth's and let himself in. A man with long braids and aviator glasses sitting on the couch stood up and asked him what the fuck he was doing barging in like this.

"I'm Beth's husband."

She stepped in from the kitchen. She swallowed in advance of saying something. He grabbed her car keys off the table.

"I need your car."

"I called around to some of her friends from school again," she said. "No one's seen her, Pete. No one."

Her chin creased like a ball of paper and her eyes sank to the floor.

"Give me their numbers. I'll go see if I can find out anything."

When he told the woman who he was, that he was looking for his daughter, Rachel, and he'd like to ask the woman's daughter a few questions, a quiet worry flitted across her face and then she stiffened and let him in. Her daughter was due back from track practice in a little bit. She asked did he want some sun tea.

She filled a glass with ice and poured him tea from a jug in the window, and when she turned around there was a fresh resolve in her face to say something frank.

"Thank you," he said, taking the tea. "Now go ahead and tell me what you want to tell me."

"I want to help. I want you to find your daughter, but I don't know why you're here. Why her mother called. I forbade Kristin from going over there weeks ago."

"Why?"

The woman plucked a dead frond from a fern by the window.

"Her mother. There is alcohol and drugs all over the place. People there all hours of the night. How did you not know this?"

Pete set down the glass of tea. Gazed into it.

"Heather's mom said the same thing."

"Kristin says she hasn't been in class since February."

"Well, where the hell has she been?!"

The question shot out of him unbidden, and he immediately murmured an apology and stood to go. She'd taken a step back, but now she gripped his forearm.

"When you get her, you keep her."

He said he would. He said he was sorry for disturbing her afternoon. He thanked her and he left.

He drove the city, searching all the places the social workers said to search and then the youth homes and runaway centers, showing skeptical staff his Montana DFS badge, more than a few of them asking him wasn't he way out of his jurisdiction. He said it was his daughter and to a person they turned remorsefully accommodating. A large-bosomed Texas matron offered to print him a ream of flyers if he'd leave her the picture he had of Rachel. She said a lot of the runaways could be found on the main drag near the University of Texas, panhandling and busking near campus and lying to cops.

His shirt soaked through walking the Drag. He made no progress whatever, the kids had never heard of her, the trail was as cold as the weather was hot. He didn't eat or drink, and by evening a headache cleaved his head into discrete lobes of pain. He sat outside a run-down three-story house where he'd seen college kids and younger go in and out. Visits of five or six minutes. None of them Rachel, each tiny teenage girl among them causing a hope to crest and crash in his heart.

SHE HAD ALWAYS liked to dance. Pete would strike up a beat on his chest, lap, or the walls, and she would twirl her arms and stutter-step in place like a miniflapper all of eighteen months old. She loved pears and ate fistfuls of scrambled eggs and was practically famous to all the tenants in their apartment building. Everybody knew everybody. The tenants decorated each floor on holidays, mainly for her, as there were no other children in the building among the minimum-wage earners and single widowers and working college kids like Pete and Beth. Such a pretty picture Rachel, Beth, and Pete made, as ideal as a water molecule, hydrogen, hydrogen, oxygen. Complete and entire.

The tenants would leave their doors open to her, and Pete would sit at the top of the stairs to make sure she didn't topple down them, and she ran from apartment to apartment and now he wondered did she trust the whole world because of that and did she think she could dance just anywhere at fourteen and it would be safe, and he wondered was she so foolish as that, and he thought of course she was, she has me for a father and Beth for a mother.

Long nights with thin, wakeful sleep, thick sluggish days driving around in Beth's car, walking creek beds and cemeteries and waiting on picnic tables in disheveled neighborhood parks and traipsing through bamboo warrens and squatting among the wary homeless and asking did they see a girl about fourteen, yay-tall, real cute, curly hair. They said no they didn't. Or they said yes they did because he as much as described any and all white girls who were in this kind of trouble. And among this population of the peculiar and outright insane were more than a few who Pete suspected were capable of virtually anything and he was leveled by the naked fact that there was nothing that could not happen to his little girl. Everything was permitted. This was real, not a fiction or mere case he was working at some remove from his heart. And he said to himself all these days, Oh Christ what have I done, I have let her down in every meaningful particular, above all failing to love her enough that she knew his love and would come to him.

Times he entertained the idea she was en route to Montana. Times he swore oaths, promised to die if she would come back—I'll die. I'll suffer anything but this, her absence. Her silence.

Not knowing where she was. Oh my God. An untold sorrow. He'd seen so much suffering, but he'd only ever suffered it secondarily. To have it fresh and his own. The scope of it. He'd had no idea. He'd known nothing.

Times he was sure she was dead. Times he spotted her body in city creek beds and ditches, in among the weeds at the shore or floating out in the river. He walked the muddy beds. Flotsam and detritus from floods, garments strung up in creek-side flora like scarecrows. Snakes and fleet lizards and spiderwebs the height of him. Insects of incredible size and speed. Nothing like home. This wasn't home.

He harbored the hope that she'd headed north. He wrote it on a piece of paper and kept it in a shirt pocket close to his heart.

He visited Rachel's school, her teachers, trying his best to appear . . . he didn't know how to appear. Professional or insane with worry. He went to San Antonio, which was much larger than he'd expected, and stayed a few fruitless days showing flyers, hanging them in shelters, giving them to anyone who'd take one.

Staying next door to him in the motel was a bickering couple at whom he more than once pounded on the wall. It rained one evening and when he returned from scouring the city, he found them sitting out front of their doorway sipping pleasantly from tumblers under the awning in the evening cool. The man's name was Beauregard and he gave the impression he was awaiting a call or a ride, even as he pressed a glass of rye into Pete's hand and introduced his wife. Sharla or Sharlene or Darla. She smoked and forced something short of a greeting out of her mouth when Pete held up his glass.

They were between jobs. They asked was he staying alone. Pete said he was. Beauregard removed his cap, as if to distract from his agenda in asking about Pete, and Pete's hackles went up, but the rye went down and his wariness leveled off with a companionable drink, the pleasant coolness of the rain, and the overcast sky. A birthmark ran up the inside of the bored woman's leg to an unknown terminus, like she'd pissed or bloodstained herself. He wondered who were these people really. Not just here, with him, but the world over. He saw them every day in his work and had yet to know why there were so many.

With Beauregard and Sharla, he let down his guard, come what may. He wondered was his daughter in some place similar doing something as foolhardy. More foolhardy. He found himself deaf to whatever Beauregard was saying and, sizing him up, wondered could Rachel evade such a man, the ropy muscles of his bare arms in his tank top.

He pummeled his worry down with another glass of rye. It got hotter as the sun set.

A black man arrived, thin, with large eye whites like boiled eggs. Pete looked the man over not in wariness or anxiety but in undisguised curiosity. He'd never seen someone so jet-black, skin glistening in the increasing humidity like a wet stone. Beauregard introduced them, and the man asked Pete what the fuck he was looking at. Sharla snorted. It seemed for a moment there'd be trouble as Pete stammered out that he wasn't looking at anything. Pete was ashamed and said he was sorry and that he'd better be heading in to hit the sack. They just looked at him like he was crazy saying that, and Beauregard said for Pete to wait with Sharla, he and Douglas here had to go on an errand and he sure as shit wasn't leaving Douglas alone with Sharla. It wasn't clear that this was a joke or at whose expense if it was.

They were gone an hour. Pete and the woman smoked, not a pleasantry passing between them.

"My daughter is missing," he said.

The woman looked at him with no compassion whatsoever.

"She ran away from her mother's. I can't find her."

"How old?"

"Fourteen."

She pulled on her cigarette and looked into her glass and if she had a thought for him, she didn't share it.

"We're shitty parents. Her mother is just over at her house getting drunk. And I'm sitting here getting drunk. But there's nothing we can do. I've looked everywhere."

"You check the Drag?"

He nodded. "We were young. We weren't ready for a kid. No one tells you that the mother of your child will resent the child and resent you. I am saying what you are not allowed to say: we did not love our child enough. God, I didn't protect her. I didn't protect her from us. I go into homes all the time and I save children. It's what I do for a living, you see? And I didn't save my own daughter."

The woman had sat up, and now she went inside. She came back out with the bottle of rye. She squeezed his wrist as she filled his glass.

"Beau will be back soon," she said. "We'll all feel better in a little bit."

When they returned, Beauregard oiled the party into Pete's motel room and dialed in some music on the clock radio. He jiggered at the tinny sounds from the tiny speakers. Douglas removed a length of glass the color of maple syrup from his pants and Beauregard removed a pocket of foil from his shirt, folded it open, and plucked out a white pellet that Pete thought was a pill that the woman smoked. She sat serenely and Beauregard took the pipe from her open palm and bent to kiss her. She blew the smoke into his mouth. When he exhaled, she grabbed the back of his head and kissed him and pulled him onto the bed, wrapping her stained leg around him. Douglas shared with Pete a look of approval, of arousal. Beauregard disentangled himself and rose with the foil and the pipe. He loaded it again and handed it to Pete.

They called it base. Pete set down his cigarette and drink, and took the hit. He was unprepared for the exhilaration and he laughed ferociously. His vision filled with bright magnesium fires. He immediately wanted another one and finished his drink and cigarette waiting for the pipe to come around. It did. He and Douglas now became bosom. The music was soulful and invigorating. They spoke and spoke and spoke, most of it lies and heightened opinions. When the time came, Pete handed over some of his money, and Beauregard and Douglas left again. He and Sharla watched television, as quiet as people waiting in an ER. Douglas and Beauregard returned, the room filling with sound.

The hours shriveled into new smallnesses.

The rye was gone, they were out of cigarettes. Douglas had disappeared. Beauregard and Sharla argued about a scab she was picking at on her leg. They seemed to have forgotten they were in Pete's room. He stepped between them to get his wallet and his keys, and still they argued. He went outside. He walked up the empty street. A strip club, railroad tracks. A police car sped by. He walked the tracks and then down a causeway to and around the shore of a pond.

He sat on the limestone in the dark. Felt the notches carved by water into the rock. He'd have wept but for the cocaine and the numbness and the queer sensation that the stones all around him were subtly shifting position. The very ground seemed to writhe. Nearby something slipped into the water. He wondered was he both seeing and hearing things. He'd had so little sleep. No more than an hour at a stretch since Beth had called.

A foot away a rock shuddered. He reached a shaking hand to the stone and it collapsed a half inch, socketed into the ground. He wondered was he going crazy. Had he already gone crazy. He touched the stone and the grooves on the dome of it—

A fucking turtle. Dozens of them all around. A bale of turtles crawling to water.

Two days later he came back to Beth's house with her car and her keys but not with her little girl. Not that she expected him to. She didn't hear him pull up or climb onto the porch. He sat exhausted against the wall and was out of her sight and he listened to her shuffle on flip-flops into the living room. He was about to call to her when she started to cry. She bawled so hard he felt witness to a vile pornography of grief and then he wondered was she crying because the cops had found Rachel's body or a piece of her clothing in the water or were the dogs searching the fields or were divers dredging the river. Fear paralyzed him, he didn't want to know. And then her sobs puttered into a soft blubbering and she lit a cigarette.

She came onto the porch and into the muggy afternoon, bugs screaming something terrific in the trees, coming and going in waves, he didn't know they were cicadas or how loud they were, just that some incredible call-and-response was at work, a crackling choir that reminded him of baseball cards in bike spokes. She noticed him there and started crying anew.

"What is it?" he whispered. "What's happened?"

He cringed as though waiting for her to hit him with a hammer.

"Nothing's happened," she said. "She's still just gone."

His relief was itself almost sickening and he wondered would this be the shape of his life. Constant worry. Images of her foot tangled in river flora, her contused and naked back, her hair in the dirt. Her teeth. Would these pictures forever turn on the carousel slide projector of his mind.

"Where have you been?"

"Everywhere. San Antonio. Just driving and looking and asking. I talked to kids all over the city, Beth. If she's here . . . Hell, she's not here. Or she's . . ."

"Pete, don't."

" . . . or she's in a hole . . ."

He wept on his knees like a man begging for his life. She pulled him inside and held him, swaying under the ceiling fan until his grief emptied out. She took his head and looked at him and said I know I know I know honey. It was he who kissed her. She tasted like salt and beer. She led him into the bedroom through the stages of their disrobing. He wasn't tender with her, but neither was he rough. The lovemaking was necessarily urgent, ashamed. They would not have been able to abide another moment's reflection. They were too sore, and there was no longer much surface to them, just a thin layer of skin and the raw pith beneath. If fucking could be frank, this was, and so was everything they said afterward. She exclaimed with some woe and wonder that this was how Rachel came to be. With these two people here.

She reached for a glass on the bedside table and drank. She handed it to him. It was bourbon and melted ice and still cool and watery and almost slaking.

"I keep calling the police station," she said. "They sent an officer over. He said it sounds like she'd run away, not been kidnapped. I think she ran away, Pete. I think she ran away from me. I let her get away with everything and then when I tried to rein her in, she bolted. I think she's okay."

She turned and grabbed his chin to have him look at her. "Right? She's just run away, right?"

"I'm sorry I left," he said.

"I'm sorry too," she said. "I am. I drove you away. I did it knowing that."

"I think I knew what you were going to do. When you got dressed that night, when you went out."

She sat up.

"I knew too," she said. "I knew that you'd leave if I slept with someone. That you'd go exactly like you did. Pack a bag and vanish. Why did I do that?"

She reached over and took two cigarettes from the pack and lit one for him and handed it to him and then one for herself. She got out of the bed and walked naked into the hall and returned with a bottle. He felt the force of this uncanny tableau. As though they had no child. As though this were a different version of things. He took a small comfort that somewhere such an iteration as this one existed, where Rachel had never been born and the only damage he and Beth did was to each other.

"I was already gone," Pete said.

She poured him a glass, and he took it and drank.

"You were. Why were you already gone, Pete? What happened to us?"

He held up the glass of bourbon.

"I don't know. I'm an alcoholic, Beth. You're an alcoholic. Shit, I smoked *cocaine* the other night. I take kids away from people like us."

"We're not that bad. People fuck up. They get forgiven."

She frowned into her drink. She set it on the dresser and went to him on the bed and took his hand. Up close he could see the gray stretched rays on her little paunch and breasts. How her body had served their child. And her habits.

"I've been thinking of something," she said. "But I don't want you to laugh at me."

"I'm not capable of laughter now."

She took his hand into both of hers.

"I think we should go to church."

She waited for his reaction.

"I know, with your family and everything . . . that you feel like it's bullshit."

She waited again. He wondered did she know his father was dead, had she read his letter to Rachel. Did Rachel read it. He told her it was okay to say what she wanted to say. She folded her legs under and took his hand.

"I've been feeling, like, this hole inside? For a long time now. I don't think we have a center. The other day I was here all by myself and I was waiting for you to come. I had all these pills and I was thinking of taking them. So I knew I had to get out of the house. And I went out and was walking around, and I dunno, I was already kind of fucked up. And I came by this church and I thought I'd just feel it out. And the people in there were singing and this lady in the back row sees me and she pats the pew and scoots down for me. But I knew if I sat still a minute I'd lose it. I'd embarrass myself even worse than I normally do."

She pushed her curls behind her ears.

"I feel like I've been busted. Like the cops have pulled me over. Like God has pulled me over and I got to sit here with my hands at ten and two. And I got to get right or something is gonna happen to Rachel—if it hasn't already. It's God who's the social worker, Pete. And he's taken our kid away, you know?"

She squeezed his hands and trembled.

"You probably think it's stupid."

Pete closed his eyes and thumped the headboard and when he opened them she looked terrified that he was going to say something hurtful. This shamed him more than she could know.

"It's not stupid," he said.

She took a shuddering breath.

"Will you go to church with me?"

She took his silence for assent and kissed his forehead. She said she'd take a bath and then maybe they could eat and then they'd go find a service.

He was frightened for her and what was about to happen to her and felt the fullest burden of the fact that he was indeed a thing that had happened to her too and was happening to her yet and would be for a long time to come.

He listened to the water run and when he was quite sure she was in the tub, he dressed, walked up the street to the convenience store, and called a cab.

✦　✦　✦

Did Booth rape her?

Who?

The guy who broke into her room, the night she ran away.

No. He just kept saying *Hey, hey* . . . like he wanted to wake her but at the same time not.

It was a million degrees already in March. She slept in her underwear and a tank top, no blanket, no sheet. She fell asleep to the hum and thump of some corn-fed redneck noise, a breaking glass, and laughter.

Booth going *Hey, hey,* and she woke up to his hand on her thigh and she shot up and out into the hall screaming and crying, and Booth came out shielding his eyes in the light because he must've been in there a long time just looking at her, maybe touching her, his hairy arms, his stubbleblue sweaty shamefaced face. She wouldn't stop screaming until they dragged him out of the house. She slapped her mother, slammed her door, started to throw her things into a bag.

Was Booth just a pretext?

A what?

An excuse. To run away.

Yes.

Where did she run away to?

Cheatham, ultimately. But first a party in South Austin looking for him. A few of the wrong kind of high school girls knocked around the room as invisible as moths. Guys who knew their inhalants.

She literally had nowhere else to go. The party at its embers. Kids splayed in shadowy attitudes of sleep all over the floor. She had a cigarette with a boy on the back step. She could barely see what he looked like. The cars shook with the sex happening inside them.

Did he use a condom?

No.

Did he hurt her?

A little. She bore it with what felt to her like a mixture of grace and sophistication. She pushed out shame, brooked no doubts.

What was its main consolation?

Feeling grown. To have had a second lover.

What about Cheatham?

She found him the next day.

TWENTY-ONE

There were a few skirts of snow up around his house, but the larch needles had come in, neon green and soft to the touch. Raccoons meandered around his property for a few days but couldn't get in the house and moved on.

His bank account was nearly empty and he thought he might have been fired, but his check was in the splay of mail shoved under his door at the courthouse. It didn't matter if he was at work or not. He had no minders.

He left the rest of his mail unopened and took the check to First Interstate, cashed it, and went for lunch at the Sunrise. He drank coffee all morning just trying to wake up from an exhaustion that coffee could not fix. Fear had worn him to a nub. What happened to her. Where she was. He worried he was forgetting things about his daughter every day, trying hard to score into memory's bedrock the way she looked at different ages, the things they did. Cross-country skiing up at Lolo Pass. The tunnels they dug into twelve-foot snowbanks. Suppers he cooked for just the two of them and the steam from the boiled noodles and teaching her letters in the steam on the windows.

A time she got a septic knee and couldn't even stand and they put her on antibiotics and hoped all her blood wasn't infected. She was pale and sweaty and his heart wrung like a wet towel, like now. Times it would unwind and his heart would race to remind him that something was terrifically wrong.

He kept asking himself where is she what is she doing please be alive why won't she call just come home baby.

A morning, waking in his cabin, he thought he felt a lot better, happier, okay, even good. Rachel would reach out at some point. He'd gotten himself sure of that. He imagined her toughness and what resilience he'd witnessed in her, and again and again in all his cases. Children who had suffered unstinting hells, their toughness intact. A wryness, a wisdom some had earned. He imagined Rachel making it, meal to meal, shelter to shelter. That people would treat her kindly. That she had guardians at every pass. Things he believed because he had to, and believe them he did.

But when he went out in the chilled morning to his car, tiny hand-prints from some prior removal preserved in the frost on his windows promptly undid him. He slumped against the car door into the crusty snow and howled out griefs that had come on as sudden and frighten-ing as earthquakes, and even after they emptied out, left him in fear of aftershocks, of unseen cracks in the load-bearing trestles of his mind. He wondered could he go on, but there was little else to do. And what did that mean anyway. To kill himself or to just sit in the snow against the car or to go inside his cabin and never come out.

Just the thought of going to work. The Pearls. Cecil in stir. What good could he be to anyone at all.

He called agencies in Dallas, San Antonio, Houston, and El Paso. Then he spent the next couple days on the phone calling agencies radiating outward from Austin. Oklahoma City, Phoenix, Iowa City, Indianapolis, Denver, Reno, Sacramento, Seattle. He had flyers made and prepared packages for the social services agents of varying sympathy that he spoke to, agents and supervisors who seemed keen to help and those who left him on hold for an hour and the majority, who made him doubt his entire profession.

He stayed with Mary, and when he bothered to notice it, sensed her irritation in the way she moved about the place, the way she would look idly in the cupboards, the way she paced. As he addressed packages of flyers for midwestern social workers, he felt her watching him with magazines open on her lap.

He said he would stay somewhere else.

She said of course not.

He asked her to stop watching him and do whatever.

She set the magazine aside and said it was like he was in parentheses.

"You'll have to explain that to me."

"Never mind."

He tried hard not to sound sarcastic when he told her he was just busy. *Busy looking for his daughter.*

"I know that, Pete. Let me help you."

He licked an envelope and closed it. His ears were hot with an anger he didn't understand, or know from where it came, except the whole situation, his entire life.

"This is weird," she said. "Say something."

All he could tell her was that he was fine.

He could see her crossing off things to say as she stood there. At last she took a shower.

He sat before the envelopes and handwritten letters and the stacks of flyers. He got up for a cup of coffee so cold it made him look at the clock. It was five-thirty. He'd been at this almost twelve hours now.

When she came out buttoning her shirt and toweling her hair, he apologized and asked her to come over and he showed her the map of all the places he'd sent packages and all the places he'd yet to call. He said he was hanging on by threads of hope, and these packages were those threads. It was all he could do to get these materials together and make the calls and wait for word. He asked would she help him.

She said nothing to that, and he tried to determine her thoughts from her watery reflection in the old glass of the apartment window. She seemed to wait another moment for him to address her loneliness, or desire or whatever was bothering her. This had happened before, but he hadn't noticed. She'd go dark as an empty house.

She rose without a word and went into the bathroom, brushed her teeth, and then into the bedroom. He listened to her undress and climb into bed, the springs moaning. He wondered did she worry or sense that he'd slept with Beth, did she figure something out just now. Had something else occurred.

He joined her in bed. She climbed onto him and made love to him, tended to him with her entire body. She stayed locked around him and bore into him with her eyes until he was pieces, then shards, smithereens, motes, iotas. She said she loved him, she'd fallen in love. He was dust, swept away. Did he love her. Was there any he at all.

He groped around for himself. His spirit.

You are here, she said with her body. *Right here.*

And so he was. And he could love her.

He drove to Spokane in the hopes that if Rachel had headed straight for Montana she might have made it that far. But no one at the shelters had seen her, nor downtown where a few bums begged for change. He sat in his car for a couple hours at the bus station and observed the hustlers making their rounds. He approached a few of the homeless, the addicts and rail riders. No one was any help. Not even lies to elicit a few dollars. His anguish so evident that even the bus station tramps and riverside bridge dwellers wouldn't ply him with fictions.

Back in Tenmile, he spent a whole day organizing his files, and several more catching up—sometimes making up—his case notes. Had someone been there to see, his efforts would have been mistaken for enthusiasm, professionalism, and alacrity.

Portly Judge Dyson called his office and invited him up for a drink. He passed. Another invite came in the evening. He passed again. That night, as Pete wrote out false case notes, the judge darkened his office doorway, let himself in, and dropped into the chair. Pie-eyed and irritated at having to come down, the prospect of reascending all those stairs on his fat little legs.

"What's your dyshfunction, son?"

Pete explained what had happened and where he'd been and what all he'd done to find his daughter.

The judge held his head in his hands as Pete spoke, and when he finished, told Pete that he had a friend in the Fraternal Order of Police and that he would put in a call. He'd think on what else could be done. He was reeking drunk when he arrived, but when he stood to leave he was as still as a post. His eyes were no longer bloodshot. He looked ready to lynch somebody.

Pete went to check on Cecil's mother, sister, but they weren't home. He picked through the notices from the power and water companies, catalogs, and junk mail. Left a note on the back of his card for Katie to call him.

He drove to Pine Hills to see Cecil. He hadn't visited since he'd dropped him off the previous October. It was now coming on April. He waited in the visiting area at the small round tables. Sullen toughs posed for their fathers and brothers, while Indian kids and pale white farm boys came in and sat stone-faced before their weeping mothers. The only boy who didn't have this manufactured toughness was a fat and guileless retard who had an open gentleness to his movements and expression that cast doubt on his guilt of anything at all. He played with his mother's necklace and when it was time to go, wouldn't give it back and had to be restrained. His mother faced the wall as they took him away. She left caterwauling not unlike her son.

Finally an official came to Pete and said that Cecil wouldn't be able to visit. Pete asked was the boy in trouble or just refusing visitors. The man didn't know.

. . .

On a clear warm day, he headed up the National Forest road toward the Pearls' camp. He brought packages of rice and instant noodles, Kool-Aid, and dried beans. For the children, he brought bags of raisins and cinnamon candies, a few coloring books, a little packet of crayons, and a small cardboard puzzle of a bulldozer. Handkerchiefs for the wife or Pearl or whoever needed one.

It took a full day to hike to where they'd been camped when the father'd gone blind. Birds shot out the canvas flap of their tent in the hillside when he pulled it back. Inside was a nest with a few eggs, so he stayed the night on the ground by the fire, and remained as long as he could the next day. He was halfway down to his car before he realized he should have left some of the food. Or a note.

He drove and then went to the rocks where he'd left things for them. Everything in the cleft was gone. He put the dried foods in there and the next day went to see if they'd been to their old house up Fourth of July Creek. The meadow was filled with wildflowers, and he ate a sack lunch among the bumblebees and butterflies and saw now how pleasant it was and also the layout and how the property could be defended from the house on the rock bench, from the escarpment behind the house, and from the dense trees on the sides of the meadow.

About a hundred yards away was an overgrown earthwork or root cellar. He crossed through the marshy horsemint and skullcap, was muddied to his ankles getting to it. It took him a few minutes to determine that it was a burned-out Airstream trailer, blackened and now almost completely napped with moss and wild cress. Orange in places where it rusted. He sat a while in hypothesis about it.

He called around to social services offices, police stations, and shelters in Denver, Oklahoma City, Las Vegas. He wondered at the map where Rachel had gone.

A weekend full blotto. Arguing with Mary on the dance floor of the Top Hat. He went to the wall and pulled another beer from the pitcher, and she knocked it out of his hand. He laughed. He went outside into the evening air and started for his car. She followed and he let her in.

"Take me for a drive," she said, digging into the paper sack of schnapps on the floor.

They were halfway to Evaro when she started to throw some kind of fit. He simply pulled over, got out, and started to walk down the hill toward town. The asphalt reflected blue and red, and he turned around and hiked back up to his car. She was crying, sitting on the rear bumper.

"Is this your car?" the highway patrolman asked.

Pete said it was.

"Any particular reason you decided to leave it?"

Another patrol car U-turned and pulled in behind the first.

"We were having an argument."

"You can't abandon your car."

"Okay."

"Okay?"

"Yes. I shouldn't have abandoned it."

The second patrolman touched Mary on the knee to see about her and then came up on the other side of Pete's car and shined a light inside of it.

"We're both in the Department of Family Services. We're just, uh, stressed."

"Yeah, I'd say the *stress* is what's gotten to her."

"I'm—"

"Shut up. You're lucky. Because I am a softie about you DFS people. My sister did this work and she drank like a dang fish. Consider this your talking-to."

Pete nodded. The cop pulled a tiny green New Testament from inside his coat pocket.

"You got one of these?"

"Yup."

"Take this one anyway," he said, pressing the book into Pete's hand. "And gitcher poop in a group."

. . .

Another week went by before he had the time to hike to the Pearls' camp again, and by the new ashes in the fire pit he figured he'd missed them by a day, no more than two.

He slept over and dreamt of Rachel. Neutral dreams that were mostly altered memories or wishes and didn't augur anything good or bad.

When he woke, Jeremiah was sitting on a stump, leaning forward holding his rifle.

"Good morning, Pearl," Pete said. "How're your eyes?"

"Where you been?" Pearl asked, meaning the last few weeks. Pete couldn't remember if he'd said when he'd be back. He'd intended to return sooner than now, but he hadn't made promises. He didn't think. He couldn't remember.

"Texas, actually."

"Doing what?"

Pete let the question hang there for a moment while he buttoned his jeans and slipped on his coat against the April morning cool.

"I asked you a question," Pearl said.

"I heard you."

Pearl squeezed the rifle barrel, stood, and started for the forest. He was crossing the creek when Pete caught up to him. He yelled for Jeremiah to wait. The man stopped in the middle of the water that had widened by several feet with the snowmelt. Ice water ran over boots that Pete knew to be thin and surely no longer watertight. He beckoned Pearl out.

"I brought some food. Things for your kids. Come on."

"You think I'm stupid?"

"I think you're paranoid."

"You tell me where you really were."

"I had to go to Texas."

Pearl crossed the creek.

"My wife and daughter are down there."

Pearl's expression flickered like a candle flame. "In Texas," he said, as if trying out the concept.

"She left me."

Pearl seemed to believe this was feasible.

"What for?" he asked.

"Jesus, Pearl. Because she was angry with me."

"Don't take the Lord's name."

"Just come get some food."

"You go down there to get them back?"

Pete didn't know if he wanted to tell Pearl about his daughter. He didn't come up here to talk about this. He'd come up to leave himself behind. Yet here he was anyway. There was no getting away.

"My daughter ran away. I was down there looking for her."

Pete's voice had dropped, and Pearl tilted toward him to hear him over the tumbling water.

"You didn't find her?"

"No. Not yet."

Pearl set the stock of his rifle on the rocks, and hung on it like a walking stick. The battered weapon looked like it might not fire at all.

"What are you doing up here then?"

Pete pointed over his shoulder back toward the camp.

"Like I said. I brought some things for your family."

"So she just took off?" Genuine wonderment colored his voice. He looked at Pete like he was from an alien country. "From her mama?"

"Yes."

"I'm sorry to hear that."

"Yeah, well."

Pearl crossed the water toward Pete and seemed unable to give expression to the sentiments churning behind the queer expression under his beard. His eyes and mouth pursed as against a strong wind or thick black smoke. He clapped Pete on the shoulder and said they needed to get moving if they were gonna make it.

They hiked two long miles up through devil's club and ivy and then snowbrush and cinquefoil and up the rocky backbone of a high ridge that looked out over a small lake, a blue color so ideal that at this distance it looked like spilled paint. Pearl sat beneath a skeletal wind-blown cedar clawing at the sky. He looked at his watch and closed his eyes and murmured through his beard, in prayer it seemed. Pete stood a few minutes waiting and asked what they were doing. Pearl said to sit, it would be a half hour.

"What will?"

"Until we can go on."

Pete squatted and ate jerky from his bag, but Pearl shook his head when Pete offered it to him.

At the half hour, Pearl raised his rifle and looked through the scope down at the lake. Pete peered down to see, but wherever Pearl aimed was too far to make out. Pearl set aside his rifle and made a series of large gestures, contacting his family using a semaphore they'd worked out.

Pearl looked through the scope again and grunted. He walked along the ridge a ways and then took a broken trail down the mountainside away from the water. Pete hurried after. They kept descending.

"Aren't we going to the lake?"

"Nope."

"Isn't your family down there?"

"Just the boy."

"Why aren't we going to meet him?"

"We are."

"It doesn't seem like it."

Pearl stopped.

"We aren't camped there. Just follow me."

He shouldered his rifle, and they carried on.

After a while Pete asked Pearl again how were his eyes. Pearl raised his hand to say they were okay. They didn't speak for the rest of the way.

It was evening when they arrived, and Pearl issued a hoot and a few seconds later came an identical answer. In a small clearing in the trees, the boy raised up at the sight of Pete.

"Howdy, Pete," he said, shaking his hand.

Pete squatted down to see how he was. Filthy. Some cuts on his hands. Otherwise hale.

"Can I see your belly a second?"

The child obliged.

There were no liver spots on his skin. He looked fed and under the dirt had good color.

"You look A-OK, kid," Pete said.

Ben grinned. His father told him to get firewood and start a fire.

Pete took in the camp. It was much like the other. More crude, hasty. Their things were strung up in catenary lines between the trees where bears could not reach them. Benjamin started a fire and, as he fed it lightwood, kept glancing up at Pete as if he couldn't help it.

"I have an eagle feather," he said.

"You do?"

"Yeah. It's in my bag."

He retrieved the feather and showed it to Pete, running it the length of his arm like a jeweler presenting a necklace. Pete whistled.

"It's nice. Where did you get it?"

Ben watched his father now. Pearl had shielded his eyes and was gazing skyward.

"What in the hell is that?" he asked Pete, pointing up.

Pete stepped out from under the alder boughs and saw the contrail of a jet directly overhead, the white line bisecting the emerging stars.

"A plane?" Pete said.

"Put out the fire," Pearl said to the boy. "Pack everything up."

The boy hesitated, and Pearl cuffed him upside the head. Ben scampered to, kicking hunks of dirt and moss onto the fire.

"Whoa!" Pete hollered. "It's just a plane."

"Directly overhead. I'm not stupid. How do you think we're still alive?" Pearl said, ripping up carpets of moss and covering the fire himself.

"I'd love to know what the hell happened to you, why you are like this."

Pearl stopped stomping out the fire. He looked hard at Pete.

"What are you looking at?" Pete asked.

Pearl went to him and took his backpack right off his back. He dumped the contents onto the ground. He furiously pawed through everything.

"What the hell are you looking for?"

Pearl mumbled to himself, tore into the plastic bags of beans, the boxes of rice. He picked up the puzzle and cut it open with a knife and fingered through the pieces. He shook out the bags of raisins and cinnamon candies and weighed the cans with his hands. Shook them next to his ear.

"It's just food," Pete said. "A few things for the kids."

Pearl squatted regarding the mess he'd made. Poked it with his finger. The boy was standing nearby, watching, slowly putting his sleeping bag back into its sack.

"What things?" Ben asked.

Pearl threw a handful of small rocks at his son, and the child cried out, and immediately covered his mouth. Pete stepped between Pearl and the boy.

"Jeremiah! Don't do that—"

Pearl swept up his rifle and leveled it at Pete's face.

"Don't tell me what to do. I will bury you."

"Jeremiah."

"I'm all right," Benjamin stammered. "I'm all right, Pete. It's all right, Papa."

"Benjamin," Pearl said, and it was all he needed to say. The boy furiously packed their things, shoving his bag into the sack and pulling the drawstring closed.

Pearl kept the rifle trained on Pete.

"I don't like guns pointed at me," Pete said, level. Flat.

"I don't like jets flying directly over my position."

"I'm not . . . I'm just a social worker. That is just a plane."

"You disappeared on us."

"I told you the truth. I was in Texas looking for my daughter."

Pearl stepped forward, the barrel inches from Pete's face.

"Why aren't you still looking for her?" He poked Pete in the ribs with the rifle, hard. "Don't you care where she is?"

When he poked him again, Pete grabbed the rifle barrel and pressed the muzzle into his chest.

"You think I'd be out here if there was one thing I could do to get her?"

Pearl pulled on the gun, and Pete stepped forward, still gripping it, still touching it to his heart.

"You think I don't spend every second wondering what's happened to her? Do you have any idea what that's like? Go ahead, put me out of my misery."

Pearl yanked the rifle out of Pete's hands, and backed away. He and Pete regarded one another, something wordless and true shaping up out of the moment. Empathy even.

"Put these things back in Pete's bag," Pearl said to this son. "We're moving out in five."

The boy released his head, his handfuls of hair, and Pete told him it was okay, and they put the cans and puzzle pieces in Pete's backpack together. Pete said to leave the spilled things. He'd bring more. Then they followed Pearl into the wilderness.

They stepped cautiously in the moonless dark and finally set down for what was left of the night at some arbitrary hillside location that had no discernible advantage. It grew very cold in the depths of night, and Pearl allowed his son to fetch out their sleeping bags. They sat in them under the stars, watchful as stooped cats. Soft nutritious duff under them like a mattress. Just before dawn the boy was asleep.

"President Reagan was shot," Pete said.

"Is that the truth?"

"He survived, though."

Pearl nodded.

"I always thought it would be a European. Someone from Hollywood."

"Thought who would be European?"

"The Antichrist will survive an attempt on his life."

"Reagan's the Antichrist?"

"He's from Hollywood."

"Well, there you go," Pete said.

"Don't patronize me," Pearl said. "I know you don't believe any of this."

The boy stirred where he lay between them, and Pearl leaned over and petted his head.

"I see a lot of different people with a lot of different beliefs. Native Americans and Mormons—"

"*Mormons*," Pearl said, shaking his head. "That's not a faith. That's a company."

"Best neighbors I ever had were Mormons."

"Gnaw Bone was lousy with Jehovah's Witnesses coming by every week, selling a map to hell. A man comes to your house to give you something—a service, a good, a belief—you best set him back on his way."

"Gnaw Bone?"

Pearl frowned, as though he'd given something unintended away.

"Indiana."

"Your people from there?"

Pearl volunteered no more.

The birds began to trill at a dawn that couldn't yet be seen. Pete asked was it all right if he smoked and Pearl nodded. He rolled and lit a cigarette. When he was finished there was enough light to see how thick and close the trees were. Snags and huge sheets of moss.

"How long you gonna stay out here?"

Pearl spat.

"Till we die."

"Until you're killed, you mean."

"My soul will live forever."

"What about him?" Pete nodded toward Benjamin.

"He's fine."

"What about your wife and other children?"

Pearl spat.

"Look, I'm just trying to do my job."

"You're not here because of your job."

"You're right," Pete said. "I'm sitting up here in the sticks with you two for the sheer pleasure of it."

Jeremiah Pearl smiled and leaned back against the hillside with his hands laced, cradling his head, and closed his eyes. As if in the coming light of day he could now rest. "We all have a part to play. We're all instruments of His will."

"You're a lunatic," Pete said.

Pearl grunted. In moments, he snored.

The boy ran ahead and told Pete to hurry and they emerged from the brush and arrived at a thin and shallow creek that ran through a narrowing canyon. Boulders strewn like the toppled bulwarks of an old castle. The banks soon gave way to sheer rock and the child clambered up the ledges of the canyon on small footholds and disappeared around a jutting face about thirty feet high. The water was only ankle deep. Shot-through tin cans lay among the pebbles in the bed. Dried bits of paper and what looked like runny scat stained the walls. They arrived under a waney set of planks. The boy called down to him from somewhere in the dark ahead. Pete ventured forward and could just make out the green streak of the creek's origin somewhere above. He walked between timbers supporting the queer structure, a kind of fort straddling the creek at the top of the rock walls. Pearl pointed to a crude wooden ladder wedged underneath, and Pete climbed up.

The floor creaked beneath him and there was no room to stand. He touched the canvas roof. It was ably waxed to wick away water. When Pearl came up, it was evident that the whole space was barely big enough to seat them all. Even though it had been empty for many days, the air was heavy with the smell of the Pearls, of smoke and grease and pine sap.

"Is that the only way out?" Pete asked, pointing to the hole.

The boy crawled around him and propped open the canvas at the rear on a stick. Pete crawled out with him onto a ledge the size of a small patio. A vista of the wilderness, alder and cedar. Greater cloud-kissed mountains rearing up many miles away. A bed of white coals lay under a blackened overhang where they cooked. Pete peered over the ledge down a forty-foot face that aproned into a scree.

"Nice view," Pete said.

The boy slipped down the side of the cliff face to a foot-wide ledge.

"Okay, okay. Get back up here."

"I'm not gonna fall, Pete."

"Just come back."

The boy pulled himself up with a self-satisfied dexterity and sat with his legs over the edge.

"You afraid of heights?" Ben asked.

"Just falling from them."

Ben digested the joke and then chortled like a donkey.

He watched Pete squat and take off his pack. He took in every detail of Pete, and Pete understood now why he'd been lured into the school. The boy was terrifically bored.

Pearl pitched out some firewood from within the shelter and the boy went and started the fire. The man came out with three open cans and set them inside the fire pit next to the flames and crouched back inside. The ledge was small enough that someone was always at the lip, usually the boy. Pete was terrified the child would fall, and never got used to him walking along the edge.

They ate beans quietly. Ben watching to see if his father or Pete would talk, knowing that he himself should not. The back wall of the shelter was a rock face where the water ran like a leaky tap, which of a sort it was. You put a cup against the green slick and in a few moments it was full of potable water. At the other end of the shelter was a hole like an old-time jakes where they defecated down into the creek. Pearl took their cans and pitched them down the hole. The boy went out to piss off the ledge, leaning and twisting like he had a trout at the end of his line of urine. When Pete went to piss, the boy asked how far out could he could do it, he wanted to see.

"I can't go with you standing there," Pete said.

The boy laughed at this preposterousness.

"I mean it," Pete said.

His father called him inside and Pete could see the man's amusement by the lamplight.

"You can't pee with me standing there?" Ben said when he got back inside. "That's so hilarious."

"Hand me my backpack."

The boy pulled it out from the corner and slid it over to him. Pete opened it and plucked out a handful of loose crayons and the coloring book. He set them in front of Ben. But the boy didn't touch any of it.

"It's a coloring book," Pete said. "You've seen a coloring book, right?"

The boy nodded.

"Go ahead. It's yours."

"I can't."

"Why not?"

"It's graven images."

"Graven images?"

Pearl didn't look up from the knife he sharpened on a small whetstone.

"It's just trains and things. Look," Pete said, opening the book and beginning to color a race car. The kid sat there.

"It's not allowed," Ben said.

"Deuteronomy Four," Pearl added.

"Sorry, but you'll have to refresh me."

"It's forbidden to make a likeness."

"A likeness."

"A likeness is a distraction from God."

"A coloring book. Is a distraction from God."

"Everything. Television, trees, and animals themselves. Everything."

"This explains a great deal, Jeremiah."

"The world is a just grain of sand in all of everything that truly is. To linger on this world is foolish. To linger is to stare at your navel."

Pete sat a moment stock-still in the wake of this, the silliest thing he'd ever heard.

"Tell me something," he said, shoving the coloring book and crayons back in his bag. "Did Adam have a navel?"

Pearl smiled.

"Of course not."

They spotted a black bear sniffing up at them from the base of the cliff. Benjamin threw rocks down at it, and the animal bolted up the hillside opposite and disappeared in the trees. They ate fish and what food Pete had brought them. Pearl mended the boy's shirt, and when Pete said he could bring them some new clothes, Pearl supposed that would be all right. A sign the man had begun to trust him. And the boy's trust in him had blossomed into a fuller effort to impress Pete, about to the point of nuisance. He sought Pete's opinion on how he ought to climb that tree or how far he could throw that rock. He took Pete by the arm to inspect things, rotted tree stumps and bear shit. Black centipedes twisting all their tar-black thoraxes sent him about into ecstasy. The child was an insatiable collector of stones and bits of driftwood, pockets to bursting. A steady discourse poured out of him concerning the flora and fauna, anthills and snowberries and bobcat prints. Pearl seemed inured to it, quiet. Or maybe he was simply grateful for the fresh set of ears the boy now had handy.

A thunderstorm trekked in on gray curdled clouds, and the rock wall at the back of the shelter wept with rainwater. Pearl warmed his hands by cupping the lamp and he darkled the shelter, made capes of shadow on the walls.

All evening he worked his little mint on a round in the corner. Over and over, he'd set a penny on a railroad fishplate and with a punch and hammer knock a hole through Lincoln's temple, then chuck the coin into a coffee can. He did this to a few more presidents and then put a thin blade through the hole of one of them and affixed the blade and coin to a small jeweler's saw. He carefully adjusted the screws so as not to break the blade. Pete could see he only had a few of them left in the cardboard drawer. He waxed the blade with a small bar of yellow wax and then set the coin over the crotch of a wooden V-shaped bench pin and began to saw, turning the coin or the bench pin to suit the angles of his imagination. When it was done, he unscrewed one end of the blade from the saw and slipped the coin into his palm and held it up to the lantern, casting a watery pentagram on the back wall. All of it accomplished much easier by Pearl than the pawnbroker had thought possible.

Pete asked to see. The coin was warm, a perfect five-point star in the copper of Lincoln's head.

Pearl held up a paper sack of coins.

"I will have these punched and scored by tomorrow."

He tossed another sack made of felt and full of coins to Pete and told him to put the penny in with them. Pete dropped it in and fingered through the others. More stars and exclamation points and question marks and swastikas. Clovers. What looked like a scythe.

"I'd like you to disperse them," Pearl said as he threaded another coin onto the blade and then screwed it shut. "You can travel more widely than we can."

"I thought you were finished with the coins," Pete said. "Just a whimper, you said."

"This is it." Pearl rubbed his finger on the fishplate and his finger turned gray with the dust of the coins he'd vandalized. "The last money I'll ever touch."

He began to saw the next coin, a soft almost pleasing sound that for Pete immediately recalled Rachel pulling the zipper on her jacket up and down. Sitting in his car. Waiting for the light to change.

"Why do you want me to distribute these?"

"It'll be over soon."

"What will?"

Benjamin picked dirty sap from his hands.

"They will come and kill us."

"No one's coming to kill you—"

"Someone shot the president, Pete."

"So?"

"The Secret Service is an arm of the Treasury. They have two missions: keep the president alive and protect the integrity of the US dollar. And the latter, I assure you, is more important than the former. They know all about me, Pete."

"That's pretty grandiose, don't you think?"

"Obviously, I do not."

Pete looked at Benjamin, who continued to pick at his palm. A completely normal conversation.

"I won't take the coins," Pete said. "I won't take part in this."

"You'll do it," Pearl said, sawing into the coin. "And I know you'll do it because you don't want anything bad to happen to us. To him. And you'll do it because if you don't, you'll never see us again. And you'll do it because you believe you'll talk us out of these mountains and back into that society of yours. Because you're the nice face of things. The kind, caring face." Pearl stopped sawing, fixed his dark eyes on Pete. "The devil, I know how he comes. With cans of food and fresh clothes and coloring books."

"I'm just a person, Pearl. You gotta stop with all this paranoia."

"I'd ask you to entertain a notion for a little bit."

"What's that?"

"I'd have you consider that I might not be as stupid and backward as you think."

"I don't think you're stupid."

"Then I'd like you to be sincere in your desire to help us, and do what I'm asking of you rather than what you think is best for us."

Benjamin had ceased picking at his hands.

"Where's the rest of your family, Jeremiah?"

At this, Benjamin turned over in his sleeping bag away from them.

"Where are your other children?"

Pete swung the sack back to Pearl and it landed with a heavy plash of metal.

"Well now," Pearl said, "there's the difference between you and me. I can answer that question, and you cannot."

In the morning they got ready to set out and Pearl and his son went together onto the ledge and when they came back in Benjamin's nose

was running and he'd been crying. He bravely told Pete it was good to
see him and thanked him for the things he'd brought.

"You're not coming?"

"He's headed in the other direction," Pearl said. "Dry up," he told
his son.

The boy wiped his nose.

"I'll come see you again," Pete said. "Okay?"

The boy nodded at the floor.

"Let's go," Pearl said.

They descended one after another down the ladder and into the late
April rainwater that was now up to his thighs, the boy's waist. It was cool
and overcast. The boy didn't climb along the walls, and when they got out
of the water he was shivering and chattering on the opposite bank.

"So long, Pete," he said.

"You're freezing," Pete said.

"He'll be all right," Pearl said. "Now, go on."

Ben disappeared into the brush.

They walked all day and didn't say a word, even when they stopped
to eat or rest. When evening fell they kept marching and Pete had no
idea where they were in the trim and waxing moon. It was some deep
middle of the night when they made a road that stood out chalky in
the dark.

"You're just down there," Pearl said.

They were barely able to see one another.

"Give me the coins," Pete said.

Pearl dug them out of his small canvas bag.

"I'm gonna come up here in a week. I'll bring some more fruit and
dried beans and rice."

Pearl said all right. Then he did a peculiar thing. He clapped his
hand on the side of Pete's neck and touched their foreheads together.

"I'm praying for your family," he whispered before he turned around
and loped up the road.

＊　＊　＊

Where did she find Cheatham?

He found her. Sitting with her backpack at a taco stand in East Austin.

How was she?

She was sick. It hurt when she peed, probably because of the guy at the party. She felt like this meant she'd lost Cheatham. She didn't want to lose him. She just wanted to be someplace else. She just wanted to go. With him. Nobody else.

Did she tell him?

Are you kidding?

What did they do?

They looked at each other a few minutes. They ate and talked. She asked did he love her, and he said he didn't know. She asked did he want to find out. She wanted to find out.

They stayed at his place a few weeks, a bedroom in a house he shared with three other musicians. The walls were spray-painted silver.

She stayed in hiding, in plain sight. Afraid her mother would roll up Congress or the Drag by UT where Cheatham would go to play his guitar. She avoided cop cars like she was holding, like she was a fugitive, which of a sort she was.

Did she pester him to leave town?

No. A little.

When did they go?

When his friends started calling her Lines.

As in?

State Lines. As in don't take a minor across them. When they started calling him Chuck.

As in?

Chuck Berry. A musician who took a girl across state lines.

Where did they go?

Oklahoma.

He came from some money. Was independently wealthy for a nineteen-year-old dropout. His father owned dealerships or gas stations. He had friends all over the lower Midwest. From Arkadelphia to Nashville.

What did they see?

They saw county fairs. Prize-winning hens and pumpkins and hogs. Quilts and lace and art made of construction paper and painted macaroni. They saw panoplies of whirled lights. Barking underweight carnies. Racing horses yearning against the lash and the night.

The saw kicked-up chaff on the horizon like the froth on a beer. Purple thunderheads opening up like head wounds, violences of wind and rain. A gray tornado made of hailstones and earth, of trailers, stock animals, and tractors.

They saw trees wrapped by corrugated siding like the signage of the route to ruin.

Was ruin what they came to?

Of a kind.

What kind?

Indianapolis.

TWENTY-TWO

He called Beth to see had she heard anything, but she wasn't home or didn't answer, and listening to her phone ring and ring he felt how strange it was that she and he and Rachel had been scattered and sent off, aliens to one another, a broken valence, who knew a family was so fragile as that. And his father and mother gone, and his brother off in Oregon, and he was alone and he left work for Missoula to see Mary to see her to have her to be with her it was something at least.

The elevator in the Wilma was open and empty. No car, no cables. Pete leaned in and looked up the shaft to see the bottom of the car, lit from below by an open door several floors up. A repairman in a leather belt came down the stairs with blackened hands and said it was stuck, everybody'd need to use the stairs.

Mary's door was ajar. He rapped it with his knuckle. It swung open and gave onto a view of her fellating the lawyer in the kitchen. The man he'd followed. His eyes were closed and he clutched a juice glass. A hiccup of laughter from Pete put a halt to everything. She rose and spoke, pulling closed her shirt. The lawyer replaced his cock in his boxers and zipped up and tucked in his shirt and, thus composed, affected nonchalance. He drank from the glass, set it in the sink. Mary was saying something to the lawyer now and then they were both looking at Pete, and he realized that they were waiting for him to leave or move out of the doorway, and he wondered what expression he wore that made them stand in abeyance like that, what feelings authored this expression. He wondered did the lawyer recognize him, was Pete being made a fool of. He punched a framed picture several times, and it shattered and fell to the floor. Mary and the lawyer didn't move. He sat against the wall in the broken glass.

The lawyer could leave. The blow job was over. This was Pete's. It was over with Mary, but this moment was his. He realized he was saying these things aloud. The lawyer was asking Mary did she want him to stay. Then he was stepping around Pete and out the door. She reached the doorway of her apartment, asking was Pete quite finished. Her neighbors were in the hall, onlooking. He'd been yelling, he supposed.

She told him he was bleeding. She left the door open and a balding layabout in a stained T-shirt grinned at him as Mary went to the kitchen for a rag. She returned to him like she might a wounded animal, low-toned, flat-affected. She gingerly took his hand and plucked the glass from his knuckles and winced as she did so. It began with tending his hand, and it would end with tending his hand.

He felt sick. Then he kissed her. The mouth that had just had the lawyer's cock in it and the rivalry inherent in that. She was caught off guard and perhaps felt guilty or obliged, and he knew there was no affection or desire to win her back in this kissing, now on her neck— she sucked in air through her teeth like his lips were ice, as if this were all some kind of dare—and he thought to fuck her right there on the floor in the broken glass, but something subtly shifted between them and the spell or whatever it was was broken.

She let go of his hand, stood, and veered into the kitchen and drank a glass of water. From over the refrigerator, she got a pack of cigarettes and waited for the electric coil on the stove to light it. She seemed to be barricading herself in there. He kicked closed the front door.

Then she came out of the kitchen. She'd acquired a new self-possession. Even her posture was frank. She said she wanted to talk. Would he listen.

She said she needed things in her life to be separate. That she had a way she organized herself. Would he just listen. Would he just shut up a minute and listen.

Did he have any idea how many times she'd been raped. What a number it did on her mind. How much she's just out there coping. And the way she copes is, she's a bureau. Like a dresser.

Would he please just shut up for a minute.

There was this old couple. There was a room the old man took her in. An old-time dresser in there, like an apothecary cabinet. Dozens of little drawers. She wasn't allowed to play with it, it was antique. She wasn't even allowed in the room. But the old man would take her in there. She'd watch the dresser. Think about what was in the drawers.

She knows it's a totem. A way of organizing her life. But it was useful to see how the things that had happened and were happening to her could be sorted. When the man was on her, she said, *This just goes in that drawer there. . . .*

She put the bad things in those drawers, like little buttons. Then the good things too. She knows it's just a metaphor or symbol. It's just an organizing principle. It's repression.

She had this therapist who tried to get her to describe the drawers, what was in them. He made her do it. And all the drawers fell open and the buttons spilled all over the floor and by the time she got home, she was worse off than before, buttons everywhere. She had to pick them up one by one and put them all back. Took her two years. Ninety minutes with a psychiatrist and she's out two years, sometimes getting more new buttons faster than she can put the old ones away.

These rugby players, for instance. Reno, for instance. The Wind River Facility in California, for instance.

Would he look at her. Would he see she's telling the truth.

There was a time when a guy like him would be somewhere on the floor. Lost there for a long while. She'd forget who'd come to see her. Wouldn't be able to tell the one who had money from the one who had drugs from the one who liked to dance from the one who liked to make her feel like shit from the one who was kind and only ever pulled her hair, and even only when she needed him to.

She said she had a drawer for guys she could love. A few buttons in there. And he's in that drawer. And when he comes over, she gets so excited to open that drawer and take him out—

The lawyer is from a kind of bad drawer. Not the worst drawer. A bad one.

No, he doesn't hurt her. Not in a typical way. What he does is between him and his conscience. It barely has anything to do with her. In a way.

Would he look at her.

She does, she does probably love him like a normal person might love someone. But he's on the floor. And he has to get back in his drawer. The good drawer. Would he please just get back in his drawer. Just pretend this didn't happen. That it doesn't happen. Please.

He stood up.

"Mary," he said.

"What."

He opened the door.

"Fuck you."

He left.

Bender.

The shit they pulled.

Spoils on the curb explaining things to the cops. A man wants to knock out the windows of his own car, it's his business, Spoils says. Glass and blood all over Pete's file folders. The cops checking his license and registration, uncuffing him, telling Spoils to take him on home.

Pete on the dog-smelling bed with all the dogs and waking among the dogs and throwing up, and the dogs sniffing it and not hazarding to even taste it, these fine mongrels.

A call came from Indianapolis that social services there had picked up a girl that met Rachel's description. Pete drove eighty-five the whole way to Spokane and rode a red-eye to Salt Lake, slept in the terminal and touched down in Indianapolis thirty-six hours after he got the message. He took a taxi to the Child Welfare Office and was referred to a shelter on the north side of town, an ugly pale building shoved among the brick houses. A black man sitting on a bucket smoking looked down his nose at him.

By now coming on evening, the sun sidling and flashing up the windows under the discouraging clouds. Somehow he knew she wasn't going to be there, that it wouldn't be her, or that she'd be gone.

The shelter hadn't admitted anyone by her name, and when they escorted him through the wing of teenagers no one had seen a girl by the name of Rachel. He showed the staff a picture, and a savvy black girl slipped over to them and said she knew Rachel and said she knew where she was and could take him there right now. Soon all the girls said they saw her, lying to him, every last one. Their black city speech rushed by his Montana ears like freeway cars and he realized that if he was himself a country mouse what a small and bewildered thing Rachel must be.

The first girl was saying she did so see Rachel, fuck y'all, she did so see the girl, the girl was in here two weeks ago, had her hair cut all stupid with short bangs and long bangs like it didn't grow out at the same speed. The other girls' insults and insinuations redounded and amplified off the concrete walls, and the girl said Rachel was let out three days ago and wouldn't shut up about some dude, name of Cheatham.

"Cheatham? Cheatham what?"

"Last name."

"Rachel was with a guy named Cheatham."

"Yes. But she didn't say her name wasn't no Rachel. But that was her. In yer pitcher."

"What did she say her name was?"

"Shit, I dunno. It just wasn't no Rachel," the girl said.

The staff muttered to Pete that the girls were all liars.

"Wait. I think it was Rose. Yeah, it was Rose."

The wing manager wouldn't let him look at the intake books and smirked at his request in such a way that said the books were themselves a bit of a shared joke. Then a girl came in with a square of naked, bloody scalp and they said Pete had to go, meaning this was his fault, he'd riled the girls and their rickety routine, he'd taken staff from the floor and now look.

He stayed in a small hotel and the next day rented a car. First he tried to find out who had called him from the Child Welfare Office, but in the massive warren of cubicles there seemed to be neither accountability nor culpability, and from every nook emanated some sob or outrage or pleading that seemed to literally hover in a physical murmur over the cubicles and, condensing on the fogged windows, ran in beads like tears. The shift managers couldn't help him, no one knew who contacted him, and they all had calls to make themselves.

He located his poster of Rachel on the bulletin board, her face obscured by a new notice. He pulled Rachel's down and tacked it on top of the others and made for downtown. A few hours of walking and a few hours by the fountain at the base of the sailors and soldiers monument, watching the cars and the people go round the roundabout. He cruised the city, the clapboard neighborhoods and tenements and downtown alleys. Into the wholesale district. He saw vagrants of every age and description around the old Union Station. He parked and circled the abandoned brick and granite structure. Stern bartizans like watchtowers. The voices within. He went around the corner and knocked in the plywood over a broken window and pulled himself inside. He tread over a rime of pigeon shit on the ornate marble floors, footsteps echoing throughout the barrel vaults and so did his voice calling out for Rachel, for Cheatham. People hid in here and he said that he was just looking for his daughter, did they have any sympathy at all. He called out that she was with someone named Cheatham. Or Booth. Whispers carried on the dusty claustral air. Someone tell me something, he said.

A bottle shot over the iron railing toward him with a tail of dregs and exploded with a terse pop and fanned across the smooth floor in thousands of discrete shards around and between his feet with the fineness of rock salt.

He was a few days in the hotel, going crazy. He didn't drink, he didn't leave the room, he let the television talk at him. He wasn't going to lose it. He wasn't going to kill himself. He wasn't going to give up.

But what was there to do. Useless.

He went to a liquor store and bought a handle of bourbon and then to a grocery and fixed himself up with a packet of razors and a six-pack of Coca-Cola. He filled the ice bucket. He observed the television like a foreigner. He made a drink and the inanities of the game shows began to wear on him. When he looked away from the screen and out the window, the glass warped and rainbowed in his vision like a huge soap bubble and he realized he was hallucinating or crying or both. He took long drafts from the bourbon at the sink. He drew a bath. He wiped away the steam and regarded the man behind it, thin and pale, the maculate sunken eyes. It had grown dark. The water was lukewarm too, and he had lost hours and he was sure that he'd gone insane.

He climbed into the tub in his clothes. He drank and fumbled open the razors from their cardboard box. He practiced cutting through his jeans into his thigh. He felt nothing. A small pink bloom in the water.

Do it.

I can't.

Do it.

He leapt out of the tub and flung himself down the hallway into the raining night and through the parking lot, his wet feet slapping the pavement and on into a copse of trees where he fell and started pounding the mud with his fists like something might be accomplished this way and then screamed at the weeping sky what am I that I want to die. The leaves like shuddering lids of tin and razors of lightning and how could anything be okay in all this, the world is a blade and dread is hope cut open and spread inside out.

He woke to conversation.

"Door was open."

"What's that all over him?"

"Mud."

"What should we do?"

"Wake up, mister."

"Look at his knuckles."

"That lamp is smithereens."

"Get out," Pete said.

"It lives."

"GET OUT!"

"Box the motherfucker's car in. He ain't going nowhere till he pays for this shit."

It occurred to him to look at a map. Gnaw Bone, Indiana, was only an hour away.

It was scarcely a place at all on the way to Bloomington. A few houses, a closed barbecue joint, and a scrap yard with a man sweeping out front. He asked the narrow-faced proprietor was there a family by the name of Pearl in the area. The man said the only Pearls left a few years ago, but the missus had some people up the Clay Lick Road and gave Pete directions.

The house sat among blooming tulip trees. He was met at the screen by a compact barefoot woman in jeans and a stained sweatshirt. Pete said he was a social worker from Montana and just happened to be in the area and wondered if by chance anybody on the property was kin to Jeremiah Pearl or his wife.

His eyes adjusted to the low light in the house. An older, papery version of the woman at the door heaved herself from a recliner.

"Has something happened to my Veronica?" she asked, mashing out a cigarette on an ashtray by the door. The woman's daughter pushed open the screen and the thin old thing stood in the doorway and searched Pete's eyes for what he knew.

"I don't—"

"Something's happened. What's happened?"

"I haven't seen anything. I haven't seen her. But I have seen Jeremiah. And Benjamin."

"Benjamin," she said, as if the thought of the boy pained her.

"Yes."

She gathered the wattles of skin at her throat and looked liable to cry. She forced a grin on her face. It wouldn't be polite to do otherwise. Then she said for Pete to come in, and he followed her into the house.

He spoke with the woman and her daughter for several hours. They gave him strawberry soda. The women had sugar diabetes and couldn't have more than a sip, so they split a can three ways and the women sipped and smoked, the older through wrinkled and furry lips. They got out an old scrapbook and showed him pictures of the family.

VERONICA AS A CHILD and then as a blurry teenager, she hates having her picture taken. A healthy girl, handsome rather than pretty, country-pious, more than her sisters or mother or her father. God bless him. Heart attack last fall.

They showed him young-man Pearl, what he looked like without a beard. Doughy, pudging out around the belly. Given to spells of talk that end in sheer drops of hours-long silences. Times you can't shut him up, times he's stone still. He claims to have been a Green Beret but was in fact only a truck driver in Vietnam. He seethed in that heat and came back ginned up to do something with his life now that the war wasn't going to do it to him or for him.

He meets Veronica on a hayride of all goddamn things. At this point a woman of twenty. Not yet severe and with all the personality of a hatchet, but she has had religion since a tent revival four summers previous.

At the drive-in, she asks is he saved. Does he want to be. He answers sincerely. He's just out of the army and accustomed to being told what to do, craves it in fact, but couldn't take orders from a body as fucked up as the US Army, and sure as shit no church.

But Veronica, he'd eat glass for her, he says.

She tells him to come see her when he doesn't have the beer on his breath.

They are engaged inside of ten days and married when he has enough for a gold band and a down payment on a little place in Gnaw Bone. They don't answer their phone. Her family hardly sees her anymore, except at the movies. They are always at the movies. He meets her after work and they neck in the back of the theater or in the front seat of his convertible on summer nights, the grasshoppers leaping away from the headlights as they drive in the dark fields to the quarry to night swim and sleep under the stars.

He buys a Super 8 camera and they make little films. Goofy, typical stuff. People waving at the camera as they fix hot dogs. Kids flying off the rope swing into the shining river. Fireworks. Snow angels.

Twenty months later, two little ones, and she is a third time pregnant. They announce this at a barbecue of her extended family, hardy Irish farmers. Catholics. An uncle jokes, *Christ, it's a womb not a clown car.* They have to use tweezers to remove the bits of his eyeglasses from his eyebrow. The way her cousins hold Jeremiah back, Veronica's about sick with love for him. She doesn't hate her uncle, but that Jeremiah would kill for her seems to please her in an unhealthy way.

The next time Jeremiah and Veronica visit they come with a film projector and boxes. Her whole extended family on folding chairs set up in the living room, smoking, drinking a little beer, thinking they are about to watch some home movies. Veronica sets out mixed nuts. Soap and sundries. American Way—Amway, for short. Jeremiah explains the versatility and breadth of the brand. He goes to her mother, sisters, and aunts, squirting dollops of milky lotion in their palms. The men notice his light feet, his mincing step. He is not yet at ease with himself as an orator. He explains how such a tiny amount of this here soap will clean a whole load in the Kenmore. Try the mixed nuts. Now lookit the business plan. When he glances at her, Veronica gestures for him to mop his brow with his handkerchief and then she nods—he's doing just fine—to go on. He draws closed the jalousies and plays them the promotional film. A great opportunity to get in on the ground floor. A good start would be only a thousand dollars, maybe two.

My God, someone whispers loud enough for everyone to hear, *they want us to sell this shit.*

A winter later, they give silver coins for Christmas. Only precious metals ever keep their value, what with oil prices and the dollar, which buys less every year. The *fiat dollar* he calls it. The government's taken all the silver out of new coins, don't you know. Replaced it with the copper sandwich, don't you know. There are pamphlets out in the car, just a second.

Then for a few-month spell, all this money stuff seems like a phase. He gets a job at the Cummins plant. A damn good wage. Just the phrase *good wage* passing his lips is astonishing. He drinks beer, smokes cigars, wears cologne. They buy a Z28 and a pair of motorcycles. She gets a big TV and Kenmore appliances. New cameras. Polaroids and long-lenses and tripods.

"The movies," the sister said. "That's what did it."

Pete asked did what.

"She comes over crying her eyes out one day. The lab that develops all their film called. Said they didn't want her husband's money, that they are good Christians over there. Veronica knows immediately why. He's been taking 'private' pictures of her. I tell her not to worry about it, but when she goes home, they have this big fight. A couple days she sleeps in her old room here at the house. Leaves the kids with him and everything."

"And then . . ."

"He bought her a car."

The old woman nodded and the sister went for another strawberry soda and poured them new pink portions. After the car, something else happened, she said. Pete asked what.

JEREMIAH COMES ACROSS A stack of Jack Chick comics and a copy of *The Late Great Planet Earth* in the break room at the plant. He has a feeling he should take them home, and home they go, where Veronica devours them in a day. He returns from the graveyard shift the next morning to a wife afire with the Spirit of the Lord. Everything is in place for the Tribulation, she says. So much has been predicted, so little has yet come to pass. She talks about the things that she will talk about constantly from now on. The Six-Day War and the consolidation of Jerusalem. How the oil crisis of 1973 was predicted by Zachariah. How Israel will become a burdensome stone. The Antichrist is probably alive right now. Right now, she says.

Half the time no one knows what the hell she's talking about. Except Jeremiah. They come over and put on coffee. Want to talk to the whole family. He holds her a minute as it percolates. She fairly vibrates in his arms. It's like with Amway, the Tupperware, only it's the both of them going a mile a minute about the End Times and Revelations. Like they're on uppers. At some point, Jeremiah's outside with her father. The father, he's never bought into a single line of this stuff. He tells Jeremiah flat out that this is bullshit. That there's something wrong with the two of them. In the head. Jeremiah isn't upset by this. He hears the old man out. Then he says, *Either there is something wrong with her or there is something wrong with the world. I choose the world is wrong.*

Everybody else in the family quickly has it up to their eyeballs, this holier than thou and the politics. The sister, she plays along, just to keep them close. She attends church with them from time to time. But they have trouble finding a congregation with any fire to it. They go to tiny, weird churches in Ogilville and Walesboro led by emaciated unkempt burnouts and longhairs. They attend services for alcoholics and the homeless in a repurposed movie theater in Edinburgh. Drunks throw up in the pews and ask parishioners for money directly. A certain disheveled preacher in downtown Indianapolis shows them his .22 pistol under his corduroy jacket and asks can't they find a service for normal people, don't they see his flock is demented. They spend a few Sundays at a house-basement ministry in Bedford. The naked bulb, electric keyboard, handwritten hymnals, and fresh supply of drunks largely mumbling to themselves on the metal folding chairs. Invalids and muttering halfwits pass the empty plate.

For a time they don't even go to church, and take their cues from Hal Lindsey's book, and from the Bible directly. They give up shellfish and Christmas.

Christmas! With all those children they have now.

Then they remove all the images from their house. The teddy bears and television go on the front lawn for the trash pickers. Her mother hears what she is doing and rushes down for the picture albums, and Sarah sends her back with them and the cameras, and too the nice china, the flatware with the images of the Clydesdales, and the paintings of covered bridges.

By now they're hardly talking to anyone. They've started in with a new church, raving about Pastor Don, and you never see them.

And she's not Veronica anymore.

"I can imagine," Pete said.

"No, I mean she's changed her name. She's Sarah now."

"Her middle name," the mother said. "More biblical, she says."

"Pastor Don?"

They didn't know much about him. He led a small church outside of Martinsville. But they loved the congregation. They gave away dog-eared copies of books. The sister went to a shelf and pulled a few paperbacks down for Pete. *Coin's Financial School* by William Harvey.

America's Road to Ruin by Chet Hart, *The Startlingly True Visions of Isaiah* by Jan Meyer. In the back you can see how to order still more.

VERONICA—SARAH—IS MAKING pen pals with like minds, every week an obscure new tome in the mail, some of them ditto-copied in aniline blue and lashed together with rubber bands, dog-eared and coffee stained.

Some of them have swastikas.

You talk to her now and half of what she says is out of the King James. She says she feels pristine, original. That is, the book and the reading of the book answer an unput-to question that has been rattling around inside her for years, a doubt and anxiety that she was too late for everything, that history was over, that the era of miracles was past, that the world was altogether discovered.

But now is the beginning of the End. Now is the At-Hand Completion. Now the evening news reveals the great engine of His devise. When the Israelis are murdered at the Munich games there is riveting horror to be sure; but you can feel another piece of The Plan slide into place too. Armageddon unfolding right there on the *Wide World of Sports*. What dazzling events gestate, what will come, befall, occur, what is yet is only just yet.

Selah.

Now.

They fall out with Pastor Don's congregation. Their circle shrinks.

She's been having these grave headaches that she says go off like bombs behind her eyes, and there are times she has to rush to the sink or the toilet to throw up they are so bad. Times she is in her terry cloth robe on the bathroom floor, palms up, weeping at the ceiling and the kids pee outside on the side of the house. Days at a stretch she hides in the murk of her bedroom, afghans nailed over the windows, talking in tongues and singing only to emerge pale and quaking on stilted legs, begging their

father to *take them all, all of the children, just away for a few hours,* each discrete
noise is like a gun going off, and her ears are ringing, *Jeremiah, just take
them somewhere, just for a little while please I got to get a little sleep if I can. If I can.*

A summer day the sister drops in, finds Veronica on the kitchen floor,
flushed and nearly gibbering. Her dress is sodden with sweat and urine.
She'd been putting clothes on the line, so many clothes now with the five
kids, another—Ethan—on the way, when a headache crept on, a dull and
growing throe in the meat of her skull, and it pulsed behind her eyes. She
fell in the hugeness of it. She concentrated on her breathing. She was terrified something was terrifically wrong. There was a blade of grass in her
narrowed field of vision and on the blade was a droplet of dew. The sunlight
shattering through the tiny bulb of water. Too much.

She clambered inside, pulled closed the curtains, and sat in the cool
of the open refrigerator. The phone rang, and she ripped the cord out
of the wall. All her senses were fire. The hot, the bright. *This is crazy,
I'm goin crazy.* She tried to pass out. She prayed to pass out. She prayed
to die. She prayed to take her children, her husband, make everything
ash, just stop the pain.

I made a covenant with death, she says to her sister.

The sister asks what the hell she is talking about.

Veronica says, *With hell I am at agreement.*

She babbles about a vision, a vision that came in the cool wake of the
fire she passed through, everything scorched away. *The fire was a siren,
His way of getting my attention.* She saw mountains. She saw such priva-
tion. Hardship. It was the Tribulation.

Let them which be in Judea flee into the mountains, she says. *We must go.*

A month later, they are headed to Montana.

Pete took a sip from the syrupy soda out of politeness and then reached
for one of the albums asking "May I?" and flipped to the pages he was
looking for. Pictures of Veronica's mother and father with the kids in
the woods. Five kids, and the baby.

"Is this in Montana?"

The women nodded.

"The baby is little Ethan. Paula is five or six in this. Then there's Benjamin, Ruth is the second-oldest girl. Then there's Jacob—the oldest boy—and Esther, the oldest girl." She gazed at them a moment and then looked up at Pete. "You haven't seen any of them but Ben?"

"No, I'm afraid not. But Jeremiah says they're up there."

"You don't believe him," the woman said, staring into Pete.

"I just haven't seen them is all." He pointed at the picture. "When did they send this picture?"

"I took it."

"Tell me about it."

THEY VISIT WHEN the house is going up. Some friends they'd made are helping them out. Veronica's father is helping.

When the kids get back from Bible Camp, they have a dinner at a big table in the meadow down from the house, the better that they might look at their work. Fried chicken and watermelon and cucumber and iceberg lettuce salad with cream dressing and onions. The boys have crew cuts. The girls all wear dresses—they aren't allowed in pants. Veronica makes them bonnets. They look like homesteaders. Worse, they let the kids climb up on the new roof, those sheets of aluminum slick from a misty rain. Jeremiah only goes up there to get them down after she hectors him to do it, and when he comes back he says they ought to paint the roof because it can be seen from the air.

One evening, Jeremiah's holding forth on the porch. Some of those tattooed friends and the kids and Veronica's father. You could hear the whole conversation from inside. The usual stuff from Jeremiah. How it was the 1980s now and it was very, very late. How every man will soon have the Mark of the Beast. How that meant computers, how all the banks will be connected with computers, and did anyone doubt that at all. Credit cards. How the cards in their wallets were the Mark of the Beast.

Veronica's father asks what the hell that means.

Jeremiah says all the numbers are derivative of 666.

Veronica's father gets out his American Express and asks Jeremiah to show him, to use actual math.

Jeremiah begs off, says American money isn't worth anything.

It's the same old saw from back after the Amway days, the old man says. *Just like when you and Veronica first got together.*

It's Sarah.

Her middle name is Sarah.

Veronica's father is getting real hot by now. Then someone says something about Jewish bankers. Greedy fuckers. Holocaust was a fake.

Bullshit, I was in Dachau during the war, the old man says.

Thousands is all that were killed, Jeremiah says. *It's been blown all out of proportion.*

Do you know that for a fact?

Hell yes, I know it's a fact. Because it is a fact. It's established by historians, John. What historians?

"What historians" he says.

You mean the crackpots. Because credentialed historians—

"Credentialed"? Just who gives these credentials?

The universities.

Oh, riiiiight, the Ivory Tower. You gotta move out of power structures if you want—

Just give me a name. One name. A book by a real historian that says the Holocaust was a fake—

Guy by the name of Stussel has a fantastic book laying out the whole conspiracy. You have to do a little research, John. Just because they give you a shit sandwich to eat doesn't mean you put it in your mouth.

Why you—I sat in frozen mud for six weeks getting shot at by murdering Krauts and you want to tell me I don't know what I saw with my own damn eyes?! I was there—

Look, I'm no Nazi. But—

—and I know what I saw, and—

—you got to understand that if you make a country's money worthless and let the banks control everything, some people are going to stand up to keep what's theirs—

*I had friends killed by those Nazi sons of bitches and I'll be goddamned if
you'll shit on their memory! I ought to kick your ass! Get up! Get up right now!*

Just then Veronica says to come inside.

The old man is quaking and nearly plum with rage.

Veronica calls him again.

He squeezes the bridge of his nose. He squeezes his legs and stands.
Says the way Jeremiah is talking, somebody is gonna get hurt.

So be it, Jeremiah says.

You're insane.

Some people won't see the light until they feel the heat, John. It's just the way it is.

The old man is asking what the hell does that mean, but Veronica is
pulling him into the house, sitting him down with a plate of pie.

Jeremiah and his friends are quiet a minute.

Then you hear Jeremiah say, *The thing that needs to get done is someone
needs to kill the Supreme Court.*

They insisted Pete eat. They made him a baloney sandwich and chips
and more strawberry soda, they couldn't get enough of the stuff. It had
gotten on to dark and fireflies sparked outside the window. He'd never
seen them before and the mother and the daughter were amused that
he went out to watch.

When he came back inside, the daughter had set up the projector.
There were boxes and boxes of film. They screened a few of the Pearls'
movies before the old woman snored in her chair and the daughter took
her up to bed and left him alone to watch. There was no telling what
was on any of the reels. He just put them on and let them play. Canoes
on the water. Parades. A great many people balancing on things, sticking out their tongues.

Then reel after reel of babies, toddlers, children. Pearl walking
them, dancing with his little girls. Veronica with a sleeping newborn,
blushing. Blushing alone. Her naked shoulder. A short clip of Uncle
Sam on stilts, and then nothing but her skin. Her brown thigh and her
belly and the between of her breasts. The ridge of her collarbone and
valley in her neck. Pearl's country, his homeland.

✦   ✦   ✦

Where'd Cheatham go?

Knoxville to see a cousin.

Why didn't she go too?

He'd been moody going on a few weeks now. They would hit a truck stop cafe and he wouldn't talk to her through the meal. He'd brood at the windshield for the whole day. They'd pull into a KOA and he'd set up the tent and say he was going to get something to eat or a six-pack and he'd come back long after she'd not fallen asleep.

What did he smell like?

Like brown. Like whiskey, tobacco, and river water. He'd sleep until noon and then play his guitar all morning, and when she asked him could they go or was there anything to eat, he'd punish her another day with utter silence.

Then what?

Then of a sunset or a morning hard-on he'd finally try to kiss her, and she'd push him away, and he'd go sweet, and she'd give in, and he'd be happy and funny, and she'd be afraid to say anything about his deserts of inattention for fear of visiting another one.

And Indianapolis?

They got a motel. She sat by the pool some. He watched television and smoked and plucked at the guitar. She said she was bored, what was he doing, weren't they going to do anything besides sit in this hotel and not even talk to each other.

He put his guitar in his case and said he was going to go play outside for a while and that when he came back they could go get something to eat.

But he didn't come back.

Nope.

What did she do?

She wyomed. Hard. For a few days.

Did she call her mother?

She was thinking about it. Thinking about could she stand to go back. Thinking about how she preferred this freedom to that not-freedom, even though she was abandoned, but also it wasn't like she wasn't basically abandoned at home anyway.

She was holding the phone when the motel manager knocked on the door and then asked through the door if she was going to check out and she wouldn't answer. He left, came back, and opened the door with a master key. She said she needed to stay a few more days. That Cheatham had just stepped out and would be back. The manager said he needed payment, and she started crying and said Cheatham would be back and she couldn't see his expression with the sun silhouetting him like that, but he left.

Did the manager return with a police officer?

Yes. She tried to run, but the manager grabbed her arm and when she hit him the cop arrested her. She had no identification.

When did she go to the shelter?

After a night in the juvie jail. The black girls explaining their contempt of her to her. A couple of them pulling her hair, trying to get her to fight back. She just cornered herself, tucked herself into a ball.

How long was she at the shelter?

So briefly. Two days. It was a joke.

A fight in the cafeteria, the clatter of trays and silverware on the concrete floor, the staff rushing in, she wedged a fork in the closing door, waited for the commotion to crescendo, and slipped into the hall. A row of doors. Offices. Someone talking on the phone. Somehow she knew to simply walk to the end and out the back door onto the concrete patio where the staff smoked and up the alley onto the street, unhurried.

Did it work?

Of course.

But then what?

She walked an hour in what she hoped was the direction of the motel and then another hour when she started to recognize the surroundings.

Did she find Cheatham?

She scanned the lot for his car. She wyomed for a while in the grass.

Did she think of going home?

She did. And if she had the coins to make the call, she would have.

Her mother or father?

Her mother, probably.

What did she do instead?

She waited for an unfamiliar desk clerk to come on shift. By then it was dark. She asked was there a Cheatham checked in here. The clerk said no, but was she Rose. There was a letter for her.

From Cheatham?

Yes. A letter she couldn't finish through her wyoming. She threw the letter away and pocketed the cash.

What did she do?

She quit wyoming and went after him.

TWENTY-THREE

Pete had begun to feel like he was being watched. Glancing up on more than one occasion expecting his office doorway to darken, to hear a knock. He'd get home and think things had been moved on his porch. At night, he'd hear footsteps outside his house, an approaching car that never came up the road. He wondered was it his daughter was it his brother was it a ghost of his dead father his dead mother. Was it Pearl or his son.

Then sitting on the gallery at the Yaak country store he realized that if it was anyone, it was probably his brother's parole officer. The mercury had topped ninety and Pete drank an orange soda enjoying the heat and the shade when Wes Reynolds pulled up in his pickup. He put his sunglasses up under the visor, got out, and joined Pete on the bench. They watched the kids leaping from the bridge into the freezing Yaak River.

"You're pretty far afield of Choteau," Pete said.

"I followed you up here."

"The hell for?"

"You ain't been home for a while."

"I don't know where Luke is, Wes."

Wes grinned. His tooth was still chipped.

"Who said anything about him?"

"It's what you're doing."

"Why are you way up here in the Yaak?"

"Work."

Wes stood away from the railing and hooked his thumbs in his jeans and spat.

"What work?"

"I have clients . . . damnit, it's confidential. Quit snooping around my house. He ain't there. He ain't here. He ain't anywhere I know of."

"Fucker jumped me in the parking lot," Wes said. "He put me in the hospital."

"I'm gonna put you in the hospital too, you don't stay away from me."

"You know where he is, Pete."

"Fine, Wes. I do. I do know."

"Tell me where."

"Let me be perfectly clear: I'm *never* going to tell you. And you'll *never* find him, I'll make sure of that."

Wes stared at Pete a minute and then shook his head and ejected a laugh.

"You just fucked up, man."

"That some kind of threat?"

Wes got in his truck.

"Enjoy your pop."

Pete held up the bottle, took a swig, and with Wes watching him, walked down to river, disrobed to his underwear, and jumped off the bridge into the water.

The cold shocked him, but he swam down to the bottom and pulled himself along the rocks and moss. He lay in the long grass and warmed in the sun. Dragonflies hovered over him. In the shade of the gallery, drinking another pop, he was pleasantly chilled, smelling of river water and sunshine.

For a minute, he forgot all about Luke, but then he thought of Rachel—the way one might remember the disease ravaging his insides—and was compelled to get up and go to his car and do something, anything. He drove east, first for no reason, and then on to Pine Hills, as though it were on some calendar that he had just consulted. Ah yes, go see Cecil.

Pete again wasn't allowed to visit Cecil, so he asked to talk to the head of the facility, explaining that he was the boy's social worker and wanted to speak with him in order to file updates on the case. The facility head had the ashen pallor of someone very ill, someone no longer in possession of the will to resist requests like Pete's. Though they both knew that once Cecil was in the facility Pete's role in the boy's life was effectively finished, everyone answered to their paperwork.

They took him through an increasingly loud and scuffed series of halls and locked doors until they reached a kind of dayroom. Concrete tables and concrete chairs, concrete shelves. A pitted drain in the middle of the floor. Shelves held duct-taped board games and 1960s editions of *Boys' Life*. Many pristine Bibles. Around the octagonal space were arranged two floors of rooms, a high railing. The whole place was empty. The guard said everyone was at activity and Cecil would be sent for.

The fluorescents hummed. There were small windows in the concrete cupola and even those had chicken wire in them and only pale blue sky could be seen without, the sky itself perhaps a pane of paint.

A different guard escorted Cecil in, set him at the table, and stood by the door from the hall. Cecil's head was freshly shaved and pink and stippled black, and he had a black eye with an areola the color of margarine.

"Christ, what happened, Cecil?"

"They give me an X-ray. It ain't fractured they said."

"You in a fight?"

Cecil smiled. Nodded back toward the guard.

"He did that?"

The guard could hear them.

"You did this?" Pete asked. "Did you hit him?"

The guard removed a stick of gum, threw the wrapper on the floor, and said to Cecil that he had three more minutes.

"Bullshit," Pete said. "I'm his case worker."

The guard blew a bubble.

Cecil leaned forward, spread his fingers over the concrete, appeared about to say something, but didn't.

"This is fucked up," Pete said. "I had no idea it was like this."

"This is exactly what you said it was like," Cecil said. "Remember? I was gonna turn into a 'bad man'? Or did you forget the talk you gave me at my uncle's?"

"I barely slugged you. I didn't nearly fracture your face. I was only trying to get through to you—"

"He was only trying to get through to me too," Cecil called over his shoulder.

"Tick tock," the guard replied.

Cecil smiled, scratched his skull, picked at some scab, and then inspected the nail.

"Look, I came a while ago, but they said I couldn't see you," Pete said.

"I got in trouble."

"For what?"

"I burned somebody."

"Excuse me?"

"I saved my chocolate and I burned the shit out of him."

"Why'd you burn this guy?"

Cecil stared dementedly at the table.

"There's this microwave in the kitchen," Cecil said. "And I was on dishes and I put my commissary chocolate in a cup and microwaved it. And when he come up to turn in his tray I threw the hot chocolate in his eyes, man."

"Jesus."

"Fucker's face looks like a melted candle."

"Jesus."

"Get a chance, I'll have to kill him."

"No."

"No?" Cecil grinned.

"Cecil, look. I'm gonna see about getting you out of here. This is—"

"It's cool. Nobody fucks with me. Not now. Except staff, right, boss?" he shouted.

"Time's up," the guard said, rapping the door with his knuckles. Someone opened it from the hall. Cecil stood and started automatically for the door.

"Hold on! I haven't even gotten *three* minutes," Pete said, and the guard and Cecil both soughed, like they didn't have time to indulge him.

"I'm gonna go see your mom and talk to the judge, all right?"

"Sure."

The guard pointed at the gum wrapper he'd thrown to the floor. Cecil squatted, picked it up, and put it in the bin right nearby. Then, with just his fingertips on Cecil's tailbone, the guard directed him into the hall.

◆ ◆ ◆

Did she find him?

She waited in Nashville at his friend's house for a few days stretched into weeks.

Then what?

Hide nor hair.

Caught a ride west in a Volkswagen split window chasing the Dead. Kansas City to St. Paul to Denver. A few weeks at a commune outside of Boulder. Swimming. Sunning. The mountains again. A feeling of home to it, but no family, just whoever was around, she tried to be useful, she lent a hand until she felt like it was time she moved on.

Where did she stay?

She stayed where there were parties and if there were no parties, she stayed where there had been a party and then with someone who'd been at the party. She sought out fellow travelers.

Did that work?

More or less. There were detours, but then could you call them detours if you weren't headed anywhere?

Detours where?

Places. Situations. The Republic of California. She made advocates. Sometimes she just waited. Someone always came along. She could make him like her. She was tall for her age and had nice tits. The other girls said so, said she had nice tits. She got condoms and she put out. It was like the boys could tell she was up for it, and she always went for the nice ones. College soccer players and adorable stoners. She had a fake ID for buying beer and she had tops that fell off her shoulder and showed her bra strap or didn't show a bra strap at all. She wore mirrored sunglasses. She smoked.

So she gave up on Cheatham?

He was the one who ran off, not her. What're you gonna do, a person doesn't want to get found?

TWENTY-FOUR

He had a lead in Reno. The cops stopped a car near Lake Tahoe, the youngest girl inside went by the name of Heather but was the spitting image of the girl in his flyers. When she called, the social worker said she'd put a Polaroid of the girl in the mail. Pete didn't wait. He drove sixteen straight hours to the Washoe County Department of Family Services office and told them who he was and waited in the lobby, studying the stains on the carpet through bloodshot eyes. The blotches on the fabric pulsed in his vision, in his road-weary exhaustion, like amoebas, split and divided in a hallucination of life.

The social worker he'd spoken to emerged from the plantation of cubicles and introduced herself—"Jenny Lovejoy," she said—and then asked was he all right.

"Not exactly," Pete told her. "I mean, you can imagine."

She cocked her head.

"I drove straight down."

"Right," she said. "Why don't you ride with me."

She was thin and tired-looking herself and drove him to the Plato

House emergency shelter in a silence that may have been respectful of him but was probably for her own benefit.

When they got out of the car, the sunlight shimmered off the hoods and Pete thought he might fall over. He leaned against a pickup and scalded his elbow on the fender. The woman was already at the door and she came back across the skillet of pavement and asked him again what was the matter. He said everything was the matter and that his father had died. Everything was the matter. She was quiet like she didn't know what to say or perhaps had just employed a therapeutic method or was quite simply annoyed. The way she squinted in the sun, her hooded eyes like caves. *I'm goin crazy*, he thought.

"It's so hot," he said.

"Let's go inside."

"I don't think I can take it if it isn't my daughter in there."

She looked in the direction of the building, the windows palely mirroring back the scorched tableau of the two of them, the lot, the untouchable cars.

"There'll be a picture in her file. I'll get it. That way you don't have to go in."

The unceasing sun coruscated off the windows of the buildings and the chrome and even the heat-hammered pavement that shone in places around the lot like slicks of hot oil. He paced out the few minutes it took the woman to come back. She handed the picture to him, the same featureless squint making her face look like it had melted some. He cupped the photo in his palm. The girl looked exactly like Rachel. They could pass for sisters.

He spent Saturday, the Fourth of July, in the casinos, earning comps right at the bar. Idly selecting lucky integers on the number pad beneath the smoky glass under his drink. He slipped coins by the handful into the machine and sometimes some of Pearl's coins, which the machine spat out in the metal tray at his knees. In this way he left all manner of Pearl's scrip at a few bars in Reno. It was something to do and then it felt like he was doing something. Like he was really sticking it to somebody.

At a hotel casino, a lank guard confronted him about the coins.

"You the one leaving these in the machines?" he asked, holding up one of Pearl's quarters.

"Yes."

"You need to come with me," the guard said.

Pete took his drink with him and sat in a plush chair waiting for the casino manager to come.

The man arrived toting a tank and breathed from an oxygen mask for a few minutes before he croaked out that it was against the law to put anything but legal tender into the machines.

"Those are real coins."

"They are . . . marred. You . . . need to . . . leave."

"The hotel too?"

"Reno."

"You can throw me out of your joint, but not town."

"What . . . are you even . . . doing . . . here?" the man asked, sucking oxygen and regarding Pete with a measure of interest. The coins. He had to wonder what Pete was trying to accomplish with the coins.

"That's a good question," Pete answered.

Three days later, he was sleeping under the stars, deep in the Yaak with Jeremiah and Benjamin Pearl.

They were all out poaching together. Pearl made a crude blind in a thicket of thimbleberry upwind of a muddy meadow while Pete and the boy walked a little farther to a shaded spot where they could bugle in some elk. Pete knew the elk weren't in rut and would, if anything, wonder what the hell all the hollering was about, but he kept his mouth shut. Maybe they'd get lucky.

As it turned out, Benjamin was pretty good with the bugle, better than Pete at achieving the breathy moan that curls at the end into a lonesome scream of the rut. The sound put him in mind of his father. At the bugle. Blowing. Watching through the binoculars. A time he and Luke are hunting with the old man, *them elk'll be right over this ridge, you two be ready* and sure enough there stands a royal bull, his breath in thick handkerchief exhalations. Something aristocratic about the animal, as though it might slap you with a glove and challenge you to a duel. They all quietly kneel and aim and shoot at once and the bull's forelegs drop and then the rest of it, and when they get to the animal, steam and pink and bubbles issue from a hole no bigger than your pinkie finger and the elk is very neatly dead, and only one of them hit it, no one can take credit.

But the old man says, *Nice shot, Luke.*

And you, you still remember this slight.

Of course, Benjamin called in no elk or other animals, though several large creatures of opportunity—vultures, hawks—gripped the power lines running from a metal tower that bisected the meadow. When Jeremiah gave up on the elk, he let Ben run over to gawk at the tower. The boy was only gone a few minutes when he shrieked, and Pearl and Pete looked at one another and sprinted toward him, both hollering that they were coming.

The scene at which they arrived was macabre. The boy stood at the edge of an area no bigger than a patio where the grass had been walked flat, and on which several dead animals lay in a writhing smoke of flies. There lay a turkey with a parcel of naked black skin near what looked to be the desiccated corpse of a raccoon. Not far away a deer with its throat ripped open lay next to a coyote. The coyote on its side like an exhausted, sleeping dog. Next to it a fox. Strangest of all, the black bear. Flat on its back, legs and arms spread wide, as though it were playing dead or at a kind of profane joke. Huge bluebottle flies worked over everything and the air hummed with them, the air was charged as by a television picture tube with the sound all the way down.

Pearl squatted near the turkey and plucked a loose feather from the bird, the feather's vane burned away.

"Don't touch anything," Pete said. He put his palms in the air in front of him. "You feel that?"

Pearl stood. Gripped Ben. A power line snaked down from the tower into the grass and Pete pointed to it.

"That's a line down."

"Ho shit, let's step back, Benjamin," Pearl said.

They paced backward the way they came, but this time gingerly as sappers, and stopped and looked back and talked animatedly about the electrocuted animals and then retreated to the far side of the meadow and up the hill to a naked outcropping where they could watch what might happen next. The turkey vultures turned in slow circles, black and cruciate, waiting for them to leave. The men and boy were as giddy as princes.

"It seems cruel to watch," Pearl said, chuckling.

He pulled the binoculars from his eyes and handed them to Benjamin.

"You ever seen such a thing?" Pete asked. "This is nuts."

"Here they go," Benjamin whispered, as the first of the vultures landed and waddled awkwardly toward the carcasses. Drawn by their own natural valence toward death. Several more landed in proximity, and immediately the birds began to jostle for position, all six or seven of them hopping and striving, at last perching on the bear, the coyote, their wings folding in and fanning out like black umbrellas triggered to open according to their enthusiasms.

Pearl took the binoculars from his son.

"Maybe they shut off the power."

"Nah. You could feel—"

There came the flash and a millisecond later the air clapped with electrocution as two of the vultures stiffened in attitudes black and fixed as logos before they fell over smoking. The remaining birds heaved into the air. The Pearls and Pete gasped at one another like twelve-year-old boys. Then they rollicked with laughter. They waited a half hour for the vultures to land again, and though the birds circled in the air and perched and longed from the tower, they seemed to have learned their lesson. What a thing to see, Pete, Pearl, and the boy were saying as they headed back to camp, and when the evening air cracked again they laughed again too and wondered aloud were vultures that stupid or what manner of opportunist had been killed this time.

What a thing to see.

.   .   .

Pete had brought a cloth checkerboard, and Pearl allowed him to teach the boy to play, as it didn't seem to represent anything except for war, and war was what Pearl was teaching Benjamin. Pearl was all right with war in the abstract. Chess, with its icons of castles and knights, was out. Checkers, okay. Pure.

Pete showed Benjamin the rules, how to avoid getting jumped. It was a wonder that the boy had never played it. But consider the child's abbreviated understanding of the world, the fences round his experience. He'd heard that men had gone to the moon, but only in passing and said he did not believe it. He believed that demons coursed through the woods but were drawn to the cities, where they mostly performed their devilry among the coloreds and people who worked for the government and spoke foreign languages in their homes. He could count very high and spell a great many words, but he knew better all the apostles and the books of the Bible in order. He'd never stepped foot inside a public school classroom. Homeschooled, he never played with a child outside his immediate family or the families of various churches they'd gone to, and even then it seemed obvious that his shy and ponderous nature prevented him much interaction with anybody, young or old. Except for the time, the one time, he'd gone to the school in Tenmile.

The boy studied the board in the dirt by the fire.

"Hey, Ben. Can I ask you something?"

Benjamin nodded.

"Why'd you go into that school that day?"

The boy leaned over to examine his positions on the board.

"The lady on the playground said I had to."

"But why were you on the playground?"

"I dunno."

Benjamin jumped one of Pete's pieces.

"You can keep going," Pete said, showing where he could jump again.

"That's all right. I don't want to take all your pieces."

"I think you have to, if you can."

Pete moved the piece for him and set another red checker in the boy's hand. Benjamin stacked them neatly with the others.

"Did you find your little girl?" he asked.

"Nope."

"I'm sorry, Pete."

"Thanks."

They played a few minutes more, and Benjamin glanced in the direction of the creek where his father had gone.

"I ran away this one time," Ben said.

Pete folded his arms and asked was that so.

IT WAS A SUMMER CAMP at Hayden Lake, Idaho. He didn't want to go, but Mama and Papa made him and his brother and sisters too. The camp is all right. Games, and you can earn candy if you do your chores and all your Bible lessons. Songs around the campfire. Fishing the lake. Tubing the ice-cold creek.

One afternoon they are made to hike up to a clearing with only the pastor to hear some more about Chinese Communists. How they kill little girl babies and how the people are rounded up into camps, not like this camp not at all, but like—

The pastor is interrupted as men on horseback come from every direction firing guns in the air, throwing smoke bombs. Some of the older children laugh, stand up. The little girls are crying before the pastor is dragged away, hollering, kicking up dirt. Now all the girls scream and the littler boys too. At the edge of the clearing, just before the trees, the pastor gets loose. He's at a dead sprint and one of the men pulls a pistol out from under his duster and everybody screams and he is shot and falls and now everybody is grabbing everybody else and bunching up like spooked sheep.

The men's bandanas cover their yelling mouths. There's smoke coming from somewhere, everywhere. The horses step in place at all of this carrying-on, the children dashing around, huddling, the young ones by now blubbering. Then a pickup and trailer come barreling through the meadow and more men get out and order the children to climb in back.

Ben's big brother Jacob breaks for it. His sister Esther screams for him not to, but he's running across the meadow. Two men on horseback go after him and sweep him up and for a moment he dangles in the air between the two horses his legs pumping, it looks almost like they'd tear him in two. Then he is thrown across a pommel and taken to the trailer. Ben's big sister Esther is already lifting his little sisters Ruth and then Paula into the trailer. She reaches for Ben, says to come on. *It's just pretend*, she says. The smoke has cleared and she points to where the pastor is pulling on a duster, covering his face with a bandana. It's okay, she says.

But Ben drops and crawls under the trailer, his belly wet from the grass, and then to the hitch and no one has seen him and he keeps on crawling, under the truck and out from under the front of it. He's almost to the forest by the time anyone spots him, but in no time, hoofs fall behind him, all around him. He feels a hand on his back, he's lifted by his shirt. He throws up his arms and slips out and keeps running. He doesn't know how he knows how to do this, he just does it. He scampers into the trees and into the brush cutting at him and the horses don't or can't follow, not directly. He's hopping and trip-ping down a ravine and into some more brush. He drops flat onto the ground. Pine needles all in his chest and neck and chin. Panting on the ground, trying to be quiet. Dirt in his mouth. The fat of his palms bleed. The men are distant. Esther yells for him. Hoofs pound by a few yards away, go far, swing near again. He's breathing heavy and trying not to breathe heavy. He stays put. Horses charge past. Men say *Get him!* and *Gotta find that boy!* and such things.

He tucks his knees under him and peeks through the brush. Now he knows it's not real, but he's afraid of getting into a different kind of trouble. He hears the truck leave the meadow. But the men on horses still search for him. They ride through the woods. They ride right by. They call to him. It's okay, they tell him. It's just a lesson. The other kids are okay. Nothing bad is gonna happen to him.

He doesn't move. He can hear them talking about him. What a

little bugger he is. He knows it's safe, it's okay to come out, but he don't want to. Maybe it's bad of him, but really it's not bad because even when he wants to get up, he can't.

He can't make himself obey.

He realizes then what all his mama and papa have been talking about all these years. How they will be hunted down and killed and what that will be like, and it's okay because what comes after is heaven and they'll all be together it's not for us to question only to obey. He *is* an obedient boy. Obedient to God. He knows what he's supposed to do.

Now the men are on foot and Benjamin is standing there waiting for them. The man's bandana is around his neck, and his chin and jaw are almost blue where he shaves them. The man has Ben's shirt, and when Ben goes to him, he helps him on with it. They give him some water from a canteen, and the man lifts him onto the horse and climbs up into the saddle behind him. They ride slowly across the meadow, the man's hand on his belly. He's never been on a horse, and the animal swaying under him and the grasshoppers leaping away from the footfalls of the horse steady his heart. Everything runs from a horse.

Pete said that sounded like it was scary.

Pearl returned with a tarp, fishing line, and a needle. He sat within earshot and began to mend a hole in the canvas.

The boy was quiet, but maybe not because of his father. This was the longest he'd ever spoken to Pete and he seemed depleted. He told Pete it was his turn.

They jumped one another's pieces until only a few kings remained on the board.

Benjamin sat cross-legged with his chin in his hands.

"Do you miss her?"

"Of course I do."

"Why did *she* run away?"

Pearl glanced up, but didn't say anything.

"It's sorta complicated."

Now the expectant boy was looking at him.

"She and her mother went to Texas," Pete said.

"How come?"

"Her mother and I weren't getting along."

"How come?"

"Benjamin," Pearl said.

"It's okay," Pete said. "Her mother did something she oughtn't have, and it made me really upset."

"Was she bad?"

"Benjamin, leave him alone," Pearl said.

"It's all right, Jeremiah," Pete said. "She did a bad thing. She's not a bad person."

"Sometimes God needs you to do a real bad thing, only it's not a bad thing when He wants you to do it, because nothing that God commands you to do is a bad thing. Was it like that?"

Pearl had stood. From where he was, he couldn't see Benjamin's face. Neither, for that matter, could Pete. The boy's eyes were trained on the board. Pearl was waiting to hear what the boy would say next. Just then, Ben looked up at Pete, a whorl of notions spinning behind his eyes. Things he'd seen and done and had happen to him.

"You all right?" Pete asked. Pearl cocked his head back and his mouth fell open as if he were watching a doorknob turning and he was just waiting to see who would walk in.

"Would you like me to pray for your daughter?" Benjamin asked.

"I think that'd be all right."

Benjamin closed his eyes and laced his fingers together over his heart.

"You don't need to do it this second," Pete said.

Pearl sat back down, folded his hands on his lap, and closed his eyes too.

"Lord, we ask that you in your wisdom, that you keep Pete's little daughter—"

Ben peeked one eye open.

"Rachel," Pete said.

"—that you keep Rachel in your safety, Lord, and you watch over her in her journey from persecution Lord so that she can be reunited with her father Lord. Amen."

"Amen."

"Amen."

Benjamin sighed with satisfaction.

"I forget whose turn it is," he said.

Pete moved his last king toward Ben's last king, and for a while they evaded one another in silence.

Under the boughs of a larch Benjamin found a freshly killed and mostly eaten deer. Pearl spoke endlessly of catamounts. How they are the only creature that kills for sport. How their survival requires murder.

And, my word, the wolves.

He'd been to a Fish and Game meeting in Libby where a wire-rimmed geek proposed repopulating the Yaak with Canadian wolves. Pearl stood and promised he'd shoot them on sight. Said he'd lace roadkill with strychnine. These people from the universities and DC were out of their fuckin minds, he said. What pox they would call "endangered" next.

The boy took the skull and the antlers from the deer and they walked down out of the mountains along a gray belt rock face. They could hear a falls somewhere upstream and the boy wanted to see it and so they went. They sat and sunned themselves as the boy ran up and down the rock stairs of the cascade, Pete worrying the whole time he'd fall in and be swept away.

They skulked across Highway 2 and back into the Cabinet Mountains. Another part of the Pearls' circuit opening up to Pete. A country cut by glaciers into humongous serrated mountains and scalloped peaks.

They shot a small deer and spent a few days in the dilapidated remnants of an old mining camp, sleeping in the shallow shaft. Pete and the boy performed amateur archaeology on the site, digging up Chinese potsherds and even a lion of carved ivory. The boy wouldn't keep it, wouldn't let Pete keep it, and discarded it somewhere in the woods.

The second day they found fabric and weaved grasses and charcoal, and inside the last threads of a burlap sack a watch, corked and stained glass vials, and a dense black talon the size of Pete's palm.

"The mountain lion that came from must've been huge."

Pete laughed.

"What?"

"This isn't from a mountain lion. It's a fossil. It's a dinosaur claw."

Benjamin swallowed, leaned away from it, then asked could he hold it. Pete set it in his hand. The boy's arm sank a touch under the weight of it.

"It's heavy."

"It's a fossil. It's rock."

He'd never seen anything so evil, he said, then ran uphill to where his father was hammering around in the mine. When Pete trudged up to them at the mouth of the hole, they'd set it on the ground and were squatting before it like two boys at a dead snake.

"Pretty cool, huh?" Pete said. He conjectured that it was found in the Sawtooths. There were quite a few fossils in that range. Or perhaps the Chinese settlers had brought it from China. Neither Pearl said one single thing.

"You two all right?"

"It's just amazing," Pearl said. "The power of Satan. Whoa."

Pearl went on to explain to Benjamin how Satan had left these all over the Earth.

"You're fucking kidding me."

To confuse people and put them in doubt, Pearl said. Such is Satan's power.

"Of course," Pete said. "You don't believe the world is old as it is."

"As they say. As old as they say. No, I don't."

"How old is it then?"

"Six thousand years, tops."

Pete asked for the canteen. Pearl handed it over, and Pete glared at him as he drank. He wiped his arm on his sleeve and handed it back.

"Do you know they can tell how old a rock is by the carbon—"

"Radiocarbon dating. Yes. Radiometric dating too. I know about these. I also know they yield all kinds of conflicting results. When you get back to town, I'd encourage you to look into a book called *The Prehistory Lie*. By . . ." Pearl tapped his skull, trying to remember this author. Obscure and self-published, doubtless.

"So that talon right there, it never existed."

"Yes."

"And it was put in the rock by Satan, right?"

"It's what we're up against. The Deceiver is powerful."

"Christ," Pete said. "Sorry—*Cripes*."

Pearl smiled.

"That's all right. It's your soul to do with whatever you wish," Pearl said. "Though taking the Lord's name in vain is annoying. What with so many perfectly good curse words like *fuck* and *shit*, and even *holy shit* . . ."

When the boy laughed, Pete realized Pearl was teasing him.

"There *is* a great deal of scholarship that goes ignored in the universities," Pearl said. "Serious scholarship that does not comport with the Zionist agenda."

Pete saw a harangue coming on and sat. Pearl cited the work of Dr. Jones and Archbishop James Ussher, who, though he was certainly burning in hell, calculated backward from the reigns of the kings of Israel to the Creation. He allowed there was some divergence of opinion on the exact age of the Earth, what with the cumulative uncertainty from verse to verse.

Pete realized that to Pearl, Satan had staged the world in this and every ancient particular. Pete imagined what it would feel like to believe such a thing, to see the very Devil ranging about the Earth like an art director, crafting fictions in the schists and coal seams and limestone. All to cast doubt on the Bible's timeline. All for the harvest of lost souls. Maybe it would be worth it for the Devil. You could almost picture it. Almost. You could almost believe a book more real than the real, more actual and relevant than terra firma and all the dull laws that govern it.

"You know, Jeremiah," Pete said, "if I believed the things you did, I'd act at least as batshit as you do."

"Rawls," Pearl said.

"Rawls what?"

"*The Prehistory Lie*. It's by Rawls."

They spent a day climbing up into the floor of a glacial cirque. They hiked an esker that cackled with snowmelt and camped in the dark on the shore and in the morning washed their clothing in the turquoise tarn. Pearl fished, caught nothing in the blue milk water. The setting sunlight bled up the mountain past the bands of gray sill that bisected that massive rock.

They ate deer meat and rice and dried fruit. Pete and the boy played checkers again by the fire and then the boy wordlessly joined his father, sitting between his legs. In time he was asleep, Pearl petting his head.

"That's a good kid," Pete said.

Pearl nodded. It may have pleased him to hear so.

Pete thought about asking where the rest of the Pearls were. But Pearl would answer with a question: *where is your daughter?* And these absences were twinned in Pete's mind as if the one could not be solved without the other, and he harbored the absurd hope that the revelation of the one would reveal the other.

It made sense in his heart and his heart only.

"I left some of your coins in Reno," Pete said. "When I was looking for Rachel."

"I'm sorry you haven't found her."

Pete nodded, swallowed, gazed into the fire. He fetched a flask from his backpack.

"I don't suppose—?" he asked, holding up the liquor.

"No," Pearl said. "No thanks."

Pete unscrewed the lid and took a pull from the metal container and set it on the stump, reflecting warped fire in its shiny and scored surface. He rolled a cigarette.

"Is your wife looking for her too?" Pearl asked.

"She's messed up." He stopped rolling the smoke, but thinking of how to explain her to Pearl made him tired. "Let's just say I've been to Washington, Texas, Nevada, and Indiana looking for Rachel, and Beth hasn't even left Austin. I dunno. She's . . . I dunno."

He resumed rolling the cigarette. Felt Pearl's silence like an open oven, and when Pete looked up, Pearl was staring at him, hard.

"Where in Indiana?"

"Indianapolis."

"You went to Gnaw Bone," Pearl growled.

Pete's mouth went dry. He tucked his hair behind his ear and the cigarette with it.

Fuck.

"Go on," Pearl said. "What did you find there?"

"I need some water," Pete said.

"I'll bet you do."

Pete fetched the canteen from nearby and drank under Pearl's calculating gaze and wondered if he should run. But it would be across all these stones and he'd be easy to hear and easy to fell and if he made the woods Pearl would track him down eventually, certainly.

Stupid, stupid, stupid.

Pete drank some more.

This is how you die.

He set the canteen by.

"Yeah, I went to Gnaw Bone. Only because I was already in Indiana. Only because I couldn't find Rachel and I was sitting in a motel room going crazy. And yes, I was curious about you and your family. I met your mother-in-law and sister-in-law. They were nice folks."

Pearl touched his fingers to his son's skull, traced his forehead.

"Do you even have a child? This Rachel. Is she even real?"

"Yes." Pete leaned over the fire so Pearl could see his eyes. "Look at me. On my mother's grave. I am *not* lying to you. I got a call that they'd found my daughter. But she wasn't there."

"You went to fill your file on us."

"My office doesn't have the budget to fly me—"

"What office? How do I know who you are? Your badge?"

"Well if you don't trust me, why let me be with you and Benjamin?"

Pearl sat up. The boy stirred in his arms.

"Because I know that out here, the moment I need to, I can kill you. But just because I've made us safe from you doesn't mean you're not a snake."

Pearl carried the boy to his sleeping bag. Pete listened to them murmuring and wondered would Pearl kill him, but knew somehow that he would not. Instead, Pearl sat back down and asked was there anything left in Pete's flask. Pete palmed it to him across the fire. Pearl regarded his dished reflection in the metal before he took a drink.

They sat quietly in the dark for a long time, Pearl sipping from time to time. Pete felt like a midwife, waiting, waiting.

"I spoke to each and every one of them," Pearl finally said, wiping a sleeve across his mouth. "And to a man they said to my face they would join us. I told them I was going to buy the land and that I was selling my house and I spoke to them about the proper preparations. They said nothing against these preparations. I sold my motorcycles and pickup. I provided literature on how to convert property to gold. . . ."

His eyes drifted down to the flames lashing upward.

"A man manages to salt away a little something for a rainy day. A farmer, first time in ten years he's been able to put something in the bank. A year of all this God-given rain and the kernels of corn in all their thousands on that acreage, and that corn arriving at market when prices are at an all-time high . . . and he means to put the proceeds in the bank?! And I'm the crazy one."

Pearl read the fire for a while longer.

"And Pastor Don. Liar. 'I do not suffer a woman to teach, nor usurp the authority over the man, but to be in silence,' he says. She dreamed that we would find a building in Gnaw Bone to make our church, and we did. She dreamed that the Soviets would launch a space station and that there would be an earthquake behind the Iron Curtain, and lo, there was an earthquake in Romania. I'd never heard of Romania until she dreamed of a disaster there. She dreamed of the air crash in the Canary Islands as clear as she had been there. And she dreamed of the mountains and the only fat pasture in them, and we found that fat pasture in Montana."

The wind churned starlights in the water. It grew colder.

"She was a prophet and I a watchman to that congregation. But they would not suffer a woman."

Pearl looked at the flask as though he'd just discovered it in his hand.

"I used to drink a lot. Too much. When I met her, I didn't want to anymore."

He tossed the flask back to Pete. It clattered empty on the rocks.

Pearl left him alone. The sky clouded over and in the perfect starless dark the fire made Pete feel naked and he let it burn out and huddled in his own bag listening the night long to the wind and the occasional owl and other things unseen knocking and cracking among the sticks and stones.

The next day a pair of fishermen descended the rocky moraine to the water and waved to them from the other side of the tarn. The men were a long time coming around, and Pearl was cautious and brusque with them and lied that the fishless water teemed with trout. Pearl and Benjamin packed up, and in a quarter hour they were hiking out of the cirque and down into the forest. Pete stayed behind. He watched the men fish and spent the night with them and when they gave up on the tarn the next morning, hiked out with them and got a ride to Libby and called the judge to come get him and take him to Tenmile.

Did she arrive in Seattle?

Yes. She stayed. At last she stayed.

Why?

She had begun making a different kind of first impression. She made people uncomfortable. A worrying aura about her. She felt their hesitations.

And she was burned out. But in Seattle, she was off the hot blacktop. She thought she might settle down. She'd met a boy in Fresno who flopped in an apartment subsidized by a Quaker church. A thin thing named Pomeroy who had her dye his hair jet-black and was the only one in the past months and a year to ask her about herself.

Where you from, girl?

Montana.

Montana. Shit. Hell's from there?

Me, I guess. Texas too.

Texas too, what?

What?

Texas too? How you from two places?

Don't tease me.

Why you out here on the streets?

I was with a boy from San Antonio for a while. He took me to Indiana.

What boy?

Just some boy.

Maybe I know him.

Cheatham.

She rubbed the dye into his hair and a black tear ran down his forehead toward his eyes. She daubed it with the washcloth.

What's he look like?

Sit still.

I don't want none of this dye on my pillow.

I got a towel.

Don't you get dye on my pillow.

Hold still then.

He asked her to turn off the lamp's naked bulb. When she did the light from the small kitchen was all they could see by and it wasn't much over on the bed.

How long's it take?

She read the box. A dark-haired woman on the cover.

The directions are on the side, dummy.

She slapped a red handprint onto his bare chest.

Ow, damn.

Don't call me dummy. It says to leave it for a half hour.

She threw the box on the floor.

That's gonna leave a mark, he said, peering down in the half-light at his chest, where he smarted.

I should get going, she said, standing.

Wait, wait. Where you gonna go?

She didn't know. She didn't feel like she could stay. He got up on one elbow and reached for her wrist and got her rubber bracelet by his middle finger. He drew her arm to him and began to touch it all over.

You got a girlfriend? she asked when they were face-to-face.

You got a boyfriend?

His smile was incredible.

I saw some woman things in the bathroom.

I've never had a girlfriend.

His fingers ran up the inside of her arm and when he said, *I like you*, she laughed and turned her face up to the ceiling and swallows flew out of her chest it felt like and she helped him rinse his hair in the kitchen sink and when he turned around with a towel turbaned up on his head and kissed her, she kissed him back. He asked how old she was. She lied and said that she was sixteen. He said sure she was. He told her that he'd go slow or not at all, and she asked would he mind if they laid on the bed awhile first. It was like the other times in that it wasn't very long at all before he had his hands on her and then his fingers up in her and her body was going too fast for her too, her mouth slick and her cooch too and his fingers were in her mouth and rubbing her cooch and then around her anus and pulling at her butt like he was trying to rip a loaf of French bread and then holding it like he was resting an open phone book on his forearm as he cradled her head to his like a receiver in a pay phone. She felt like a phone booth. Her body was a booth that a person could get into and call long-distance from inside of, call her dad Pete maybe, she wondered why did she think of him now, Pomeroy wasn't like her father, not like Cheatham kind of was.

It was gross to think of your dad and she put that away.

Pomeroy moved her body for her, tilting her pelvis so that it sometimes felt in new places inside of her and she gasped because it hurt, which surprised her because it hadn't hurt down there in a long time.

Did she tell him to stop?

Yes.

Did he?

Yes. In the half-light from the kitchen with the pipes groaning in the other Quaker apartments and the cars shishing on the wet pavement outside. It must've rained.

Men were animals, he said. Some animals have to run, some animals have to chase. She was an animal who would have to run. Unless.

Unless what.

I can keep those animals away, he said.

But who'll keep you away?

She was teasing him and he didn't care for it. He sat up.

I said I don't have girlfriends. You do me if you want. If not, you don't.

She wrapped herself around his torso. He smelled like black dye. Like a blot. Like black water. Wet hot water. She asked him how old he was.

Twenty. Go get them cigarettes.

She was all the way over at the table, naked and dribbling his cum out of her before she realized she'd just hopped to when he said so. He said wait let's have a look at you and flipped on the bulb. She covered up with her hands and then dropped them so he wouldn't have to ask her to and also because it felt immature to cover up and she wanted to be sophisticated. And it didn't bother her, him looking her up and down a moment, nodding like he liked what he saw or just that she'd grown up in that moment. She didn't care, or she told herself she didn't care, if there was a difference, which perhaps there wasn't. Men were supposed to look at women. They were supposed to.

Christ, he said, reaching for the smokes.

What? she said, horrified. Looking herself over.

He explained that she was so damn fine his heart did backflips. Shit her not.

TWENTY-FIVE

He went to visit Cecil's mother, intending to get him back into her home. There were so many cars parked on her block, he thought maybe she'd died, that he'd happened upon her wake. But of course there wouldn't be anyone at her wake.

And Katie. Was she eating. Had she been to school at all this spring. Was she alive.

He parked and mounted the steps to the front door. A balding man with a mustache and a polyester brown suit cornered the house and climbed over the railing with a black single-barrel pump-action shotgun. He put a finger to his lips, pointed at the ground, smoothing his tie back into his coat. Pete looked dumbly at where he'd pointed and then started to back away. Several things occurred at once. Men in suits and tactical gear with pistols and submachine guns streamed through the tall grass toward the front porch. Pete's knees buckled and the back of his hand was wrenched up between his shoulder blades by someone who'd come from behind.

He started to protest, but the man with the shotgun punched the stock into Pete's gut, and he doubled over on his way down, his face striking the porch. His teeth rang in his skull like tines of a tuning fork as a couple hundred pounds compressed into a single kneecap in the middle of his back. He coughed and gagged at once and thought he was suffocating as someone cuffed him. Now someone straddled him. There were shouts from inside the house.

"There's a kid in there!" Pete croaked.

"Shut up!"

"I'm a social worker! There's a CHILD in there!"

The world rang and spangled. Something hard as iron had struck the back of his head, smashed his teeth into the porch again. Blood, metal, salt, a hot pain radiating from a point on the rear equator of his skull. He was collared up onto his knees, his head rolling, lifted to his feet. From within the house there were shouts, there were shots, quick POP-POP-POPs, and he was kicked back down. Boots on the porch all around him. Screams. Scuffles. He lay still, gonged and wincing.

From the back of the unmarked sedan in which he'd been placed, he could see plainclothes cops, cops in DEA jackets, and local law enforcement. Pacing in and out of the house, puffed up in their adrenaline and bulletproof vests. All this contemptible hard-assery. An ambulance at last arrived and weaved among the cars flashing its lights. Paramedics rushed inside.

The back of Pete's neck was moist with blood. Indentures of his teeth scored the inside of his lips. The cuffs cut into his wrist bones. He was by now half-crazed with worry about Katie. Had she been shot. Hurt in any way whatsoever. He should've removed her from the home too. Instead of Cecil. She was the one he should've taken to the Cloningers.

He'd gotten it all wrong. Once again.

Idiot.

Is there anything you touch doesn't turn to shit.

He knocked his head against the rear window. A nearby cop turned around, looked at him, shook his head no, and resumed speaking to his fellows.

"Fucker!" Pete shouted. He pounded his head against the window. To break it if he must.

The balding cop who'd hit him with the shotgun flung open the door.

"There's a little girl—"

The cop punched him in the mouth. He toppled backward, stunned and squirming.

"Shut the fuck up."

Slam went the door. Pete turned over onto his knees and watched the runnel of blood out his nose splotch the fabric of the backseat. This was a nice sedan with a cloth interior, not some county squad car of vinyl. He blew blood all over the upholstery. He sat up and spat at this road show of federal law enforcement, and a bubbly red slug drew down the window.

They searched Pete's car, set things from his glove box and passenger seat on the roof. For no ostensible reason a federal agent removed the cardboard Pete had taped over his broken window. Just being thorough. A file folder opened in the breeze and several sheets of paperwork blew away. The citizens standing across the street taking everything in picked up the loose papers and inspected them.

"Shit's confidential," Pete hollered. No one heard him or looked his way if they did. When the cop emptying his glove box discovered it, he opened and took a sniff from Pete's flask, capped it, and set it on the folder.

A Tenmile police officer emerged from the house with Katie in his arms, and the girl rode him in mute shock to the squad car parked alongside the one Pete was in. He could see someone put a blanket around her and then stand next to her where she sat, legs out the back door. She was eye level with Pete and when she saw him she knew him, and he said to her it was okay it would all be okay though she couldn't hear him. She locked her eyes on his. She tethered herself to him in this way, and he could see her wonder why he didn't come out of the car for her, why he was so very bloody too. He said he was very, very sorry. Someone nudged her over into the seat and got in back with her, and the car pulled away.

Debbie out the front door now, performance in full, leaping and arching her back against her captors and handcuffs and falling backward into the arms of the cop behind her. T-shirt torn at the neck and sliding over her shoulder, a sagging tit flopping out as she twisted and dug in, her feet running halfway up the porch post. For a moment she strained perpendicular to the floor like a bow aimed at the sky before another cop took her by the feet and with the one holding her by the armpits bore her snapping, kicking, and squirming, and quickly folded her into a sedan. Then it pulled away too.

The fed who'd had the shotgun opened Pete's door. He double-took the bloody mess on Pete's face, parted his jacket and set his hands on his hips.

"Jesus," he said, and took a handkerchief from his jacket. "What did you do to my car?"

Pete edged away from him.

"Fuck off, pig."

The fed tossed the handkerchief at Pete and closed the door.

They were soon on Highway 2, heading east into a brilliant day, clear skies, warm.

Pete asked who got shot. It occurred to him that if Cecil had been there, he'd be dead. Maybe he had been there. Maybe he'd been released. Pete asked was it a teenager they'd shot.

The fed glanced in his rearview at Pete but didn't say anything.

"You realize I'm their social worker, right, dipshit?"

The agent drove in silence. Pete sat back. His head throbbed, front and back, bulbs of pain like a flashing string of Christmas lights around his skull.

"I know my rights. And you straight fucked up."

The fed adjusted his mirror and tried to settle in for the drive, but Pete harried him with insults. He asked how long the DEA had been hiring retards. Was it a quota thing or was there a special squad of them. He complimented the man's comb-over. He asked was he philosophically a fascist or was this just the consequence of being hung like a thumb. Was he missing a testicle like Hitler. What it was like to have been aborted. Was his mother a good kisser. Was his father. Did the little fellas he fellated mind his mustache.

Pete flew into the side of the door, struck his head against the window as the fed suddenly turned. They rumbled over gravel and then skidded to a stop and the fed killed the engine. In the brief subsequent silence Pete could hear the man breathe through his nose, the very dust settle. Then the fed got out. Pete heaved himself up and his door was open. The fed grinned. He took a handful of Pete's long hair and yanked him out. He stood Pete in front of the rear tire and most officially slugged him in the stomach. Pete pitched forward. The man caught him, and Pete could smell his lunch. Meat, gravy, bitter coffee.

He slugged Pete under the opposite rib and standing so close kept him on his feet as he pumped fists into his guts dexter and sinister and when he stepped back, Pete dropped to his knees and then onto his side convulsing and cacking on the gravel. His breath croaked to and fro, like it wouldn't take, like he was trying to find a way to breathe sideways.

The fed panted from his efforts and asked Pete whatever had happened to his smart-ass mouth. Then he spat onto Pete's face and fetched his handkerchief off the ground where it had fallen and knelt in front of him. He sat Pete up, spat into the handkerchief directly, and wiped Pete's face clean. He said it was a good old spitwash like Mama used to do. He asked could Pete believe the pain he was in. He pulled up Pete's shirt and exclaimed, my, what little indication there was of any assault. How long it would take before he would bruise there if at all.

He stood Pete up. By now, the handkerchief was covered with blood. He spat on Pete's face directly again and used his thumb to clean the last bit of dried blood from the grooves around his nostrils. Tilted Pete's head this way and that, pulled back Pete's lips to have a look at his teeth and gums. Like a man inspecting a horse or hunting dog. The cop's bitter breath reeked all over Pete's face. He stepped back, had a good look at him, and asked Pete had he had quite enough.

Pete closed his eyes and hung his head yes. His rearranged guts churned.

The fed straightened him, said that was too bad, and whaled on him a little more.

The basement of a post office in Kalispell. They uncuffed him and deposited him in a chain-link cell in the corner that was concrete walls on two sides and a few folding chairs and that was all. A metal desk stood outside the makeshift cell and a map of Tenmile was taped to a free-standing chalkboard on wheels.

Debbie's high hysterical voice cantered behind a door across the room. After a while the cops ushered her upstairs and she looked at Pete as if she couldn't quite place him.

The sole remaining DEA agent removed his gun, put it in the drawer in his desk, and commenced with paperwork. Pete asked could he have something to drink. The officer trudged upstairs, came down with a Coke, and forced it under the chain link with his foot. Just drinking made Pete's stomach quake. Even sips. He pounded the cola anyway and burped in a novel kind of agony bent over on his folding chair. He lay flat on his back and still his insides ached all the way through to his spine.

It was too cold in this basement to sleep through the hours. There were no windows to tell the time by, and when Pete asked him, the agent would not tell him.

"That woman you got, she's too fucked up to be whoever you think she is."

"And who exactly do you think we think she is?" the agent asked, not turning around.

"Fuck if I know. Some kind of kingpin, by all the heat you brought. Unless that was for whoever you shot."

The agent kept at his paperwork.

"And killed?"

The agent moved some papers into a manila folder, stood, and left Pete alone.

Two agents came downstairs and let themselves into the cell with Pete. One of the men was clean-shaven and serious and wore a dark suit and carried a briefcase that he set on the concrete floor next to him. FBI, Pete guessed. The man crossed one leg over the other, pants pressed and neatly creased, and regarded Pete, mildly bouncing his dangling foot in its wingtip.

The other man wore jeans and a black jacket with an ATF badge sewn over the zipper pocket. He took off his black baseball cap and scratched his thinned hair and fixed the hat back on his head. He was sitting on the chair backward and, at a gesture from the man in the suit, reached into his coat pocket and dropped Pearl's sack of coins on the floor. The sack that had been in Pete's car. The man in the suit smirked at whatever Pete's expression said. Then he uncrossed his legs, leaned over, and opened the sack. He fingered through the coins and picked one shot through with a swastika.

"Lovely," he said of the coin, holding it up to the fluorescent light. He had a wry and cocksure expression that would irritate anyone at all.

"Where did these come from?" the ATF agent asked.

Pete decided he wasn't going to say a thing. He said, "I'm not saying shit about shit until I get a lawyer."

He coughed. His stomach muscles convulsed painfully. He held his side wincing.

The suit's mouth turned up at its corners in an expectant grin.

Pete said again that he wanted counsel.

"Been to Reno recently?" the suit asked.

From the agents' expressions Pete was certain that his face showed that he had. He swallowed, winced again. Shit. He swallowed and he winced.

"Lawyer," he croaked.

"Look," the suit said, "every bank in the country is watching for these coins. They get one, they call the Secret Service. The Treasury Department runs it down to Jim here and Jim calls me. I'm FBI. So you got Justice and Treasury crawling up your ass right now. You and Jeremiah Pearl and the Posse Comitatus and Truppe Schweigen have the federal government's full fucking attention. Congratulations."

"You lost me," Pete said. "I don't know what you're talking about."

The suit opened his briefcase and removed a file folder and handed Pete a photograph. A burnt-out armored truck. Another color photo of two dead security guards prone in livid pools of blood. He handed over another and another, told Pete of the robberies depicted in them, and also of bombings and murders. A synagogue. A little girl who bled out from the holes made by the nails and screws of a pipe bomb. He told Pete about Posse Comitatus, the separatist organization behind it, about the clandestine arm or offshoot called Truppe Schweigen, which was German for "Silent Corps" and which specialized in the financial activities, mainly counterfeiting. Piles of phony tens and twenties. They defaced currency and clogged the courts with spurious liens.

Pete looked from the ATF to the FBI agent and snorted weirdly in astonishment.

"You really think I'm one of these guys?" Pete asked. "I'm a social worker. That fucked-up woman you got, I'm her social worker."

"But how do you know Pearl?" the ATF agent asked.

"How do you think? *I'm a social worker.* He has no job and many kids."

Pete thrust the pictures back, but the suit wouldn't take them. Pete turned them over and dropped them on the concrete.

"Why were you in Texas the day the president was shot?" the suit asked him.

"What? How did you—?"

"Just answer the question. What were you doing in Texas?"

"This is insane. I want a lawyer."

"And Indiana? Did you visit Pearl's family in Gnaw Bone? Or is Jeremiah Pearl hiding somewhere in Gnaw Bone right now? Is that why you went there?"

The agents both watched him impassively. The suit leaned forward with his hands on his knees.

"You already admitted to leaving a hundred of these coins in Reno, which you know is illegal—"

"No, I *don't* know that's illegal—you can flatten a penny in one of those machines down in Yellowstone and stamp a buffalo on—"

"Nobody tries to pass one of those. You put *dozens* of these coins in the slot machines down there—"

"And they fell right through into the tray—"

"So you were in Reno."

"I want a lawyer."

"You can get five years for this."

"Counsel," Pete said flatly.

The FBI agent cleared his throat and sat up.

"Why don't you have a case on Jeremiah Pearl in all that paperwork in your car?"

"Counsel."

"I'll be honest," the FBI agent said. "You don't look like a neo-Nazi. You don't look like a gunrunner. But you do look like a goddamn hippie anarchist. The hair and the jacket and the fuckin attitude. And here you are swept up in an amphetamine bust, and . . . I just don't know. What the hell are you, Peter Snow?"

Pete stared at the floor, thinking, concentrating on the idea that there wasn't anything to be afraid of. Do not be scared. It's not like you knowingly did anything wrong. Assuming it was illegal to pass Pearl's fucked-up coins. Five years. That couldn't be right. Fuck this guy. Fuck him all day. They'd have to be crazy to think you're moonlighting as some kind of separatist. You're a social worker.

"I want a lawyer."

Several moments passed.

The suit bent over and plucked the photos off the floor.

"Come on, Jim," he said.

"Be a minute," the ATF agent said.

The suit shrugged and left the cage, and the ATF agent and Pete sat together in silence until the suit departed up the stairs. The desk agent returned and began hunting and pecking at a typewriter. Each keystroke shot off the concrete walls and floor. The ATF agent stood, went to the cage door, and asked the desk agent if he would mind grabbing them a couple coffees. The man sighed heavily, pushed himself up, clomped to the door, and left them alone.

The ATF agent returned to his chair.

"My name's Jim. Jim Pinkerton, Department of Alcohol, Tobacco, and Firearms. Division of the Treasury. I am the liaison to the Secret Service on all matters regarding currency as it pertains to Jeremiah Pearl."

"I'm delighted all to pieces, Jim."

"The point I'm making is I have nothing to do with the investigations regarding his threats to the president."

"Thanks for clearing that up."

"You're pretty punchy today aren't you?"

"Interesting word choice."

"Why?"

"I want a lawyer."

Pinkerton leaned back, holding the armrests of the chair, and sighed at the ceiling.

"The people in the house, they were clients of yours."

Pete nodded.

"You didn't know the guy who was killed."

"I have no idea who you killed."

"Speed supplier out of Denver. Two years of DEA work and no conviction because the fucker wouldn't stand down."

"My condolences."

"But you were just there to check on the girl."

Pete sighed.

"What's gonna happen to her?" Pinkerton asked. "I mean, now that her mother is in custody."

"Someone will call my office and wait for me to come and get her."

"They won't call someone here in Kalispell?"

"I'm the someone in Kalispell. This is my region."

"From Tenmile all the way to here? That's a lot of area for you to cover." Pinkerton chewed his cheek. "So, you need to get out of here. To help the girl. Maybe we can make a deal so you can do that."

The desk officer returned with two coffees, and Pinkerton sipped his. He spat it back into the cup and set it on the floor.

"I don't know where Pearl is," Pete said.

"Do you know where we can get something that isn't burnt and lukewarm?" he asked.

Pete swirled the brown water in his cup. He didn't want to drink anything. He was tired, very tired.

"Come on, Snow. Take me somewhere and hear me out."

Pinkerton got up to call the FBI agent and explain what cafe they were in. When he came back to the table, he waved the waitress over and ordered a slice of meringue and asked did Pete want anything.

Pete said he was fine.

"Get some fries or whatever. On me. You haven't even touched your coffee."

"It hurts to drink."

"You have a cavity or something?"

Pete gingerly brushed his stomach with his fingertips.

"Heartburn?" Pinkerton said. "I get that."

"One of your colleagues kicked the shit out of me on the way here. But thanks for asking."

Pinkerton looked Pete up and down.

"He was careful," Pete said, lifting his shirt, "just to beat my guts all to hell."

Grayish bruises along the ridge of his ribs stood out in the last of the evening light through the windows. Pinkerton sighed.

"You want to get that checked out?"

"I wanna take a pipe to that piece of shit."

The waitress had returned with the pie and looked askance at Pete.

"Fair enough," Pinkerton said. "Thanks, hon."

He cut a piece of pie, put it in his mouth and chewed. He took a swallow of coffee.

"I can make this go away, but you and I have to come to an understanding."

"Make what go away? I haven't done a goddamn thing."

"That's not how we're gonna see it. But if you and I come to an understanding . . ."

"About?"

"Jeremiah Pearl."

"What exactly do I need to understand?"

"Well, first you need to know what happened up there," he said, chewing, his voice thick with yellow meringue.

How did she meet Pomeroy's girlfriend?

At the bus station in Tacoma they went to get into a locker where he'd put his watch, some hairspray, his brass knuckles (he showed her these for some time, fondled them), and a carton of Pall Malls. They'd hitchhiked down from Seattle in a semi with a blockhead truck driver who kept eyeing her legs. Later in the bus station, he said she could have made him quit that looking if she just gave him what he wanted.

What?

You could just put your little paw on his meat and he'd prolly cum in two seconds, he said, going through his things.

She stood. He smelled a shirt from the locker and shoved it into his duffel.

Fuck this, she said. She strode out and among the buses idling in the station, felt then how meager was her freedom, that no one worried over her.

What about her mother and father?

She was too busy crying to think of them. They would have ruined the perfect lonesomeness that she felt seeping into all her past—this was the story, she was always ever alone even at home—and her prospects too. She wyomed on the aluminum side of the bus and left swells of breath there. Riders watched her. A driver was behind her asking did she need any help, what was the matter, he could help figure it out. But she was embarrassed to have run out because she was a proud and independent girl, and said she was fine and paced among the rumbling, idling buses not yet going anywhere. She took a look at herself in the windows of the station. Her hair a shag, and she was wearing a blue ski jacket and a white denim skirt and how she looked was the only thing she had going on. When she went back inside the girl straddling Pomeroy spotted her right away and chewed on his ear and then said something into it. She was stunned. Not really jealous. Just surprised. She knew she looked better than this girl, who was at once used up and flush with youth. She had baby fat in her face and a small tire around her belly like she'd had children at a young age. Pomeroy leaned back to see Rose and called her over, and said, *This is my old lady, Yolanda.*

I thought you didn't have a girlfriend.

Come off it.

You can call me Yo, Yo said.

She went back out to the buses again. She had fourteen dollars in her pocket. It wasn't enough to go anywhere for real. Her legs were cold. At least it wasn't raining. She made up her mind, but this time she really thought about what she wanted and what she had to do and what was the best thing between those two poles.

Where did the three of them go?

They rode to Seattle in a car that Yo had borrowed from an old homo named Jorge. They drove through a city like a gray and linear crystallization of the raw slab of clouds overhead. It was going on night when Yo killed the engine, let the car roll, and parked in front of a house on Capitol Hill. Yo said to just get out and not close the doors. Then Yo quietly clicked the car doors closed herself, and snuck up to the house. Pomeroy took Rose across the street.

Jorge didn't give her permission, did he?

Pomeroy smiled. *That Yo.*

The house was reached by a row of concrete steps that went up from the sidewalk, and Yo looked especially squat sneaking up them, slipping in the front door.

Yo's pretty, she said. Sounding his feelings about her, the depth of them.

She has nice lips.

And nice eyes.

They're slanty. She's a little Eskimo or something.

Yeah.

Yolanda slunk down the stairs in her purple flats, slapping across the street to them. She said to walk, pointing up the street. She got between them and put her arms through theirs and they trundled down the hill, past the wrought-iron fences and Victorian houses, on into the night traffic at Highway 5, under the highway and into a liquor store. Street kids and castoffs and whatever miscreants had called out *Hey Pomeroy!* and Pomeroy sashayed for them and when he had his bottle, shared and shared alike with a group of slack kids drinking beer and smoking weed in a small lot on Thomas Street.

That's Dee and Jules and Custer and there's Kenny and Curt, Yolanda said, and they nodded at her and checked her out. Yolanda turned her into the light and said, *You look about like Sissy Spacek to me, but with darker skin tone,* and Rose asked was she the coal miner's daughter, and Yo said yep.

A cop rolled past and no one hid the bottle. That was exhilarating.

What's happening tonight?

The kids looked around as if something might be evident in their immediate surroundings and finally someone said they were thinking of heading to the Monastery later.

The bottle had gotten to Rose. Someone had lit a joint and it was going around too. The Talking Heads hiccupped out of a passing car. One of them—Kenny—was a tall black kid who looked at her with vague intensity. She tugged on Yolanda's arm, but Yolanda was talking to someone and just handed her a cigarette.

You gonna drink from that or what, girl? Kenny asked her.

She clutched the bottle to her mouth—it was heavy as a brick—and took a swallow and passed it on. Kenny kept his eyes on her, half-listening to Pomeroy.

Yo headed off giggling with Dee and Jules, so Rose went over to Pomeroy's side with a cigarette in her mouth and let him light it, and felt in her silence quite adult. Kenny offered her the joint, but she held up her cigarette to say she would smoke this instead. Again, adult. She tucked in under Pomeroy's arm and murmured just loud enough for him to hear that she was cold. He let his arm go around her and nobody noticed her there, the slight thing. A soft bird she felt like. Not even Yolanda really noticed her when she came back—she just took the cigarette from her and dragged off it and gave it back, and then complained about the assholes on Pike, and told Dee and Jules to watch themselves down there.

Let's go, Pomeroy said.

Did Pomeroy keep her under his arm all the way down Minor as they moved through the night in this bouncing, laughing pack, sometimes harassing passers-by for spare change and getting none because they didn't conceal their happiness, even though they were to a person underfed and a little sick with inflamed lungs or swollen glands or limped a little on thin shoes and worn socks, and the girls flirted like they were the age they were and the boys were the grossest things they knew about, and the most pretty boy, Pomeroy, squeezing her close, so close, even Kenny who now looked a little jealous of Pomeroy with her under his arm the whole way did he keep her there?

Yes. And Rose wondered did Yolanda care and wondered when she herself wouldn't care, wouldn't feel a hot spot in her chest and her arms go a little numb when Yolanda would kiss him again, which she surely would.

And they passed a girl talking on a pay phone. The coiled metal cord in a loop under her bare arm, and the way she was or had been crying, her foot in its checkered sneaker on the glass, and her fist on the glass.

Was the girl talking to her daddy?

Rose thought maybe she was.

Was there a dull thudding of music and purple lights from the

bell tower, from this white clapboard church on the corner of Boren and Stewart throbbing within?

Like some kind of demented midnight mass. The lot filled with cars and milling kids.

What is this? she asked.

The Monastery, Yo said.

Bearded ladies came through the lot in pink tutus and wands and sparkling blue and green eye shadow, footing steadily on shaven monkey legs in heels across the littered lot. Nigh a parade of apish slatterns and ladyboys and mustached musclemen in denim and sport socks. A lesbian sauntered by in a zoot suit. And milling all about them like fruit flies were these street kids in ski jackets and sweaters, dressed for the cold. The steady pulse of disco and Pomeroy peeled his arm off Rose and strode to the front step.

Where's he going? Rose asked. She felt unsafe without Pomeroy, unchaperoned.

Yo pulled her aside and gave her another cigarette. They shared it awhile before they spoke, Rose's eyes flashing from time to time at the door. Yo sat on the hood of an old Cadillac and beckoned Rose up there and they perched together, passing the smoke and watching the new arrivals dash around. They looked as young as twelve, some of them. They wore hooded sweatshirts and some were done up in cheap costumes, cardboard wings and tiaras and halos of tinfoil and other such getups as you might find at a school play. They shrieked and clutched one another in hysterics, in greeting. Everything was amplified. The music, the lights, these outlandish children.

See? Yo said. *It's all right. Everybody around here is cool. Everybody knows everybody.*

Rose folded her legs under her and sat full on the hood of the car. She was so thin now that she didn't dent the hood.

You don't have to go with me and Pom. You find some other people you want to hang with, that's cool.

Oh, I like you guys fine, she said meaningfully. A skosh of worry in it. *Really, I like you and Pomeroy a lot. I'm not jealous of you two or nothing.*

Yo exhaled smoke and smiled.

We like you.

You do?

Yeah. I knew I would from the way Pom was telling me about you. It could be weird or it could be cool, and with Pom it's always cool.

Rose didn't know what to say or to ask.

You want a beer?

Yes.

Yo ran off. Rose rubbed her legs. Yo returned with a number of girls and they gave Rose beer from a sack, Yo making introductions, the girls checking Rose out. The night turned cold as they spoke about people Rose didn't know and places she hadn't been.

And when Pomeroy came back out, a few hours later, pink in the eyes, and aweave in his foot placement, and grinning, colliding gently into the coterie of girls around the car, what did he do?

He threw up, nearly on Kenny. A short bolt of laughter escaped Rose that she clipped off when Kenny looked to see who it was.

Yolanda took him off through the lot and Rose hurried after. They dropped next to a chain-link fence that jangled where Pomeroy fell into it, laughing himself. It was moist in the weeds from the nightdew.

I'm cold, Rose said.

Too much beers, Pomeroy muttered. *I'm about like to trip out.*

He had to arc up his ass to get his hand into his jeans pocket—Rose resisted the urge to touch his naked stomach—and pull out a plastic Baggie. The light on it fairly glowed white and illicit in the dark.

Was it coke?

No.

Was it MDA?

Maybe.

What was it?

What it was was Yolanda taking a sniff off a matchbook and shaking her head and handing the Baggie to Rose who looked at it and then over among the cars where there was a scuffle happening and then toward the street and then back into the Baggie and taking it up like she's seen Yolanda do.

What it was was a sweet knife of tingling and then a slow drip of jitters, and handing it back to Pomeroy who was vaguely nearby asking for it and the sound of him taking a short blast and saying oh man and hot rushes up and down her arms that she imagined was Braille, some text in her body, but was only goose bumps.

What it was was Yolanda laughing and standing and Rose was up and standing and walking as liquid blurs slithered past.

What it was was they were in the Monastery now. Pomeroy had her by the wrist as they birthed themselves again and again through the wet and heated throng. A strobe froze each posture in giddy eternities, a mandarin and a geisha with elongated faces. Sparkling beards. Howling caryatids of pale shirtless boys. Dark gauntlets. What it was was an arm thrown round her shoulder and pulling her up under her armpit to bounce, and Rose lost Pomeroy's grip and gave over to the mass of arms and sweat and stomp. Completely naked men on the speakers, the small gyre of their cocks as they danced. She was hefted up, passed from fag to fag and deposited in a bank of airline seats.

She could not stop laughing.

A furry animal tossed up and down in the lap of the man next to her.

She tapped his arm. He didn't look over.

You have something there! she yelled.

The man opened his eyes and smiled at her and said, *Yes, yes I do.*

She looked again and the man clutched the animal and it was a human head giving him head. There was a bottle under her. She unscrewed the cap and drank hot fire and nearly threw up. She stood and heaved herself back into the mass. Disappeared into it.

TWENTY-SIX

Pinkerton had met Pearl at a loggers' swap meet in the Idaho woods. He was undercover, had been coming and going in the area for the past three months by the name of Joe Stacks. He'd done odd jobs—every man was a handyman up here—and lived in a cabin the ATF had bought just the other side of the Montana border in Boundary County, Idaho. He'd gone to the meetup with a swarthy dimwit by the name of Ruffin, a big-talking hyperactive conspiracy freak.

This is where he meets Pearl, a country roundup where the folks in the region trade stories and sell chain saws, rhubarb, and crafts made of pie tin and rope. There was nothing inherently political about the gathering, just rumors that so-and-so was Posse Comitatus, Truppe Schweigen. Or not. And among the people Ruffin introduced Stacks to was one Jeremiah Pearl. The real deal, Ruffin says. Tribulation-ready, Race War–ready. Set up to handle the National Guard, the Shit-Covered Fan, the feds, the unraveling of the social compact.

Pearl introduces the missus, the kids. Missus is rubber-gloved to the elbows stirring a pot of preserves over a campfire. Grins wanly, waves.

A quiet, serious woman. Gorgeous kids, knees as ruddy as red apples. They sit arrayed around Pearl in the pickup bed like a kinder court. The baby boy in Pearl's lap and little Paula and Ben right close, and Ruth and Esther sitting beside him and the oldest boy, Jacob, standing on the ground between where his father's legs dangle off the tailgate. It was like Pearl drew some strength from the brood, the way they climbed on him, the way he goosed them.

Joe Stacks, Pearl says. *That's an interesting name.* Asks is it a nickname.

Pinkerton says *No, no it isn't.* Asks does Pearl want to see his driver's license.

Pearl says not unless you're in need of someone to cut it up for you. Smiles.

Pinkerton's bosses want informants. The Truppe Schweigen did the synagogue job in Portland, blew the front wall and doors into kibble, killed three. Pinkerton is to run down every last lead, even though he knows Ruffin and Pearl aren't involved with anything. Ruffin's a dipshit, and Pearl, he's got all those kids. It's just obvious that he loves his family too much to get into that kind of trouble. But the ATF wants somebody inside, inside of something, anything. It's a pissing contest anyway, the Department of Treasury vying with the FBI. The ATF wants somebody up fucking in there. Yesterfuckingday.

So six weeks later, after several informal visits in truck stops, Stacks, Ruffin, and Pearl meet in Ruffin's truck in Sandpoint, Idaho. It's cold and windy on the city beach, the gusts off Lake Pend Oreille buffeting Ruffin's pickup. Ruffin's shit-talking as usual. He's gonna knock over the First Interstate branch in Boise. He's gonna pick off the marshals when they come for him. Then he's gonna find a nigger church and toss a Molotov cocktail into it.

Pearl is quiet.

Stacks mentions he's got some friends in Seattle who could use some sawed-offs for a job or two. Double-barrel, preferably.

Ruffin asks what job.

Pearl asks how much.

Stacks tells Pearl he can pay $150 for single-barrel, $200 per double. Pearl says can you go three.

Stacks says he isn't sure. Pinkerton can go three, but he doesn't want to seem too eager.

I have to have three, Pearl says, sad as hell, like he's having to ask Stacks for a set of kidneys. Pinkerton thinks maybe there's something wrong with one of the kids. The guy doesn't say a word for forty minutes of Ruffin's shit-talking and then out of nowhere, *How much, I have to get three.*

The guy is just busted-ass broke, Pinkerton realizes. He asks Pearl to give him a few days. He'll call.

I don't have a phone, Pearl says. *Call Ruffin. I need three and I gotta move quick if we're gonna do it.*

Pinkerton makes it happen.

The biggest regret of his career.

Pearl and Stacks start to meet up without Ruffin, because the deals run a lot shorter without him. Cash, shotguns, I'll meet you in two weeks for more. Seven transactions total.

Once, Pearl muses how strange it is that he could get in trouble, how he could do time for sitting under a pine tree with a hacksaw and a couple of bird guns. *Some kind of world,* he says. This is the same occasion where he announces that he needs $350. He has to be careful, buying up all these guns. He has to drive farther and farther, gas money and everything cutting into his profits. *Gas and money,* he mutters. *Shekels and oil the world over.* And Ruffin has been bitching. Thought he should've been cut in on the deal, so now he and Pearl are on the outs.

Ruffin says you're a fed, Pearl tells him. *You a fed, Stacks?*

Pearl looks sad. It's like he already knows. For a minute there, Pinkerton thinks Pearl's going to do something stupid. Pinkerton can feel the pistol in its holster against his calf, wonders can he get it out before Pearl does something stupid.

You'd be burned by now if I was, Stacks says, wedging a laugh into the air. *I bet you're the fed, you crafty fucker.*

It's always hard to tell exactly what Pearl is thinking behind that beard of his. Is he as world-weary as he looks. Is he ready to die already. Without his kids around, the guy's like a lump of oatmeal, like something on the bottom of your shoe. He's saying again he needs the $350. He just needs the money, the damn money.

The thing is, the ATF is done throwing money at Pearl. Pearl is over. Pinkerton's supposed to be setting up other buys, moving up the chain. But there isn't a chain to move up. There's just this sad guy in the sticks who will go all the way to Miles City for a shotgun to chop. $350, and it'll be worth it. The sum total of his prospects is what the ATF pays him to break federal law.

Stacks sighs, says he's been meaning to talk to Pearl about this, that his partners are flush with shotguns. But does Pearl know where to get anything with a little more bang for the buck. Does Pearl have a line on anything like that.

Don't do it, Pearl, Pinkerton is thinking. Begging. *Don't do it.*

No, he doesn't have a line on anything like that. Lump of oatmeal. Shit on your shoe.

Weeks of no word. Pearl didn't set up another meet and Ruffin's not talking to Pearl and pretty soon Ruffin isn't even talking to Stacks. His bosses decide Pinkerton's been made. They're going to relocate him to California. He did fine work, it's just time to bag it.

He's mucked out the cabin and packed everything (sleeping bag, pistols, cast-iron cookware) when Ruffin comes barreling up the road in his truck. Asks where Stacks is headed. Pinkerton thinks fast, says the owner of the cabin's selling the place from under him. *Fuckin asshole,* Ruffin says. *But you're in luck,* Ruffin says. *I just leased some property, have a trailer already up on it and everything.*

Whereabouts? Stacks asks.

Jeremiah Pearl's is where. Sweet little spot.

It's a nice Airstream trailer, on the other side of the meadow from the Pearls' house, abutting a stand of buckskin tamarack. Wild mushrooms and carpets of moss and bumblebees turning figure eights in the slashes of sun in the woods, as if they too are stupefied by the beauty of the place. It's a slice of heaven, Pinkerton can see right away.

Ruffin racks out a couple nights with Stacks, and Pearl sloshes through the mucky meadow every evening, and they even drink a little beer together. Pearl looking over his shoulder up toward the house.

He says the old lady has the spyglasses on him. *Hand to God, she's the brains behind the whole operation.*

There's maybe a little rift there. Money worries and the stresses inherent to their worldview.

Ruffin says Pearl's allowed a beer every once in a while. Especially now he's got a job harrowing a large farm out near Three Forks and the money from the timber lease. Working puts food on the table, he can have a little beer now and again.

So Pearl is off on his harrowing gig in Three Forks. Pinkerton is whittling his time in the trailer, wondering what the hell to do with himself. How exactly to proceed. Watching the kids and the old lady. It's like the kids have been told let him alone, taking the long way around the trailer when they go by with baskets, when they come back with baskets of huckleberries and mushrooms, with fish. He kind of wishes they wouldn't. They're nice enough folks, just trying to get by. But the woman is not neighborly. He sees her watching him from the house, but she doesn't wave.

One night, he takes a walk. Full moon or nearly so. It's warm and clear and he hikes up the hill and takes in the view from the cliff overlooking the place. He's sitting on the edge and when he gets up to leave sets a few rocks tumbling over, cracking the quiet. When he climbs down, he's nearly blinded by a powerful jacklight.

What were you doing up there?

Just taking in the view, Mrs. Pearl. Could you get that light off my face?

You're not allowed up there.

Why the hell not?

I don't know you.

My name is Joe Stacks.

Are you saved, Mr. Stacks?

Saved?

Saved by the Lord?

Oh yes. Of course.

I don't believe you. I don't believe you are who you say you are.

I don't know what to say to that.

Don't be going around the property. You stay at that trailer.

She traipses away to the house, tells the kids who must be sentried there to go on in, get back to bed.

In a few days, Ruffin returns, in high psychotic spirits as usual. He's brought a used chain saw and a splitter and also a few sawhorses for some undisclosed project.

What's all this?

Firewood.

This is the first Ruffin's mentioned anything about it.

Maybe we should wait until Jeremiah gets back.

The fuck for. I have bills, you know. I need this firewood money to get liquid. Cover my nut for winter, we get cracking.

I dunno.

Ruffin asks what the hell did Stacks think he was up here to do? Drink beer and live free? This is how Stacks is gonna cover his rent on the Airstream.

That next morning, Ruffin's gone and Stacks goes to work. He gets after the deadfall, but it's wet through and some of it downright mucky inside, all the rain they've been having. For about a day and a half, he's clearing out the useless wet wood and then he starts the standing tamarack. He's cutting rounds when he feels someone near. Pearl's old lady yelling at him from ten feet away. He kills the chain saw.

Who said you could cut down our trees?

She's holding one cowboy boot that came off in the meadow and is shaking the mud out of it.

Ruffin leased it from Jeremiah.

Cutting down our trees isn't part of the lease.

That's not what he said. I was sitting right here with your husband when he and Bob were talking—

When you two were feeding him beer, you mean.

She yanks her boot back on, stomps her foot into it.

Look, Bob said for me to do it to pay my rent. He comes back and sees I haven't done it. . . .

She's already turned around and started back up to the house. Pinkerton has no idea what that means, should he stop or not. She just goes.

It's about suppertime anyway. He eats a can of chili and observes the children running around the house and then going in for dinner. There's good couple hours of light left. He figures he'll get after it again. The tree is already down. Might as well cut the rounds. Maybe talk to her tomorrow. Maybe see about finding Ruffin and squaring all this with him. Hell, the Pearls can have the firewood for their winter. It's just one log.

So he's got a barrowful of rounds and is dumping them on the high ground near the trailer for splitting. Something claps him on the eardrum real good. Sarah Pearl's open palm. She swings again. He catches her arm and she flings the other one, and he pushes her over a round into a spot of muck, and then she's up again, and he's saying he's sorry, he didn't mean to push her, and he's trying to stammer out an explanation—

Stars. Tears of light.

He's tumbled against the trailer, sliding along the siding. Everything keeling. He rights himself as the trailer window just over his head shatters. Something rattles around the countertops inside. He looks up as something nails him in the shoulder. It was the boy, throwing rocks. The eldest. Jacob. The other boy trudging with difficulty through the meadow, and Sarah Pearl, she ain't calling off her son, and Pinkerton doesn't know what to say or do. And does she know this. Does she know he won't hurt the boy.

Of course she doesn't. Or the bitch is crazy, doesn't care what happens to her kids.

He doesn't hear what he says until he sees Sarah and the boys hear him, their mouths and eyes gape wide: *I'm going in my trailer for my goddamn gun.*

Sarah Pearl runs for the house like he'd drawn down on them already. He isn't even sure if his pistol is in the trailer or down at the drive in his truck with half of his other things, but she tears off through the meadow with her boys like he's firing at them.

He should go. This very moment.

Stacks would go.

But Pinkerton, he's jammed up. He feels like he must stay, must wait until Pearl gets back, and make everything okay. Fuck the case. If he just sticks out this rough patch, he can make it square with Pearl.

Pinkerton steps inside the trailer. He's in there a minute, then a while, then it's sunset, then it's dark and there are no lights on at the house. Now leaving seems impossible. Fact is, he's afraid to go outside. If he's honest with himself. Are they watching him. Is she watching him. Are they outside right now. He can't hear a thing. Just the owl and the stream and the sighing trees. The moths kissing the screen. He locks the door and closes the curtains. Finds his pistol in his bag and beds down with it. He'll go in the morning.

His sleep is so light it's some smallness of sleep, some rumor of sleep.

He can hear the boy—somehow the footfall sounds like a boy coming through the grass and nettles at the backside of the trailer. Pinkerton moves just as the glass crashes and he's crouched behind the counter as it rains down. He fires out the window, up into the sky from his position on the floor in the glass. There's a moment in the wake of the shot where all he hears is the ring and the fade of it. There's a stone on the floor. One of the kids is throwing rocks. Again.

He yells that he doesn't want any trouble, that he'll leave in the morning.

The metal teapot caroms off the stove to the floor and pisses the carpet. The report of the gun that Sarah or one of the children shoots echoes off the mountains. Kids playing little Indians on the high ground. He thinks of carbines and face paint and warbonnets.

Another bullet hole appears in the wall near the ceiling. He can see a single night star just off center in it.

Another.

They are shooting at the trailer.

They are going to kill him.

He grabs the jacklight off the counter and flips it on. He leaps out the front door and holding it level with his pistol, sweeps the nearby area for anyone and then around the meadow. Nobody. He fires in the air and throws the light as hard as he can in the direction opposite the one he's running—to the truck—as gunfire erupts from the house. He dives in and starts the pickup and bounds across the meadow in pitch-black. Trees rear up and he hits the brakes and then pulls on the lights and turns and guns the engine spitting mud. He still gets turned around and nearly high-centered on the zigzag out but then, his heart racing, he finally bounds through the brush onto the dirt road.

Pinkerton touched crumbs of piecrust onto his finger and licked them off and burped silently into his fist. It was night now and had taken him an hour to eat the slice of pie and tell the story.

"Was anybody hurt?"

"Hurt? No. I didn't fire *at* anyone. I just wanted to get out of there."

"So you're sure none of the kids or their mother was hurt?"

"No. Of course not. I was trying to *avoid* anyone getting hurt. That's why we arrested everybody. Ruffin was bound to go up and catch hell for what happened with me—"

"Waitaminute. You *arrested* everyone?"

"Pearl and his wife, yes." Pinkerton looked at his hands a moment. "I was still thinking that if they just gave us something, just a name, I could make it all go away."

"When? Wait. How?"

"Took a few weeks, but they eventually came down the mountain to get supplies."

"And?"

"A couple agents pretended to be broke down on the side of the road when Pearl and his wife were driving into town together."

"Were you there?"

"In Spokane for the meeting with the US attorney, yes."

Pete shook his head and scoffed.

"This explains a lot."

"About?"

"About why Pearl is so paranoid."

Pinkerton sighed. He leaned forward and spoke low.

"Look, the shotguns were small fry. The FBI had never even heard of him. And we all at the ATF knew the only thing he'd possibly be good for was getting us near some real bad guys."

"After everything that happened, you really thought he'd just turn informant?"

"When we got them to Spokane, we laid out the charges and what they could do to make them go away." Pinkerton palmed the table, as though he were spreading relevant documents for Pete to see. "Most people take the deal. But they wouldn't play ball. They posted bail and blew off their lawyer and their court date. They didn't understand what a big deal this *wasn't*, how easy it would've been—"

"So why not leave them alone?"

"Are you deaf? These are *federal* charges. The US Marshals are serving the bench warrant. And it's not like Pearl is standing down. Right after this, he sent a letter threatening the president. A month before the president was *shot*. And dozens more threatening letters. Governors. The Fed chairman. The chief justice of the Supreme Court. Ranting about currency, and then these coins start showing up? Shit, Snow. You got the Secret Service involved now, as agents of the Treasury *and* as security for the president. Even if he wanted to, Pearl can't get off the radar."

Pinkerton tore his napkin in half, seemed amused that he'd done so, and set it on his plate.

"He doesn't want to get off the radar, does he?" Pinkerton asked.

Pete rubbed his eyes, then laid them dully on Pinkerton.

"You could help bring him in," Pinkerton said.

"Pearl doesn't trust me."

"He gave you all those coins. To distribute, right? He trusts you that much."

"He sees my *instrumentality*, he says."

"Did you take him to Reno?"

"No."

"Did you see him in Indiana?"

"I was looking for my daughter there. And in Reno too."

"*Your* daughter."

"Yes, she ran away. The coins were just . . . there in my car. I dropped some in the machines for the hell of it. Or I don't know why."

"Can someone verify you were looking for her there?"

"Lovejoy. Washoe County Department of Family Services. Jenny, I think."

Pinkerton got out a pen and wrote the name down on half of his napkin.

"Okay, I'll check it out."

"You can do whatever the fuck you want. This has shit to do with me."

"But you see what's coming, right? You see how bad this can all turn out."

"Yes."

"How are Pearl's kids?"

"I've only been with the middle boy. Benjamin. I haven't even seen the wife or the other children," Pete said.

"You haven't?" Pinkerton asked.

"No."

"You don't know where they are?"

"Pearl says they're away. Alive. Somewhere else."

"That's weird."

"Why?"

"You don't think it's weird?"

"Is there a single thing that's *normal* about this? Pearl already thinks the whole government is one huge conspiracy to fuck him over. And how's that *not* what we're doing right now? You want me to help you and the US Marshals and Secret Service? Christ, can we really call him paranoid at this point?"

Pete put on his coat.

"He's around the fucking bend," Pinkerton said. "Hiding up in those mountains—"

"Who wouldn't be? You put him up to committing a federal crime? You pretend to be his friend and then you arrest him and threaten him with prison if he doesn't inform on guys he doesn't even know?"

Pete slid out of his chair and stood. Pinkerton grabbed Pete's forearm.

"Look, I'll be the first to admit that this has gotten out of hand. I'm trying to avoid trouble—"

Pete pulled his arm away.

"My whole job is about helping people avoid trouble. That's what I was trying to do today. Keep somebody out of trouble. And after what's happened to me, it's pretty easy to see Pearl's side of things." Pete zipped his jacket. "So here's a novel fucking idea: *drop it*. Leave him the hell alone."

"Impossible. Where do you think you're going?"

Pete threw wide his arms, and Pinkerton looked around the restaurant at the people who had ceased eating, who were now watching the two of them.

"If you're gonna arrest me and charge me with something, then let's go back to that little makeshift jail of yours and I'll wait for my lawyer. In fact, I can't wait to get in front of a Rimrock County jury."

Pinkerton laced his fingers together, sniffed, and glared at the table.

"I'm gonna take your posture as a sign that I'm free to go," Pete said.

Then Pete announced to the room that the man sitting there was an ATF agent named Jim Pinkerton who had agreed to let him go. Pete said he just wanted to have witnesses that he wasn't being charged with anything.

When he got outside it was full dark and he was a few moments in the parking lot looking for a car that was probably still in front of Debbie's house in Tenmile if it hadn't been towed to God knows where.

And Katie. God knows where too.

＊　　＊　　＊

How did they get by?

They bummed rides to places where they stayed. They bunked with a guy named Ira in Tacoma who tried to feel Rose up and she let him because she'd had a lot to drink, but then didn't let him when she was tired and crawled into the blankets next to Pomeroy and Yolanda. When it didn't rain, they slept in a tent that Pomeroy kept in another bus station locker with his outdoor gear.

Did it always rain?

Yes.

How much did they get by on?

Nickels a day. Potatoes they cooked over small fires in Viretta Park that they were careful could not be seen from the street. They got by by being on the move at dusk and tucking into some spot or other that Pomeroy knew about, someplace where he had secreted a blanket and some cans in a plastic sack. A condemned apartment in Medina, a bridge in Clyde Hill, an overpass on Mercer Island. They got by on Pike Street simply sitting in front of a hat.

Dine-and-dashing. They took turns: Yo would eat and then break for it and, if necessary, Pomeroy would obstruct the cashier charging out after her.

Yo's got short legs, but she's quick as duck shit, Pomeroy said.

That was how they celebrated her birthday. They ate. They ran.

What about when Yolanda got pinched shoplifting gloves from the Bon?

It was a lucky thing, eventually. She was assigned a social worker, a guy named Norman Butler who wore a porkpie hat and smoked thin cigars. Because she'd turned seventeen, she was eligible for a program that got her an apartment. Pomeroy was reluctant, but when he found out they could get a bigger place if he signed up too, he did. Norman told them they'd have to take classes for job training. They said, yeah yeah, sure thing, Normal. They called him Normal to his face.

Rose cried over it. They were leaving her out. She was nearly frantic when they didn't let her help move their few things in case the social worker came by. Normal wouldn't understand their arrangement, Pomeroy and two gals. They were giving Rose the heave-ho.

She walked to a crowded diner downtown and read and reread the menu at the counter until one of the booths emptied. Then she slipped the tip into her palm and walked to another diner. Looking over her shoulder the whole way. She was near Pike and could see some kids she knew and Kenny and the girls who were getting into cars. Dates, they called them. At first she thought all they did was really go on dates. To the movies. What a sucker she was, what a country mouse.

Did she think of calling home? Her mother? Or Pete?

For a minute, but then an old guy with horn-rimmed glasses pulled a girl out of his Pontiac, and she was yelling and carrying on. Kenny and some of the street kids coming over. At the sight of Kenny, the man jumped into his car and tore off. The girl shrieking and throwing her things, her compact, her hairbrush. A cop pulled up. The crowd melted.

She went to the diner and wondered what to do until dark getting the shakes on the thirty-five-cent coffee. The neon and night sounds downright terrifying now. Catcalls and wolf whistles and the like. Tires on the road. She looked over the counter and into the kitchen. The cook at his regular job. A proper address. A Social Security number. She didn't have any of those things. She didn't even know how to do the stuff a waitress does. How to wash dishes even.

Then she spotted Pomeroy. He was in the door, scanning the room. He was wet with rain mist and his black hair shone. He looked on her like a relieved, disappointed father and that corkscrewed into her heart like the feeling of being loved. She stood. She ran to him and began to hug him, but he wrenched her around by the arm and she cried out. People watched, people did nothing.

Where the fuck you go? He was dragging her out of the place. *Where you been? Yo and I been fuckin worried. . . .*

He was rough with her all the way to the bus stop, but when they got on, he put his arm around her, and she fell into his chest and he petted her head and the sounds that came out of her were coos from before she could talk.

Did they heat chili in its can over the hot plate and pour it over hot dogs and drink Rainier beer? Did they put on the radio and hear the cartoon motorcycle purr of "Electric Avenue" for the very first time in their lives? Did Pomeroy make another beer run and return with a quarter of weed and Kenny and Dee? Did the girls brush their teeth with their fingers because Normal gave them toothpaste but forgot the brushes, and did they get in the dark with Kenny and Pomeroy and become an elegant harem, smoking from Kenny's long brass pipe?

Yes. They did.

And the next day it was like winter in August, the radiators knocking throughout the building, the hallways showing your breath and sounding your steps. The second-floor communal bathroom was wet in the mornings, and a peppered rime of stubble coated the sink that was the only evidence of other boarders. But she felt good, like a squatter, like they were getting away with something, squatting over the pissy, splattered toilet seat to pee and shuffling down the hall in Pomeroy's heavy duster and back into bed with him and Yo.

Was Yo gone for days at a time?

And Rose and Pomeroy would be quiet all week, except to play checkers with pennies and bits of paper or to have a quick fuck in the bed. She took up smoking in earnest, and Pomeroy sent her down for Camels from the machine in the lobby. A Hmong man about the size of her and four times her age made change from behind the front desk, and eyed her with suspicion, but didn't say anything.

You send me out for everything and I'm not supposed to be here, she said, tossing the cigarettes onto his bare chest.

Do you even care about me? he asked.

Yes! Yes, I do!

I'm not so sure about that. If you did, you'd just do things for me.

He fretted with the radio, trying to get stations to come in.

C'mere, she said.

What.

He didn't come over, and instead went and sat at the kitchen table. She straddled his lap and ran her hands through his hair. He leaned back and she felt perfectly adult. She lit a cigarette and gave it to him.

Your roots are coming in. Give me some money and I'll get you some dye.

He lifted her off of him, brusquely, in a mood, and stood.

Where you going?

I don't have girlfriends. He put on his coat.

I know.

So you don't get to ask me where I'm going.

Was it hard for him because he'd been falling in love with her? Had all this time without Yo brought them close, sharing cereal from the same bowl and just smiling at one another across the Formica table? Did he need to cut the cord? Not that she had anywhere else better to go, but did she stay because she thought he was falling in love? Real love and not like Cheatham's love? Was she actually acquainted with his heart in a way that he himself was not?

She worked up a belief in this.

Was she right?

Of course not. A little. Yes. Maybe.

Who knows?

Exactly.

What he did was, he left. Three days. She ate what was in the pantry and stared at the door and cried and expected any minute the Hmong man would come and kick her out onto the street.

When Pomeroy came back, he had Yo and some money.

From what?

Yo's dates.

How did she know?

Rose asked and Pom told her. He gave her some money, and sent her out for hair dye.

TWENTY-SEVEN

From her jail cell, Debbie complained ceaselessly of aches in her stomach, her head, her thin bruised limbs. She said to the cops that they had to do something about it, that she had rights. Then she just begged for relief. She trembled and wore an expression of such pained anxiety, the dayshift jailer took her seriously and brought her aspirin every two hours and, when her condition failed to improve, eventually arranged to have her taken to the hospital. After the fact, it was pretty obvious she was suffering massive withdrawal, that her body was precisely calibrated to the careful and steady administration of vodka, amphetamines, and barbiturates to maintain her.

The jailer on the second shift was a recovered alcoholic and considered sobriety his life's achievement and ministered to her, holding her hand through the bars of the cell. Her thin fingers were bulbed at the knuckles and otherworldly and tacky as drying Elmer's glue. After a while she asked for her hand back, it hurt to have it held at all. The jailer gave her half a pack of cigarettes, and when she smoked one, she threw up. But right after she puked she felt better for a little while, and so she worked the pack for the few respites of sweaty, swimmy relief that vomiting afforded her.

A hospital visit was supposed to happen just after the morning shift change, but a teacher had broken up a huge fight in the local high school parking lot, and by the time everything was sorted out Debbie's appointment had been scotched. She asked to go to the ER once, but it was a faint request made to a cop shop full of a dozen sullen high school wrestlers and officers calling their parents. She went to lie down. No one saw her spasm or heard the jouncing of the springs under the thin mattress as she had the heart attack that killed her.

Pete rode with Judge Dyson to his 1920s-era farmhouse just west of Tenmile. An old buckboard was sunk in a nap of moss in front of a collapsing barn, but the house and the dooryard were fastidiously kept. The judge got out of his car and Pete followed him around the house. The judge waddled up to a car there and pulled off the tarp, revealing a powder blue 1977 Monte Carlo.

Pete shook his head.

"Well, to hell with you then," he said, trying to snap the tarp back over the car.

"No, no," Pete said. "It's great. It's too great."

The judge let the tarp fall from his hands, walked toward the house, picking up stray items between himself and the door. A hand rake, which he tossed toward a small shed that abutted the rear stonewall of the house, then ducked inside. Pete wished the judge would invite him in, but seemed to know too that he would not.

He returned with the car keys attached to a large fob with a picture of a beaver atop a jumbled assembly of sticks. *Where did I leave the dam keys?*

"Funny," Pete said.

"Not really."

"You sure this is all right?"

"It'll be full of hornets and squirrels, I don't do something with it."

"Maybe you should sell it."

"I'm not giving her to you, Pete."

"I know."

"And if she's comes back scratched, I'll have your ass."

"Sure, I know."

"Damn right you know."

They stood a minute, Pete looking at the house he'd never set foot in, the judge into the woods.

"How long they gonna keep your car?"

"No idea. Until they find Pearl, I'm thinking. To make my life hard." He gripped his back and sighed at the sky.

"Anything on your daughter?"

"Nope."

"I got every highway patrolman in Montana and Idaho looking for her. If she turns up thisaway, we'll find her."

"Thanks," Pete said. "Have them keep an eye out for Luke too."

A nuthatch cackled.

"He doesn't know about your father," the judge realized.

"I wrote him a letter, but didn't tell him about it."

"You know where he is," the judge said, by way of asking him why Pete didn't turn him in already.

"He's my brother," Pete said, by way of answering. "Besides, after what those DEA pricks did to me, I'm done helping cops."

"Like you gave them no reason, that mouth of yours."

"It doesn't matter. No one should be able to do that to you."

The judge ran his hands along the lapels of his jacket as if he might thumb his buttonholes and hold forth, but the gesture faded into a mild self-embrace as though he were clenching an empty dress to his chest. He took in his empty house.

"She wanted a new car for a long time," the judge said. "It was just a thing she wanted to have her whole life. For some damn reason. I didn't mind she wanted it, I just couldn't understand why. It took so long for me to get her one. If she could've just explained, maybe she'd have had the pleasure of the thing for more than six months."

The judge shook his head.

"God damn it."

He headed inside.

"I'll take good care of her."

The judge waved him off, and closed the door.

The staff had packed a few things for Katie—pink pajamas, a small tube of toothpaste, a bottle of shampoo, a pink comb and toothbrush—and put them in a paper sack to take with her. The rest of her things were still at the house, which was yet being gone through by law enforcement. She sat with the sack on her lap in the shelter lobby with a staff member waiting for Pete to take her to a foster home. A faulty fluorescent bulb flashed skittishly. How she felt about going to a new home was not any more clear than how she felt about living in a shelter. No one had even asked what she saw happen in her house when the cops busted in and shot the man who was there. She was quiet and untroublesome, and at the shelter she garnered little attention.

When Pete arrived for her, she sat up straight and kicked her legs as a dog might wag its tail. Pete asked the woman sitting with Katie if there was a room where he could be alone with the girl. Katie was in his arms at once and he carried her into the office, sat her on the table, and took a seat near her. She was hoping he would be her father. He had to look up into her eyes, but for a few moments he couldn't and he just touched her leg.

"I have some very bad news, Katie."

He said what had happened to her mother.

The girl covered her face.

He said he was sorry and was presently astonished that he shook under hot sobs himself. *Now you gotta cry*, he said to himself. *Now of all times.* He was able to think of himself critically in this way, and at the same time seize and nearly hyperventilate in sadness. In fact, it was she who reached across the short distance between them and clutched at the nape of his neck, and in a single swoop he had her in his arms again as they both wept together, the child and her social worker.

His grief kept almost guttering out as it should have but the thought that this was so unfair kept aggravating his sadness afresh. His bruised stomach was sore with the effort. That he'd been beaten wasn't fair. The girl was undersized and orphaned, that wasn't fair either. His daughter was gone so long now. That wasn't fair. Her father had left her in Missoula with an alcoholic mother. His parents were dead. His brother was gone.

Pete was alone.

There was the thing. The total lonesome. How that could be.

He noticed as in a dream that she was petting his head. Her touch helped him put himself back together. Right now, he was necessary. For the girl, vice versa, or both.

Pete carried Katie from his car to the Cloningers' door and into the house. The children showed her where she would be sleeping and where she could keep her things. Cloninger's wife suppressed her surprise that the girl had only a paper sack of belongings and wondered aloud what they would need to get for her, and silently began to make a list. The kids emptied out toys from the closet for Katie to partake of.

They all went into the living room for coffee and then out onto the back porch where it was cooler as the late afternoon sun set behind the mountain. The dog came up and as Katie knelt to pet it, Pete and Cloninger shared an awkward glance that bloomed for each into a private grin about Cecil. Time had passed and the boy's outrageous fondling of the animal now seemed remote and safely amusing.

"Thanks for this," Pete said.

"How's the other one?"

Pete covered Katie's ears as he would when he was talking to her mother.

"He's in stir. Got in more trouble after his stay with you."

"I shouldn't have . . . I overreacted."

"Oh, I dunno about that."

"Is he going to get out?"

A breeze picked up and the weeping willow in the yard shivered its ropes of leaves.

"It's not fair that he's locked up. I let him down."

"He's welcome back here if you can get him out."

"That's kind of you."

Pete uncovered Katie's ears and she asked would Pete be staying the night and he said he'd stay until bedtime, which seemed all right to her, but she sat with him as Pete and Cloninger chatted. After a while, though, he quietly nudged her off his lap, and she inspected the porch, the terra-cotta-potted plants, and then the yard, and finally went with Cloninger's daughter out to the garden, where they picked raspberries and returned with stained fingers and raspberry seeds on their cheeks and chins.

Pete put her to bed himself, and sat on the floor next to her and petted her hair. He found it incredibly difficult to leave her side. When he closed the door behind him and went down the hall, he couldn't help feeling like he'd forgotten something in the room where she was. He even patted his pockets.

He wanted her. For a moment he even entertained the idea. She could live with him in his cabin.

"You okay?" Cloninger called from the easy chair in his living room, and Pete was startled, as if caught out at something suspicious. He grinned sheepishly and said he'd better be going.

Cloninger joined him in the foyer, and inspected a loose coat hook made of antelope antler and tightened it to the one-by-four in which it and several other coat hooks were affixed. The hooks were waist-high and homemade by Cloninger himself for his children.

"You don't look so hot, Pete."

Pete grinned again, looked at his shoes, and scratched behind his ear. "I've been better."

Cloninger asked if it was the drug raid that was on his mind. Getting arrested. It'd been in the little Tenmile paper, talked about on the porches and storefront galleries. His name.

"Oh sure," Pete said, as if to say his arrest was but one of many things bothering him.

Cloninger clasped his hands together below his belt buckle, as though expecting Pete to say more, but Pete did not.

"We're getting a few more crazies every year," Cloninger offered. "But don't you forget that you're about the only one who's up here helping out. The kids especially."

"You help too."

"Yeah, well."

Out the screen door and across the road, the forest was alive with wind, pine limbs waving in all directions like a distressed band of tree people.

"A lot of folks come up here to get away," Pete said. "I know I did. But most of us just wind up bringing our particular trouble with us."

Cloninger nodded gravely, even though Pete was trying to joke.

"I's more talking about guys like that Jeremiah Pearl we had living up there," Cloninger said, pointing a thumb up the dirt road that ran past his house and toward Fourth of July Creek.

Pete's mouth fell open. He could kick himself for not asking Cloninger earlier. If things hadn't gone south with Cecil, if he'd just visited to patch things up—

"You know the Pearls?"

"Oh sure. He and his family'd come down. Supper or to work on his truck or something. We'd run up there from time to time too. Helped roof his house."

"Fuck."

Cloninger pursed his mouth. Pete apologized.

"Sorry. I just should've asked you sooner," Pete said. "So you know the whole family."

"Uh-huh."

"Do you have any idea where they are now? The wife and the other kids, I mean."

"They talked about heading to Alaska after he and his wife were arrested."

"They told you about that?"

Cloninger laughed.

"It was about the only subject of interest to Jeremiah. But they ain't up at their place now, are they?"

Pete explained how Benjamin had wandered into a school. Just the boy alone. He told Cloninger how he'd managed to get Pearl to trust him enough to let Pete check on them, but not enough to tell him where the rest of his family was.

"That's strange," Cloninger said.

"Why?"

"You don't think it's strange?"

"Yes, of course I do. When was the last time you saw them?"

Cloninger gazed up toward the brim of his John Deere cap, trying to remember.

"A couple weeks after he and Sarah had been arrested, I reckon. Pearl brought an elk he poached down to butcher. The whole lot of them come down because our storage freezer had about ten inches of ice built up in it, and Sarah and her kids set what all was in the freezer out on the garage floor and then she put 'em all to work chipping ice out of it."

Cloninger hit Pete on the shoulder with the back of his fingers, amused at something.

"They even made snow cones. Got some of them paper oil-change funnels I had laying around and chipped ice into 'em and shook a little Kool-Aid from the packet. Presto."

"And this is when they said they were going to Alaska."

"Oh, I dunno. That was just something they was liable to say. Maybe it was that time, maybe another."

Just then there was a noise from the back of the house—a bump, a voice—and Mrs. Cloninger got up from her sewing machine at the kitchen table and went to check on the children.

"Step outside with me a minute?" Pete asked. "I don't want Katie to know I'm still here."

Cloninger opened the screen door for them and they went out and crossed the yard to the gate and then through it to where the judge's car was parked. The American flag whipped in the wind. A thunderstorm was coming on, and a churned gray wave of clouds banked and bunched over the mountains. A tumult of thunder within them grumbled throughout the racing air.

"So when was this?" Pete nearly shouted over the wind. "When you saw them, I mean."

Cloninger started to take down his flag, the pulley knocking against the flagpole like a bell tone.

"Spring before last. Maybe April. We didn't hear from them after that. It was probably almost fall when me and the kids drove up to see how they was doing. The place looked cleared out. Everything grown over. No vehicles. The windows all dusted up. The wife, she kept a clean house, so we knew they'd been gone awhile."

Cloninger unhooked the flag and nodded for Pete to take up the end with the stars. They folded the flag in half lengthwise.

"They didn't say anything about their plans? What they were going to do about the court case or anything?"

"Fold it in half again."

Pete did, and then Cloninger took one corner on his end and neatly folded it over.

"They didn't say they had any plans. It was a good day. The kids played together. Pearl got his elk butchered and put in the freezer and we cooked up some steaks."

Cloninger folded the flag corner by corner until he arrived at Pete and then took the flag from him and folded it into a tight triangle and tucked it under his arm.

"You might be the last one who saw them before they cleared out," Pete said.

"I s'pose so."

Cloninger shifted the flag under his other arm.

"Is there anything you remember about that last visit?"

"Not really."

"Any fights or discussions—"

"The younger boy, Benjamin, got in a heap of trouble with his mama. He was watching TV with Toby. The Pearls don't allow TV. No cartoons or nothing. She paddled him and made him sit out here on the fence, and he didn't get a snow cone. That was about the high drama of the day."

A limb cracked somewhere in the woods, and the wind sounded

all around like a great surf. Cloninger clapped Pete on the shoulder.

"Well, better get out of this before it rains."

"Sure. Thanks again for taking Katie."

They shook.

"I should thank you. We'll keep her. Long as you need. We got her."

"I'll check back."

Pete climbed in the Monte Carlo. Compared to the mess of his own car, the inside of the judge's vehicle seemed almost naked. Pellets of rain spotted the dusty hood and windshield. Cloninger was now coming back out of the house, jogging toward the drive. Pete started to get out.

"Is Katie asking for me—?"

"Nah," Cloninger said. "I just remembered something."

"What's that?"

"I saw the boy. Benjamin. After the last time."

"Where?"

"He come down for something. Just him. A cup of sugar, like. But not that. Something for his mama, he said. Some herb or something. Like Epsom salts, but not that."

"Just him?"

"Yeah. It was honey maybe? Something like that. I'll have to ask the missus."

"Okay. Thanks."

"Hold on."

"What?"

Cloninger looked at the churned sky, frowned.

"It's on the tip of my tongue."

"It's all right. Call me if you remember."

Cloninger lit up. The sky cracked open and started to dump on them, pounding on the car, the woods, and Cloninger's roof and drive.

"Oil!" Cloninger shouted.

"Oil?"

"He said his mama wanted olive oil!"

And when he was sure Pete heard him, Cloninger slapped the hood and ran inside.

◆　◆　◆

When did she realize that Pomeroy would make a whore of her?

By the time she got back from the Safeway with the dye, a loaf of bread, and a carton of cigarettes. She stopped in the middle of the stairwell, saying to herself you're so stupid. A heavy door some floors below opened and closed. She left the groceries on the floor. She sat across from the Golden Arms on the curb.

A few minutes later Pomeroy was outside, shivering in his short sleeves, crossing the street right for her.

This was as far as I was gonna look. Yo said to go after you, but I was just gonna walk around and tell her I couldn't find you.

I wanna talk to Yo.

Fine. She's right up there. Talk your fuckin head off. I'm going to the bar.

She marched up the stairs and found Yo making a sandwich.

I'm not doing it. Not what you do.

Yo put down the knife and leaned against the counter.

No one asked you to.

I'll do something else.

Okay.

I'm afraid Pom's gonna kick me out.

You don't have to do anything you don't want to, Yo said.

You don't sound like you mean it.

Yo shrugged and started eating.

Did she panhandle down along the waterfront and inside the Pike Place Market, a little cup in front of her?

Yes. And the old men who worked those plum spots ran her off, and she found herself talking to a cop at an on-ramp to I-5, asking her what the hell she thought she was doing working that intersection. The cop himself calling what she did *work*.

So she found herself down between Second and First streets with the other panhandling kids and the young hookers, the old buskers who caterwauled over four-string guitars like outraged leprechauns. People who slunk into the night with huge boom boxes and strutted for one another, watching unbothered when the paramedics rolled up and tended to a freshly wounded girl who screamed and denied herself care until the pigs showed up and forced her into the ambulance.

Can't they see a girl was raped? Can't they see her date took a tire iron to her? Why they gotta make her say it? Yo would ask, and Rose would not know the answer or what Yo was expecting her to say.

Did she see when Pomeroy barreled up the block and knocked the shit out of some street rat named Vince for trying to roll Yo five weeks before? Did he come out of nowhere while Rose was hitting up strangers for nickels and dimes and take Vince by the hair and slam his face into a light pole to the surprise and muted evasion of all the civilians coming out of the fish market?

And when the cops were coming, she took him by the hand and moved him off a ways, sitting him on the curb, and then sat herself on his lap, commencing to make out with him so that the cops didn't think he was the one who'd left the street rat bloody and knocked out there on the ground.

Did Pomeroy ask if she had any money?

She left her cup over on the sidewalk and it was filched and long gone.

I forgot it when I saw you. I just came running over. I was trying to help you.

You know how to help me, he said, and he strode away.

TWENTY-EIGHT

Cecil had been living in a canvas tent with three other boys, digging trails and putting in fence under the direction of a ranch manager who was not employed by Montana Corrections, but rather worked for a friend of the warden and who had for years used the young men at Pine Hills as a private labor force. Those chosen for this detail were considered lucky. Fresh air and three squares. They were offered a cigarette every evening just after supper, and hot coffee, bacon, and eggs at dawn. The property was bordered by a dry creek bed just outside of Box Elder with the Rocky Boy Reservation on the other side. They worked miles from anything except coyotes, gophers, scrub brush, and the few dilapidated trailers and corrugated shacks that dotted the chalky wasteland reservation to the east.

The other three boys were Indians or half-Indians and shared a laconic humor that Cecil couldn't penetrate, and were in any case not disposed to proffer him any kindness. Cecil had by now acquired a reputation for viciousness, and was considered in the small violent society within the institution to be something of a comer, a real hard case who didn't give a fuck. The Indians called him No Fuck, he said it so much.

Cecil called them stupid prairie niggers, and if they'd been inside, he would've been obliged to fight them all. But the boys worked in the hammering summer sun all day chopping at the hillsides with pickaxes and shovels while the ranch manager watched them from the shade of his pickup. By bedtime they promptly passed out, and at dawn their backs ached from nape to asshole and they were sore everywhere else.

There was also a straw boss on the ranch, a kid about their age. He had a contempt for Cecil and the Indians born most likely of a significant wonder of what it was they'd done to wind up here. He supervised their efforts from his horse. He chewed tobacco, spitting poorly so that his blue shirtsleeve was constantly stained. The Indians quietly joked that he wiped his ass with his shirt cuff.

The straw boss, this nephew or some relation to the owner of the property, asked Cecil what the Indians were saying about him. Cecil told him. The next day, the straw boss didn't chew any tobacco and looked at the Indians like he dared them to say anything. Come late morning, they obliged him with some muttering and small trickles of laughter.

"What did those fuckin Indians say?" the straw boss asked Cecil.

"I didn't hear," Cecil said.

The kid rode up and asked them did they want to go back to the prison, he could arrange for that, and when they looked at him with faintly disguised indifference, he rode off to visit the ranch manager, who was dozing in his pickup a half mile away. They all watched the kid ride his horse up to the truck and then lean over and talk with the foreman. Then the pickup started up and crossed the uneven earth to where they stood by a pile of fence posts. It seemed the boom was about to come down, the way the manager exited the pickup and slammed the door and hiked his belt and marched at them bandy-legged and swole up. But the ranch manager was utterly unequipped to deal with bickering boys, was in fact astonished that these kids had any time at all to mess around talking, much less arguing, and it was immediately evident that he was as disgusted with the straw boss as with any of them.

He checked their progress on the fence. He asked Cecil to show

him how he was using the posthole digger. Before Cecil could finish, the man snatched the tool from him and demonstrated a few tips
toward using it more efficiently, as though that were the source of all
the trouble. Then he got back in the truck and watched them return
to work.

The straw boss sat on his horse, seething.

That night, the straw boss sent the Indians to bed early. Alone with
his one white prisoner, he said his name was Jeremy.

"Do you want to escape?" he asked.

"What?"

"We can take the pickup. It's mine to inherit anyway," he whispered
over the fire. "All this property belonged to my daddy before he died
and my uncle took over. He acts like it's his, but it's mine. But he can
fuckin have it. I hate it out here. I hate fuckin Indians especially."

He spat, wiped his lip with his finger, wiped his finger in the dirt.

"Do you have anywhere we could light out to?"

The spikes of campfire stabbed at the dark as Cecil contemplated
this plot and this would-be coconspirator.

"It's only a matter of time."

"What is?"

"Two of us against them three insubordinate Indians," he said.
"Only a matter of time before the dirty fuckers slit our throats."

Cecil pokerfaced his skepticism.

"You just wait, friend," Jeremy said.

At last, Cecil said that yeah he had a place they could go. But the next
day Pete showed up and took him to Tenmile for his mother's funeral.

It was two weeks to get the necessary paperwork filled out and the
approval for Cecil to attend the service. Pete had to ask Judge Dyson to
call the Kalispell morgue to keep Debbie's body on ice, then to transfer
it to the Libby morgue, then for the Libby morgue to hold on to it for
another few days. Ultimately, none of this was necessary as there was
no grave plot for her and she had to be cremated in Missoula anyway.
Her ashes hadn't even been returned in time for the small service in

the Tenmile funeral home. Her brother Elliot sent flowers and a note that curtly informed Pete that he and his wife wouldn't take either of Debbie's children.

Only Cloninger, Katie, Cecil, and Pete attended the service. Katie sat with Cloninger, resting her head on his arm. When Cloninger gave Cecil his condolences, the boy suggested he go fuck himself. Katie put her hand inside Cloninger's to take back his attention and shot her brother a quick raspberry.

The reverend said a few words about redemption and what a trial Debbie's life was. Her childhood in Colorado and a variety of military bases in California and Texas and how she settled in Tenmile with a man who'd run out on her and her children. He'd gotten the biography from Pete, but even Pete wasn't sure how much of it was true and wondered if Debbie was telling lies to the very last.

The reverend invited anyone to say anything about her, share a memory or funny story. There were no such stories. Cecil blew out a long sigh. Pete stood, pushed his hair out of his eyes, and said she was trying to get her life together, she was always at least trying. Katie cleaved to Cloninger and cried some. Cecil didn't show the slightest distress, save looking toward the door, as if someone coming for him was about to enter or so that he might flee at the first opportune moment during the service.

It wasn't until they'd crossed the Idaho panhandle that Cecil realized they weren't on the way back to the ranch outside Box Elder.

"Where are you taking me?" he asked when they passed a sign indicating they'd entered Washington.

"You want to go back to that camp?" Pete asked.

"Where are we going?"

"Spokane."

"What for?"

"You think you can make it on your own?"

"Holy shit."

"If you don't think you can, I gotta take you back."

"Hot shit. Holy shit. For real?"

Pete nodded.

"Holy fuck. Awesome."

"What I said wasn't true. About your mom trying. She never tried. I only said it for your sister."

"Sure."

Cecil's mind raced forward down the road, out of the pickup, into the Next.

"Cecil, look at me."

The boy's face was wild with freedom. He put his hands on the dashboard and was shaking his head in wonder.

"She was a piece of shit, Cecil. She didn't try a day in her life. I was wrong to have put you in the—"

"You're not fucking with me?"

"I'm trying to tell you I'm sorry."

"You're really letting me out in Spokane. For real."

"Yes. Your friend, Ell, she called to tell me to tell you they'd moved to Spokane. That you were still welcome."

"No way."

"Listen. I'm going to tell Pine Hills you ran away. You can't come back to Montana."

"This is so fucking awesome."

"You can't come back. At least not for a long time. You hear me?"

"No. Yeah. I won't." He drummed the dashboard. "This is so goddamn awesome!"

Bear had found a janitor gig in Spokane. Pete pulled up to their apartment and when Ell came out, astonishing tears ran down Cecil's face, and his nose ran, and Ell started crying as well. She twisted to hug him with the baby. Pete helped him get his bag, and Cecil bounced into her apartment with her and she showed him his room.

Pete slipped away before Cecil could say good-bye or thank him.

+   +   +

Did she watch Yo work?

On accident.

A not unhandsome forty-year-old man with a leather satchel and nice gray hair at his temples moved with purpose up the block and she followed. Paused at a mailbox, as if dropping in a letter, and then went in among the girls along the graffitied wall, girls who mashed out smokes and scurried over when he started to chat with Yo. She watched Yo walk up the street, disappear around the corner with the man, and come back surprisingly soon.

After that she watched from across the street. The girls just stood around smoking or chewing gum and then a guy would come and one of them would leave with him and come back later.

Did she follow Yo into the hotel and sneak past the front desk and find the room? Did she listen at the door as Yo serviced this man?

No.

She asked Yo about it later, as Yo douched in the apartment bathroom.

Was it less frightening than she imagined? According to Yo was it just a matter of teasing it out of the guy, so little touching really, and that you don't have to kiss the customer, you don't even have to really look him in the eye, yeah, there is a little weirdness sometimes—a guy will try put a finger in your butt or he might want to toss you around—but you just keep yourself between him and the door and keep your pepper spray nearby is all. When it comes down to it, all anybody wants is to get their rocks off and feel cool about it. Was it just a matter of being cool?

Of course it wasn't.

But it seemed that way.

She swallowed a couple of times and almost didn't ask it, but then she did: *Would you help me if I tried it?*

Yo acted as if Rose had just asked to borrow a comb, just nodded sure.

What was it like?

It was like this: Yo introduced her to other girls. To a one, they were young and kind to her. They shunted away the freaks and rough ones that were known to them. Yo told her to be confident and just ask the guy inside the car if he wanted a date. Then to do what he asked for.

How much?

Tell him it's your first time and you want as much as he's got.

Really?

Yes. Really.

The car rolled up along the curb. Yo nudged Rose, and she walked over, thinking this is the car where I will become a whore. Astonishment shivered over her. Yet most of the girls she knew were. Rose didn't feel like she was dressed right in just her regular clothes. Her sneakers looked childish and she had no idea yet that that was the idea, that she would now be trying to look childish, girlish, and whorish. Still, she couldn't imagine giving a guy head in these sneakers.

Was her first date kind?

Kind enough. He was thrilled by the claim that this was her first time—though he didn't believe it—and he tried to kiss her on the mouth, and she let him because she didn't know how to stop him. She didn't know how to stop anything. He gave her forty-five dollars, which seemed a fortune.

Yo said that wasn't too shabby.

She soon learned to climb in the car, show the date where to park, and say, *You can't kiss me. I touch you. You can't kiss me. I do all the work. You tell me what you like and I'll do it, and if it costs more, I'll tell you.*

Did she ever get in a car and feel in the way the date breathed through his nose or pinged his eyes to the rearview every few minutes that she should get out at the next light get out right away, that this one was too sketchy?

Yeah, but she didn't think it would happen to her. The dates were so goddamn grateful for her tiny hands, her wry, filthy mouth that expressed in word and act a twisted and premature craving for cum, for specific cum, for your special cum, only cum, let me get it out of there, baby, I need it, give it to me, give me your goddamn cum baby. Give it. Come on. Cum for me. Come on.

And then it was three or four in the morning, and Rose and Yo would make their way in the dark back to the Golden Arms and Yo would give Pomeroy her money and Rose would too.

And Pomeroy would buy them presents with it?

Yes. A ghetto blaster for the apartment and new velvet pillows and a box of comic books and strawberry shampoo.

He talked about getting other girls, making some real money.

Did she get diseases?

Of course. Herpes came in a series of hot pinpricks between her legs. Yo took her to the free clinic on Madison Street. After she was examined, she waited for counseling in an office jam-packed with boxes of rubbers and other contraception, douches and paperwork. She fidgeted and then a large maternal counselor came in with a clipboard.

So where are you from, Rose?

Montana.

Family there?

Not really. My mom's in Texas. That's where I was last.

Bad situation at home?

She didn't want to talk about it.

Where do you live?

Rose looked at the counselor with suspicion.

What's with all the questions? Are you gonna give me medicine or not?

The counselor pulled off her cardigan sweater and pumped her collar up and down to cool off.

This is all just so I can help. I could maybe get you a place to stay for a little bit if you're interested. Do you ever use protection?

I don't like rubbers.

Do you like herpes?

Rose closed her eyes, gripped the armrests of her chair.

When was your last period?

I only ever had a couple.

Well, you're young yet. Would you know if you missed one?

I guess not.

So you might be pregnant. How would you feel about having a baby, Rose?

I dunno.

Would you consider an abortion?

No. The baby didn't do anything wrong.

How would you take care of a child?

I dunno. You got some services I bet. Or is all you do abortions?

The woman sighed and leaned forward. Sweat was beading over her lip.

You're getting services right now. One of the services is trying to head off a pregnancy that both of us know you're not prepared to handle.

Rose couldn't concentrate on what the woman was saying. Her brain just wouldn't engage with it.

You got sweat on your lip.

The woman set the clipboard in front of her and didn't wipe off the sweat or even acknowledge that Rose had noticed it. She handed Rose a packet of pamphlets bound by a rubber band.

This is some literature. Read it and then sign down here. Here's a box of condoms. Use them.

What about . . . ?
The herpes?
Yeah.
Go to the drugstore and get some aspirin. Take a hot bath.
That's it?
That's it.
The woman's grin was faint, serene, maddening.

TWENTY-NINE

Just back from dropping Cecil off in Spokane, Pete was stopped at a crosswalk in Tenmile waiting for an old cowboy to shuffle across the street when the judge spotted him from the courthouse lawn. The judge had taken a rake from a groundskeeper and was demonstrating some aspect of lawncraft when he noticed his own car and shouted at him and waddled over on his fat legs. Pete could tell the man had bad news.

"What is it?"

"You haven't been to your place."

"No, I was out of town. Why? What's going on?"

"It's gone, Pete."

"What's gone?"

"Your house."

When they got there, the earth around the cabin was wet, and everything Pete had owned was now ash or burned beyond recognition in the charred crater. His heat-warped bed frame and coils of mattress springs sat in the dirt and black remnants of the wood floor. He climbed down onto the cast-iron stove where it had fallen into his cellar. He pulled several blackened potatoes from the earthen shelf and touched around the still-warm molten glass of a burst jar of pickles. That was all that was left. His books, his pictures of Rachel, his leather chair. A curl of his daughter's hair he kept in a small jar on the shelf in his room. Love letters. His baby book. Quilts his mother had made him. His rifles and his great-grandfather's .22 pistol.

For some reason, he thought of the piece of paper with his brother's address on it, and then vaguely recalled putting it in his wallet. He looked and there it was, along with a small school picture of his daughter when she was ten, the scrawled phone number of some woman he no longer remembered, and several business cards. This and forty-odd dollars. His possessions entire.

The judge watched him thumbing through his wallet and then told him to come on out of there, and when he did his hands were black all over and he started chuckling.

The judge remarked sarcastically that Pete was taking the fire well.

Pete gripped his knees and shook in his helpless chortling.

"You've gone around the goddamn bend," the judge said. "Come on, let's get over to the courthouse and have a drink."

Pete sat on the hood of the Monte Carlo and started to roll a cigarette.

"That's all right, I'm good."

"Nonsense. You come with me. You can stay with me."

Pete smiled.

"Thanks, but no."

"You gonna stay in Missoula?"

"Nah."

"Your father's?"

"God no."

The judge shoved his hands in his pants pockets and watched Pete roll the cigarette and begin to smoke with diminishing acknowledgment at the things the judge said, how it'd be all right, how these things happen, that Pete would get on his feet again. How it was damn lucky that Jim McGinnis just happened to have his water tenders back from the fires outside of Whitefish. Could've lit up the whole mountain.

Pete nodded.

The judge said again that Pete should stay with him, and Pete again begged off. Smoking and grinning like a lunatic. The judge finally said for Pete to go to hell then, and climbed in the car.

He went to Pearl's house up Fourth of July Creek. There were mice and a hornet's nest and more than a few barn spiders fat as cotton balls, but when the Pearls lit out they'd left their home more or less furnished and Pete was able to make it clean and comfortable inside of a week. He swept up the dust and pellets of rodent shit and flushed the bats from the eaves. A bird's nest caught fire inside the stovepipe the first time he lit it, and he went outside and chased down the large burning ashes of leaves and scrap paper that floated away from the house, glowing malefic in the dark and sometimes catching in the trees and burning the witches moss and other times landing in the dry grasses around the house. He wondered the while was he fated to burn down the forest.

Cloninger lived a few miles down the road and Pete was able to visit Katie and never left without a plate of Mrs. Cloninger's corn bread or a tureen of casserole or soup. He held an old margarine container of corn and pumpkin chowder when his brother's parole officer rolled by, slow and then suddenly accelerating, kicking up a plume of dust meant for Pete.

Wes Reynolds followed him up to the Pearls' house. Pete looked on as Wes inspected the Pearls' home for signs of Luke, opening cupboards and thumbing through dog-eared Bibles and then as he went out and shined a flashlight under the house.

"How many times do I have to tell you I don't know where he is?"

"No, you said you *did* know. And that you would never tell me."

Wes crossed the meadow to the burnt-out Airstream trailer and walked to the cliff. Replaying their last exchange up at the Yaak country store made Pete wonder if Wes was the one who'd burned down his cabin.

I'm never going to tell you. And you'll never find him, I'll make sure of that.

You just fucked up, man.

That some kind of threat?

It certainly had been some kind of threat. By the time Wes went up the hill behind Pearl's house, Pete was all but sure he'd set his home afire. Wes spent some time at a pile of loose stones near the empty chicken coop and asked about it when he got back, wanting to know how they got there.

"You torched my house."

Wes put a thumb through a belt loop and tipped back his hat.

"Maybe your brother left a cigarette going up there."

"All because you got *beat up*? Don't you have a sense of proportion?"

"You should've told me where he is."

"You think I'm going to now?"

"Of course not," Wes said, heading down the hill. "But the fucker has one less place to rack out."

He sipped coffee and watched a pair of deer eat in the meadow. The morning had been downright cold and Pete wondered did deer worry about that, were they eating quickly, did they hate the cold. He realized this worry about the deer was a worry for Rachel. Some of the larch shed their needles, showering yellow and orange pins in each brisk, pining gust.

Pete cleared his throat. The deer lifted their heads and ceased chewing. In a brindled blur they leapt into the forest, and then he saw Benjamin jump over a stump, followed by Jeremiah, who stepped on it, surveyed the meadow, the tree line, the sky, and then strode out after his boy.

Pete's heart lifted, sang a little. He went outside and waved at them and was honestly moved to see them, it felt like such a long time. Grasshoppers sprang away from Benjamin in dozens like a herald in miniature, and when he got to the stream he squatted down and in a moment had something cupped in his hands. Pete asked to see what it was when he got up to the house, and the boy put a green and yellow frog in Pete's palms. The two of them petted it and felt its frightened, urging heart.

Ben looked good. He had a scrape over his eye that had mostly healed, his hands were filthy, and he reeked of campfire, but he had color in his face, weight too. Pete told him so.

"There's frogs all down there," Benjamin said. His eyes were bright as new pennies. "You can get one anytime you want."

"I will," Pete said, touching the boy's head.

Pearl hiked up the rocks to where Pete and Ben stood by the house and scanned the meadow for a moment again, then nodded and grunted a greeting when Pete said hello. Pete handed the frog back to Ben and reached out to shake Pearl's hand, and the man took it and pumped it succinctly.

"I'm squatting," Pete said, answering Pearl's unasked question. "My cabin burned down."

"How'd it burn down?" Benjamin asked, thrilled.

"I was away. It was cinders when I got back."

"Maybe lightning hit it."

"Maybe. Can I get you a cup of coffee, Jeremiah?"

The man had been listening to Pete answer the boy's questions about the fire and now looked about uneasily.

"There wasn't no storm."

"I can be out of here pronto," Pete said. "I'll git if you want to winter here."

"Passing through," Pearl said.

"You should stay."

"We most certainly should not."

"Let me fix you a cup of coffee."

"It's all right."

"I wish you'd visit a little."

"Well," he said flatly.

"Let me get you a cup. It's fresh."

Benjamin was already back in the meadow for more frogs. A small sigh from Pearl.

"I take it black. Put in a little water to cool it off. I don't want to wait on it."

Pete did as the man asked and brought out the coffee and again invited Pearl into his own house. Pearl sat on the ground cross-legged and sipped the coffee.

"There's a little firewood out behind the chicken coop," Pearl said. "Not enough for winter, but some."

Pete thanked him, asked how the coffee was. Pearl grunted.

"I met Stacks," Pete announced.

Pearl paused briefly, sipping his coffee, and then took a swallow and said, "Pinkerton, you mean."

"Yes."

"I assume you had a meeting about me."

"I was arrested actually. Mistakenly."

Pearl was surprised by this. Then suspicious. Then he sipped his coffee.

"They don't make mistakes," he said.

Pete told what had happened. The raid. The man with the shotgun on Debbie's porch. Some DEA clusterfuck. The girl he'd been going to see. Getting the shit kicked out of him. Going to the cafe with Pinkerton.

"He asked me to help catch you—"

"I bet he did."

"—but I told him to fuck off."

"Wouldn't matter if you agreed to try and bring us in."

"I know."

"There's no going in."

"I know."

Pearl sipped some more coffee and gazed across the meadow to the remains of the trailer. A remote expression like a cloud passing before the sun crossed his face as he entertained some memory.

"What are you thinking?"

"Sarah had a vision that said I had to burn that trailer. Pinkerton and Ruffin and the rest weren't coming back. We could've sold it, had a little money." He looked into his coffee, closed his eyes, his mouth moved. He seemed to be saying a short prayer. He nodded at something he asked himself or perhaps was just saying amen. "But she was right. She was right."

"Are they in Alaska now?"

Pearl faced him.

"Every time I see you, you know another piece of my business. How is that?"

"I know Mr. Cloninger."

"Cloninger. Good man. For a civilian."

"Why's Benjamin out here with you?"

"It's not for us to question why we were chosen, but only to carry the burden."

"I know you don't trust me, but you can."

He looked Pete full in the face. His own was as filthy as if he'd just crawled out of the ground. Lines of grime like black rays around his eyes from times he'd squinted.

"That's not something I'm ever going to do."

"All right."

He handed Pete the empty cup with a nod and stood. His whistle ricocheted off the rocks and across the meadow and Benjamin sat up holding two fat frogs. He set them free and came walking through the grasses toward the house, wiping his hands on his pants.

"We might be up at Deerwater a day or two," Pearl said, hitching up his rifle. "I know Ben would appreciate it if you'd come play checkers. I just don't have the patience."

Pearl headed toward the boy, touched his shoulder, and they walked together to the twisted and overgrown wreckage of the Airstream. Pete wondered was Pearl remembering his wife sending him to commit arson on his own property. Did Pearl go inside with a jerry can of gas and open the windows and did the fuel splash onto the screen in small rainbows. Did he back out the door, pouring. Did he strike a kitchen match against his jeans and drop it on the ground and did the flame hasten into the trailer, the inside light up like Stacks himself had flipped the switch, and did fire dance in obscene chemic colors as the polyester curtains went up in green and cerise flashes like magicians' smoke.

How did she get busted?

A date pulled up in a Plymouth and didn't lean over to roll down the window. The rain was small and persistent. She climbed in. He had a crew cut and was extremely nervous.

You want a date, baby?

Yes. He looked at her and his brows creased. *How much?*

Eighty. She'd never done this, but she figured she'd pocket the difference. Fuck Pomeroy. *You see that parking lot over there. Just pull in. We got people who keep an eye out there, so it's safe.*

He swallowed, and put the car in gear, stalled out, restarted the car and pulled into traffic. She noticed Pomeroy didn't have anyone on the corner, but she didn't tell the date to drive on. She didn't want to spook him. She wanted the sixty goddamn dollars for herself.

He parked. *What do I get for eighty?* He killed the engine.

You get off. In my pussy.

He sighed. *Okay,* he said, and reached into his coat for his wallet.

It's raining like a mother out there, she said, unbuttoning her coat.

What was he holding when she turned to him?

A snub-nosed .38. She started to speak, her door flung open, and she was yanked so hard out of the car that she flew out onto the lot.

They put her in cuffs, and then in a hard plastic backseat of the police cruiser, a small processing room with the spastic overhead fluorescent panel, and now with this detective and his stubble and acrid coffee breath and sidearm, and this undercover greenie who was getting ribbed by his fellows—*Christ, Cunningham, did you really draw down on this poor kid?*—and then in the booking room, her purple fingertips, this oversize coarse pink jumpsuit that nearly fell off her shoulders, these paper slippers . . .

Was she surprised that no one was mad?

Yes. She expected someone to yell at her, this was the first time the cops had her in custody, but they simply directed her from one room to another, one holding cell to another, until they put her in a van with about seven similarly reserved girls and shipped her to Pioneer House.

Was she aware of the charges against her?

Yes. Prostitution.

Did she wish to make a statement at that time?

Frustratingly no. There's nothing in the file.

Did she give her DOB and her POB and her next of kin?

No. She volunteered nothing but her name. Rose Snow. She was a whore. Did they get it? They could put her in jail for all she cared. They could go ahead and shoot her in the head.

For.

All.

She.

Cared.

THIRTY

Despite seventy years of abandonment to the weather, to eaves-high snow and the ceaseless drizzle and storm and winds that made a deadfall of so many trees, many dwellings and public houses in the ghost town of Deerwater remained upright all these years, if not safely habitable. The chinking had fallen from all the cabins where summer wasps nested in their coolnesses, and every building shone in the sunlight the otherworldly silver of sun-bleached pine, all the exposed woodwork napped in a gray velvet. But the buildings stood in testament to the hardy, hurried skill of the people who built them.

The town had burned down twice in its short history and both times was rebuilt in roughly the same configuration, running straight up the narrow gut of the ravine. There was a graveyard. There was a gallows. A jail dug into the hillside that was still locked shut with a rusted padlock.

The two-story clapboard hotel was the most sound and true of all the several dilapidations, and it was here where Benjamin Pearl watched a spider gingerly wrap a struggling bluebottle fly, expertly swaddling it in silk and tucking it in the corner among the others, as in a nursery. This spider's pantry.

"Your turn, man," Pete said.

"I'm a boy."

"Term of endearment. Go."

Benjamin looked at the board and lifted a black checker, moving it forward to where Pete could jump it.

"You sure about that?"

"Is it okay if we don't play no more?"

"I was starting to wonder if we'd make it to a dozen games."

"Will you stay awhile, though?"

"Yeah, sure."

They were on the floor. A few iron bed frames with mattresses of straw and striped canvas ticking were jammed unevenly into the corner, and the Pearls' things were spread out on the pine that was scored and scuffed with the boot marks of hundreds of long-dead men. A flashlight and Bible lay near the opening of Pearl's sleeping bag. Collapsible plastic cups. The toothbrushes Pete had gotten them. A small camp stove and cans of food he'd brought stood in a neat stack along the wall. MINA, MINA, SHEKEL, HALF-MINA etched into the door.

"Why didn't you two each take a bed?" Pete asked.

"Centipedes all in them. I like centipedes fine in the daylight, but I don't care for them crawling on me when I'm asleep."

"Fair enough."

"There's earwigs in 'em too and they'll get into your brains."

"Is that right."

"Yup. It's completely true."

"I told your father, I'd clear out if you two wanted to come back to your house."

Benjamin stood. The spider sat motionless in the middle of its web. Benjamin touched one of the spokes of it and the spider held on, but when Ben plucked it again, the spider sped to the edge, along the sill, near his food.

"We won't go back. We're cast into the wilderness."

"And why is that exactly?"

Pete smiled as though he was teasing, but Ben watched the spider.

"What is it, Ben?"

He sniffed.

"They was all like in the cartoon. That's when I knew."

"You're losing me, kid."

"Paula was the sneezing one, and Ruth was silly and couldn't move her arms right. And Jacob was like the one that was laughing all the time. And Rhea was grumpy. Just like in the cartoon."

"The cartoon? What cartoon?"

Pete slid along the floor to where he could see Ben's face. The boy gazed through the smoky glass or at the mottled surface of it.

"Ethan was sleepy. Mama couldn't get him to wake up, and he was the littlest."

"They were sick?"

"He did it to punish me."

"Did what? What did he do?"

"Papa's coming."

Through the smoked translucent glass they made out the shape of Pearl hurrying up the still-rutted main street overgrown with bear grass. As he got closer, they could see his jaw moving like he was talking to himself. Pete wondered did they spend a lot of their time just muttering near one another. Did they even hear one another.

Pearl made the hotel steps two at a time to the second floor and shoved through the single-hinged door in a hurry, in a fury.

"Up! We're getting out of here," Pearl said.

"What's going on?" Pete asked.

Jeremiah strode into the room, took his rifle from where it leaned against the wall, and went over to the window Benjamin had just been looking through. The boy had begun packing. Pearl rubbed the glass, but the stubborn accumulation of dust seemed to have melded permanently to the window in all these years and the view was warped and dim as through a glass of beer. He knocked out a few panes with the rifle butt with efficient pops. The boy hesitated, and Pearl sensed it immediately.

"I said pack it up, Ben."

The child gathered their cups and shoved their loose clothing into their sacks and put on his coat and his boots.

"There's someone coming," Pearl muttered, scanning the overgrown ghost town, poking his head out the window to see left and right. "What I get for telling you we were here."

"I'm sure it's nobody. Kids come up to drink beer and people come to look at the old—"

"This was no kid. Some fucker with a sidearm. You report us to your superiors?"

"Jeremiah, I don't think I have said more than two words to a superior in a year."

Pearl scoped the meadow between the ghostly cabins and mercantiles, a roadway once choked with cart, hoof, and foot traffic. Where children had dashed between wagons on their way to the school.

Pearl whipped around.

"Is this it? Is this how you decided to end it?"

Pete opened his face to Pearl, let play every honest naked thought and let Pearl read them.

"Do you really think I want something like that?"

Pearl slung his rifle over his shoulder, told Benjamin to hurry up, and dragged a canvas bag of their things out of the room and down the hall toward the stairs. Pete followed. He needed to talk to him. About the kids being sick. About Ben thinking it was his fault—

Pete stopped on the landing when he realized what Benjamin had been telling him.

That they died.

That the children got sick and died. And Pearl told the boy it was his fault.

Pearl started down the stairs.

"Jeremiah!"

Pearl ignored him.

"Wait a minute!" Pete shouted. "They're dead, aren't they?"

He gripped the banister and just the weight of his hand made the rail come free and the balusters helixed away out over the stairs, pieces falling in front of Pearl. Pearl stopped on the steps, his breathing heavy. Pete could see his face in profile—the man wouldn't turn all the way around—breathing heavy through his nose, like a bull. His jaw moved queerly and his whiskers shook. He was otherwise still.

"Why'd you tell Ben it was his fault?"

Pearl heaved the canvas bag to the bottom of the stairs where it thudded to the wood floor and sent up a plume of chalky dust. Then he descended himself, his footfalls heavy on the steps. Pete went after him.

"What did you do, Jeremiah? Those kids—"

Pearl whipped around and struck Pete's face with an open palm. The blow threw him back and into the newel at the bottom of the stairs. Pearl hit him again and Pete fell onto the floor. He crabwalked backward as Pearl rained down slaps and then fists, starbursts of pain, klaxons of pain, as Pearl shouted that he would bury all of them for what they did, that he was the Lord's avenger, that none would be spared His wrath.

Then his face shuddered like a broken engine coming to rest.

Pete's head toned, an aching bell.

Then Pearl had Pete's shirt in his fist and he spoke into his face.

"I am dynamite, Mr. Snow. And you, you are a functionary of Satan. You cannot say you were not told. You cannot say that no one told you what you are."

He punched Pete in the nose and all over his face and all was white and loud and blurred.

The boy was shouting from upstairs. His voice composed itself.

"Papa! PAPA!"

Pete lay flat on his back in the settling dust. He'd been gone a moment, but now he sat up on his elbows, working a diskiltered jaw. His vision mildly quaked. His teeth hurt. His ear pulsed like a burning coal. He tasted blood.

Pearl knelt in the doorway, his rifle aimed somewhere out into Deerwater.

"Hold it right there!" he ordered, his voice clear and plain.

Pete flipped onto his stomach. Christ. What was happening now.

He pulled himself up on the wall and along it and then stood behind Pearl.

His heart sank at what he saw.

Wes.

His brother's PO had halted in the middle of the exposed roadway between the old buildings. He tilted his head to see better who was yelling at him, but he couldn't make anyone out in the shadowed interior of the hotel. Pearl trained his rifle on Wes.

"Okay, look," Pete said steadily to Pearl.

"Shut up."

"Now listen. That's my brother's parole officer."

Pearl took his left hand from the forestock and yanked Pete forward and out the front door by his belt loop.

"You two get out of here," Pearl said. "Now. Or I will kill him. And you."

Pete stood in the sunshine and horseflies. He shielded his eyes.

"Wes!" Pete shouted.

Wes threw out his palms, wordlessly asking what the hell was this. Pete jogged to where he stood about 150 feet in front of him, waving his palms the whole way. Wes craned his neck to look up into the window overhead. Pete glanced up and back. Shit. Ben's rifle barrel appeared out the window as well.

"Get Ben down from there!" Pete shouted to Pearl as he advanced toward Wes.

Wes reached down and unsnapped his holster.

"Christ!" Pete yelled. "Let's don't escalate, Wes."

"Just tell your brother to come out," Wes replied.

"My brother isn't here, Wes," Pete said when he was close enough to talk plain to him. "These are just—"

"A couple idiots drawing down on an officer of the law. Luke! Luke Snow, you get your ass out here!"

Wes advanced, removing his .38.

"I said to *stop* right there!" Pearl screamed and the ferocity of it stalled Wes, but only just, and Pete stepped directly in front of him, palms up.

"Please, Wes. Just listen."

Wes advanced yet. The fool.

"Wes! Stop!"

"You better fuckin stop him, Pete!" Pearl shouted.

"Wes, please! Just hold up a goddamn minute!"

Wes halted a few feet from Pete, who stole a quick look over his shoulder. Benjamin was still at the window. Pearl had moved outside, taken a new position at the corner of the hotel, where he drew a fresh bead on them. Pete again put himself between the two men.

"I'll put a bullet in the both of you cocksuckers!" Pearl yelled.

"Jeremiah, just let me talk to him!"

Pete stepped forward, just to the left of Wes. Close enough to touch him.

When Pete reached for his shoulder, Wes leaned away, aimed the pistol at Pete's chest.

"Look, I'll tell you where Luke—"

Wes shuddered, unevenly, like he was having trouble with a dance step, and lowered the gun. Crows started from an old barn roof. Wes reached around as if to scratch his back and then belched up a long red tongue that Pete still didn't recognize as blood. Then he did, and the long suctionlike fade as the rifle report diminished away into the trees, the wind in the trees.

Hearing himself say *oh shit it's all right it's all right*.

Seeing himself stepping forward.

Wes pointed the pistol at Pete again, his wide eyes glassy with shock or pain or perhaps something only known to the nearly dead. Then the man's head yanked backward as if on a string. A red cataract flipped out behind his ear. He toppled down.

Pete spun around. To yell at Pearl to stop. But there was only the boy in the upstairs window, a ghost of smoke there. Pete looked at Wes helplessly. Through the open front door he heard Ben bound down the stairs. He paused at the doorway to look out at what he'd done, and his father yanked him down the hall, toward the back. Another moment and they were headlong to an old broken fence. Pearl ran and the boy chased after.

Hearing himself shouting at them.

Feeling himself neither going after them nor staying put, just moving about within his senseless, ceaseless invective.

Hearing himself asking them what did they do, what did they do. Why. Why didn't they let him take care of it. He would have taken care of it.

Benjamin stopped at Pete's garbled screaming and turned around. Pearl had made the fence and seeing that his son had lagged, ran back and plucked Ben by the ear and led the crying child in front of him and fairly barked at him until the boy began to run.

All was quiet save the gentle aspiration of the man on the ground. Pete went to where he lay faceup, his eyes partly shut like someone squinting at a menu. His plaid shirtfront black with a saucerful of blood. He called to the Wes within the body, and inspected him to see what could be done. A good portion of the man's skull and brains were gone. Yet he breathed. Wet, thin breaths that spoke to the suddenness and inappropriateness of his death stealing over him.

Pete felt a cold churning in his bowels and his testes, and he moved some feet away. He guessed there was no remedy, and then thought maybe he should gather the pieces of bone and brains, but he knew he was just torturing himself.

He steeled himself to sit next to this person he'd known as a boy, went to him. He took his hand and told him it was all right to go on and that he was sorry and asked him why he had been such a stupid son of a bitch, was it worth it, of course it wasn't.

This was September. Autumn was gathering itself up and the feeling all around was of happy things departing.

Sometime later it occurred to Pete that Wes could perhaps be dying for days. He thought of President Lincoln, breathing unbidden a whole night, and much older than Wes when he'd been shot. He thought about Benjamin becoming a murderer. A boy that age.

When it had gotten dark, the man choked but would not die. Suffocating but not yet dead. It was unbearable to hear, and finally Pete palmed the dying man's nose and mouth, thinking, I'll bear some of this, some of this is my fault, maybe the better part of it. But when the man's breathing ceased, nothing stirred in the woods, and Pete was even more profoundly alone. That was unbearable too. But there was nothing to do about it.

THIRTY-ONE

He left the man's body in the night. He worried someone would see the judge's car at the trailhead. In the dark he trod the old Deerwater road where wagons would haul ice, ice cream, lamp oil, and prostitutes. He mused idly on whether Wes was the last murder in this town or were there a few more unlikely deaths yet making their way here.

A pale fingertip moon eased up over the tree line. A spotlight. A night for bandits.

In the morning, he waited for Neil to open the Ten High. Neil sipped coffee watching Pete drink beers.

"You want anything to eat?"

"No thanks."

"What the hell's the matter with you?"

"That question's bigger than I can properly answer right now."

Neil watched Pete's hands run along the bar like he was admiring the tail fin of an old Chevy.

"Mind I put the TV on?"

"No."

"Will you stop that?"

Pete put his hands around his beer. Neil shook his head and turned on the television with a pool cue cut down for the purpose and watched the morning news with one foot high on the cooler and the other on the duckboards. From time to time he glanced at Pete.

The judge waddled in shy of noon, waited for his eyes to adjust to the gloom, and then went straight for Pete.

"The police are looking for you."

"That was quick."

"What happened?" the judge asked. "Fuck off, Neil."

Neil shot the judge a wounded look and then went out from behind the bar, got a broom from the closet, and went out front to sweep.

"They came to my house, Pete. Everybody knows that car is mine."

"Who found him?"

"Couple kids cutting class." He waited for Pete to say something. "What the hell happened?"

"He's the one burned down my house."

"Jesus Christ. Where'd Neil go? I want a drink."

The judge went behind the bar, poured himself a rye and then another one.

"You got cause now. Heat-of-the-moment kind of deal. A jury would—"

"I didn't kill him. I was there, but I didn't kill him."

"Luke?"

"No."

"Who then?"

Pete leaned over the bar and filled his beer from the tap, sipped off the foam.

"I need you to find someone for me."

Pete had a few more big swallows of beer. Burped. The judge took it from his hand and set it aside.

"The cops are going to talk to you any minute. Don't say shit. I already called Jim Uhlen. You'll probably want to get somebody better, this goes to trial. But he's already on his way from Kalispell."

Pete grinned somberly.

"You're welcome, Pete."

"I don't need a lawyer."

"Yeah. You fuckin do."

"There's this ATF agent I need you to find for me. Name of Pinkerton. He's the one I need to see."

Trucks and vans full of armed federal agents, marshals, and officers commandeered Pearl's house and set a pair of snipers on the cliff. They ran dogs. The once-impregnable mountain meadow was taken without a shot fired in defense of it.

Pete rode in a helicopter, pointing out as best he could the places where they'd camped, but the Yaak was virtually impenetrable from the air. He showed Pinkerton where he'd cached food and clothes for the Pearls, and tried to discern on their topo maps all the places he'd been with them. He'd covered a lot of ground with them, and Pete was sure he hadn't seen the half of it. They traipsed the Purcells, Whitefish, Salish, and Cabinet mountain ranges. They slipped into Glacier Park, maybe Canada. When he'd first met them, they'd been having a rough go of it, and the wilderness was winning, but with a little help from Pete they'd gotten healthier. He assured the feds that they had provisions, first aid, medicines, plenty of bullets, and in the thick forests and untracked roadless areas of the Yaak in particular, they were virtually invisible.

Nights he sat on the porch of the house, half-wishing Pearl would shoot him from somewhere in the trees. Agents inside smoking, talking about their kids, about professional football, the Soviet Union. Worlds and worlds away from here.

He felt an odd but true yearning to apologize to someone. For what was happening. What all he'd done wrong.

His life.

. . .

The wardens from Fish, Wildlife, and Parks had jurisdiction but handed it over to the FBI and ATF. The Tenmile police interviewed Pete, but mostly, it seemed, to satisfy a morbid curiosity. Even a brief meeting with his lawyer only amounted to Pete again sharing his story and the man sharing his business card. As far as everyone was concerned, Wes had followed Pete up to Deerwater and touched off a confrontation with a mountain lunatic who'd begun to trust Pete and reacted violently to the appearance of an armed agent of the state. And except for the fact that it was the boy who'd fired the shots, all of what Pete said was true.

But the Department of Corrections was still institutionally convinced that Pete was hiding his brother, and one windy day the judge and a man from Corrections sat down at Pete's table in the Sunrise Cafe. The winter cold had come early and fierce—no snow, just an unceasing front of arctic air—and when the judge opened the cafe door people jumped at the cold as though he'd laid on a car horn. A family decamped with their French dips and grilled cheeses for warmer reaches near the kitchen.

The man from Corrections introduced himself, but Pete was far gone within his thoughts and immediately lost the man's name. He said that although it was generally believed that Pete was telling the truth about who had killed their colleague, it was hard to ignore Officer Reynolds's own documented opinions on the matter of Luke Snow's whereabouts.

"I won't speak ill of the dead," Pete said.

"I'm not asking you to. But you should tell me where your brother is. Wes was certain that you know."

Pete had Luke's address in his wallet when he said he hadn't the slightest idea where his brother was. The man from Corrections put his cowboy hat back on, slid out of the booth, and walked out the door. The judge remained, didn't even bid the man good-bye, and quietly stirred his coffee.

"You hell-bent on going to jail too?"

Pete looked through the fractals of frost on the big front window and out on the deserted square.

"Everyone goes to all this trouble to find a degenerate like Luke or track down some madman in the woods," Pete said, "but no one can tell me where Rachel is."

The judge took in his haggard face, but couldn't look Pete long in the eye.

"Right now, where the hell is she?"

There was nothing to say. The waitress came and the judge ordered. When his food arrived the judge split a dinner roll with his red fingers and spread butter into the steaming innards and shoved half the thing into his mouth, chewing with his eyes closed. He drank from his coffee, and Pete sat with him, and then they went to the Ten High for drinks, and Pete listened to him tell broad lies. Late afternoon the judge went back across the street to practice jurisprudence.

September gave over to October. Still no snow. Pinkerton came calling on him, knocking on Pete's office door. He stood in the doorway holding his cap and wore an unhappy expression like he'd come to evict someone.

"You got a little bit to take a ride?" Pinkerton asked.

Pete asked him what happened. He asked had they found Pearl, the boy. Pinkerton ran a finger along the brim of his hat.

"You're just gonna need to see."

They drove through Tenmile in silence, then out of town. They turned on the road to Fourth of July Creek. As they passed Cloninger's place, Pete watched for him and for Katie but they were not anywhere abroad the property nor together astride one of Cloninger's horses, which of late Pete had seen them doing. Sometimes clopping through town. He hoped she was well. He knew she was. That was something good.

They rounded a corner and nearly struck a pickup barreling down the dirt road.

"Fuck you," Pinkerton said, pumping closed his window as they sped into the truck's cloud of road dust. "You people drive like shit up here."

He was about to blow past the Pearls' and Pete said so. He skidded to slow down and make the turn.

"Thanks."

"It's easy to miss."

They went back and forth up the rucked drive and then cut through a swath of sawn saplings and truck-trampled ninebark. They pulled up through the uneven meadow, which was now filled with unmarked cars and a few trailers with federal acronyms.

"I said for you to leave the Pearls alone," Pete said, taking it all in. "If I'd listened to my own advice, none of this would be happening."

"You didn't cause any of this."

"A social worker darkens your door, you hightail it out the back."

Pinkerton didn't smile, didn't wander his eyes from what was ahead on the road.

An ATF agent assembled an Uzi submachine gun. Others spoke on walkie-talkies. Pinkerton escorted Pete up behind the house and the chicken coop. A cold dry wind bore out of the north and through the trees with a wrathful noise, and tarps held to the ground by stones puffed up where the wind shucked under them so they rose into blue pontoons and deflated and rose again like some kind of industrial bladders. The rock pile behind the chicken coop had been removed from the front of what was now revealed to be a cellar dug out of the mountainside just to the left of the cliff. Lights flared in the cellar—flashbulbs, Pete realized—and a moment later a man backed out with a gurney, and he and the man on the other end of the gurney set it down on the ground next to the tarps.

Pete didn't understand what he beheld.

The agent with the camera exited the cellar, bent, and then knelt taking pictures. Pinkerton had gone over to the tarps, but Pete found that he could not. Pete saw the sole of a child's nylon sock, and even from several yards away that it was darned and pushed down around the ankle bone and he had the tremendous urge that someone—not him but someone—lift it up. He couldn't go over until someone pulled it up. Instead, the men covered the gurney with another tarp.

Pinkerton realized then that Pete had not come with him, that he was sitting on the hillside overlooking the meadow and all the police vehicles and the federal police, and went over to him.

"I knew they were dead. Ben said the baby wouldn't wake up and the others were acting funny, like cartoons, he said—"

"They were executed, Pete."

Pete turned around.

"That's not true. Jeremiah wouldn't have—"

"Every one of them." Pinkerton gestured toward the tarps. "Go see for yourself. Shot in the temple."

"Fuck they were. They were *sick*."

"Sick with what?"

"I don't know. They were just sick. And I'm sure they . . . they were afraid to come to town to the doctor. Because of the arrest. They—"

Pinkerton grabbed Pete's arm.

"Come on. Come see. With your own eyes."

Pete yanked his arm free but went with Pinkerton to look. At impossibly small wrist bones and metal zippers and plastic barrettes. Everything of cotton was gone to decomposition, but the cotton-polyester pajama top, the nylon yarn socks, the buttons all remained.

They were so exquisitely little.

"I didn't bring you here because I'm morbid, Pete. I wanted you to see who you were dealing with all this time. A man who killed his own wife and children."

"I gotta get out of here."

Pete got up and started to walk down the hill.

"If there's anything you're not telling us, now's the time. You see what he's capable of? Do you see?"

Pete kept walking, through the cars and vans and trailers, down through stamped earth and trampled gooseberry and then the alder and larch. He descended the mountain on the gravel road and after a while arrived at the mucky shore of a pond at the back of Cloninger's property. The dog came barking through Cloninger's pasture as Pete approached. He showed the animal his palms and walked on as the dog fell in with him and then practically escorted him to the back door. Cloninger's children played tag in the yard. Katie slid out of the tire swing and ran over to him as if it was the most normal thing in the world, Pete coming out of the woods to see her. Maybe it was fairy tales that inured her to such weirdness, or her mother. Maybe it was the state of childhood to not question and fear everything, it'd been so long, Pete couldn't remember.

♦   ♦   ♦

Does it say in her case notes that she attacked a staff member?
Did they revoke her privileges? Does it say that she was given mood
stabilizers for several weeks? Does it recommend that she be trans-
ferred to the state hospital in Lakewood for evaluation?

Yes. But Washington law stipulated that a court must order such a
move within thirty days of an official request, and the official request
was lost or misprocessed.

So she settled into a routine. She ate her meals and went to
her meetings and did craftwork. She played checkers with the girls,
so many girls. Weepy girls, angry girls, mutually molesting girls,
cutting girls, sneaking girls, arguing girls, hugging girls, girly girls,
womanly girls, crazy girls. She tried to be the mature girl. The
solid girl. The quiet girl who did the program. She talked during
circle time but only in generalities or manufactured specifics.
What kinds of people you meet out there. Hard-core pervs and
gentle souls who will give you anything so that you wonder how
they survived everything. It's what the world is going to look like
someday, she says. A world of chasers and just a few runners.
Takers. No carers.

Everybody wyoming.

She sat on a cot and wailed. She wasn't ashamed of anything.

So was she released to Butler?

The social worker? Yes.

And when she told Butler she had friends staying at the Golden Arms, his eyes lit up, and she could see he felt like he'd accomplished something bringing her back to her pimp's apartment. Something true about all of life in that irony, in Butler idly surveying the apartment. In asking where was Pomeroy and not really listening to the answer. In saying that he'd check back in a week.

And where had Pomeroy been?

California again.

Yo and Rose went to get him at the bus station. When they asked if he had anything on the bus—meaning bags—he said, "Just that" and pointed at a blond girl so tall she seemed a rebuke of Rose and Yo. Her name was Brenda. She had bruises on her legs and seemed half crazy to listen to, chattering ohmigod choke me out already totally they were all insane and I was like whatever and they were so totally pissed but I was out of there it was like goddamn cannibals in Sacramento know what I mean everybody out for themselves thank God for Pomeroy. You know? Smacking her gum.

She was a whore too. She hoped the guys she was with didn't come after her. They didn't give up any girls down in Sacramento. They'd fuck up her face if they found her.

Really? Rose asked. *What would they do?*

Cut me up probably, totally, they would. No shit. So I couldn't work for nobody.

Did Rose decide then to get the hell out?

Yes.

She told Yo she was going to quit. Going to move out of the Golden Arms.

Pom's not gonna let you.

I'll talk to him.

Sure. You do that.

When she tried to leave—had her few things packed up in a green rucksack and ready on the bed, and sat waiting for Pomeroy to come home so she could tell him—did he walk in and say, *Take off your clothes?*

Yes.

And did she?

She never saw him move so fast: he knocked her upside the head with an open palm that set her jaw funny in her head for a few days and had a wire hanger stretched out on the hot plate when she could see straight.

You still in your clothes, he said plainly.

She just looked at him, wondering did he think he would break her this way. Did he think she would stay. Did he realize what a stupid thing it was to do. How all he had to do was talk her out of it, that he could talk her out of it if he wanted. How he could simply say she was a beautiful woman, so many men wanted her. Even that might've switched her.

But instead he came over with a red-hot hanger and stood so close to her face she could feel the heat of him through her closed eyelids the whole time she unbuttoned her shirt. He told her she better not ever charge more than he says and pocket the difference. Told her she wasn't going anywhere.

Did he have to burn her?

Nah. She said just get through this and then you'll go.

So she ran?

She was going to, but something happened and she didn't need to.

What?

Sacramento came for Brenda.

A van pulled up, and three guys jumped out. Rose didn't even know what she was seeing until they grabbed Brenda and hit her in the mouth and dragged her into the van with startling expertise, the back doors swinging shut as it sped around the block.

What did she do, standing there on the street?

She ran to the Golden Arms, stuffed her things into a garbage bag, and left before Pomeroy and Yo could get there.

Why?

She saw how to make Pomeroy pay.

How?

Sacramento.

THIRTY-TWO

Word of Rachel came in a letter from the Seattle Department of Social and Health Services, which had languished on his desk in the stack of pamphlets and newsletters and official correspondence he'd all but ceased even leafing through. He'd knocked over a stack of mail and his eyes lit on the Seattle DSHS seal on the envelope, and realizing what it might contain, ripped it open. The words swept by, he comprehended in bursts.

Dear Mr. Snow . . . not sure, but I believe we have your daughter, a girl by the name of Rose . . . Rose! . . . matches her description . . . in our Bremerton facility . . . would like you to reunite. . . . please feel free to contact me directly . . . Norman Butler, DSHS . . .

The letter was dated in August, a few days after the raid. Pete couldn't understand why the guy bothered to type up a letter when he could have called. For a moment, he was too furious to read it again. Maybe he'd tried to call. Fuck. He probably did call and couldn't get him. He should've left a Missoula number, the main office.

Rose.

The girl in Indianapolis had said she went by Rose. This was her.

He picked up his phone and dialed Butler at Seattle DSHS. It rang and rang and no one answered. He hung up, tried again. He listened until the ring tone through the speaker turned into a babble of water. He grabbed his keys, and drove ten hours to Seattle.

It was deep in the night when he arrived. He drove through downtown, got turned around, then properly lost. He stopped at a light, rubbed his temples and eyes.

Several blocks away, someone in a wheelchair hurtled down the paved hill. A figment of his quaking sleep-deprived vision. Or not. The chair and its occupant cut a long swath through the street, down and down like a suicidal star, and homed in on the judge's car. The blinking streetlights lit the man amber as he continued on his trajectory through the intersection. He braked with fingerless gloves and knocked into the wheel well of Pete's car, skidding alongside and coming to a rude stop at Pete's window. A ribald assemblage of crooked, parted teeth, and cracked lips under a cankerous thin-haired skull. Pete tingled with inchoate terror. Was this motherfucker even real. The man put a gloved palm on Pete's window and moaned out a few sentiments.

Pete gunned his car through the empty red light. The image of the lunatic was a long time leaving his mind. A revenant, a bad omen.

He caught a ferry to Bremerton. The DSHS offices were in an old marble building and caseworkers streamed in with the morning traffic and the lot soon filled. It began to rain, the sunrise overcome by gray slabs of stormwork, ominous thunder.

Pete ran inside. Clients already sat banked on the benches by the door, watching him shake water off his coat. The glass rattled in the panes at the rumbling outside like the concussions of a besieged city. Phones rang out unanswered it seemed. Pete slipped by the empty front desk with his lanyard badge around his neck and paced the floor, scanning cubicles and office nameplates for Butler's desk. He found the cubicle and waited in a chair near it until the man himself approached, stirring a Styrofoam cup of coffee. A mustache like bowed longhorns, a doleful exaggeration of the expression produced by his jowls and chins, his sagged hangdog eyes, as though in some fundamental way the man were melting.

"Norman Butler?"

The man nodded.

"I'm Pete Snow. You sent me a letter about my daughter."

Even Butler's smile when he shook Pete's hand had a somnolent quality, a kind of surrender to it, as if a handshake and greeting were a formality he'd rather not observe, but would be far too much trouble to rid from his human routine.

Pete explained who he was. Butler listened with narrow nods, his head tucked down as though it might turtle back into his chest cavity.

"So have you seen her?"

"Personally?"

"I mean is she here."

"Hard saying."

Pete waited for more explanation that was not immediately forthcoming. The man sat down at his desk almost as if they'd completed their business.

"Look, I just drove all the way from Montana. Waited all night for your office to open. I want to go wherever she is. Can you find out what facility she's in?"

"When did you say you got my letter?"

"Yesterday. But you sent it in August. I didn't realize what it was until yesterday."

Butler leaned back, his chair cracking like a pair of knuckles.

"Well, there's no telling where she is now."

"Surely you can find out. A file?"

"The letter," Butler said, thrusting out a large palm, fine long fingers. Pete gave it over. Butler sat at his desk and opened a thin drawer and plucked out a pair of reading glasses and took a good deal of time situating them on his face. He started to read, took the glasses off, cleaned them, put them back on, and resumed reading.

"I asked you to call." Butler put his finger on this instruction in the letter, as if he would have Pete read the passage again.

"I know. I did. There was no answer."

"I don't work Mondays."

"Right."

They looked at one another. A realization crept over Pete that there was something deeply amiss with this man.

"I asked you to call so I could avoid having you take a trip if she wasn't here—"

"Can you just tell me if she's in your facility or not?"

"We have more than one facility, but none of them would have her for this long."

"Well, where is she?"

"She could have had a court date and then would be in the juvenile facility. She could have been sent to one of the treatment centers. I have so many cases, you see."

"Yes—"

"Or a long-term facility."

"Okay, but—"

"Or she may have been released to an adult guardian in the community—"

"Norman," Pete said, covering his eyes.

"Yes?"

"I don't expect you to know where she is off the top of your head."

"I'm just trying to tell you the possible outcomes, Mr. Snow."

"Is there a way we can find out the actual outcome?"

Norman sighed out of his nose and stood. Pete followed him around the corner and down a row of cubicles to a locked door. He thumbed through several dozen keys on several interlocked key rings for several minutes. When the door swung open, he flipped on the light and stepped aside. A card table strained under the weight of hundreds of manila folders between two walls of filing cabinets.

"Her file is there," Butler said.

Pete took off his coat and set it on the floor, there was nowhere else in the smallness of the space.

"There's coffee in the break room," Butler said.

. . .

Two pages. She'd given her name as Rose Snow. It made him think of blood, of someone dying in the snow. She'd been arrested for prostitution.

Prostitution.

He scanned the rest of the document in a fugue, without affiliation to what it described.

It was the only way.

"What did she need to go to the clinic for?" Pete asked.

Butler looked up at Pete and then took the file and read it over with his glasses and handed it back.

"It doesn't say."

"I *know* it doesn't fucking say. Who's this Yolando Purvis you released her to?"

"Purvis . . . ," he said, chewing on his pen. "Why do I remember her name?"

"I don't know."

"There's an address here, I'll just go—"

"Let me see."

Pete handed the file over. Again with the fetching of his glasses from his shirt, the reading. Pete wanted to punch him in the face, he was so slow.

"Ah, right," Butler said, nodding to himself like he'd figured out a portion of a crossword.

"What is it?"

"The Golden Arms is a young-adult transition facility. A place we have set up for street kids so they have an address, so they can get a job, et cetera."

Pete pulled on his coat.

"You should go there," Butler suggested.

No one answered when he knocked on the apartment door, so Pete waited in the hall. A wallpaper of repeating roses. A fire extinguisher

behind glass. The powerful odor of something canned and meaty cooking on a hot plate.

No one came by, so he went out to a cafe around the corner. He
ordered a brothy chowder of rubbery seafood that turned in his stomach. He watched through the bleary windows for her.

There was no answer at the apartment again. He searched for signs
of Rachel, as if she'd have left behind a clue or written her name on
the wall for some reason. As if she'd have left a trail of bread crumbs.
Fairy tales bore troubling resonance now. Wolves and dark forests. He
wondered was she scared, how scared.

His chest clenched around his heart and it wouldn't release, and for
a few moments he thought he would faint right there in the lobby, his
rib cage slowly suffocating him like a great bony hand. He sat on the
hall runner worn to a napless gray and swallowed deep breaths. Told
himself things he would tell a client. That the anxiety would pass. That
all was not as it seemed. Not as dire.

But it was as dire. Exactly as dire.

In the lobby, he thought about calling Beth.

He didn't want to talk to her.

He didn't want to be alone.

He dialed.

She answered and he told her where he was.

"I'm outside her place, waiting for her to turn up."

"Where?"

A couple came in the front door of the apartment and crossed the
lobby. A guy with shoulder-length black hair and a short and over-
weight vaguely Asian girl. They went up the stairs together. The only
people he'd seen come or go.

"Seattle."

"Seattle."

She'd begun to softly sob.

"Is she okay?"

He thumped the receiver against his forehead.

"Is she okay?"

"Yes. This place is nice. She's living with some people."

"What people?"

"I don't know yet."

"How did you find her?"

He explained. Partially. Nothing about Rachel's arrest.

"I've been praying for her every night, Pete. He's been protecting her."

She began to cry again. They were quiet a few minutes like this, him listening to her cry. He felt like bawling as well, but he was too keyed up watching the door. For her to walk in any minute.

"Why did you leave, Pete?"

"When?"

"When you were here. In Austin."

"It . . . was time to go, Beth."

"You should've come to church with me."

"I'm gonna find Rachel. And then I'm gonna take her home."

"With you?"

"She can live in Tenmile with me or Missoula or wherever she wants."

His head swam, and he had to sit in the phone booth with his head between his legs.

"I keep feeling like I'm going to faint. My hands are tingling."

"Pete?"

"Yeah."

"I want to tell you about Jesus, Pete."

He blew out long breaths.

"That's where we lost our way, Pete. We gotta get right with Jesus."

"Okay, Beth."

"Keep your heart open."

"Wide open, Beth."

"Are you listening?"

"Yes."

He set the receiver on top of the phone. Concentrated on his breathing.

. . .

RACHEL NEVER SHOWED UP. This did not prevent him from depicting it.

She comes in shaking off an umbrella.

She comes in shivering cold.

She comes in with someone else.

Then she sees Pete. She starts to cry. He goes to her.

Or she runs away. He runs her down, outside. She cries. He has her.

All night he sat there. People came and left, none of them her.

He tried the apartment again on the chance that she'd come in a back way. He was startled to see the black-haired kid that he'd observed in the lobby with the other girl answer the door. Up close it was apparent that his hair was dyed. He had the face of a skeptical cartoon rat.

"I'm looking for Rachel Snow," Pete said.

The kid was twenty, early twenties.

"Sorry, man, wrong apartment."

He started to close the door, but Pete stopped him.

"Rose. She goes by Rose."

The kid wore no shirt, and a few bright scars rose on an otherwise immaculate pale torso. Pete could hear the girl at something inside, running water. There were candles. Cigarette smoke.

"Can I come in?"

"Nah, man, you can't come in," he said with a trace of amusement.

"You know her. Come on."

The kid looked down and black dyed hair fell over his eye.

"I know she stays here."

The girl from inside asked who it was. Pete half-hollered into the place that he was Rachel's—Rose's—father. Was she Yolanda. Was she the one to whom Rose was released when she got out of juvie.

The girl came to the door and glanced at Pete, and then she and the guy had a wordless exchange that verged into wordless argument. The guy threw up his hands and retreated inside. Yolanda invited Pete in.

"This is Pomeroy," Yolanda said. Pete sat on the edge of the bed because there was no place else to sit except at the table in the kitchen, and Pomeroy occupied the sole chair, smoking and turning his cigarette in the ashtray to a throbbing red point.

"Your daughter isn't here."

"Do you know where she's staying?"

"Nope."

Yolanda tugged off her pajama pants and pulled on a pair of jeans. She took off her shirt, slung herself into a bra, and buttoned herself into a blouse. Pete looked at the floor.

"You might find her at the Monastery or down around Pike's Place."

Pete procured a small pad and pencil from inside his coat and wrote this down.

Pomeroy lit another cigarette and avoided looking at Pete directly. A panoply of bottles, compacts, brushes and combs, and jewelry on Yolanda's bureau tinkled as she walked to him.

"How long was she with you two?"

Yolanda glanced toward Pomeroy who sat and studied the ashtray.

"Since August, I guess," she said.

Pete stood and thanked them both. Told them what hotel he'd be staying in and asked that if they saw Rachel would they tell her that he was looking for her. Tell her where he was staying. Pomeroy mashed out his cigarette.

"Sure, man," he said. "We'll tell her."

He went to Pike Street and Pine and trod all over Capitol Hill. Nights he stood outside the Monastery and watched the kids and homosexuals and dancers mince about and smoke and trot off in small groups to do drugs or get some drugs or drinks. Kids who in Tenmile would have been at the Dairy Queen plotting quaint kinds of trouble, snapping bra straps, necking with second cousins. So young, these kids. Some of them looking no more than twelve, some riding skates. Occasionally a girl would cry or there would be a fight, a bloody upper lip, once a seizure, an ambulance, paramedics soaked in rainwater and amber light, the scene melting like a sand castle, rose-colored snow.

She was here.

He sat on a concrete berm just up the street from where very young girls got into cars with strange men and returned a half hour later. He doubted what he was seeing when Pomeroy and Yolanda arrived. Yolanda sat on a bike rack by the boom box, smoking and chewing gum, the girls shuttling between positions on the rack like ravens on a power line. Pomeroy off talking with other girls, young girls who seemed to be feeling out the scene, practically shouting to be heard over the traffic. Pete could hear snatches of the things Pomeroy said.

A whore turns eighteen, she can give blood instead of head.

I don't play no games. You do what you want.

Sure, maybe we can use you later, come back around ten.

Yolanda slipped into the open door of a sedan. He wondered where were the police. What city would permit this outrage. Then a squad car pulled up and Pomeroy talked with the cops inside it pleasantly, leaning over the passenger door, pushing his jet hair behind his ear. Like he'd called them to report suspicious activity.

Pete harbored two contradictory thoughts: he wanted Rachel to appear, he thanked God she didn't.

All day it threatened to drizzle but never much did. Pomeroy appeared on the concrete berm next to Pete, startling him.

"Are we gonna have a problem?" Pomeroy asked.

"Took me a while to realize what you were."

Pomeroy shook his head.

"Monna need to know if we have a problem, man."

"Yeah, we have problem," Pete said. "I'm a disaster can't wait to happen."

Pomeroy squinted at him.

"You might oughta second-guess that. You lift a finger in my direction and that big Afro-American dude and that other one'll be over here so fast you'll shit running."

The two directly across the street observed them with elevated attention.

"Not to mention what I'll do to you," Pomeroy added. "Assuming you wanna go in that direction."

"You know where Rachel is."

"I don't know no fuckin Rachel."

"*Rose*. You know who I mean!"

"And I don't give a fuck. And if I did give a fuck, does it look like she's around to be given a fuck over? I told you she's gone."

Pete looked about for something he could use, a rock, a stick. He thought, *just use your bare hands. Put your fingers to soft parts of his face, his skull.* What damage he could do before anyone could stop him. What a ruin he could make of this one face.

Then Pomeroy said he had a story to tell Pete.

Pete asked what story.

Pomeroy said a true story.

"What story?"

"You gotta calm down first."

"What cocksucking story."

Pomeroy grinned. *Cocksucking.* Interesting word choice.

"It's not that kind of story."

"Speak."

HE AND ROSE GO to breakfast, a little cafe not far from here. Great pancakes et cetera. They're eating, and the whole time this lady at the counter is staring at them. At Pomeroy or at Rose, he can't tell.

But when Rose hits the head, the woman tracks her going through the restaurant. So Pomeroy wonders is this woman a relative, is there gonna be trouble. Just like he's wondering now with Pete.

Rose comes back from the bathroom. He asks her does she know the lady at the counter. Does she look familiar. Rose looks over her shoulder. She has no idea. The whole deal is starting to piss Pomeroy off. He doesn't have time for a fuckin mystery.

He's gonna go ask her what the fuck, when the woman, she slides her plate away, finishes her coffee, and comes over to their table. Right over, even though Pomeroy is staring knives at her. The balls on this bitch.

Thing is, she's almost crying. Her eyes are watering and her face is all fucked up, and she covers it.

Rose says *what's wrong, can I help you.*

The woman holds up a finger for them to give her a minute.

When she finally gets her shit together, she says she's sorry, but that Rose is just the spitting image of the woman's daughter at that age. The girl had died. Run over by a car or some accident or some shit. Rose is a sweetheart as usual. She says, *My gosh, I'm so sorry.* Et cetera. Not that there's much she can say. Then Rose thinks to ask what was the girl's name.

The woman says it was Becky or something like that.

Becky, Rose says. *That's nice.*

Then the woman says can you do me a favor. Rose says what. My daughter, I never got to say good-bye. Would you do me just a little favor. Would you wave good-bye to me. When I get to the door, I'll just turn around and would you wave good-bye?

Rose says of course. She even gets up and gives the woman a hug. A big long hug. Woman's got a tattoo on her finger. Like a ring. Pomeroy notices this.

So the lady goes up to the counter and gets her check and does her business at the register and looks over at them. Rose smiles over her shoulder at the woman and waves. The bitch waves back, out the door she goes, covering her face, making that clipped, strangled noise of someone about to wail.

Pomeroy says to Rose *you're too nice.* Rose smiles, Rose shrugs. He says, *no I mean it, you're gonna get messed up being nice like that.*

So they finish eating and get the check, and when Pomeroy goes up to the register, the cashier rings up, like, twice what it should be.

Pomeroy says, *Whoa, we had pancakes, two coffees, bacon, whatever. It wasn't this much.*

The cashier says, *But the other breakfast. What breakfast,* Pomeroy asks and he knows as soon as he says it. A scam.

.   .   .

Pete studied the kid's ratty face for guile and lies, for some deeper strat-
agem in his eyes, his pubescent mustache.

"I'm her father."

"Or you're some guy who just wants fuckin breakfast," Pomeroy
said. "I don't give a shit."

"I am *her father!*" Pete roared. Whores and Pomeroy's heavies and
johns watching to see what might happen.

"It don't matter," Pomeroy said. "I can't have you out here."

He hopped off the berm.

"She's hiding from you," Pete said. The truth of it startling Pete.
"She is. What did you do to her?!"

Pomeroy walked through traffic like it couldn't touch him. Which
it didn't.

"Maybe she's hiding from *you*, motherfucker," Pomeroy called from
the middle of the street.

"That's a lie! That's a fucking lie!" He started into the street, but
the traffic, it would touch him, and the cars swerved and horns startled
him into stopping just off the curb. Pomeroy kept walking, his boys
kept watching.

"I'm gonna tune you up, you fuckers! I'm gonna . . ."

He felt like he was choking. Like he would suffocate.

The very idea of her having breakfast. Giving a hug. He wasn't suffocating, it was just the story, just the fullness of the pictures of his
daughter it put in his head.

According to the map Luke had given him, his brother's place was a
half-day away in the woods in Oregon, not close to anything, a ways up
a dirt road that in places had boards laid across muddy washouts.

There was a cabin lime green with moss, ferns feathering all around,
the soil black and rich. When he got out of his car, a dog was already
coming up followed by an alarmed white-haired coot yanking up his
suspenders.

"Is Luke Snow here?" Pete called. He knelt and the dog sniffed him warily.

"It's just me," the man said. "You get back in your car and—"

"It's all right, Theo," Luke said, coming around the side of the cabin. "It's my brother."

Luke clapped the old man on the shoulder, and when he got to Pete, threw his arms around him and hugged him tight.

They went inside and Luke showed him around a cabin that seemed to be partly under construction, partly mid-demolition. The back wall was nothing but a tarp and beyond that a stack of two-by-fours and a pallet of concrete. Luke said they were planning on pouring a foundation but it had been raining and they were waiting for everything to dry out, if it would. In back of the house stood a greenhouse, a tractor, and a half-acre of corn.

"You look good," Pete said.

Luke took Pete by the arm.

"And you look like shit."

"Why's everyone keep saying that?"

"All these bastards must have eyes in 'em or something."

He took Pete into the greenhouse and showed him the tomatoes and peppers and flowers he had growing. Herbs. A thriving marijuana plant he winked at Pete about, glancing out at Theo in the cabin.

"Old coot has no sense of smell. Not that he'd know weed by smell."

"So you can fart around him too."

"Nah, any change in air pressure messes with his trick knee."

"Well, you can't have everything."

"Still. It's the life of Riley out here."

"Just you and the handsome octogenarian."

"Is that a Latin joke?"

"I said he was eighty years old."

"Damn close."

They grinned near one another, at the ground. Luke pulled dead leaves from the tomato plant by running his hand along the stem.

"I'm afraid to ask," Luke said.

"Ask what?"

"Why you're here."

Luke took all the news worse than Pete expected. He sat in a bed of moss and dangled his hands out over his knees and spat between his legs.

"This is my fault, my mistakes are still rippling outward. The damage I done isn't done."

Pete sat next to him. Pete told him the old man's death wasn't anybody's fault. And Wes, that was more due to himself and Pearl than anything.

He found himself talking more about Pearl, about the strange Pearl boy and how everything went down to get them to this point. How the man had murdered his wife and children and was there any accounting for that.

Then he began to tell Luke about Rachel. To take for instance his daughter. How long she'd been gone, and still had not come home. How strange it was people calling her Rose. Like she was a fiction. How some of this was of her own mistaken volition. How there was always more than one source to any trouble. How it required two parents to let her down. That was his point. Nothing was any one person's fault.

"No idea where she is?"

"She's in Seattle. Somewhere. There's this kid, this twentyish kid. A pimp."

"You're not saying—"

"I am."

"No."

"I met him. She lived with him. And another girl."

"No. Not Rachel. She's a child."

"The last time you saw her maybe. Now—"

"No."

"A little girl doesn't hitchhike from Texas to Indiana to Washington, Luke. She doesn't survive . . . out there . . ."

The thought of her. He stood, staggered off to the trees and threw up. Then his face poured. Tears. Snot. Drool.

When he came back, Luke was lacing up a pair of boots.

"All right," he said. "Let's go find this motherfucker."

Night they waited on a bench across the street from the Golden Arms. He thought perhaps he'd missed Pomeroy's arrival—the front door to the Golden Arms closed behind someone. He watched the apartment window.

"You see that van?"

"The Chevy?"

"Uh-huh."

They watched it idling a few parking spaces up the street from the front door.

"Been around the block a few times," Luke said.

"You think it's him?"

"Let's watch a minute."

The driver killed the engine, and after a few moments, four men jumped out. None of them Pomeroy. The men zipped up their coats, looked up and down the street, and then went in a group into the Golden Arms.

"Come on," Luke said.

They jogged across the street to inspect the van. Pete put cupped hands on the driver's side window and looked inside. A can of chew. Some empty beers. A baseball bat.

"He ain't in here," Luke said from the rear of the vehicle.

They went back across the street to watch the apartment window. The men exited the building and, again looking up and down the street, got into the van.

"What'd you think the chances are they're looking for this piece of shit?" Pete asked.

"I dunno. This guy ever been to California?"

"Why?"

Luke pointed at the departing vehicle.

"California plates."

·   ·   ·

They went to Pike Street and the Monastery but mainly watched the young whores come and go. They went over together and asked if any of them had seen Pomeroy and received in reply only cautious ignorance.

They saw the van again. Luke pointed it out.

"I'm starting to wonder what are the chances," Pete said, "of that van being here and at that fucker's apartment?"

"Some coincidence, that."

"I think someone else is looking for him."

"Let's get the car."

They were parked two spaces back from the van when Pomeroy exited the Triangle Tavern. Even then, as they leapt out of the car, Pete felt a strange pull. Even as Luke ran to tackle him, even as the men from California—from Sacramento, to be precise—spotted Pomeroy and themselves scrambled out the back of their van to attack him, and even as Pomeroy saw them coming at him and turned around and then saw Luke and Pete running toward him as well, even in this moment of high action, Pete still felt, strangely, that this was all some kind of non-sense, that he was missing something quite more important than these Californians now clubbing Pomeroy to the ground with their bats.

He stopped dead in his tracks and turned around.

She was across the street. It had begun to not so much rain as mist upward, the slishing traffic making a kind of street-level fog that he immediately worried was she cold in. He actually reached toward her, the very gesture that set her off on a dead sprint as it might a doe. He chased her up the block on the opposite side of the street, yelling her name, shouting for her to just wait, he just wanted to talk, pleading and running and thwarted by the cars from crossing. He shot into the halted traffic at a stoplight and screamed when he couldn't see her. He scanned the shop windows, and ran two blocks at a dead sprint and then into an evening throng leaving work, and onto the street when the sidewalk clogged. He didn't see her. He clambered into a parked pickup bed and then onto the roof. Next to him a horn blared and did not puncture his panic. It was only when Luke yelled his name that he came somewhat to his senses and leapt down and into the car.

"Did you see her?"

"Rachel?! Is that what you—?"

"Drive! Go!"

Luke put the car in gear and Pete scanned the sidewalks. All too soon they came to a halt just before the freeway. Red brake lights blurred and spangled through the windshield.

"Wipers! I can't see!"

Luke fumbled with them, and Pete reached over to do it himself and with the first pass spotted his daughter striding to the corner, glancing from time to time over her shoulder. He jumped out of the car.

"Pete, wait," Luke said, but Pete slammed the door and started for her.

He'd have to grab her. Sneak up and just grab her.

He slunk behind the idling cars, startling not a few of their inhabitants with his skulking. When the light changed, he had to get out of traffic and for a moment the noise of it disguised his coming up behind her. Her hair hung in loose curls, wet against the back of a thin jacket. She had a small drawstring backpack of moist canvas. Low-top sneakers. No socks. She hugged herself at the crosswalk, and then turned full around to see him, what was he saying was he saying anything she just ran into the traffic, the on-ramp, cars skidding, and he went headlong after her. She scampered up the grassy incline and he slipped in the steps she made so effortlessly, he clawed at the earth hand and foot and when he reached the highway she was running along it and he after and she looked back to see was he coming and when she saw he was, she ran into the highway and down the median between the cars. He thought he'd seen her killed, heedless semis slicing past her, but he drew even of her and still she ran, she didn't look over and he dared not cross over to her for fear a car a truck a van would, in swerving to avoid a man, run his daughter down. He waved at the traffic to stop but they only saw a hysteric and maybe the girl in the mist. She darted to the concrete divider between the northbound and southbound lanes and she stopped a moment to catch her breath or to see was he coming and he held up his hand as though to say *I'm not coming, I give up, I won't chase you just stay there a minute* but she leapt over the divider and ran into traffic again and his heart dropped and the only way he knew she made it was by a smear of her going over the guardrail on the other side of the highway.

In the motel, they made plans to search the city together, Pete in a kind of stupor, watching the news, not really watching the news. The next day, they drove all over Seattle, Luke drinking coffee, saying that she'd turn up, he was sure.

Everything observed through rain. They watched it fall in ribbons of streetwater from underpasses and from the broken gutters of abandoned apartment buildings. They watched it fall on a popular place in Belltown where homeless kids came and went, bartered, and otherwise idled away the days. No sign of her. Just the low hum of sleeplessness behind the eyes. Of worry. Pete wondered could a person drown in it, as in a ceaseless rain, a flood.

A squad car eased up alongside them. Luke gripped the wheel as the officer interrogated them, asking flat out were the two of them here to score some pussy or some dope. Or some dick. He didn't even ask for their IDs, just ordered them to move on.

Luke lost his nerve, speculated and then was certain that the cop had remembered his mug shot after he told them to go, that there was now an APB out for him. He backed into the parking spaces for a faster getaway, certain it would come to that. Walking along the pier, he hunched his shoulders, folded up his collar, tugged his cap low, utterly spooked.

Pete didn't notice any of this. He couldn't stop thinking of Rachel running from him. How he just about got her killed.

"I can't be out here," Luke said, his head swiveling around like they were being tailed.

Pete couldn't evict that scene from his head—those trucks and cars, her lithe body in the wet traffic. Everything was soaked and shining and hard. Except her. You were killing her, chasing her like that. You were as much as killing her. If you found her up here, she'd jump off the pier, swim to the middle of the Pacific—

"Pete. Wait."

Pete halted, but not because Luke told him to.

"Jesus, there's cops all over, Pete."

There were. All of them headed to the water, edging through the crowd lined up along the railing, looking over, pointing at something in the water. Someone in the water.

It was like he'd willed it to happen. Like she'd sensed him.

"I gotta get out of here," Luke said.

But Pete ran to the throng and pushed through it to the railing and looked over. Thirty, forty feet below. He was sure it was her in there, bobbing akimbo facedown in the greenblack swells knocking gently against the great log pillars but it wasn't, the girl was too tall, too tall and even in the dark water so blond and so utterly dead. Rachel was not tall. Not so blond. Not dead.

Luke was waiting for him at the car.

"Pete, I can't—"

"Me neither," he said. "I'll take you home."

He meant to go home too but found himself in Belltown again at the abandoned apartment. It had been freshly boarded up by the owner or the city and had no ingress. He circled it until he discovered the fire escape. The metal teetered away from the wall in places where it was poorly or no longer affixed to the brick and mortar, but it held him, and on the third flight, he pushed in the padlocked door. A narrow trash-filled hall. A gray light leaked in from foggy skylights. Seepage stained the walls.

After several rooms, he thought he found it. How did he know. There was a mattress and a pair of skates, a notebook, a bag of makeup and cheap jewelry. A duffel held skirts and girls' underwear. A sock-monkey doll and a pack of cigarettes and within it, a small Baggie of marijuana dust.

He opened the notebook. He took it to be her handwriting but wasn't sure. What time this girl rose and the weather that met her. How hard it was to write at all. Her sincere intention to keep her thoughts in here but how when it came time to write she didn't have anything to say or so much to say that she didn't know where to begin and how she couldn't stay put long enough to express it in any case.

An entry about how she left P+Y and she would have to write more about that later, she was too happy to write about sad stuff and bum herself out.

A list of thing she needs to do. Stop chewing her nails. Find a job. Find a place. Try to sleep at least eight hours. Get up early. No arguments.

An inexplicable gratitude swells. The floor pulls away from your crossed legs, but it's just a light-headedness. Of late you've been through so much. More than can be borne. You'd seen a man die. You'd learned your daughter was a prostitute. And as the weak sunlight went darker yet in advance of another rainstorm, you find yourself in the midst of a strange peace that seems to emanate from the middle of your chest, a warm spot that reminds you, to your mild amusement, of peeing in a pool or wetting the bed or wetting the diaper and finally, of course, of being in your mother's womb. Even the thought of your mother and father buried in the ground doesn't trouble the serenity that now strobes in the atmosphere around you.

You see your daughter now in toto, from a vantage not even fatherhood has given you, a new place. You don't know her trajectory, weren't meant to know it, because of her or by circumstance. You simply wish her well. A voice in you is saying to keep her safe, warm, to light her way, for her to know little fear and to have bravery and joy.

After a while it occurs to you that this is a prayer.

◆   ◆   ◆

How did she set up Pomeroy?

She watched for the van and when it came around again, she ran up, startled the driver into rolling down his window, and told him that she would call them at the pay phone on Second and Pike. When she did, it'd be to tell them where Pomeroy was.

Why did she run from her father?

She was surprised ashamed couldn't go back wanted to die rather than have him see her like this wanted to go south, she had it all set up.

Set up with who?

. . .

Did she leave Seattle right away?

She went to see Pomeroy first.

Would Seattle General let her?

No, so she waited until the nurse changed shifts, stole a large duffel from one of the rooms, and told the new nurse her name was Rose Pomeroy, that she just rode in from Spokane to see her brother.

Pomeroy had two arms in casts and one leg was elevated, and bandages covered the top of his head. He looked like a purple infant, his face was so swollen up. She pulled a stool over and sat down. He didn't move when she spoke to him. She put herself up to his ear and said that he shouldn't have treated her that way. He shouldn't have made her fear for her life.

Did she hurt him?

She found a place on his arm where the bandages ended just above his elbow and wanted to bite into his flesh, she wanted to gnaw until she tasted blood.

Instead?

She kissed his wrist. A small shudder passed over him.

Did it feel good to still have her kindness?

It did. Very much so.

And Brenda, what became of her?

The girl Pomeroy brought up from Sacramento? The reason they'd nearly killed him?

Yes.

The Sound. They pulled her from the Sound.

THIRTY-THREE

Dinner with Spoils and Shane and Yance and sundry women from Butte, from Wyoming, from the university. An artist who smokes and speaks at length of an encounter with Bob Dylan at last pins Pete to the wall and in the small hours fucks him on the stairs. She goes upstairs to douche, his head sloshing from his spent efforts. He tumbles outside, falls, and somehow makes his feet, the sidewalk, his way, almost by feel through the snowy blue and gray tableau, across the Clark Fork River on the Higgins Street Bridge. The Wilma looms up on the north shore of the river like a hewn obelisk. He hollers for Mary, once, twice.

He's on a bed. A girl or perhaps a woman in attendance. Working loose of her clothes, a satiny fabric, a thunderstorm of sparks as it passes over her head. His nose somehow in her waxy, stubbly armpit.

"The fuck are you doing?"

"Huh?"

"My lips are over here."

"I'll pass."

"You'll *what?*"

"A joke. Come here."

He is shook.

He is in another room.

He is peeing in a closet.

He is peeing on someone's bed.

He is peeing into a bottle in a car, missing, pissing on the floor.

He is among many angry strangers.

He is walking on the roadside under a transom of falling stars, the sky streaked in a kind of agony, white grooves, his eyes can't brake their casters.

Come Halloween he is back in Tenmile, coaxing the judge into or out of a booth, bar crawling in a Santa suit. The judge a laggard in the plush velvet seats of the War Bonnet, holding a sky blue orb of liqueur like a seer's bauble. A disordered air hangs about him like he might fling the glass at the first offensive target. Or no target at all.

There are stories of hens laying fewer eggs. Things out of place up at lakeside cabins. Unexplained spikes in electric usage. Break-ins where the thieves only make off with boots, ammo, and maps. Near a residence up Question Creek a dog keeps finding pelts, a beaver, a coyote, many rabbits. This same dog is discovered dead near a bowl of sweet lime green antifreeze. A snowshoer comes across a few wet quilts and sleeping bags hung up to dry, stiff and frozen in the cold. A hunter comes across an ember and turns over a hastily buried campfire with his boot. He swears later he felt crosshairs on him. He walks backward twenty feet, turns, and runs back to his car.

All of these are attributed to Pearl. The assumption is that he's close to Tenmile, slipping into town as needed. Dogs and horsemen from the Department of Corrections are brought in. They find a shelter a couple miles from the highway made of planks and plastic, and they surveil it, but only arrest a pair of poachers who camp there.

After they hand down an indictment for the murder of Wes Reynolds, they begin to buzz the woods where they think Pearl's hiding with helicopters and C-130s. The people who live in the cabins complain.

Demented Harold goes down to Kalispell with an idea etched on a napkin and comes back with fifty T-shirts that say JEREMIAH PEARL: HIDE AND SEEK CHAMPION 1981. The ATF guys buy out his stock and he comes back with fifty more and another fifty that have a quarter with a hole in it and read RUN, JERRY, RUN!

A throng gathers up at Fourth of July Creek and then a permanent camp of neo-Nazis and Christian Identity and various bands of sepa-ratists and sympathizers. There are new protocols for going up that road. There are complaints in the local paper about the federal occupa-tion. Some graffiti. Some leafletting. Some media from the smaller sta-tions in Idaho and eastern Washington. A combative Jewish reporter from New York appears and promptly disappears after a brick goes through his car window. The motels and cabin rentals do brisk busi-ness and the Sunrise hires a fourth waitress. Helicopters continue to hazard the crisp night air.

Then there's trouble.

Snow falls in white floc like the ashy precipitate of a yonder fire, in discrete spirals and helixes on a haphazardry of vehicles, squad cars, and motorcycles on the way to Fourth of July Creek. A man wearing a turtleneck, pince-nez, and a sidearm like some kind of Nazi intellectual runs a Confederate flag up the flagpole on his motor home. A cam-eraman from a Spokane television station films him from just across the way atop his own news van. And a cordon of police stand down a mostly shouting rabble of unemployed loggers and handymen, denimed teenagers with domes shaved and naked in the vailing snow. They hol-ler. Angry women quote scripture and legal precedent and jeer the cops, calling them pigs and jackbooted Nazis with no irony whatever.

Some one hundred of them, now closing the gap toward the line of police. The cops retreat uphill toward an area cleared of trees, a muddy,

rooty, churned-up scar of soft Yaak earth. Behind them, several vans
and motor homes constitute the federal occupation of Fourth of July
Creek, the source of all this outrage.

Shattered chants and ceaseless invective morph into a nearly simian
cacophony of hoots and throaty shrieks as a white cloud of gas com-
poses and insinuates itself into the small crowd that yet churns forward
from the rear and backward from the front as the agitators break into
two scattering bodies, fanning and choking and wild-eyed, coursing up
and down the road. In the close quarters the cops swing batons at the
remainder of the mob recalling, strangely, a swath of Hutterites scyth-
ing a field of grain. A man bursts from the crowd covering his eye, blood
running from his ear, and caroms into the parked cars and falls over
like a windup figure. The batons keep on until there remain only pockets of conflict. A woman flashes by with a baby pressed to her chest. A
cop appears, swings his baton between a biker's shoulder blades, and
sends him to earth with a sad thud. Another cop sweeps down to help
beat him.

The cameraman, from atop his van, captures it all.

There is a thwarted bombing in Libby—a patrolman stops a Truppe
Schweigen member with a box of pipe bombs on his pickup bench
seat—and then an unthwarted bombing at the federal courthouse in
Spokane.

There are death threats, and every so often Pete must evacuate his
office and stand outside in the cold with Judge Dyson muttering and
complaining as the meager Tenmile police sweep the building. It gets
to be silly.

One morning a madman tosses a stick of dynamite into the post office.
The windows blow out and a postman is killed, and another man stumbles outside burned and bleeding and naked save the tops of his overalls
that hang on him like a denim bib. He staggers across the street holding his insides inside. He makes the courthouse lawn just in time for

Pete to exit his office and see what's the matter. Then he pitches over, smoking, dying from his injuries on a thin crust of rime and old snow.

People appear from all over, go to the man. A woman runs to her car and comes back with a quilt, and a doctor arrives, addresses the man's injuries for a time, and then covers his head with the blanket. The shock is palpable. Weeping. The brick post office is still somewhat afire but only somewhat, as a volunteer fireman puts out most of it with the Sunrise Cafe's kitchen fire extinguisher. A squad car races up the street, presumably hard after the terrorist. The mayor and the judge consult with the chief of police not twenty feet from the dead man. Clerks and secretaries hold closed their coats, waiting to be told what to do.

Pete crosses the street to the Sunrise. Old boys stand outside smoking, darkly delighted that something so outrageous has occurred. Even they are doing their part, comparing it to the bank robbery of 1905, contextualizing this event in the history of the place, making the first stabs at rendering it for all time.

Pete sits in a booth by the window. His finger idles around the tabletop a nickel with a swastika in it when the waitress at last comes over with a water, a place setting, and a menu. She observes the paramedics loading the dead man's body into an ambulance.

"I heard he's dead."

"I believe that's right."

"I could just spit."

"I bet you could do better'n that."

She has had a hard life—you can tell from the way her face has aged, the frowns etched there—but Pete's remark elicits an endangered smile. He's recognized her, something deeply true about her, and it is a pleasant thing to be seen and for her toughness to be acknowledged.

"Yeah, I could do better than that. What'll you have, hon?"

THIRTY-FOUR

Pinkerton was sitting in a wooden chair outside of Pete's office. He had his hat in his hand. He stood when Pete came in.

"We got the boy. I want him to see you when he wakes up."

He'd been standing in the middle of the highway. The semi driver slammed on his brakes and the trailer skidded around parallel to the cab, but the whole assemblage managed to stay on the road and halt just a few yards in front of Benjamin. He was in a fever. He didn't seem to recognize he'd almost been crushed by tons of firewood, rubber, and metal. The trucker chewed him out, then saw how sick he was and took him to the hospital in Libby.

The ATF found a lean-to shelter in the catface of an enormous larch. A burn scar tall enough to stand in, not far from the highway. A small cook fire had burned itself out. There was a sleeping bag, a sack of cooked rice, and a thermos full of an awful-smelling tea. The boy's rifle stood at hand.

The ATF set up a perimeter to wait for Pearl. It snowed and they saw things all night, none of them materializing into the man. Come morning, it felt palpably obvious he'd been spooked and wasn't coming back. They left Pearl a note that they had taken his son. Pinkerton said he went up there personally and shouted into the trees the same thing.

Still. It was still.

A fat deputy sat backward on a folding chair reading a Billy Graham paperback. Pinkerton showed the deputy his badge, and they went in. Benjamin slept on the hospital bed. An IV of clear liquid ran to his arm. There were scabs everywhere on his body, small cuts from running through the brush, clambering up clattered rockslides, and sleeping under cedar. His eyes moved under their lids and cracked as they flashed partly open. He murmured hoarsely. Pete touched his hair, and the boy tilted his face toward the contact. The heart's living tropism. His eyes stopped moving as his dream ceased or the pictures on his eyelids turned pacific.

The deputy called Pinkerton to the door and he spoke with some other agents outside.

Pinkerton came back in.

"Someone took shots at our HQ downtown."

"Anybody hurt?"

"I don't know. I gotta go."

"That wasn't Pearl."

Pinkerton pulled his cap onto his head.

"But I wish it were," he said.

Pete sat by Ben for hours. Logging trucks from the highway running their Jake Brakes were the only sound that disturbed the room. Pete slept too, his chin resting on his chest. He dreamed as well. A diamond turned on his forehead. A tree. He was a landscape. He was covered with trees. He was the Yaak. He was Glacier. He was all the tremendous valleys of western Montana, cloud shadows grazing over him. Storm fronts broke against his nose. He was sparsely populated. He was a city. He teemed with highways and lights. He dreamed he had a sister, a beautiful girl, and in the dream he reasoned out that the girl was Rachel and what he was actually dreaming was a spirit inside of his, a sibling she'd never had, a son. He dreamed that we all contain so many masses and that people are simply potentialities, instances, cases. That all of life can be understood as casework. That DFS was a kind of priesthood.

The boy's eyes were open.

They grinned at one another.

"Hey, kid."

"Pete," Benjamin said.

Pete sat up. The boy's eyelids sagged closed again and then opened partway to look at him.

"How's it sleeping in a real bed?"

"Is Papa here?"

"Not now."

"He didn't come back. He told me to stay because I was sick. But I got scared something happened to him. Is he here?"

"He's fine. Look, it's still dark out. Why don't you go back to sleep?"

The boy turned his head and the snowfall just outside the window was hundreds and thousands of little turning white lights.

"He said he'd come back, Pete, but he didn't. I thought I had the same cold as Mama and Esther and Jacob and everybody."

"You just have a fever. Pneumonia. You should rest."

The boy took a deep breath and sat up.

"I feel better."

Pete went and poured him some water from a pitcher on a tray table and gave the boy the glass. Ben sat with it in his lap, looking vaguely at a spot on the blanket.

"You guys were on the run a little bit, huh?"

A change deepened the child's expression, as though what was on his mind was itself difficult to think.

"Were you scared? There were helicopters and things. Dogs. It's scary to—"

"Did that man die?"

Pete cast about for something else to talk about, but didn't find anything.

"Yeah."

"Papa was mad at me for it. But that man was going to shoot you, Pete. Right?"

"You saved me, Ben. That's right."

"He was bad?"

"Yeah."

"So I'm not in trouble for it?"

Pete looked over his shoulder at the cop just outside. The man licked his finger and turned a page. Pete wondered should he tell the boy. Should he explain how he'd blamed his father for the man's death.

"Nobody knows that you shot him."

"They don't?"

"No. And we're gonna keep it a secret, okay?"

"But if he was bad, then it was okay."

"We're gonna keep it a secret, Benjamin. You ever pinkie swear?"

"No."

Pete took the boy's hand and made a fist out of it and then untucked the boy's pinkie and hooked it with his own.

"Say you pinkie swear to keep it a secret. That no matter what they say, you won't tell them you did it."

"I pinkie swear I won't tell."

He touched the boy's face with his hand. His hair had gotten longer and knotted, and Pete couldn't pull his hand through it. He tugged on the kid's ear.

"Pete?"

"Yeah?"

"Are they gonna kill me?"

"Of course not. You're in a hospital. They're taking care of you."

"They gonna kill Papa?"

"No. They're just scared he's gonna hurt somebody. That's all. We're gonna try and keep that from happening."

"He never hurt anybody."

"Not on purpose, I know."

"No. Never. He never hurt anybody."

"He hurt you a little, didn't he? Didn't take very good care of you. And your brothers and sisters . . ."

Ben sat back against the pillows. Pete took the glass that he still had between his legs and set it on the table. Then he put himself on the edge of the bed. What thoughts roiled in the boy's head.

"That was Mama."

"What was Mama?"

The boy looked askance at Pete and pulled a pillow to his chest. He gathered the covers over his folded knees. He said he didn't mean it, it was his fault. He let the poison in. Pete asked him what he was talking about, but the boy didn't say anything, and for a long time Pete waited, as if the thing he wanted to draw out of the child was something frozen in ice and it would only be a matter of time as the room temperature did its slow work.

Pete leaned out over his knees and regarded the tile and the cop reading outside, and when he sat back again, he said for the boy to please tell him what happened, one thing after another, just plain.

At last Benjamin began to speak. He didn't move as he did so except to occasionally scratch where the intravenous needle was taped to his arm.

HE SAID IT WAS because of TV, of likenesses. The Cloninger boy alone in the den and Ben using the bathroom real quick and when he comes out the TV draws him in. The dwarves hi-ho, hi-ho-ing and now he's sitting on the rug in the blue glow of the cartoon. He drools he's so enraptured.

Then by his ear his mama has him. She drags him into the yard yelping like a kicked dog. She swats him a couple times and sets him on the fence. How his ear burns. He's too old to cry about it, but he knows he did bad.

His father's in the barn butchering two deer. Ben can see him pulling the skin from the carcass where it hangs from the rafters. He looks curiously at his son sitting on the fence, scowls, gets back to work.

From the fence Ben can also see into Cloninger's garage, where his mother and siblings work on the freezer. Ruth and Esther stand inside it with butter knives, chipping at the buildup of ice, little flakes of white flashing with their silverware. It's full of ice and they need to make room for the deer meat Cloninger's letting them keep here. His brother and sisters are making snow cones with Mama, putting handfuls of the new shavings into paper funnels from Cloninger's tool bench and flavoring them with Kool-Aid packets from Mrs. Cloninger's kitchen. No, Ben can't have any. Don't even ask. He sulks on the fence, he's been bad, shouldn't of been watching the likenesses no matter how funny, how colorful, he shouldn't of been in there.

At bedtime, Mama tells him he's done a grave thing. That he's put their souls at hazard. That you let some poison into your eyes and it can spread to your heart and to those you love. That evil is contagious. That every single thing you do matters, and matters forever.

Baby Ethan falls sick first. Fever, crying, then not crying.

Then all his brothers and sisters are sick. Mama too. High high fevers. Chills. Slipping around the house like it's a ward.

Nobody wants to play.

They pray. Smear mentholated ointments, pastes that Mama pestles in the middle of her own fever. Saying that this might be it, this might be how Satan comes at the last. With poisons and toxicants. What won't they do, these forces arrayed against them. Entrapment, fiat currency, lawyers. Now this. Sickening the family.

Except for Ben and Papa. They don't get sick.

"Because of the ice," Pete thought aloud.

"What?" Benjamin asked.

"The ice, there was something in it."

Benjamin shook his head.

"No, it was the cartoon. The likenesses!"

Pete looked over at the cop, still enraptured by Billy Graham's book. "Okay, sure. No yelling. Just go on."

The boy gathered some blanket about him, and Pete asked him to please keep telling what happened. That it was okay. Everything was okay.

SEVERAL DAYS OF THIS, these fevers, and Papa says they should think maybe of going to the doctor, but the temperatures stop climbing. Maybe because a person can't get any hotter.

Mama says any day now, they'll begin to mend up properly.

The Lord is strong in them, Mama says. *He shan't let them perish, not now.*

Mama says to remember that these bodies they inhabit are thin things compared to the stuff of their souls.

A night they wake to sneezing. Paula, she can't stop, not for three hours, the little girl is crying until she just passes out, hot as a skillet. They don't know should they wake her or allow her the relief. Not that she can come full around anyway, her fever is so high.

Papa says he's going for a doctor now.

Mama makes him promise not to. Would he make it easy for them to just finish us off, right there in the hospital. Just let a doctor come and assassinate them with a needle. Put them down like a vet would an old dog.

Papa says he's not just gonna sit there and watch them suffer.

She waves him off, says she'll pray, she'll have a vision, she always does.

She's running hot as a teakettle herself, but she totes the baby outside with her in the cool spring night and she prays under the stars in the meadow. Come dawn she's in the meadow yet, talking in tongues in the mist, clutching the baby.

Papa says for Ben to do his chores. He fetches the eggs. He sweeps the porch. He cooks the eggs because Mama's still in the meadow. He doesn't know how to cook very well. There are shells.

When he brings him his eggs, Papa says the baby hasn't made a sound in hours. Says she won't let him come down to her—*I get within thirty yards of her and she says "Benjamin Pearl you take one more step and so help me God . . ." Like the Lord put eyes in the back of her head.*

What else can he do, he says.

Benjamin doesn't know what to tell him.

I wish—

You wish what.

I wish I was sick too, Papa.

It's quiet in the house. Jacob's muttering sometimes and Esther tells him to shut up, even though it's not nice to say. No one comes to eat, not even Papa, he just paces the porch.

The flies get all on the eggs and Ben shoos them into a cloud, and they knock around and descend onto the eggs and the apples he cut. The flies in like poison. Like the poison you let in here. It's because of the likenesses they're all sick. You did put them at hazard.

Mama dances up to the house. *Joy,* she says, *joy. It's all joy. The glory,* she says, *you can see His glory on everything like new snow.*

But the children, Pearl says. *They're laid out. That isn't glory, Sarah.*

They just need to anoint them with oil. She says God said to anoint them. They are as kings and queens each one. She says for Benjamin to go get oil from the Cloningers.

He looks at Papa.

She cuffs him suddenly, weakly, her arm has no power. Shouts, *I said to go!*

Papa waves helplessly for him to do it.

He returns with a Tupperware of olive oil, Ruth can't walk right, can't even hold a pencil, it slides out of her hand and she bawls, she wants to say something and she can't and she can't write either. So Mama anoints her first, pours oil into her hair and kisses her head, and Papa carries her to bed and sits with her and ministers to her. She just wants to say something.

Benjamin helps Mama anoint the others. Baby Ethan whose eyes only open, just. Mama carries the little sleeper to Jacob's bed, she won't let anyone have the baby, and Benjamin bears the oil.

Jacob isn't himself. He can't stop laughing. *The joy*, Mama says, *you have the glory and the joy.* He laughs and they wet his head with oil.

Esther won't let them anoint her. She bows up like a tomcat, and then dashes through the house and tucks herself behind the stove, which has gone cold because everyone is boiled with fever. She hisses at them. She spits.

She's just grumpy, Mama says, laughing, rocking the baby on the floor so her dress hikes up and bare red legs show, she's never shown her legs before, how come they are so red. *Esther's just grumpy*, Mama says, *the oldest carries the most burden, you see.*

Jacob cackles from his bed.

Paula sneezes again.

Ruth comes for a glass of water and she can't grip the cup. She can't walk right.

It's the *cartoon*. The Seven Dwarfs. Ben says to Mama, *Ethan is Sleepy and Paula is Sneezy and Ruth is Dopey and Jacob is Happy and Esther is Grumpy.* He says, *This is my fault, God is punishing me.* He's turned them into likenesses of cartoons, which are likenesses of people, it's all inside out now, it's all hell now.

Ben knows that this is his doing.

But what to do.

Papa wants the baby but she won't let him. He says the baby Ethan is not alive. His open eyes are still and his arm won't remain where Mama places it, it keeps spilling out and she keeps tucking it back.

They argue.

She scratches Papa with her free hand when he reaches.

They scream at one another and Ben covers his ears and faces the wall.

Jacob laughs.

Ruth cries. She cries for Papa, and Papa goes.

Now Mama hisses to him, *Ben come here.* He does and she tells him to go remove the battery from the truck.

He says he doesn't know how.

She says to come here closer.

He's afraid.

Come on, damnit, you're afire.

He says, *Mama I'm okay,* and she says, *get over here, so help me.* He slips over to her and she slaps out the fire only she sees and says he'll be okay. She straightens his shirt. Kisses his cheek. Her face is like a hot coal, like passing too near the stove.

She squints at him now, *Why are you on fire?*

Papa has the keys to the truck. At the sound of them dimly jangling she says to not do it, and she crawls toward him on one arm, the other with the baby tucked to her, but he just steps around her and jogs out to the truck.

He guns the engine, rattles down through the trees.

Mama leans against the cold black stove. She sets the baby by like a piece of firewood, sits there with her palms open in her lap. Head thrown back. Exhausted. It's quiet. There's peace.

Then she moves to her knees, pulls herself up, stands on knocking legs. She takes a rifle from the wall. The barrel swings down, pounds the floor like it weighs a hundred pounds. It takes all her strength to bear it.

Ben watches through the unfinished walls, through the two-by-fours, as she staggers to Esther's bed. She coaxes her to sit up. Esther's shivering as they head out together and Mama stumbles back for a blanket. Esther is working her jaw around something that she might say, but she doesn't. Ben calls her name. Mama looks over, says, *Shut up, Benjamin Pearl. Just shut the hell up.*

Mama puts the blanket over her and together they go out.

She explains that they are already dead and she can't let them fall into the hands of . . . she gestures down the mountain. *Them*, she says. Does he understand.

He says *I let in the poison.*

Yes yes you did.

The first time, the rifle spins her around and she lands on it like a crutch. Jacob is led out by the wrist, takes the steps like a baby colt. Jacob's bare feet stepping in place in the moonlight. A hoot owl after Mama kills him. When it's Ruth's and Paula's turn, they clasp hands. The afghan spread over Esther. Shells spill out of Mama's pockets and she has trouble closing the bolt. She says for Ben to sit down next to the others.

She says, *Waitaminute no. You're chosen out. Go inside.*

There's one more shot and then no more shots.

What film played behind the boy's eyes, Pete could not guess. But his eyes ranged across the bed and the walls as though he were witnessing everything afresh.

"What happened when your father came back with a doctor?"

It seemed it took a moment for the boy to even hear the question.

"He didn't bring a doctor. He come back up to the house when he was stopped at the highway. Heard the rifle all the way down there. Didn't make it back in time." The boy's eyes were tethered to some section of the blanket, that far-off night. "He went up and looked. And then come back and sat on the ground with me."

"What did he say?"

"I don't think we said nothing."

"I'm so sorry. I can't imagine how scary that was."

"Naw. She did what God said to. Papa was wrong to go to the doctor. She'd put it in God's hands and he and I's what made her have to do it. It's why we were chose out."

"No."

"Yes. We were chose out."

"The ice," Pete said.

"What?"

"The ice from the freezer. You didn't have any. Neither did your father."

He left the Libby hospital and drove to see Pinkerton. To explain. But because of the shooting, the headquarters was a slew of flashing squad cars, paramedics, and every stripe of law enforcement taking pictures and making notes or just standing around fuming. An officer in front of the command centered regarded Pete angrily. Glass spangled and crunched underfoot, and he could just make out a long brown bloodstain on the tile inside.

"This is a crime scene now," the officer said. "You can't stand here."

Through a plywood gap Pete could see ATF agents giving interviews to FBI agents. A spot of hair on the floor that Pete only in his waiting realized must be part of someone's skull.

"I need to see Agent Pinkerton."

"You gotta clear out."

"Look, I have information about Jeremiah Pearl."

"Go to the police station, give your statement there." The officer shoved Pete off the curb and took his position back in front of the building. Pete loitered, but then word got around that the shooter was holed up in a barn and the place cleared out in a mass. If Pinkerton left with them, Pete didn't see him go.

He went back to the hospital, but visiting hours were over. He dozed in the lobby and paced and smoked outside and in the morning, the cop with the Billy Graham book was gone. And so was Benjamin.

THIRTY-FIVE

T he standoff at the barn failed to occur. If the shooter had been
there at all, he slipped away just as quickly as they'd cornered
him. The collective wisdom around the bar at the Ten High
was that Pearl would never be caught either. It was surmised he'd left
the boy and lit out for Canada or an unreachable remove deep in the
Yaak, which was more like a rain forest, a jungle really, only partially
known even to locals. He was long gone.

That the feds should leave was just as plain. They were licked and
nothing good would come of staying, billeted in the town like an occupy-
ing army. Locals getting pulled over at checkpoints. Made a person want
to have done something to deserve it. That's why the dynamite and the
riot and now the shooting at their headquarters. And whatever was next.

Pete was two days trying to find out where Benjamin Pearl had been
taken. He wasn't in the Tenmile jail, so there was no telling in what
vague lawyerless custody he was secreted. It was only when Pete trolled
the motels looking for vehicles bearing federal plates that he finally
sussed the boy's whereabouts. He noticed a television on the patio in

back of one of the ten cabins of the Sandman Motel. A man with a chest holster and service revolver answered his knock.

"Where's Pinkerton?" Pete asked.

"The hell are you?"

"The boy's social worker."

The agent moved his gum to the other side of his jaw and resumed chewing.

"What boy?"

"Tell Pinkerton that Pearl didn't kill his kids." Pete pointed over his shoulder. "See that Monte Carlo? I'll be waiting right there."

A few hours later Pinkerton pulled in and walked into the motel room from his car. Pete watched him tug aside the curtain and look out, and then come alone, hunched into his thin windbreaker against the mist and new slivers of rain.

"Jesus, it's freezing. Can you turn on the heat?"

"This is nothing," Pete said. "Where you from?"

"Virginia. What do you want?"

"To put Ben in a foster home."

Pinkerton fingered the upholstery.

"New car?"

"Loaner. Since you have mine. You can't just keep him in a hotel. He's still just a kid for fucksake."

Pinkerton's finger stopped. "Pearl didn't shoot that PO," he said. "Did he?"

"He did."

"Forensics, Pete. We have the kid's rifle."

"They must've swapped at some—"

"You know the kid did it. You were there."

Pete's skin hummed. Wondered how much trouble the boy was in. "Look, the boy tried to protect me. Wes had his pistol aimed at me—"

"I were you, I'd shut up. You're gonna need a lawyer before we have this conversation." Pinkerton blew on his hands. "Turn on the fucking car."

Pete started the engine, turned up the heat, which blew cold, then lukewarm.

"Maybe Pearl will cop to shooting a parole officer when we catch him," Pinkerton said. "Then your . . . *version* of events will hold up. More than likely, he'll get himself killed. And again, your version will stand." Pinkerton cupped his palms over the air vents. "But as far as I'm concerned, that kid's just as dangerous as his old man."

"He's not like that. His—"

"He sits in that motel room and doesn't say a word. He's been *trained*, Pete."

"He's terrified! He's stuck in a motel with armed federal agents. The only adults he trusts are me and his father—"

"The one who murdered his mother and brothers and sisters? *That* father?"

Pete handed Pinkerton some papers from his dash.

"Pearl didn't kill his kids. She did it. The mother."

Pinkerton read the first page, looked at Pete.

"Lister . . ."

"*Listeriosis.* It's a disease. They got it from eating contaminated ice chips from a freezer. Probably from deer blood according to the doctor. What you have there is a description of the symptoms."

Pinkerton read.

"It had to be something in the ice. Pearl and Benjamin were the only ones who didn't eat the ice chips." He watched Pinkerton read. "You hear of people getting sick from deer blood. But with listeriosis, you get all sorts of nasty shit. Read the next section on meningitis."

Pinkerton flipped the pages.

"Jesus."

He told Pinkerton what happened. How Pearl went for a doctor and she, feverish and paranoid, took the kids outside, shot them one by one, before killing herself.

Pinkerton covered his eyes.

"Jesus. The kid told you this? He saw his own mother—"

"He needs therapy. Let's get him out of a motel room and with some real people."

"I told them." Pinkerton tossed the papers onto the dash. Then he punched it. "Goddamnit! I told them Pearl wasn't anybody. We never should've built a case. . . ."

"Just go, then. Shut it down."

Pinkerton wasn't listening to him. He picked the papers back up, read them again.

"You're losing," Pete said. "You're making more enemies than friends out here as it is. Get your guys to draw down."

Pinkerton chuckled morosely.

"What?"

"You're talking like this is up to me, Pete. Or anyone."

"Someone's in charge."

"That'd be Jeremiah Pearl. And he wants to die up here. And for some reason we're unable to not oblige him."

They watched it rain.

"Can he live through the winter, you think?" Pinkerton asked. "Christ, I don't wanna spend Christmas up here. I got kids too—"

"Can I have the boy or not?"

Pete carried Ben's bags to the car. The federal agents had given him sacks of toys, unopened packets of race cars and action figures.

They sat in the car a minute. Pete didn't know exactly what to do with him. Or he knew exactly what to do with him, which for the first time made him uneasy. Because he wanted to do something else. He kept wanting to take these kids home. An urge to atone for Rachel.

"Are we going to see Papa?"

"He's not . . . I don't know where he is."

"Oh."

"He's still out there. People are trying to find him. Trying to get him to come in."

"He won't."

"I know."

"So where are we going?"

Pete gripped the wheel. Turned to face the boy, his coat groaning against the leather upholstery. He didn't want to be in this priesthood anymore.

"If you had a choice, would you rather stay at Cloninger's or . . . ?"

Take him, Pete thought. *Take him to your home . . .*

"Or what?"

. . . your shitty little apartment over the bar where you get pasted every night.

"Never mind. The other thing won't work."

The boy tucked his new tennis shoes under his corduroy pants. His oversize ski jacket engulfed him.

"What are you laughing at?"

"You look like a tortoise in that coat."

"It's warm."

"You all right with staying at the Cloningers'?"

"Will Papa know I'm there?"

"I'll tell him when he turns up."

"I dunno."

"I'll do everything I can. Anything I can. If I can get him to you, I will."

The boy looked hard at him.

"You fuckin promise?"

"I fuckin promise."

He faced forward. In profile, the child looked older.

"You ready?"

The boy nodded. Somehow he was.

THIRTY-SIX

He visited the Cloningers. Benjamin and Katie had settled in nicely, Katie more so. Benjamin wouldn't even enter the living room where the television was. Wouldn't play with the toys. The missus had him at multiplication and reading the Bible, and besides that he would go out and watch the animals hours at a stretch and not really play so much as tolerate the play going on around him.

They walked through the snow in the pasture, the sun hammering their eyes squinted shut. The kid turtled up into his great red coat. They arrived at the creek, water tumbling under the sheen of ice. Ben stood at the water's edge, his hood up, remote. His breath on the air.

"What's gonna happen to me, Pete?"

"Nothing."

"How's he gonna find me?"

"He has to come out of the mountains first."

"Where will we go? Where will we live?"

"I don't know."

He shoved his hands into his coat and burrowed deeper into it.

"Maybe . . . I was thinking if you wanted, we could try you living with me," Pete said, but Ben had already started back for the house and if he heard Pete's offer, he didn't care.

Winter was sudden, the snowfall fat and heavy. The judge called Pete to come shovel his roof before the whole thing caved in. Believing that the Monte Carlo entitled him to Pete's labor. Pete was hot and coatless and in the perfect quiet of the day wondered where everybody went. Then the judge emerged from inside and told him to hurry up, he wanted to get to Tenmile for a drink.

All that remained of the federal presence was a skeleton crew of agents who sipped coffee in the Sunrise and read newspapers they had sent from back east. A fool calling himself a bounty hunter came and chatted up the old boys at the counter, and soon they were mutually flattering one another.

When Pete sat, the waitress asked was the judge joining him for lunch. He told her to bring two coffees just to be safe, and when she did, he stirred in creamer and listened to the bounty hunter tell lies. Pete ate lunch listening to the badinage, paid, and asked the waitress to tell the judge to come get him at his apartment.

He'd just lain down when the judge knocked at his door.

But it wasn't the judge. Some wild-eyed vagrant stared back at him, clothed in too-large miner's coveralls. The man's face was splotched red in places with gin blossoms or bad chilblains under a trucker's hat.

"Jeremiah," Pete whispered.

"Where's Benjamin?"

"Come in."

"My son, Pete."

"He's fine. He's safe."

"Let's go."

"I'm not going anywhere. Come in and sit down."

Pete threw wide his door and went and sat at the little table in the middle of the studio apartment.

Pearl stepped inside, closed the door, and inspected the room. Opened the broom closet, the bathroom. Studied the street through the window, flush to the wall. Then pulled down the blinds and sat. He didn't look like Pearl at all. His viscous naked face shone with sweat. Where it didn't glow nearly red from what must've been a crude and rushed shave with an old razor and creek water was stippled gunmetal blue. The coveralls were coated in vermiculite dust, and he must've grabbed them off some miner's back step or pickup.

"You're going to take me to my son."

He produced a .38 from inside his pocket.

"Jeremiah, I know what Sarah did."

Pearl's beardless face gave Pete access to a startling gout of disordered thoughts. Anger. Racing fear. Then a brittle conviction. Pearl closed his eyes. A long time. Pete could've taken the gun.

"They were sick and you were going for help. She thought they'd been poisoned and she—"

Pearl's eyes snapped open.

"They *were* poisoned," he hissed. "How does every one of them get so sick like that . . . ?"

The thought guttered out like a candle. Like an old lie. They sat facing one another for a long time, as though at a card game that had taken a strange turn, and neither one quite knew the rules. Then Pearl leveled the pistol at Pete's face, looking almost surprised at this outcome himself.

"Take me to my son."

Pete thought he'd be scared in such a moment as this, if it ever came. But he wasn't. Whatever fear nested in him dissipated the moment Pearl lifted the gun.

"Taking you to him, right now, like this," Pete said, "would go against everything that's sacred to me."

"I will kill you."

"I know what it's like, Jeremiah. Losing a kid. I know some of your pain. I'd do anything to get Rachel home. So I *understand* you, but I will not hand over your boy at gunpoint."

Pete stood slowly and wasn't killed. And he wasn't killed when he fetched out the black case and the box and carried them onto the table. Pearl sat with the pistol in his palm and watched Pete open the case, set up the projector, and thread in the film. Pete told him he'd asked his mother-in-law if he could borrow these. Pete didn't look at Pearl as he turned out the lights, nor when he flipped on the projector. A square of white on the bare wall over his bed and then the children. Out of focus and waving. With Sarah in a green canoe on a stony shore. Little feet off the edge of a dock. Pearl himself in cannonball. Holding a Coke. Holding a cigarette, no, a piece of chalk, that he uses to trace the shapes of his children on the pink wall of a quarry. Their outlines. Their faces so close now. Their very freckles. A campfire, a snake in a bucket, a reaching hand. A motorcycle burns rubber, Sarah waves the smoke away from the baby—

The film slaps the projector. The fan. The glowing white square in the wall.

Pete threads in another film.

A baby bottle. Sacks of candy. A baptism in a flashing river.

Every lovely silliness composed of light, every good coin of time in Pearl's life.

It is dark out when they've finished the box. Pete turns off the projector and the fan quits, leaving them in a novel quiet. Pete opens the shades to let in a little streetlight, winter's stillnesses.

"You weren't sure. You argued. As the kids got sicker. You wanted to take them to the hospital."

Pearl turns his head and looks out the window. He says her name. Sarah.

That is all. Just her name.

"When you saw your baby boy was dead, you quit arguing, and you went to get a doctor."

"I wanted, I wanted . . ." Pearl touches his chest with his fingertips and then lets fall his hand into his lap. "I couldn't put all those sick kids in the bed of the pickup. They weren't . . . they couldn't . . . Esther's neck was so stiff, she couldn't move her head and . . ."

Pearl takes a deep breath and a single sob falls out of him like an ingot thudding on the table. He breathes unevenly, like the air won't take.

"You didn't think she'd do that, Jeremiah. You never thought that. How would you?"

Pearl is leaning forward, whispering. As though the opinions he has are secrets. He whispers that he still loves her, can you believe that, after what she's done. That he misses her yet. His helpmeet. His one. That if she walked in the door right now, even now, he'd sit with her and start over with her. Whispers how pathetic that is. How evil. He whispers he misses his children, that of course he misses his children. He's failed his children. He'd as killed them himself. That he doesn't deserve them. Because of her. Because of a love that does not see madness.

"My God," he says. He takes his head in his hands and kneads it like a foreign object, some tumor he must get the feel of, that he might remove with his bare hands.

"I don't know what I'd do if I were you—"

Pearl looks startled, alarmed to be here. He sweeps himself up. He turns in the apartment, still holding his head like a person in thrall of migraine, someone insane with auditory hallucinations. He leans over to vomit but nothing comes up as he seizes. He keeps bending over into empty retching.

"Jeremiah, it's okay."

It is through wasted eyes, red and scalded round, like he'd been all this time staring into a white sun, that Pearl at last sees him. The man is burned through, cauterized, a scar, and for all that, familiar as whatever it is Pete sees in any mirror. Pearl is Snow is himself is everyone.

When he went to look, did he sob there and ask her why? And did he hold her yet?

Or did he bound into the night? Did he rend his shirt? Did he hear his own strangled sobs and sorrow echoing off the shallow mountainsides? Did the pine martens and hares flee his screams?

Did he run up a fallen log and squat there and hold his knees like he would explode if he let them go?

Did he search his heart and ask what he'd done? Did he wonder was the universe a cruelty?

And did he put the children in the cellar alone or did Benjamin help him?

Did they roll the stones and how long did it take?

Were they still doing it even now?

For this were they chose out?

Chose out for this?

For this?

This?

THIRTY-SEVEN

Pete's brother stood some ways off, showing Jeremiah Pearl the teepee that he and the boy would live in. Pearl walked around the structure, looking off into the trees, the area around, warily. Luke beckoned him into the tent and he smiled back at Pete and the boy, and took Pearl inside.

"My brother's a pretty nice guy," Pete said.

Ben sat on the back porch next to him. The sky was heavy with dark clouds and it rained a lot here, but things could be gotten used to.

"Will you visit?"

"Of course."

"When?"

"Sometimes. I'll just come out."

He put a piece of grass in his teeth.

"Papa looks weird."

"You'll get used to it."

"I want him to grow it back."

"Maybe he will. Think you'll like it here?"

"I dunno."

"I think you will."

"Do you have to go right away?"

"Later. I got a long drive back to Montana."

"Can we play checkers?"

"I think the board is still in the car," Pete said.

The kid scampered around the house. Pete was alone a moment, the heel of his palm against his eye. The other heel, the other eye. Pete removed his hands and the gray sky shuddered in his vision, a dread pulsing of his blood, his ichor. He turned and there was the boy inside the back door, profoundly alive, saying the board was on the table. To come inside and play.

EPILOGUE

Pete drove by the camp twice before he spotted the car, the green tarp deep in the ninebark. An early spring cold front bore down, and when he walked off the main road above them and down through the brush to where they were parked they didn't hear him in the wind. The man stood and then the woman when they saw him. Their unsmiling mouths looked like they'd been hacked into a flat and uncomplicated wariness by a dull knife. Their boy sat a few yards away in fine sand by the water, and a silent infant lay in a stroller held level by a stone where a wheel was missing. A tarp stretched out from the back of the station wagon and was tethered to a couple of trees. A thin fire in the fire pit burned clear and orange, and a pair of fishing poles against the tree suggested how they got by.

"Howdy," Pete said.

"Howdy," said the woman and the man both, and they looked at each other as if they'd already done something they hadn't intended and needed to look at one another to remind the other of the plan or contingency.

"My name's Pete. Just right up front, let me tell you I'm not a police officer or anything like that, and the last thing I want to do is cause you any trouble."

They looked at each other again, and then the man said, "Okay."

Pete took out his badge.

"This says I'm with the Department of Family Services for the State of Montana."

At this the woman covered her mouth. The man set his hands on his hips as Pete came forward. Pete showed the badge to both of them and they looked at it and nodded, the woman still covering her mouth. The man and boy had upshot hair, and when he got closer they smelled of kerosene and trout. The woman uncovered her haggard downslung mouth and wiped her eyes.

"So we got a call that there might be some folks staying down here."

"What call?" the man asked.

"Just someone who seen you down here," Pete told him.

"Who was it?"

"It was anonymous. I just get the information to check out the situation."

"Because we haven't bothered anybody," the woman said with a voice that crackled with shame. She had by now gotten close to her husband and wrapped her arm around his, and looked back at the boy who was sitting by the fire with a toy truck watching to see what would happen next.

"I'm sure you haven't bothered anyone," Pete said. "Looks to me like you are making out fine here. It's just when there's a call it means somebody's concerned—"

"Why are they concerned?"

The man seemed genuinely surprised that someone would look upon this situation as odd.

"Mind if I have a look around?" Pete asked.

"Suit yourself."

Pete stepped over to the fire. The boy watched him. The mother went nearby, which Pete took as a good sign. Protective. He squatted down. The boy had no marks other than an old scratch on his arm. It was cool, but he was in a vest, shoes and socks.

"Hi," Pete said warmly, stirring the fire with a stick and then tossing the stick onto the coals.

The kid mutely stood and went to his mother and grabbed her leg.

"How old?" he asked the mother.

"This one's four and the little one is eighteen months," she answered. "Do we need to go somewhere else?"

Pete stood.

"No. Like I said, I'm not a police officer. Now, I'm not sure what the law is about staying right here, but *I'm* not telling you that you need to go."

"It's just if someone called, maybe someone else will call the police."

Pete had worked his way over to the baby in the stroller and he leaned to have a look at her, and the mother came over with the boy. The baby's blue eyes were in themselves an astonishment, as lovely as anything in creation. A too-big sweater enveloped her and there was a blanket over her. Her snot ran clear. No infection.

"She's really lovely," Pete said. "What's her name?"

"Erin."

He touched her on the nose and stood next to the car to see in back. Paper sacks of clothing. Playing cards. A ukulele. A box of cereal, hot dog buns, and a jar of peanut butter.

Pete stood away from the car to have a look at it.

"Is this a Buick Sport Wagon? They have a little something under the hood, don't they?"

"She runs."

The man had his hands in his jeans and was watching his wife when Pete turned to them.

"You were asking a question about the cops," Pete said to her.

Her nod chopped the air. She shook. He tried to sigh warmly, nonchalantly, as though there was nothing to worry about, but couldn't tell if it helped or not.

"I don't know that someone won't call the cops to come out here and give you a ticket or something. I don't know if this is anybody's property."

The boy wanted up, and she lifted him onto her hip and how her skirt hiked down revealed the upper bones of her pelvis. She was pretty, overrun and weary, like a pet come in from the weather.

"So where you guys out of?" Pete asked.

"We don't have to tell you anything, do we?" the man said. Pete turned full to him and the man was holding a stick. Pete glanced at it, and the man tossed the stick aside.

"Of course not. I'm just here to see that you're okay. That's all."

"We're okay."

Pete put his hands together.

"Sure looks like it. Why don't I go on and get out of your hair."

He shook the man's hand and waved at the children each and then the mother. He stopped at the hood of the car.

"We used to take these road trips," Pete said. "We're from out in Choteau—middle of nowhere, you know—and so Great Falls was like the big city, right? You can imagine what I thought of Minneapolis. Of Seattle. There's just nothing better than being a kid and going to new places. And how you could sleep so good in a moving car . . . and when you got home or to the hotel or the campsite and your dad would wake you up and carry you to bed. . . . It was just the best, you know?"

She had taken her man's hand.

"Hey," Pete said, "I happen to have some stuff up in my car that I was running down to the office—some blankets and coats and diapers and things. Maybe you all would want some of those things? It's just gonna sit in my office."

The man didn't look up.

"Tom," she said.

The man moved his weight to his other leg.

"Tom," she said again.

The man touched his temple with his free hand like he was trying to figure a difficult sum. Pete and the man's wife and son watched him work it out. He ran a sleeve under his nose and nodded.

"Maybe we'd have a look at what all you got," he said.

＋　　＋　　＋

Does he ever find her?

She wyoms to California. There are stories in this, but they are her stories.

Good stories? Bad?

A mixed bag.

But it's hurtful for her to be gone so long. She needs to forgive him and come back. He's so alone.

It's difficult. Wyoming is hard on everybody.

I don't think I can take it, she doesn't go back, she doesn't at least call? Her parents are good people. They meant well. Pete helps everyone. He's not perfect, but he tries. He'd make up for it, for lost time.

Time, yes. These things take time.

So she does come back. Eventually.

You gotta believe. You can't just go through life acting like there are answers to every—

ACKNOWLEDGMENTS

Much gratitude to my agent, Nicole Aragi, and to my editor, Lee Boudreaux.

Deepest thanks to all my colleagues and confidants for their taste and wisdom, especially Jon Marc Smith, Kevin Jones, and Becca Wadlinger.

This book has benefitted from countless readers, but I'd like to thank the following people, who were especially generous with their discernment and encouragement: Michael Adams, Rebecca Calavan, Peter Carey, Jessica Hansen, Stephen Harrigan, Jim Magnuson, Patrick McGrath, and Neil Winberg.

Thanks to the following organizations for providing me with the time and resources to complete this work: the Michener Center for Writers, the PEN American Center, the Stadler Center at Bucknell University, and the Jentel Artist Residency Program.

This book would not have been possible without the sustained support of Melissa Stephenson. You are made of iron or something quite like it.

Additional thanks to the following people and organizations for their crucial help over these past several years: Tom Grimes and Texas State University, Glen and Janet Stephenson, Steve Sullivan, Jo and Dan Beck, Sue and Jim Polich, Jesse Donaldson, the Interlochen Arts Academy, Mutt, and Wieden+Kennedy.

Finally, I'd like to thank the social work professionals in Texas and Montana as well as the researchers at the schools of social work at the University of Texas and the University of Montana. Thank you for your insights, but above all for your service to the most vulnerable among us.